Black Ace Books, POB 6557
Forfar, DD8 2YS, Scotland
Tel: (44) (0)1307–465096
Fax: (44) (0)1307–465494
www.blackacebooks.com

COUNT DRACULA

Count Dracula

the authorized version

Hagen Slawkberg

BLACK ACE BOOKS

First published in 1998 by
Black Ace Books, PO Box 6557, Forfar
DD8 2YS, Scotland

© Black Ace Enterprises 1997

Typeset in Scotland by Black Ace Editorial

Printed in England by Redwood Books
Kennet House, Kennet Way, Trowbridge, BA14 8RN

A CIP catalogue record for this book
is available from the British Library

ISBN   1–872988–96–2

For my dear patients everywhere
Past, present and future

CONTENTS

Part I

JONATHAN HARKER'S DIARY

Transylvania

1

In Search of Dracula

3 May.

Left Munich at 8.35 p.m. on 1st May, arriving in Vienna early next morning. Should have arrived at 6.46, but train was an hour late. Budapest seems a wonderful place, from the glimpse I got from the train and the little I could walk through the streets. I feared to go far from the station – having arrived late, we were to re-start promptly.

Impression of leaving the West and entering the East.

The most Western of splendid bridges over the Danube, which is here of noble width and depth, took us among the traditions of Turkish rule.

We left in pretty good time, and came after nightfall to Klausenburgh. Stopped for the night at the Hotel Royale, and had for supper a chicken done up some way with red pepper. Very good, but makes one thirsty.

(Mem., get recipe for Mina.)

I asked the waiter, and he said it was called 'paprika hendl' and that, as it was a national dish, I should be able to get it anywhere along the Carpathians. My smattering of German is very useful here. Indeed, I should be lost without it.

In the British Museum I had found that Count Dracula's district is in the extreme east of the country, just on the borders of three states – Transylvania, Moldavia, and Bukovina – in the midst of the Carpathian mountains. One of the wildest and least known portions of Europe. I was not able to light on the exact locality of Castle Dracula, as there are no maps of this country as yet to compare with our own Ordnance Survey; but I found that Bistritz, the post town named by the Count, is a fairly well known place. I shall enter here some of my notes, as they may refresh my memory when I talk over my travels with Mina.

In the population of Transylvania there are four distinct nationalities: Saxons in the south, and mixed with them the Walachs, who are the descendants of the Dacians; Magyars in the west, and Szekelys in the east and north. I am going among the latter, who claim to be descended from

Attila and the Huns. This may be so, for when the Magyars conquered the country in the eleventh century they found the Huns settled in it. I read that every known superstition in the world is gathered into the horseshoe of the Carpathians, as if it were the centre of some sort of imaginative whirlpool. If so, my stay may be very interesting.

(Mem., I must ask the Count all about them.)

I did not sleep well, though my bed was comfortable enough, for I had all sorts of queer dreams. There was a dog howling all night under my window, which may have had something to do with it. Or it may have been the paprika, for I had to drink up all the water in my carafe, and was still thirsty. Towards morning I was wakened by a continuous knocking at my door, so I must have been sleeping soundly by then. I had for breakfast more paprika, and a sort of porridge of maize flour which they said was 'mamaliga', and eggplant stuffed with forcemeat, a very excellent dish, which they call 'impletata'.

(Mem., get recipe for this also.)

Had to hurry breakfast, for the train started a little before eight, or rather it *ought* to have done so, for after rushing to the station at 7.30 I had to sit in the carriage for more than an hour before we began to move. It seems to me that the further East you go the more unpunctual are the trains. What ought they to be in China?

All day long we seemed to dawdle through a country full of beauty of every kind. Sometimes we saw little towns or castles on the tops of steep hills such as we see in old missals. Sometimes we ran by rivers and streams which seemed from their wide stony margins to be subject to great floods. It takes a lot of water, and running strong, to sweep the outside edge of a river clear.

At every station there were groups of people, sometimes crowds, and in all sorts of attire. Some were just like the peasants in and Germany, with short jackets and round hats and home-made trousers. Others were very picturesque. The women looked pretty, except when you got near them, but they were very clumsy about the waist. They had all full white sleeves of some kind or other, and most of them had big belts with a lot of strips of something fluttering from them like the dresses in a ballet, but of course petticoats under them.

The strangest figures were the Slovaks, more barbarian than the rest, with their big cowboy hats, great baggy dirty-white trousers, white linen shirts, and enormous heavy leather belts, nearly a foot wide, all studded over with brass nails. They wear high boots, with their trousers tucked into them, and have long black hair and heavy black moustaches. They are very picturesque and on the stage would be set down at once as some old band of Oriental brigands. They are, however, I am told, very harmless and rather wanting in self-assertion.

It was past twilight when we got to Bistritz, which is a very interesting old place. Being virtually on the frontier – for the Borgo Pass leads from it into Bukovina – it has had a very stormy existence, and certainly shows marks of it. Early in the seventeenth century it underwent a siege of three weeks and lost 53,000 people, the casualties of war proper being assisted by famine and disease. And only fifty years ago a series of forest fires wrought terrible havoc on five separate occasions.

Count Dracula had directed me to the Golden Krone Hotel, which I found, to my great delight, to be thoroughly old-fashioned. I was evidently expected, for at the door a cheery-looking elderly woman in the usual peasant dress – white undergarment with long double apron, front and back, of coloured stuff fitting almost too tight for modesty – bowed to me and said:

'The Herr English?'

'Yes,' I said. 'Herr Jonathan Harker.'

She smiled, and gave some message to an elderly man in white shirtsleeves, who had followed her to the door. He went, but immediately returned with a letter:

> Dear Friend,
>
> Welcome to the Carpathians. I am anxiously expecting you. Sleep well tonight. At three tomorrow the diligence will start for Bukovina; a place on it is kept for you. At the Borgo Pass my carriage will await you and will bring you to me. I trust that your journey from London has been a happy one, and that you will enjoy your stay in my beautiful land.
>
> Cordially,
> DRACULA.

4 May.

My landlord had a letter from the Count, directing him to secure the best place on the coach for me. Yet he seemed somewhat reticent, and pretended he could not understand my German, though up to then he had understood it perfectly. He and his wife, the old lady who had received me, looked at each other in evident fear. He mumbled that the money had been sent in a letter, and that was all he knew.

When I asked if he knew Count Dracula, and his castle, both he and his wife crossed themselves, and, saying that they knew nothing at all, simply refused to speak further. Then, just before I left, the old lady came up to my room and said in a very hysterical way:

'Must you go? Oh, young Herr! Must you go?'

She was so excited that she seemed to have lost her grip on German, and mixed it up with some other language which I did not know. I was just able to follow her by asking many questions. When I told her I must go at once, on important business, she asked insistently:

'Do you know what day it is?'

I answered that it was the fourth of May.

She shook her head as she said again:

'Yes, yes! But do you know what *day* it is?'

On my saying that I did not understand, she went on:

'It is the eve of St George's Day. Do you not know that tonight, when the clock strikes midnight, all the evil things in the world will have full sway? And where you are going?'

She was in such distress that I tried to comfort her, but without effect. Finally she went down on her knees and implored me not to go. It was all very ridiculous, but I did not feel comfortable. However, there was business and I therefore raised her up, and thanked her, but said my duty was imperative.

She dried her eyes, took a crucifix from her neck and offered it to me. I did not know what to do, for, as a good English Churchman, I have been taught to regard such things as idolatrous, and yet it seemed so ungracious to refuse an old lady meaning so well and in such distress.

Seeing my doubt, she put the rosary round my neck, and said:

'For your mother's sake.' Then she left the room.

I am writing this while waiting for the coach, which is of course late, and the crucifix is still round my neck. Whether it is the old lady's fear, I do not know, but I am feeling a little uneasy. If only Mina – but here comes the coach!

5 May.

The grey of the morning has passed, and the sun is high over the distant horizon, which seems jagged, whether with trees or hills I know not, for it is so far off that big things and little are mixed. I am not sleepy, and will write till sleep comes. There are many odd things to put down, beginning with my meal. I dined on what they call 'robber steak' — bits of bacon, onion, and beef, seasoned with red pepper, and strung on sticks and roasted over the fire, in the simple style of the London cat's-meat! The wine was Golden Mediasch, which produces a queer sting on the tongue. It is, however, not disagreeable. I drank only a couple of glasses of this, and nothing else.

When I got on the coach the driver had not taken his seat, and I saw him talking with the landlady — evidently of me, for now and then they looked at me, and some of the people who were sitting on the bench outside — which they call 'word-bearer' — came and listened, then looked at me. I could hear a lot of words often repeated — queer words, for there were many nationalities in the crowd — so I quietly got my polyglot dictionary from my bag and looked them up. I must say they were hardly cheering, for amongst them were 'Ordog' — Satan, 'pokol' — hell, 'stregoica' — witch, 'vrolok' and 'vlkoslak' — both of which mean the same thing, one being Slovak and the other Serbian for something that is either werewolf or vampire.

(Mem., I must ask the Count about these superstitions.)

When we started, the crowd round the inn door, which had by this time swelled to a considerable size, all made the sign of the cross and pointed two fingers towards me. With some difficulty I got a fellow passenger to tell me what they meant. He explained that it was a charm against the evil eye. This was not very pleasant for me, just starting for an unknown place to meet an unknown man, but everyone seemed so kind-hearted, sorrowful and sympathetic that I could not but be touched.

I shall never forget my last glimpse of the inn-yard amid its crowd of picturesque figures, all crossing themselves, as they stood round the wide archway, with its background of rich foliage of oleander and orange trees in green tubs clustered in the centre of the yard. Then our driver, whose wide linen drawers covered the whole front of the box-seat — 'gotza', they call them — cracked his big whip over his four small horses, which ran abreast, and off we set.

I soon lost sight and recollection of ghostly fears in the beauty of the scene as we drove along, although had I known the language, or rather languages, which my fellow-passengers were speaking, I might not have been so serene. Before us lay a green sloping land full of forests and woods, with here and there steep hills crowned with clumps of trees and farmhouses, their blank gable-ends to the road. There was everywhere a bewildering mass of fruit blossom – apple, plum, pear, cherry – and the green grass under the trees was brightly spangled with the fallen petals.

Amongst these green hills of the 'Mittel Land' ran the road, weaving round grassy curves and through the straggling ends of pine woods, which licked down the hillsides like tongues of green flame. The road was rugged, but still we seemed to fly over it with a feverish haste, the driver being evidently bent on losing no time in reaching Borgo Prund.

I was told that this road is in summertime excellent, but had not yet been put in order after the winter snows. In this respect it is different from most roads in the Carpathians, for it is an old tradition that they are not to be kept too well. Of old the Hospodars would not repair them, lest the Turk should think they were preparing to bring in foreign troops, and so hasten the war which was ever at loading point.

Beyond the green swelling hills of the Mittel Land rose mighty slopes of forest up to the lofty Carpathians themselves. Right and left they towered, with the afternoon sun bringing out all the glorious colours of this beautiful range, deep blue and purple in the shadows of the peaks, green and brown where grass and rock mingle, and an endless perspective of jagged rock and pointed crags, till these were themselves lost in the distance, where the snowy peaks rose grandly. Here and there seemed mighty rifts in the mountains, through which, as the sun began to sink, gleamed a whiteness of falling water.

One of my companions touched my arm as we swept round the base of a hill and into view of a snow-peaked mountain:

'Look! *Isten szek!* – God's seat!' And he crossed himself reverently.

As we wound on our seemingly endless way, and the sun sank low behind us, the creeping shadows of evening were emphasized by the sunset still on the summit snows, which glowed a delicate cool pink. Several times we passed Czechs and Slovaks, all in picturesque attire, but I noticed that goitre was painfully prevalent. By the roadside were many crosses, which caused my companions all to cross themselves. Occasionally we saw a peasant man or woman kneeling down before a shrine. They would not look round as we approached, but seemed, in their self-surrender of devotion, to have neither eyes nor ears for the outer world.

There were many things new to me: hay ricks in the trees, and beautiful masses of weeping birch, their white stems shining like silver through the delicate green of the leaves. Now and again we passed a leiter-wagon – the ordinary peasant's cart – with its long, snakelike vertebrae, built for the uneven roads. On this were sure to be seated quite a group of home-coming peasants; the Czechs in their white, and the Slovaks with their coloured sheepskins; the latter carrying their long staves lance-fashion, with axes at their ends.

As evening fell it got very cold, and the growing twilight seemed to merge into one dark composite mistiness the gloom of all the trees – oak, beech, and pine – though in the valleys which ran deep between the spurs of the hills, as we ascended through the Pass, the dark firs stood out against the background of late-lying snow. Sometimes, as the road cut through the pine woods that seemed in the darkness to be closing down upon us, great masses of greyness bestrewed the trees and produced a peculiarly weird and solemn effect, which revived grim fancies engendered earlier, when the falling sunset had thrown into strange relief the ghost-like clouds which amongst the Carpathians seem to wind ceaselessly through the valleys.

Sometimes the hills were so steep that, despite our driver's haste, the horses could only go slowly. I wished then to get down and walk, as we do at home, but the driver would not hear of it.

'No, no!' he said. 'The dogs here are too fierce.' Then he added, with what he evidently meant for grim pleasantry – for he looked round to catch the approving smile of the rest:

'And you may have enough of such matters before you go to sleep.'

The only stop he would make was a moment's pause to light his lamps.

When it grew dark there seemed to be some excitement amongst the passengers, and they kept speaking to him, one after the other, as though urging him to further speed. He lashed the horses unmercifully with his long whip, and with wild cries of encouragement urged them on to further exertions. Then through the darkness I saw a patch of grey light ahead of us, as though there were a cleft in the hills. The excitement of the passengers grew greater, and the crazy coach rocked on its great leather springs and swayed like a boat in a storm. I had to hold on. The road grew more level, and we appeared to fly along.

Soon the mountains loomed nearer and seemed to frown down upon us. We were entering the Borgo Pass. Several of the passengers now offered me gifts – indeed, would take no refusal. Their offerings were of an odd and varied kind, but given with a kindly word, and a blessing, and that strange mixture of fear-meaning movements which I had seen outside the Bistritz hotel – the sign of the cross and the guard against the evil eye. Presently the driver leaned forward, and on each side the passengers, craning through the coach windows, peered eagerly into the darkness.

It was evident that something very exciting was expected, but no-one would give me the slightest explanation. This excitement kept on for some time, and at last we saw before us the Pass opening out on the eastern side. There were dark, rolling clouds overhead, and in the air a heavy, oppressive sense of thunder.

I was now looking out for Count Dracula's carriage. Each moment I expected to see the glare of lamps through the blackness, but still the only light was the flickering of our lamps, in which steam from our hard-driven horses rose in a white cloud.

The other passengers drew back with a sigh of gladness, which seemed to mock my own disappointment. I was wondering what to do, when the driver, looking at his watch, muttered to the others something which I could not understand. Turning to me, he said in German worse than my own:

'There is no carriage here. The Herr is not expected, after all. He will now come on to Bukovina, and return tomorrow. Or the next day. Better the next day.'

While he was speaking the horses began to neigh and snort and plunge so wildly that the driver had to rein them cruelly hard. A chorus of screams from the peasants accompanied frantic crossing of their breasts, as a calash with four horses drew up beside our coach. I could see from the flash of our lamps that the horses – splendid-looking animals – were all coal-black. They were driven by a tall man with a long brown beard and a great black hat, which seemed to hide his face – so that only a pair of very bright eyes gleamed brightly red in the lamplight. To our driver he said:

'You are early tonight, my friend.'

The man stammered back:

'The English Herr was in a hurry.'

The stranger replied:

'That is why, I suppose, you wished him to go on to Bukovina?' As he spoke he smiled. The lamplight fell on a hard-looking mouth, with very red lips and sharp-looking teeth, white as ivory.

One of my companions whispered to another that line from Burger's 'Lenore':

For the dead travel fast.

The strange driver evidently heard the words, for he looked up with a glinting grin. The passenger turned his face away, crossing himself yet again.

'Give me the Herr's luggage,' said the stranger.

With exceeding alacrity my bags were handed out and put in the calash.

Then I descended from the coach and the calash driver helped me up with a grip of steel. Without a word he shook his reins. The black horses turned, and we swept into the darkness of the Pass. As I looked back I glimpsed in the lamplight the steam from the coach horses, and projected against it the figures of my late companions – crossing themselves. Their driver cracked his whip and called to his horses, and they rumbled away towards Bukovina.

As they disappeared into the darkness I felt a strange chill, and a lonely feeling came over me; but a cloak was thrown over my shoulders, a rug across my knees, and the driver said in excellent German:

'The night is chill, mein Herr, and my master the Count bade me take all care of you. There is a flask of slivovitz (plum brandy) underneath the seat.'

I did not take any, but it was a comfort to know it was there. I felt a little strange, and not a little frightened. Had there been any alternative to that unknown night journey I should have taken it. The carriage went at a hard pace for some time, then took a sharp turn down another straight road. It seemed to me that we were going over the same ground again and again, so I took note of some salient points, and my suspicions were confirmed. I wanted to ask the driver what this all meant, but I feared to do so. Curious to know how the time was passing, I struck a match and looked at my watch.

It was a few minutes before midnight.

This gave me a shock which I could not explain, and I waited with a sick feeling of suspense.

Then a dog began to howl far down the road – a long, agonized wailing, as if from fear. The howl was taken up by another dog, then another, and another, until, borne on the wind sighing through the Pass, a wild cacophony filled the air. At the first howl the horses began to strain and rear, but the driver spoke to them soothingly, and they quieted down, but shivered and sweated as though after a fearful runaway. And now, far up the mountains on each side of us, began the louder and sharper howling of wolves, which affected both the horses and myself in the same way – for I was minded to jump from the calash and run, while they reared again and plunged madly, so that the driver had to use all his great strength to keep them from bolting.

In a few minutes, however, my ears got accustomed to the sound, and the horses calmed enough for the driver to descend and soothe them. Petting them, he whispered something in their ears, as I have heard of horse-tamers doing, and with extraordinary effect, for under his caresses they became manageable again, though still they trembled.

The driver again took his seat. Shaking his reins, he started us off at a great pace. This time, after the Pass, he suddenly turned up a narrow roadway to the right.

Soon we were hemmed in by trees, which in places arched right over the roadway till we passed as through a tunnel, with great frowning rocks guarding us boldly on either side. Though we were in shelter, we could hear the rising wind moan and whistle through the rocks, and the branches of the trees crashed together as we swept along.

It grew colder still and fine, powdery snow began to fall. Soon we, and all around us, were blanketed with white. The keen wind still carried the howling of the dogs, though this grew fainter as we went on.

Meanwhile the baying of the wolves sounded ever nearer, as though they were closing round us. I grew dreadfully afraid, and the horses shared my fear.

But the driver seemed not in the least disturbed. He kept turning his head left and right, but I could not see anything through the darkness.

Suddenly, away on our left, I saw a faint blue flame.

The driver, seeing it at the same moment, at once checked the horses, jumped to the ground, and disappeared. I did not know what to do, the less as the howling of wolves grew closer; but while I wondered the driver suddenly appeared again, silently took his seat, and we resumed our journey.

I must have fallen asleep and kept dreaming of the incident, for it seemed to repeat endlessly, and now it is like a recurrent awful nightmare:

The flame appears so near the road that even in the darkness I can follow the driver's movements. He goes rapidly towards the blue flame. It must be very faint, for it does not illumine the place around it at all. The driver gathers a few stones and forms them into some strange device. Then a curious effect: when he stands between me and the flame he does not obstruct it, I can see its ghostly flicker all the same. This startles me, but as the effect is only momentary, I take it that my straining eyes deceive me. For a time there are no blue flames, and we speed onwards through the gloom, with the howling wolves in a circle all around us.

Soon the driver descends again, and this time he goes further afield.

During his absence the horses begin to tremble worse than ever and to snort and scream with fright. I cannot see any cause for it, for the wolves have fallen silent. Suddenly the moon, sailing through the black clouds, appears behind the jagged crest of a beetling, pine-clad rock. By its light I see around us a ring of wolves, with white teeth and lolling red tongues; with long, sinewy limbs and shaggy hair. In the ghastly silence which holds them they are a hundred times more terrible than when they howled, and I feel paralysed by fear.

All at once the wolves howl together again, as though triggered by the moonlight. The horses rear about and roll helpless eyes that are painful to look upon — the ring of living terror encompassing them on every side. I shout to the coachman then beat the side of the calash, hoping by the noise to scare the wolves away — yet they slink ever closer. Suddenly — I know not how — the coachman reappears in the roadway, his voice raised harshly in imperious command.

As he waves his long arms the wolves fall back. Just then a heavy cloud obscures the moon, and again we are in darkness.

My next memory is of the driver climbing back into the calash, the wolves having disappeared. This was all so uncanny that a dreadful fear came over me, and I was afraid to move or speak. The time seemed interminable as we swept on our way, now in dreadful utter darkness, for the rolling clouds concealed the moon. We kept on, ever upward, until suddenly the driver was pulling up the horses in the courtyard of a vast ruined castle, from whose tall black windows came no ray of light, and whose broken battlements showed only as a jagged line against the sky — moonlit above the clouds.

2

Castle Dracula

6 May.

In the gloom the courtyard looked huge — several dark alleys leading off under great round arches. But perhaps it seemed bigger than it really is. Daylight will surely tell.

When the calash stopped, the driver jumped down to assist me, and again I noted his prodigious strength — his hand round mine like a vice of steel. Then he placed my bags on the ground beside me as I stood close to a great door, old and studded with large iron nails, and set in a projecting doorway of massive stone. I could see even in the dim light that the stone carving had been much worn by time and weather. As I stood, the driver jumped back into his seat and shook the reins. The horses started forward, and the carriage disappeared down one of the dark openings.

I stood in silence, for of bell or knocker there was no sign, and through these frowning walls and dark windows my voice could hardly penetrate. My wait seemed endless, and doubts and fears crowded round me. What sort of place had I come to, and among what people? What sort of grim adventure was this, indeed, for a solicitor's clerk sent out to explain the purchase of a London estate?

Solicitor's clerk!

Mina would not like that, for just before leaving London I had word that my examination was successful: now I was a full-blown *solicitor!*

Wasn't I?

To see if I were really awake, I began to rub my eyes and pinch myself. It all seemed like a horrible nightmare, and I expected that I should suddenly awake and find myself at home, with the dawn struggling in through the windows. But my flesh answered the pinching test, and my eyes were not to be deceived. I was indeed among the Carpathians. All I could do now was be patient, and await the coming morn.

Just as I reached this conclusion a heavy step approached behind the great door, and through the chinks came a gleam of light. Then the sound of rattling chains and the clanking of massive bolts drawn back. A key was turned with the loud grating noise of long disuse, and the huge door swung back.

Within stood a tall old man, clean-shaven save for a long white moustache, and clad in black from head to foot, without a single speck of colour about him. In his hand was an antique silver lamp, in which the flame burned without chimney or globe of any kind, throwing long, quivering shadows as it flickered in the draught of the open door. The old man motioned me in with a courtly gesture, saying in excellent English, but with a strange intonation:

'Welcome to my house! Enter freely, and of your own will!' He made no motion of stepping to meet me, but stood like a statue – as though his gesture of welcome had fixed him into stone. The instant, however, that I had stepped over the threshold, he moved impulsively forward and grasped my hand with a strength which made me wince, an effect not lessened by his hand feeling cold as ice – like the hand of a corpse.

Again he said:

'Welcome. Come freely. Go safely. And leave something of the happiness you bring!'

'Count Dracula?'

He bowed as he replied:

'I am Dracula. And you, Mr Harker, must come in. The night air is chill, and you need to eat and rest.' As he spoke he lodged the lamp in a bracket on the wall, then stepped out and took my luggage.

I protested.

He insisted:

'Sir, you are my guest! Since it is late, and my people are not available . . . ' He carried my bags along the passage, then up a great winding stair and along a further passage, on whose stone floor our steps rang heavily. At the end of this he threw open a heavy door, and I rejoiced to see within a well-lit room and a table spread for supper, while a mass of logs blazed and crackled in a mighty hearth.

The Count halted, put down my bags, and closed the door. Then he crossed the room and opened a second door, which led into a small octagonal room lit by a single lamp, and seemingly without a window. Passing through this, he opened another door, and motioned me to enter. It was a welcome sight: a great bedroom well lighted and warmed with another log fire, which sent a hollow roar up the wide chimney. The Count left my luggage inside and withdrew, saying:

'You will need, after your journey, to refresh yourself. I trust you will find all you wish. When you are ready . . . your supper awaits you.'

The light and warmth and the Count's courteous welcome had allayed my fears, and I realized I was famished – so I made a hasty toilet, and went back to the other room.

My host, who stood leaning against the great fireplace, waved gracefully at the table, and said:

'Be seated. Sup heartily. Excuse my not joining you – I have dined already.'

I handed him the sealed letter Mr Hawkins had entrusted to me.

He opened it, read it gravely, then, with a charming smile, he handed it back to me. One passage made me flush with pleasure:

'I much regret that an attack of gout forbids absolutely my travelling; but I am happy to send in my place Mr Jonathan Harker, in whom I have every confidence. He is a talented young man, full of energy, and of a very faithful and discreet disposition, having grown into manhood in my service. He shall attend on you when you will, and shall take your instructions in all matters.'

The Count came forward and took the cover off a dish, and I fell to at once on an excellent roast chicken. This, with some cheese, a salad, and two glasses of old Tokay, was my supper. While I ate, the Count asked me many questions as to my journey. After my supper he desired me to draw up a chair by the fire and smoke a cigar.

(Mem., strange that he did not smoke himself.)

I had now an opportunity of observing him, and found him of a very marked physiognomy.

His face was strong – *very* strong. Nose aquiline, with a high bridge and peculiarly arched nostrils; lofty domed forehead; hair growing scantily round the temples, but profusely elsewhere; eyebrows almost meeting over the nose, with bushy hair that seemed to curl in its own profusion. The mouth, so far as I could see it under the heavy moustache, was fixed and rather cruel-looking, with peculiarly sharp white teeth protruding over the lips, whose remarkable ruddiness showed astonishing vitality in a man of his years. For the rest, his ears were pale and at the tops extremely pointed; chin broad and strong; cheeks firm though thin. The general effect was one of extraordinary pallor.

Hitherto I had noticed the backs of his hands as they lay on his knees in the firelight, and they had seemed rather white and fine. But now I saw that they were rather coarse – broad, with squat fingers, and hairs in the centre of his palms. The nails were long and fine, and cut to sharp points.

As the Count leaned over me, and his hands touched me, I could not repress a shudder. It may have been that his breath was rank, but a horrible feeling of nausea came over me, which I simply could not conceal.

The Count, noticing, drew back. With a grimly sharp-toothed smile he sat down again on the far side of the fire. In the tense silence that followed I looked towards the window and saw the first dim streak of dawn. Moments later I heard a strange distant howling of many wolves.

The Count's eyes gleamed, and he said:

'The children of the night! What music they make!' Seeing the expression in my face, he added:

'You dwellers of the city cannot feel as does the hunter.' Then he rose and said:

'But you are tired, and your bedroom is all ready. I have to be away till the afternoon, so sleep as late as you will. And dream well!' With a courteous bow he opened the door to the octagonal room, and I entered my bedroom.

Later:

I am at sea in doubts and fears. I think strange things which I dare not confess to my own soul. God keep me.

7 May.

It is again early morning, but I have rested and enjoyed the last twenty-four hours. I slept till late, and awoke of my own accord. When I had dressed I went into the room where we had supped, and found a cold breakfast laid out, with coffee kept hot on the hearth. On the table was a card:

'I have to be absent for a while. Do not wait for me. D.'

So I tucked in to a hearty meal. Then I looked for a bell, to let the servants know I had finished; but I could not find one. There are certainly odd deficiencies in the house, considering its extraordinary evidences of wealth. The table service, for example, is of beautifully wrought gold, and must be of immense value. The curtains and upholstery of the chairs and sofas and the hanging of my bed are of the costliest and most beautiful fabrics, and are in excellent order even though they must be centuries old.

Yet nowhere is there a mirror – not even a toilet glass on my table – and I had to get the little shaving-glass from my bag before I could shave. I have not yet seen a servant anywhere, or heard any sound except the howling of wolves. After my 'breakfast' – it was between five and six o'clock – I looked about for something to read, for I did not like to roam about the castle until I had asked the Count's permission. There was absolutely nothing in the room – no books or newspapers; not even writing materials – so I opened another door and found a sort of library. The door opposite mine I tried, but found it locked.

In the library I found, to my great delight, a vast number of English books, whole shelves full of them, and bound volumes of magazines and newspapers. A table in the centre was littered with English magazines and newspapers, though none of them were recent. The books were of the most varied kind – history, geography, politics, political economy, botany, geology, law – all relating to English life and customs. There were even the London Directory, Whitaker's Almanack, the Army and Navy Lists, and – which somehow gladdened my heart – the Law List.

While I was looking at the books, the far door was unlocked, and in came the Count. He saluted me in a hearty way, and hoped that I had had a good night's rest. Then he went on:

'I am glad you found your way in here, for I am sure there is much that will interest you. These' – he laid his hand on some of the books – 'have been good friends to me, and for some years past, ever since I had the idea of going to London, have given me many hours of pleasure. Through them I have come to know your great England; and to know her is to love her. How I long to go through the crowded streets of your mighty London, to be in the midst of the whirl and rush of humanity, to share its life, its change, its death, and all that makes it what it is. But alas! As yet I only know your tongue through books. To you, my friend, I look that I know it to speak.'

'But, Count,' I said, 'your English is first-class!'

He bowed gravely:

'True, I know the grammar, and the words – yet I know not how to speak them.'

'Indeed,' I said, 'you speak excellently.'

He answered:

'Did I speak in your London, all there would know me for a stranger. That is not good enough. Here I am noble; a boyar; the master. But a stranger in a strange land, he is no-one. Myself I have been so long master that I will have none other ever master over me. So you, Mr Harker, you must tell me when I make error, even of the smallest, in my speaking. I am sorry to have been so long away today – but you will forgive one who has so many important affairs in hand.'

'Of course,' I said, then asked if I might use the library freely.

He answered:

'By all means,' and added:

'You may go anywhere in the castle, except where the doors are locked. There, in any case, you would not wish to go.'

'Of course not.'

He went on:

'We are in Transylvania, not England. Our ways are not your ways, and there shall to you be many things strange.'

This led to much conversation. Seeing he wanted to talk, I asked many questions. Sometimes I felt he pretended not to understand; but generally he answered frankly. As time passed I became bolder, and asked him why the coachman had stopped to investigate the blue flames.

The Count described the common belief that on a certain night of the year – last night, in fact, when all evil spirits are supposed to have unchecked sway – a blue flame is seen over any place where treasure has been concealed.

'That treasure *has* been hidden,' he went on, 'in the region through which you came last night, there can be little doubt. For it was the ground fought over for centuries by the Walachian, the Saxon, and the Turk.'

'But how', said I, 'could such treasure have remained so long undiscovered?'

The Count smiled, and as his lips ran back over his gums, the long, sharp, canine teeth showed out strangely. He answered:

'Because your peasant is at heart a coward and a fool! Those flames only appear one night a year, and then no man of this land will, if he can help it, stir without his doors. So the blue flames burn unseen!' Then he abruptly changed the subject:

'But tell me now of London, and the house you have procured for me.'

I went back to my bedroom to get the property papers from my bag. While I was placing them in order I heard a rattling of china and silver in the supper room. When I passed back through it, I noticed that the table had been cleared and the lamp lit. The lamps were also lit in the study, or library, and I found the Count lying on the sofa, reading, of all things, an English Bradshaw's Guide. When I came in he cleared the books and papers from the table; and with him I went into plans and deeds and figures of all sorts.

He was interested in everything and asked me a host of questions about the place and its surroundings. He clearly had studied beforehand all he could get on the neighbourhood, for he knew much more than I did. When I remarked upon this, he answered:

'Is it not needful that I should? When I go there I shall be all alone, and my friend Harker Jonathan will be in Exeter, miles away, working at the law for Mr Hawkins. So!'

We went thoroughly into the purchase of the estate at Purfleet. When I had told him the facts and got his signature to the necessary papers, and had written a letter with them ready to post to Mr Hawkins, he asked how I had come across so suitable a place. I read to him the note which I had made at the time:

'At Purfleet, on a by-road, I came across just such a place as seemed to be required, where was displayed a dilapidated notice: *For Sale*. The property is surrounded by a high wall, of ancient structure, built of heavy stones, and has not been repaired for years. The closed gates are of heavy old oak and iron, all eaten with rust.

'The estate is called Carfax, no doubt a corruption of the old *Quatre Faces*, as the house is four-sided, agreeing with the cardinal points of the compass. It contains in all some twenty acres, quite surrounded by the solid stone wall above-mentioned. There are many trees on it, which make it in places gloomy, and there is a small but deep and dark-looking lake, evidently fed by some springs, as the water is clear and flows away in a fair-sized stream.

'The house is very large and of all periods – dating back, I should say, to medieval times, for one part is of stone immensely thick, with only a few windows high up and heavily barred with iron. It looks like part of a keep, and is close to an old chapel. I could not enter it, as I had not the key of the door leading to it from the house, but I have taken Kodak views of it from various points. There are few houses close at hand, one being a very large house only recently added to and formed into a private lunatic asylum. It is not, however, visible from the grounds of Carfax.'

When I had finished, Count Dracula said:

'I am glad it is old and big. I myself am of an old family, and to live in a new house would kill me. A house cannot be made habitable in a day, and, after all, how few days go to make up a century? I rejoice also that there is an olden chapel, since we Transylvanian nobles love not to think that our bones must rest amongst the common dead. I seek not gaiety nor mirth, nor the bright sunshine and sparkling waters which so please the young and gay. For I am no longer young. And my heart, through weary years of mourning over the dead, is not attuned to mirth. Moreover, the walls of my castle are broken, the shadows many, and the wind breathes cold through the broken battlements and casements. I love the shade and the shadow, and would be alone with my thoughts.'

Somehow his words and his look did not seem to accord. Or was it the cast of face that made his smile look malignant and saturnine?

Presently, excusing himself for some minutes, he left me to arrange my papers. After half an hour I began to look at the books around me. One was an atlas, which I found opened naturally at England, as if that map had been much used. On it little rings marked certain places – one near his new estate; the other two round Exeter, and Whitby on the Yorkshire coast.

An hour later the Count returned.

'Aha!' he said. 'Still at your books? Good! But you must not work always. Come. Your supper is ready.' He took my arm, and we went into the next room, where I found an excellent meal ready on the table. The Count again excused himself, saying he had dined out. But he sat as on the previous night, and chatted while I ate.

After supper I smoked, as before, and the Count stayed with me, chatting and asking questions on every conceivable subject, hour after hour. I felt that it was getting very late indeed, but I did not say anything, for I felt obliged to meet my host's wishes in every way. I was not sleepy, as the long sleep yesterday had fortified me; but I could not help experiencing that chill of coming dawn which is like the turning of a tide. All at once we heard a cock crow rise up with preternatural shrillness through the clear morning air.

Count Dracula, jumping to his feet, said:

'Morning again! How remiss I am to keep you up so long! You must make our conversation regarding my dear new country of England less interesting, so that I may not forget how time flies by us!' And with a courtly bow he left me.

I went into my bedroom and drew back the curtains, but all I could see was a warm grey of quickening sky. So I drew the curtains again, and have written of this day.

8 May.

There is something so strange about this place that I cannot but feel uneasy. I wish I were out of it, or, better, that I never had come. Perhaps this night-existence is telling on me; but would that that were all! If there were anyone to talk to I could bear it, but there is no-one. I have only the Count to speak with, and he! – I fear I myself am the only living soul within the place. But . . . no, I must not let imagination riot. If it does, I am lost. So let me say once how I stand – or seem to.

I only slept a few hours, and, feeling that I *could* not sleep any more, got up. I had hung my glass by the window, and was just beginning to shave. Suddenly I felt a hand on my shoulder, and heard the Count's voice say:

'Good morning.'

I started, for it amazed me that I had not seen him, since the reflection of the glass covered the whole room behind me. Having answered the Count's salutation, I turned to the glass again to see if I had been mistaken. This time there could be no error, for the man was close to me, and I could see him over my shoulder.

But no reflection of him in the mirror!

The whole room behind me was displayed; but there was no man in it except myself. And in that instant I saw that I had cut myself while shaving. The cut had bled a little, and the blood was trickling over my chin. I laid down the razor, turning as I did so half-round to look for some sticking-plaster.

When the Count saw my face, his eyes blazed with a sort of fury, and he made a demoniac grab for my throat. I shrank back, and his hand touched the string of beads which held my crucifix. Immediately his fury passed – so quickly that I could hardly believe it had ever been.

'Take care', he said, 'not to cut yourself. It is more dangerous than you think in this country.' Then he seized the shaving-glass and went on:

'And this is the wretched thing that has done the mischief. Foul bauble of man's vanity, away!' Opening the heavy window with one wrench of his terrible hand, he flung out the glass, which shattered into a thousand pieces on the courtyard stones far below. Then he withdrew without a word.

It is very annoying, for I do not see how I am to shave, unless in my watch-case or the bottom of the shaving-pot, which is, fortunately, of metal.

When I went into the dining-room there was no sign of the Count, so I breakfasted alone.

(Mem., strange that I have not seen the Count eat or drink. He must be most peculiar.)

After breakfast I did a little exploring in the castle. I went out on the stairs and found a room looking south. The view was magnificent. The castle is on the edge of a terrible precipice. A stone from the window would fall a thousand feet! As far as the eye can see is a sea of green tree-tops, with occasionally a deep rift where there is a chasm. Here and there are silver threads where the rivers wind in deep gorges through the forests.

But I am not in heart to describe beauty, for when I had seen the view I explored further; doors, doors, doors everywhere, and all locked and bolted. Only through the castle windows is there any possible escape.

It is a veritable prison, and I . . . a prisoner.

3

Dracula's Prisoner

When I found I was trapped a wild feeling came over me. I rushed up and down the stairs, trying every door and peering out of every window I could find; but after a little the conviction of my helplessness overpowered me. Looking back, I think I must have been temporarily mad, for I behaved as a rat in a cage.

And yet . . . I *am* as a rat in a cage.

Hardly had I come to this conclusion when I heard the great door below shut, and knew the Count had returned. He did not come at once into the library, so I went cautiously to my room and found him making the bed. This was odd, but only confirmed what I had all along thought – that there were no servants in the castle. When later I saw him through the chink of the hinges of the door laying the table in the dining-room, I was assured of it. This gave me a fright, for if there is no-one else in the castle, it must have been the Count himself who drove the coach that brought me here. This is a terrible thought; for, if so, what does it mean that he could control the wolves, as he did, by merely raising his hand?

How was it that all the people at Bistritz and on the coach had some terrible fear for me?

What meant the giving of the crucifix, of the garlic, of the wild rose, of the mountain ash? Bless that good, good woman who hung the crucifix round my neck! For it is a comfort and a strength to me whenever I touch it. It is odd that a thing which I have been taught to regard as idolatrous should in a time of loneliness and trouble be of help. Some day I must examine this matter, but meanwhile . . . meanwhile I must find out all I can about Count Dracula, taking care, however, not to awaken his suspicion.

Midnight.

I have had a long talk with the Count. I asked him a few questions

on Transylvanian history, and he warmed to the subject wonderfully – speaking of great events, especially battles, as if he had been
present at them all. This he afterwards explained by saying that to a
boyar the pride of his house is his pride, their glory his glory, their fate
his fate. Whenever he spoke of his house he always said 'we', speaking
almost like a king. I wish I could put down all exactly as he said it, for
it was fascinating. He grew excited as he spoke, and walked about the
room pulling his great white moustache and grasping anything on which
he laid his hands as though he would crush it by main strength.

One thing he said I shall put down as nearly as I can; for it tells in its
way the story of his race:

'We Szekelys have a right to be proud, for in our veins flows the blood
of many brave races who fought as the lion fights, for lordship. Here,
in the whirlpool of European races, the Ugric tribe bore down from
Iceland the fighting spirit which Thor and Wodin gave them, which
their Berserkers displayed to such fell intent on the seaboards of Europe,
and of Asia and Africa too, till the peoples thought that the werewolves
themselves had come. Here too when they came they found the Huns,
whose warlike fury had swept the earth like a living flame, till the dying
peoples held that in their veins ran the blood of those old witches who,
expelled from Scythia, had mated with the devils in the desert.

'Fools, fools!

'What devil or witch was ever so great as Attila, whose blood is
in these veins?' He held up his arms. 'Is it a wonder that we were
a conquering race? That we were proud? That when the Magyar, the
Lombard, or the Turk poured in thousands over our frontiers, we drove
them back? Is it strange that when Arpad and his legions swept through
the Hungarian fatherland he found us here when he reached the frontier?
That the Honfoglalas was completed there? Or that, when the Hungarian
flood swept eastward, the Szekelys were claimed as kindred by the
victorious Magyars, and to *us* for centuries was trusted the guarding of
the frontier of Turkey-land?

'And who more gladly than we, throughout the Four Nations, received
the "bloody sword", or at its warlike call flocked quicker to the standard
of the King? When was redeemed that great shame of my nation, the
shame of Cassova, when the flags of the Walach and the Magyar went
down beneath the Crescent; who was it but one of my own race who as
Voivode crossed the Danube and beat the Turk on his own ground!

'There was a Dracula indeed.

'Who was it that his own unworthy brother, when he had fallen, sold his people to the Turk and brought the shame of slavery on them! Was it not this Dracula, indeed, who inspired that other of his race who in a later age again and again brought his forces over the great river into Turkey-land? Who, when he was beaten back, came again and again, though he had to come alone from the bloody field where his troops were being slaughtered, since he knew that he alone could ultimately triumph! They said that he thought only of himself. Bah! What good are peasants without a leader? Where ends the war without a brain and heart to conduct it? Again, when, after the battle of Mohacs, we threw off the Hungarian yoke, we of the Dracula blood were amongst their leaders, for our spirit would not brook that we were not free.

'Ah, young sir, the Szekelys – and the Dracula as their heart's blood, their brains, and their swords – can boast a record that mushroom growths like the Habsburgs and the Romanoffs can never reach. The war-like days are over. Blood is too precious a thing in these days of dishonourable peace. And the glories of the great races are but a tale to be told.'

It was by this time close on morning, and we went to bed.

(Mem., this diary echoes the 'Arabian Nights', for everything has to break off at cockcrow . . . or is it the ghost of Hamlet's father?)

12 May.

Let me begin with facts – bare, bald *facts*. Last evening when the Count came from his room he began by asking me questions on legal matters in relation to English business practice. I had spent the day wearily over books, and, simply to keep my mind occupied, went over some of the matters I had been examined in at Lincoln's Inn. There was a certain method in the Count's inquiries, so I shall try to put them down in sequence.

First, he asked if a man in England might have two solicitors, or more. I told him he might have a dozen if he wished, but that it would not be wise to have more than one solicitor engaged in one transaction, as only one could act at a time, and that to change would militate against his interest. He seemed thoroughly to understand, and went on to ask if there would be any practical difficulty in having one man in London to attend, say, to banking, and another, elsewhere, to look after shipping, in case local help were needed.

I asked him to explain more fully.

He said:

'I shall illustrate. Our friend Mr Peter Hawkins, from under the shadow of your beautiful cathedral at Exeter, far from London, buys for me, through your good self, my place at London. Good! Now here let me say frankly, lest you should think it strange that I have sought the services of one so far from London, that my motive was that no local interest be served. As one of London might have some purpose of himself or friend to serve I went thus afield to seek my agent, whose labours should be only to my interest. But suppose now that I, who have much of affairs, wish to ship goods, say, to Newcastle, might I not better consign to some agent in that port?'

I answered that we solicitors have a system of agency, enabling work to be done locally on instruction from the client's principal lawyer.

'But', said the Count, 'I still could be at liberty to direct myself?'

'Of course,' I replied. 'Such is often done by men of business, who do not like the whole of their affairs to be known by any one person.'

'Good!' he said, and then went on to ask about the means of making consignments, the forms to be gone through, and of all sorts of difficulties which might arise, but by forethought could be guarded against.

I answered to the best of my ability, and discovered that the Count would have made a wonderful solicitor, for there was nothing he did not foresee. For a man who had never been to England, his knowledge and acumen were wonderful. When he was satisfied that I had little more to teach him, he suddenly stood up and said:

'Have you written, since your first letter, to our friend Mr Peter Hawkins? Or to any other?'

With some bitterness in my heart I answered that I had not as yet seen any opportunity of sending letters to anybody.

'Then write now, my young friend,' he said, laying a heavy hand on my shoulder. 'Write to our friend and to any other. And say, if it please you, that you shall stay with me one month more.'

'So long?' I asked, for my heart grew cold at the thought.

'I desire it much. Nay, I will take no refusal. When your master engaged that someone should come on his behalf, it was understood that my needs only were to be consulted. I have not stinted. Is it not so?'

What could I do but bow? It was Mr Hawkins' interest at stake, not mine. Besides, while Count Dracula was speaking, there was that in his eyes and bearing which made me remember that I was already his prisoner.

The Count saw his victory in my eyes. Smoothly he continued:

'And I pray, my good young friend, that you will not discourse of things other than business in your letters. It will doubtless please your friends to know that you are well, and that you look forward to getting home to them. Is it not so?' As he spoke he handed me three sheets of notepaper and three envelopes. They were all of the thinnest foreign post, and looking at them, then at him, and noticing his quiet smile, with the sharp, canine teeth lying over the red underlip, I understood instantly that I should be careful what I wrote, for he would read it. So I determined to write only formal notes now, but to write fully to Mr Hawkins in secret, and also to Mina, for to her I could write in shorthand, which surely would baffle the Count.

When I had written my two letters I sat quiet, reading a book while the Count wrote several notes, referring as he wrote them to some books on his table. Then he took up my two and placed them with his own, and put by his writing materials. Minutes later, the moment the door had closed behind him, I leaned over and looked at his letters, which were face down on the table. I felt no compunction in doing so, sensing that in these circumstances I must protect myself in every way possible.

One of the letters was directed to a Samuel Billington, 7 The Crescent, Whitby; another to Herr Leutner, Varna; the third was to Coutts & Co, London, and the fourth to Herren Klopstock & Billreuth, bankers, Budapest. The second and fourth were unsealed. I was just about to look at them when I saw the door-handle move. I sank back in my seat, having just had time to replace the letters and resume my book before the Count, holding yet another letter in his hand, entered the room. He took up the letters on the table, stamped them carefully, and said:

'I trust you will forgive me, but I have much work to do in private this evening. You will, I hope, find all things as you wish.' At the door he turned, and after a moment's pause said:

'Let me advise you, my dear young friend – nay, let me *warn* you – never by any chance to fall to sleep in any other part of the castle. It is old, and has many memories, and there are bad dreams for those who sleep unwisely. Be warned! Should sleep ever threaten to overcome you, then haste back here to your own chamber, for your rest will then be safe. If you be not careful in this respect . . . ' He concluded with a gruesome washing of his hands.

I quite understood; my only doubt was whether any dream could be more terrible than the unnatural, horrible net of gloom and mystery which was already tightening round me.

Later.

No, I shall not fear to sleep where he is not. I have placed the crucifix over the head of my bed. I imagine that my rest is thus freer from dreams; and there it shall remain.

When he left me I went to my bedroom. Shortly, hearing no sound, I came out and went up the stone stair to where I could look out south. There was some sense of freedom in the vast expanse, inaccessible though it was to me, as compared with the narrow darkness of the courtyard. Gazing upon this I felt indeed a prisoner, and desperate for fresh air. I fear this nocturnal existence is destroying my nerve. I start at my own shadow, and am full of horrible imaginings. God knows, though, that there are grounds for terrible fear in this accursed place! I looked out over the beautiful expanse, bathed in soft yellow moonlight till it was almost as light as day. In the soft light the distant hills melted and in the valleys and gorges floated shadows of velvety blackness. The sheer beauty cheered me; there was peace and comfort in every breath I drew.

But then my eye was caught by something moving a storey below, to my left. The window at which I stood was tall and deep; stone-mullioned. Though weatherworn it was still complete; but it was evidently many a day since the case had been there. I drew back behind the stonework, and looked discreetly down.

What I saw was the Count's head emerging from a lower window. I did not see the face, but I knew his neck and the movement of his back and arms. In any case, I could never mistake those hands. I was at first somewhat amused, for it is wonderful how small a matter will interest a lonely prisoner. But my feelings changed to repulsion and terror when I saw the whole man slowly egress from the window and begin to crawl down the castle wall over that dreadful abyss, face down, with his cloak spreading out around him like great wings.

At first I could not believe my eyes.

I thought it was some trick of the moonlight, some weird effect of shadow; but I kept looking, and it could be no delusion. I saw his fingers and toes grasp the corners of the stones, worn clear of the mortar by the stress of years, and by thus using every projection and inequality he moved downwards with considerable speed, like a lizard along a wall.

What manner of man is this, or creature in the semblance of a man? The dread of this horrible place overpowers me; I am in fear – awful fear – and there is no escape; I am enveloped in terrors that I dare not contemplate . . .

15 May.

Once more have I seen the Count go forth in his lizard fashion, moving sidelong downwards, some hundred feet below and a good deal to the left. He vanished into some hole or window. When his head had disappeared I leaned out to see more, but without avail – the distance was too great. I knew he had left the castle now, and thought to use the opportunity to explore further than I had yet dared. I went back to my room, collected a lamp, and set off trying doors.

As I had expected they were all locked, and the locks were comparatively new. Next I went down the stone stairs to the hall where I had entered originally. I found I could pull back the bolts easily enough and unhook the great chains; but this door too was locked, and the key was gone!

Determined to find some means of escape, I proceeded to make a thorough examination of the various stairs and passages, and to try the doors that opened off them. One or two small rooms near the hall were open, but there was nothing in them except old furniture, dusty with age and moth-eaten. At last, however, I found one door at the top of a stairway which, though it seemed to be locked, gave a little under pressure. I tried it harder, and found that it was not really locked, but that the resistance came from the the hinges, which had fallen somewhat, so that the heavy door rested on the floor. Here was an opportunity not to miss, so I exerted myself, and with many efforts forced the door back.

I was now in a part of the castle quite distant from the rooms I knew, and a storey lower. From the windows I could see that this suite of rooms occupied a south wing, the windows of the end room looking out both west and south over the height of a terrifying precipice. The castle was built on the corner of a mountainous rock, so that on three sides it was quite impregnable, and great windows were placed here where sling, or bow, or culverin could not reach, and consequently light and comfort, impossible to a position which had to be guarded, were secured.

To the west was a long misty valley, and then, rising far away, vast jagged peaks rose endlessly, their sheer rock studded with mountain ash and thorn, whose roots clung hard in crevices of the prehistoric stone.

Here was evidently a portion of the castle occupied in bygone days, for the furniture had more the air of comfort than any I had previously seen. The windows were curtainless, and the yellow moonlight, flooding in through the diamond panes, enabled one to see even colours, while it softened the wealth of dust which lay over all and disguised in some measure the ravages of time and moth. My lamp was of little effect in the brilliant moonlight, but I was glad to have it with me, for there was a dread solitude about the place which chilled my heart and made my nerves tremble.

Still, the sense of adventure was better than fretting alone in the rooms I had come to hate, and after trying a little to school my nerves, I felt a soft quietude come over me. Here I was, sitting at a little oak table – where in old times possibly some fair lady sat to pen, with much thought and many blushes, her ill-spelt love-letter – and writing in my diary in shorthand all that has happened since I closed it last.

Later:

16 May; morning.

God preserve my sanity, for to this I am reduced. Safety is a thing of the past, and while I live on here there is but one thing to hope for: that I may not go mad. If, indeed, I be not mad already. If I be sane, then surely it is maddening to think that of all the foul things that lurk in this hateful place the Count is the least dreadful to me; that to him alone I can look for safety – so long as I serve his purpose. Merciful God, let me be calm, for in panic madness beckons indeed . . .

Calmer now, I see what Shakespeare meant when he made Hamlet say:

'My tablets! Quick, my tablets!

'Tis meet that I put it down . . . '

For now, feeling my own brain nearly unhinged, I turn to my diary for repose, and the habit of entering accurately helps to soothe me.

The Count's mysterious warning frightened me at the time; it frightens me more now when I think of it, for in future he has a fearful hold upon me. I shall fear to doubt what he may say!

When I had written up my diary, and had fortunately replaced the book and pen in my pocket, I felt sleepy. The Count's warning came into my mind, but I took a pleasure in disobeying it. The lure of sleep was upon me, and with it sleep's seductive obstinacy. The soft moonlight, and the wide expanse without, gave a sense of freedom which refreshed me. I determined not to return tonight to my gloom-haunted rooms, but to sleep here, where of old young ladies sat and sang and lived sweet lives while their gentle breasts pined for their menfolk away in the midst of remorseless wars.

So I dragged a heavy couch from a corner, in order, as I lay, to savour the lovely southern view. In this mood and posture, then, uncaring of the dust, I composed myself for sleep.

I suppose I *must* have drifted off; I *hope* so, but I fear . . . for all that followed was startlingly real – so real that now, sitting here in the broad, full sunlight of the morning, I cannot in the least believe that it was all a dream.

For I was not alone.

The room was the same, and along the floor, in the brilliant moonlight, my footsteps marked where I had disturbed the long accumulation of dust. In the moonlight opposite me were three young women, ladies by their dress and manner. I thought even at the time that I must be dreaming, for – though the moonlight was behind them – they threw no shadow on the floor. They came close and examined me for some time, then whispered together. Two were dark, and had high aquiline noses, like the Count's, and great dark, piercing eyes, that seemed almost red by the light of the pale yellow moon. The third was fair as fair as could be, with lush wavy tresses of golden hair and eyes like pale sapphires.

Somehow I seemed to know her face, and to know it in connection with some dreamy fear, but how? Where . . . ? All three had brilliant white teeth, that shone like pearls against the ruby of their voluptuous lips. There was something about them that made me uneasy, some longing and at the same time some deadly fear. I felt in my heart a wicked, burning desire that they would kiss me with those red lips. It is not good to note this down, lest some day it should cause Mina pain; but it is the truth.

They whispered together, and then they all three laughed – such a silvery, musical laugh, but hard – as though the sound never could have come through the softness of human lips. It was like the intolerable, tingling sweetness of water-glasses when played by a cunning hand. The fair girl shook her head coquettishly, and the other two urged her on. One said:

'Go on! You first; we shall follow.'

The other added:

'He is young and strong. There are kisses for us all!'

I lay quiet, looking out under my eyelashes in an agony of delightful anticipation. The fair girl advanced and bent over me till I could feel the movement of her breath upon me. Sweet it was in one sense, honey-sweet, and sent the same tingling through the nerves as her voice, but with something bitter underlying the sweet, a bitter offensiveness, as one smells in butchered blood.

I was afraid to raise my eyelids, but saw perfectly through my lashes.

The fair girl knelt over me, fairly gloating. There was a deliberate voluptuousness which was both thrilling and repulsive, and as she arched her neck she actually licked her lips like an animal, till I could see in the moonlight the moisture shining on her scarlet lips and on the red tongue as it lapped the sharp white teeth. Lower and lower came her head as her lips below my chin seemed about to fasten on my throat. Then she paused, and I could hear the churning sound of her tongue as it licked her teeth and lips, and could feel her hot breath on my neck. Now the skin of my throat began to tingle as one's flesh does when the hand that is to tickle it approaches nearer – nearer.

I could feel the soft, shivering touch of her lips on the supersensitive skin of my throat, and the hard dents of two sharp teeth, just touching. I closed my eyes in a languorous ecstasy and waited – waited with beating heart.

But at that instant another sensation swept through me, quick as lightning. I was conscious of the presence of the Count, in a storm of fury. As my eyes opened involuntarily I saw his strong hand grasp the slender neck of the fair woman and with giant's power pull her back.

Thwarted, her blue eyes blazed with rage, her white teeth chattering as her fair cheeks fumed with passion.

But the Count!

Never could I have imagined such terrible wrath, not even in the eyes of the demons of the pit. For the Count's engorged pupils were positively afire – lurid as the flames of hell – while behind them his face was deathly pale, the lines of it hard as drawn wires. The thick eyebrows that met over the nose now seemed like a heaving bar of white-hot metal. With a fierce sweep of his arm, he hurled the woman from him, then motioned to the others as though beating them back. It was the same imperious gesture I had seen used to the wolves. And in a voice which, though almost a whisper, seemed to cleave the huge dusty chamber, he exclaimed:

'How *dare* you touch him, any of you? How *dare* you cast eyes on him I had forbidden you? Back, I say! This man belongs to *me*.'

The fair girl, with a laugh of ribald coquetry, answered:

'You yourself never loved! You *never* love!'

At this the other two women joined in a mirthless hard laughter which rang so loudly round through the room that it almost made me faint.

It was the soulless laughter of fiends.

The Count looked at my face attentively, then in a whisper assured the three furies:

'Yes, I too can love. And I promise you that, when I am done with him, you too shall . . . kiss him – at your leisure. For now, go! *Go!* I must awaken him: there is work to be done.'

'Are we to have nothing tonight?' said one of the raven pair, with a low laugh, as she pointed to the bag which the Count had thrown upon the floor, and which moved as with some captured life inside it.

With a knowing leer he nodded.

The fair woman jumped forward and opened the bag.

If my ears did not deceive me there was a gasp and a low wail, as of a half-smothered child. The women closed round, while I lay aghast with horror; but as I looked they disappeared, and with them the dreadful bag. There was no door near them, and they could not have passed me without my noticing. They simply seemed to merge with the moonlight and filter through the window.

Outside I glimpsed their dim, shadowy forms for a moment before they entirely faded away.

Then the horror overcame me, and I sank down unconscious.

4

Dracula's Villainy

I awoke in my own bed.

If I was not dreaming, the Count must have carried me here. I tried to satisfy myself on the subject, but could not. To be sure, there were certain small evidences, such as that my clothes were folded in a manner which was not my habit. My watch was still unwound, whereas I always wind it last thing before going to bed. Many such details. But no proof, since perhaps my mind was disturbed. So . . . I must watch for proof. Meanwhile of one thing I am glad:

If it was the Count that carried me here and undressed me, he must have been hurried in his task, for my pockets are intact. I am sure this diary would have been a mystery which he would not have brooked. He would have taken or destroyed it. As I look round this room, although it has been to me so full of fear, it is now a sort of sanctuary, for nothing could be more dreadful than those awful women – waiting to suck my blood.

18 May.

I have been down to look at that room again in daylight, for I must know the truth. When I got to the doorway at the top of the stairs, I found it closed. It had been so forcibly driven against the jamb that part of the woodwork was splintered. I could see that the bolt of the lock had not been shot, but the door is fastened from the inside. I fear, therefore, that it was no dream, and must act on this surmise.

19 May.

I am surely in the toils. Last night the Count asked me in the suavest tones to write three letters: one saying that my work here was nearly done; another, that I was starting for home the morning following the date of the letter; and the third, that I had left the castle and arrived at Bistritz. I would fain have rebelled, but felt it would be

43

folly to quarrel openly with the Count while I am so absolutely in his power. He knows that I know too much, and he plans that I shall not live, lest I be dangerous to him. My only hope lies in apparent acquiescence. Something may occur – *must* occur – which will give me a chance to escape.

Last night I saw in his eyes an echo of that awful wrath when he hurled the fair woman from him. He explained to me that posts were few and uncertain, and that my writing now would ensure peace of mind to my friends; and he assured me he would countermand the later letters, which would be held over at Bistritz just in case it became necessary for my stay to be prolonged.

To oppose him would have been to create new suspicion. I therefore pretended to oblige, and asked him what dates I should put on the letters.

He calculated quickly, then said:

'The first should be June 12. The second, June 19. The third, June 29.'

I know now the span of my life. God help me.

28 May.

There is a chance of escape, or at least of sending word home. A band of Szgany has come to the castle, and is encamped in the courtyard. These Szgany are gypsies; I have notes on them in my book. There are thousands of them in Hungary and Transylvania and they are almost outside all law. They attach themselves as a rule to some great noble or boyar, and call themselves by his name. They are fearless and without religion, save superstition, and they talk only their own varieties of Romany.

I shall write some letters home, and try to have them posted. I have already spoken to the Szgany through my window, to establish a relationship. They took their hats off and made obeisance and many signs, which, alas, I understand no better than I could their speech.

I have written the letters.

Mina's is in shorthand, and I simply ask Mr Hawkins to communicate with her. To her I have explained my situation, but playing down the horrors. It would frighten her to death were I to expose my heart. Should the letters not carry . . .

I have given out the letters.

I threw them through the bars of my window with a gold piece, and made what signs I could to have them posted. The man who took them pressed them to his heart and bowed, then put them in his cap. I could do no more. I stole back to the study and began to read. As the Count did not come in, I have written here . . .

The Count has been. He sat down beside me, and said in his smoothest voice as he opened two letters:

'The Szgany have given me these. See! One is from you to my friend Peter Hawkins. The other' – here he caught sight of the strange symbols as he opened the envelope. The dark look came into his face, and his eyes blazed wickedly:

'The other is a *vile* thing. An outrage upon friendship and hospitality! Not signed – well, so it cannot matter to us.' And he calmly held letter and envelope in the flame of the lamp till they were consumed. Then he went on:

'The letter to Hawkins I shall, of course, send on. Since it is yours. Your letters are sacred to me. Your pardon my friend, that unknowingly I did break the seal. Will you not cover it again?' He held out the letter to me, and with a courteous bow handed me a clean envelope. I could only redirect it and hand it to him in silence. When he went out of the room I heard the key turn softly.

Two hours later, having fallen into a miserable sleep on the sofa, I was awakened by the Count's return. He was very civil, almost cheery, and seeing that I had been sleeping, he said:

'Tired, my friend? Then get to bed. There is the surest rest. I have not leisure to talk tonight, and so you shall sleep in peace.'

I passed to my room and went to bed, and, strange to say, slept without dreaming. Despair brings its own tranquillity.

31 May.

This morning, another shock. Every scrap of paper, every envelope, was gone from my bag, and with it all my notes, my memoranda relating to roadways and travel, my letter of credit, in fact, all that might be useful to me were I once outside the castle. In desperation I next made search of my portmanteau and in the wardrobe.

My travelling suit had been removed, and also my overcoat and rug. Were it not for the company of this diary – which, mercifully, I had secreted within my pillow – I fear I should already be insane.

17 June.

This morning, as I was sitting on the edge of my bed cudgelling my brains, I heard without a cracking of whips and pounding and scraping of horses' feet up the rocky path beyond the courtyard. In the joy of hope I rushed to the window, and saw drive into the yard two great leiter-wagons, each drawn by eight sturdy horses, and at the head of each pair a Slovak, with his wide hat, broad, nail-studded belt, dirty sheepskin, and high boots.

They had also their long staves in hand.

I ran to the door, intending to descend and try and join them through the main hall, as I thought that way might be opened for them. Again a shock: my door, I was cruelly reminded, had been locked from the outside.

Back to the window I ran and shouted down.

The Slovaks looked up stupidly and pointed, but just then the 'hetman' of the Szgany came out. Seeing the Slovaks pointing to my window, he sneeringly said something – at which they laughed. Henceforth, no effort of mine, no piteous cry or agonized entreaty, would make them even look at me. They resolutely turned away.

The leiter-wagons contained large oblong boxes with handles of thick rope. These, judging by the ease with which the Slovaks handled them, and by their resonance as they were roughly moved, were evidently empty. When they were all unloaded and stacked in a corner of the yard, the Slovaks were given some money by the Szgany. Spitting on their coins for luck, they lazily went each to his horse's head. Shortly afterwards I heard the cracking of their whips die away in the distance.

24 June, before dawn.

Last night the Count left me early.

Not hearing his stealthy key, and finding my door unlocked, as soon as I dared I ran up the winding stair, and looked down from the south-facing window. I thought I would watch for the Count, for there is clearly some villainy afoot. The Szgany are quartered in the castle, and now and then I hear a faraway, muffled sound as of work with mattock and spade.

I had been watching for perhaps half an hour when something moved in the Count's window. Carefully motionless, I saw the whole man emerge. When I saw he was clad in my travelling suit . . . how can I describe my feelings?

And slung over his shoulder was the terrible bag I had seen his women take away. There could be no doubt as to his quest, and in my garb. This, then, is his new scheme of evil: that others see *me*, as they think, in some nearby village, posting my own letters. And that the wickedness he does in my clothes shall be blamed entirely on *me*.

Seething with helpless rage I determined to watch for the Count's return, and for a long time sat doggedly at the window. Then I seemed to notice some quaint little specks afloat in the moonbeams. Like tiny grains of dust, they whirled and danced and gathered in nebulous clusters. As I watched them a sense of soothing calm stole over me. I leaned back in the embrasure in a more comfortable position, to enjoy more fully the spectacle of this magical aerial frolic.

Something made me start up: the low, piteous howling of a dog somewhere far in the valley below, beyond my sight. Louder it seemed to ring in my ears, and the floating motes of dust assumed new shapes to the sound as they danced. I felt myself torn by some call of my instincts; nay, my very soul was struggling, and my half-remembered sensibilities were striving to respond.

I was becoming hynotized!

Quicker and quicker danced the dust, and the moonbeams seemed to quiver as they went by me into the mass of gloom beyond. More and more they gathered into dim phantom shapes, hints of form, until suddenly I started, broad awake and in full possession of my senses, and ran screaming from the place. The phantom bodies materializing from the moonbeams were those three ghastly women by whom I was doomed by the Count to be . . . kissed.

In a panic I fled back down the stairs, and felt somewhat safer in my own room, where there was no moonlight and where the lamp was burning brightly.

After an hour of harrowing silence I heard something stirring – in the Count's room? Then a sharp wail quickly suppressed; followed by silence again. A deep, awful silence which chilled my very soul. With a thumping heart, I tried my door.

But now it was locked again.

Abandoned, helpless, trapped, I sat down and simply cried.

And as I sat I heard a sound in the courtyard without – the cry of an agonized woman. I rushed to the window and peered out between the bars. There, indeed, was a woman with dishevelled hair, holding her hands over her heart as one exhausted by running. She was leaning against a corner of the gateway. When she saw my face at the window she threw herself forward, and screamed:

'Monster, give me my child! Monster, *give me back my child!*' Then she tore her hair and beat her breast, and abandoned herself to violent emotion. Finally, she thew herself forward, and, though I could not see her, I could hear the beating of her naked hands against the door.

Somewhere high overhead, probably on the tower, I heard the Count call out a harsh, metalic summons, which was answered from far and wide by the howling of countless wolves. Minutes later a pack of them poured, like a flood through a broken dam, past the gateway into the courtyard.

From the stricken woman came not a sound as the wolves devoured her. Before long they streamed away singly, long red tongues licking blood from their foaming lips.

I could not pity her, for I knew now what had become of her child, and she was better off dead.

What shall I do? What *can* I do? How can I escape from this dreadful thrall of night and gloom and fear?

25 June. Morning.

No man knows till he has suffered from the night's dread worst how sweet the morning can be. When today's young sun touched the top of the great gateway opposite my window, it seemed as if the dove from the ark had lighted there. My fear fell from me like a vapour dissolved in the warmth. In the courage of this bright day I must *act*. Last night one of my post-dated letters went to post, the first of that fatal series which is to blot all trace of my existence from the earth.

Let me not think of it. *Action!*

It has always been at night-time that I have been molested or threatened. Never have I seen the Count in daylight. Can it be that he sleeps when others wake, that he may walk while they sleep! If I could only get into his room!

But yes!

There is a way. As I have seen him crawl out from his window; why should I not imitate him, and by the same means enter his room? The risks are desperate, but my need is more desperate still. I shall attempt it. At the worst it can only be death. And a man's death is not a calf's,

and the dread Hereafter may still be open to me. God help me in my task!
And pray look after Mina if I fail.

Same day. Later.

I went while my courage was fresh: straight to the window on the
south side, and at once got outside on the narrow ledge of stone which
runs round the building on this side. The stones are big and roughly cut,
and the mortar has been washed away between them. I took off my boots,
and ventured out on my desperate way. I looked down once, and that
sudden glimpse of the awful depth nearly overcame me, but after that I
doggedly kept my eyes up. I knew pretty well the direction and distance
of the Count's window, and made for it as fast as I could. I did not feel
dizzy – I suppose I was too excited – and within seconds, it seemed, I
found myself standing on the windowsill and trying to raise up the sash.

I was filled with agitation, however, when I bent down and slid feet
foremost in through the window. The room was barely furnished, with
odd things which seemed never to have been used. The furniture was
of the same style as that in the south rooms, and was covered with
dust. I looked for the key, but it was not in the lock. I searched for it
everywhere but found instead a heap of gold in a curtained-off corner.
Gold of all kinds – Roman, British, Austrian, Hungarian, Greek and
Turkish – covered with a film of dust, as though it had lain long
untouched. None of it was less than three hundred years old. There
were also chains and ornaments, some jewelled, but all of them old and
stained.

Feeling my way around the wall, I found a small heavy door disguised
as a panel. Finding it unlocked, I pushed through and along a stone
passage to a circular stairway, which went steeply down. I descended,
minding carefully where I went, for the stairs were dark, lit only by
loopholes in the heavy masonry. At the bottom was a dark, tunnel-like
passage, through which came the sickly, deathly odour of old earth
newly turned.

As I went along the tunnel passage the smell grew closer and heavier.
At last I pulled open an arched door which stood ajar, and found myself
in an old, ruined chapel, which had evidently been used as a graveyard.
The roof was broken, and in two places were steps leading to vaults, but
the ground had recently been dug over and the earth placed in those
large oblong boxes brought by the Slovaks. Next, although to do so

was a dread to my very soul, I went down even – the dim light ever weakening – into the vaults. In the first of these I found nothing except fragments of old coffins and piles of dust; but in the second vault . . .

There, in one of the great boxes, of which there were perhaps fifty, on a pile of newly dug earth, lay the Count! His eyes were open and stony, but without the glassiness of death – and his cheeks had the warmth of life through all their pallor, while his lips were red as ever. But there was no sign of movement; no pulse, no breath, no beating of the heart. I bent over him, listening for life, but in vain. He could not have lain there long, for the earthy smell would have passed away in a few hours. By the side of the box was its cover, pierced with holes. I thought he might have the keys on him, but when I bent to search I saw in his dead eyes such a look of hate, though unconscious of me or my presence, that I fled the vaults in terror. Leaving the Count's room by the window, I crawled again up the castle wall to my my own chamber, where I threw myself panting upon the bed and tried to think . . .

29 June.

Today is the date of my last letter, and the Count has taken steps to make it seem genuine, for again I saw him leave the castle by the same window, and in my clothes. As he went down the wall, lizard fashion, I wished I had a gun or some lethal weapon, that I might destroy him; but I fear that no weapon wrought by man would worry him. I dared not watch till his return, lest those weird sisters materialize to torment me. So I came back here to the library, and read till I fell asleep.

I was shaken awake by the Count, who informed me grimly:

'Tomorrow, my friend, we must part. You return to your beautiful England, I to . . . some work which may preclude our meeting again. Your letter home has been despatched. Tomorrow I shall not be here, but all will be ready for your journey. In the morning come the Szgany, who have some labours of their own here, and also come some Slovaks. When they have gone, my carriage shall bear you to the Borgo Pass, to meet the diligence for Bistritz.'

Struggling to mask my suspicions, I asked him point-blank:

'Why may I not go tonight?'

'Because, dear sir, my coachman and horses are away on a mission.'

'But I would walk with pleasure. I want to get away at once.'

He smiled. Such a soft, smooth, diabolical smile that I knew there was some fiendishness afoot.

'And your baggage?' he mockingly inquired.

'I can send for it later.'

The Count stood up, and said, with a sweet courtesy which made me rub my eyes, it seemed so real:

'You English have a saying which is close to my heart, for its spirit is that which rules our boyars:

'"Welcome the coming. Speed the parting guest." Come with me, my dear young friend. Not an hour shall you wait in my house against your will, though sad am I at your going, and that you so suddenly desire it. Come!' With a stately gravity, he, with the lamp, preceded me down the stairs and along the hall. Suddenly he stopped.

'Hark!'

Close at hand came the howling of countless wolves – almost as if at the raising of his hand, just as the music of a mighty orchestra obeys the baton of its conductor. After a moment he proceeded in his stately way to the door, drew back the ponderous bolts, unhooked the heavy chains, and began to draw it open.

To my intense astonishment I saw that it was unlocked. Suspiciously I looked all round, but could see no key of any kind.

As the door groaned open, the howling of the wolves without grew louder and angrier; their red jaws, with champing teeth, leered up at the doorway, and:

'Shut the door!' I cried. 'I shall wait till morning after all.' And I covered my face to hide the tears of my bitter disappointment.

With one sweep of his powerful arm, the Count threw the door shut, and the clanging bolts echoed through the hall as they shot home.

In silence we returned to the library, and after a minute or two I went to my own room. The last I saw of Count Dracula was his kissing his hand to me, with a red light of triumph in his eyes, as he smiled a smile that Judas in hell might be proud of.

When I was about to lie down, I thought I heard a whispering at my door. I tiptoed to it softly, and listened.

'Back! Back!' I heard the Count say sternly. 'Tomorrow! Tomorrow night . . . he is yours!'

There followed a low ripple of lascivious laughter.

In a rage I threw open the door, and saw without those three terrible women licking their lips. At the sight of me they all joined in a horrible laugh, and ran away.

Back in my room I fell to my knees. Is it then so near the end? 'Tomorrow!' Dear Lord, help me, and those to whom I am dear.

30 June. Morning.

These may be the last words I ever write. I slept till nearly dawn, then knelt beside my bed to pray – determined that Death should find me ready.

At last I felt that subtle change in the air which the first light of morning brings. Feeling somehow safer, with a gladder heart I opened my door and ran down to the hall. Having seen the door unlocked, I sensed that perhaps escape was now before me. With trembling hands I unhooked the chains and drew back the massive bolts.

But the door would not move. In despair I pulled and pulled and shook it till, massive as it was, it rattled in its casement. But it had been locked after I left the Count last night, and now it would not yield.

Then a wild desire took me to obtain that key at any risk, and I determined again to scale the wall to the Count's room. He might kill me, but death now seemed a lesser evil. Without a pause I rushed up to the east window and scrambled down the wall. The Count's room was empty, as before. Nowhere could I see a key, but the heap of gold remained. Next I passed through the corner door and down the winding stair, then along the dark passage to the old chapel – knowing now, well enough, where to find the monster I sought.

The great box was in the same place, close against the wall, but the lid was laid on it with the nails ready to be hammered home. I knew I must search the body for the key, so I raised the lid and laid it back against the wall. Then I saw something to fill my very soul with utter horror. There lay the Count, but as if his youth had been half-renewed: his white hair and moustache become dark iron-grey; his cheeks fuller, while that foul white skin seemed ruby-red beneath. His mouth was redder than ever, and from his lips fresh gouts of blood trickled over his chin and down across his neck. Even the deep, burning eyes seemed set amongst swollen flesh, for the lids and pouches underneath were bloated. It seemed as if the whole awful creature were simply gorged with blood; he lay there like a filthy leech, exhausted with repletion.

I shuddered as I bent over him, every sense in me revolting; but I had to search him, or the coming night might see my own body become a banquet for those fiendish females to whom he had promised me. All over his body I felt, but no sign could I find of the key. Then I stopped and looked at the Count. There was a mocking smile on the bloated face which I felt must drive me mad. This was the being I was helping to transfer to London, where, perhaps for centuries to come, he might, amongst its teeming millions, satiate his lust for blood, and create a new and ever widening circle of semi-demons to batten on the helpless. The very thought was so obscene that a terrible craving inflamed me to rid the world of such a monster.

There was no lethal weapon at hand, but I seized a shovel which the workmen had been using to fill the cases. This I swung high and aimed edge downward at the Count's hateful face. But as I did so his head rolled and his eyes turned full upon me, ablaze with basilisk malice. Somehow the sight seemed to paralyse me. The shovel slipped in my hand and struck the Count merely a glancing blow on his temple. The rebounding blade hit the coffin lid, which fell over again, and hid the bloody head of that horrible beast from my sight. The last glimpse I had was of the bloated face, bloodstained and fixed with a grin of the nethermost spite.

My brain seemed on fire and my heart unbearably heavy with despair as I heard in the distance the gipsy song of merry voices coming closer. And through their song the rolling of heavy wheels and the cracking of whips. The Szgany and the Slovaks of whom the Count had spoken were coming. With a last look around and at the box which contained the vile body, I ran from the place and gained the Count's room, determined to rush out of the castle at the moment the main door should be opened. With strained ears I listened, and heard downstairs the grinding of a key in the great lock and the creaking back of the door. Then the tramping of many feet, which died away in some echoing distant passage. I turned to run down again towards the vault but at that moment there seemed to come a violent puff of wind. The door to the winding stair blew to with a shock that set the dust from the lintels flying. When I ran to push it open, I found it was hopelessly fast.

I was again a prisoner, and the net of doom round me was tightening.

As I write there comes from the passage below a thudding of many feet and the crash of weights being set down heavily – doubtless the boxes, with their freight of fetid earth. There is a sound of hammering; surely the Count's travel coffin being nailed down. Now the heavy feet plod again along the hall, with other, lighter footsteps behind them.

The door is shut; the chains rattle. Now a grinding of the key in the lock. I hear the key withdrawn. Another door opens and shuts; I hear the creaking of lock and bolt.

Hark! In the courtyard and down the rocky track roll heavy wheels, the crack of whips, and the chorus of the Szgany.

They pass into the distance.

I am alone in the castle with those awful women. Women? Mina is a woman, and there is naught in common. These are devils from the bottommost pit – insatiable ghouls in feminine form – and I shall not remain alone with them. No. To be their toy, their fodder, their . . . Never. Rather shall I try to scale the castle wall all the perilous way to Freedom.

And then away for home! Aboard the soonest train! Away from this cursed land, where the devil and his children still walk with earthly feet! At least God's mercy is sure, and the precipice . . .

At its foot a man might sleep – as a man. Goodbye, Mina.

Everyone. Goodbye.

Oh, God.

Part II

THE HORROR HITS

England

5

Letters, Etc

MINA MURRAY TO LUCY WESTENRA
9 May.

My dearest Lucy,

Forgive my long delay in writing, but I have been simply overwhelmed with work. The life of an assistant schoolmistress is sometimes trying. I am longing to be with you, and by the sea, where we can talk together freely and build our castles in the air. I have been working very hard lately, because I want to keep up with Jonathan's studies, and I have been practising shorthand very assiduously. When we are married I shall be useful to Jonathan, and able to write out his work on the typewriter, at which I am also practising very hard.

He and I sometimes write letters in shorthand, and he is keeping a stenographic journal of his travels abroad. When I am with you I shall keep a diary in the same way. I don't mean one of those 'two pages to the week with Sunday squeezed in a corner' diaries, but a sort of journal which I can write in whenever I feel inclined. I do not suppose there will be much of interest to other people; but it is not intended for them. I may show it to Jonathan some day if there is in it anything worth sharing, but it is really an exercise-book. I shall try to do what I see lady journalists do: interviewing and writing descriptions and trying to remember conversations. I am told that, with a little practice, one can remember all that happens or is said during a day. However, we shall see.

I shall tell you all my little plans when we meet. I have just had a few hurried lines from Jonathan from Transylvania. He is well, and will be returning in about a week. I am longing to hear all his news. It must be so nice to see strange countries. I wonder if we — I mean Jonathan and I — shall ever see them together. But . . .

There is the ten o'clock bell ringing.

Goodbye.

Your loving,
Mina.
P.S. Tell me all the news when you write. You have not told me anything for a long time. I hear rumours – especially of a tall, handsome, curly-haired man!?

LUCY WESTENRA TO MINA MURRAY
17 Chatham Street,
Wednesday.
My dearest Mina,
I must say you tax me very unfairly with being a bad correspondent. I wrote to you twice since we parted, and your last letter was only your second. Besides, I have nothing to tell you. There is really nothing to say. Town is very pleasant just now, and we go a good deal to picture galleries and for walks and rides in the park. As to the tall, curly-haired man, I suppose it was the one who was with me at the last Pop. Someone has evidently been telling tales. That was Mr Holmwood. He often comes to see us, and he and Mamma get on very well; they have so much in common.

Talking of which, we met some time ago a man that would just *do for you*, if you were not already engaged to Jonathan. He is an excellent *parti*, being handsome, well off, and of good birth. He is a doctor and really clever. Just fancy! He is only twenty-nine, and he has an immense lunatic asylum all under his own care. Mr Holmwood introduced him to me, and he called here to see us, and often comes now. I think he is one of the most resolute men I ever saw, and yet the most calm. He seems absolutely imperturbable. What a wonderful power he must have over his patients. He has a curious habit of looking one straight in the face, as if trying to read one's thoughts. He tries this on very much with me, but I flatter myself he has got a tough nut to crack. I know that from my glass.

Do you ever try to read your own face? I do, and really it is less easy than one might think. He – Dr Seward – says that I afford him a curious psychological study, and I humbly think I do. As to the new fashions . . .

Dress is a bore!

That is slang again, but never mind. Arthur says that every day – there! It is all out. Mina, we have told all our secrets to each other since we were *children*. We have eaten together, slept together, and laughed and cried together. Now . . . oh Mina! Can't you guess?

I love him!

But I am blushing as I write for although I *think* he loves me, he has not told me so. Not in words. But, oh, Mina, *I* love *him*. I love him; I *love* him! There. That does me good. I wish now we were together, sitting by the fire, undressing, as we used to. Then I would try to tell you what I feel. I do not know how I am writing this even to you. I am afraid to stop, or I should tear up the letter, and I don't want to stop for I *do* so want to tell you all. Let me hear from you *at once*, and tell me what you think.

Mina, I must stop. Goodnight.

Bless me in your prayers; and, Mina, pray for my happiness.

Lucy.

P.S. I need not tell you this is a secret. Goodnight again. L.

LUCY WESTENRA TO MINA MURRAY

24 May.

My dearest Mina,

Thanks, and thanks, and thanks again for your sweet letter. It was so nice to have your sympathy.

My dear, it never rains but it pours. How true the old proverbs are. Here am I, who will be twenty in September, and yet I never had a proposal till today. Not a real proposal. And today I have had three! Just fancy! THREE proposals in one day! Isn't it awful! I feel sorry, really and truly, for two of the poor fellows. Oh, Mina, I am so happy that I don't know what to do. Three proposals! But, for goodness sake, don't tell any of the girls, or they would feel envious and slighted.

Some girls are so vain.

You and I, Mina dear, who are engaged and are going to settle down soon soberly into old married women, can despise vanity. Well, I must tell you about the three, but you must keep it a secret, dear, from *everyone*. Except, of course, Jonathan. You will tell him, because I would. I mean, in your place, I certainly would tell Arthur. A woman ought to tell her husband everything – don't you think so, dear? – and I must be fair. Men like women, certainly their wives, to be quite as fair as they. And we women, I am afraid, are not always quite as fair as we should be.

Well, my dear, number one came just before lunch. I told you of him,

Dr John Seward, the lunatic-asylum man, with the strong jaw and the good forehead. He was very cool outwardly, but was nervous all the same. He had evidently been schooling himself to be calm, yet almost managed to sit down on his silk hat, which men don't generally do when they are cool! And then when he wanted to appear at ease he kept playing with a lancet in a way that made me nearly scream. He spoke to me, Mina, very straightforwardly. He told me how dear I was to him, though he had known me so little, and what his life would be with me to help and cheer him. He was going to tell me how unhappy he would be if I did not care for him, but when he saw me cry he scolded himself for being a brute and said he would not add to my present trouble. Then he broke off and asked if I could love him in time.

When I shook my head his hands trembled, and then with some hesitation he asked me if I cared already for anyone else. He put it very nicely, saying he did not want to wring confidences from me, but only to know, because if a woman's heart was free a man might have hope. And then, Mina, I felt it a sort of duty to tell him that there *was* someone. I only told him that much, and then he stood up, looked very strong and very grave as he took both my hands in his and said he hoped I would be happy. And that if I ever wanted a friend I must count him one of my best. Oh, Mina dear, I can't help crying. And you must excuse this letter being all blotted. Being proposed to is all very nice, but it isn't at all a happy thing when you have to see a poor fellow, whom you know loves you honestly, going away looking all broken-hearted, and to know that, no matter what he may say at the moment, you are passing quite out of his life. My dear, I must stop here at present, I feel so miserable, though I am so happy.

Evening.

Arthur has just gone, and I feel in better spirits now. Well, my dear, number two came after lunch. He is such a nice fellow, an American from Texas, and he looks so young and fresh that it seems almost impossible that he has been to so many places and had such adventures. How I sympathize with poor Desdemona when she had such a dangerous stream poured in her ear, even by a black man. I suppose we women are such cowards that we think a man will save us from fears, and so we marry him. I know now what I would do if I were a man and wanted to make a girl love me. No, I don't, for there was Mr Morris telling us his stories, and Arthur never told any, and yet—

My dear, I am somewhat previous. Mr Quincey P. Morris found me alone. It seems that a man always does find a girl alone. No, he doesn't, for Arthur tried twice to *make* a chance, and I helping him all I could – I am not ashamed to say it now. I must tell you beforehand that Mr Morris doesn't always speak slang – that is to say, he never does so to strangers or before them, for he is really well educated and has exquisite manners – but he found out that it amused me to hear him talk American slang, so, whenever there was no-one else present to be shocked, he said such funny things! I do not know, though, if I myself shall ever speak slang. I do not know if Arthur likes it, and certainly I have never heard him use any.

Well, Mr Morris sat down beside me and looked as happy and jolly as he could, but I could see he was very nervous. He took my hand in his and said ever so sweetly:

'Miss Lucy, I know I ain't good enough to regulate the fixin's of your little shoes, but I guess if you wait till you find a man that is you will go join them seven young women with the lamps when you quit. Won't you just hitch up alongside of me and let us go down the long road together in double harness?'

Well, he looked so good-humoured that it didn't seem half so hard to refuse him as it did poor Dr Seward. So I said, as lightly as I could, that I did not know anything of hitching, and that I wasn't broken to harness. Then he said he had spoken in a light manner, and he hoped that if he had made a mistake in doing so on such a momentous an occasion, I would forgive him. He looked awfully serious saying that, and I couldn't help feeling a bit serious, too.

I know, Mina, you will think me a horrid flirt – though I couldn't help feeling a sort of exultation that he was number two in one day. And then, my dear, before I could say a word he began pouring out a perfect torrent of lovemaking: laying his very heart and soul at my feet, and in terrible earnest too. I suppose he saw something in my face which checked him, for suddenly he stopped, and said with a sort of manly fervour (that I could have loved him for if I had been free):

'Miss Lucy, you are an honest-hearted girl, I know. I should not be here now if I did not believe you clean grit, right down to the depths of your soul. Tell me, like one good fellow to another, is there anyone else that you care for? If there is, I'll never trouble you a hair's breadth again, but will be, if you will let me, a very faithful friend.'

Dear Mina, why are men so noble when we women are so little worthy of them? Here was I, almost making fun of this truly great-hearted gentleman. I burst into tears – am afraid, my dear, you will think this a very sloppy letter – for I really felt very badly. Why can't they let a girl marry three men, or as many as want her, and save all this trouble? But this is heresy, and I must not say it. I am glad to say that, though I was crying, I was able to look into Mr Morris's brave brown eyes, and tell him straight out:

'Yes, there is someone I love, though he has not told me yet that *he* loves *me*.' I was right to speak to him so frankly, for quite a light came into his face, and he put out both his hands and took mine, and said in a hearty way:

'That's my brave girl. Better late for a chance of winning you, than early for any other girl. Don't cry, my dear. If it's for me, I'm a hard nut to crack, and I take it standing up. If that other fellow doesn't know his happiness, well, he'd better look for it soon, or he'll have to deal with me. Little girl, your honesty and pluck have made me a friend, and that's rarer than a lover. It's more unselfish, anyways.

'Dearest Miss Lucy, I'm going to have a pretty lonely walk between here and Kingdom Come. Won't you give me just one kiss? For a flicker in the darkness now and then. You can, you know, if you like, for that other feller ain't spoken yet.'

That quite won me, Mina, for it was so noble and yet so sad. So I leant over and kissed him. He stood up with my two hands in his, and as he looked down into my face – I am afraid I was blushing scarlet – he said:

'Little girl, I hold your hand, and you've kissed me, and if these things don't make us friends nothing ever will. Thank you for your sweet honesty to me, and goodbye.' He wrung my hand, and taking up his hat, went straight out of the room without looking back, without a tear or a quiver or a pause. And I am crying like a baby. Oh, why must a man like that be made unhappy when there are lots of girls about who would worship the very ground he trod? I know I would if I were free – only . . . I don't want to be free. My dear, this has quite upset me, and I feel I cannot write of happiness just now, so will tell you of number three anon.

Ever your loving,

Lucy.

P.S. Besides, it was all so confused and . . . And only a moment from his coming into the room till both his arms were round me. And he was *kissing* me! I am very, very happy, and don't know why I deserve it. Must try in future to show grateful for all His goodness in sending me such a lover, husband, and friend.

Goodbye.

DR SEWARD'S NOTES

25 May.

Ebb tide in appetite today. Cannot eat, cannot rest, so diary instead. Since my rebuff of yesterday I have a sort of empty feeling. Nothing in the world seems worth the doing. Knowing the only cure was work, I went down amongst the patients.

Picked out one who has afforded me a study of much interest. He is so quaint in his ideas, and so unlike the normal lunatic, that I have determined to understand him. Today I seemed to get nearer than ever before to the mystery of his hallucinations. In my method there was, I now see, something of cruelty: in my keeping him to the point of his madness – a thing which normally I avoid with the patients as I would the mouth of hell.

(But under what circumstances would I *not* avoid the Pit?)

Omnia Romoe vernalia sunt.

Hell has its price.

R. M. RENFIELD

(from Dr Seward's records)

Age, 59; sanguine temperament; great physical strength; morbidly excitable; periods of gloom ending in some fixed idea which I cannot make out.

A possibly dangerous man; *probably* dangerous, if unselfish. *Because* unselfish? In selfish men caution is an armour for their foes as for themselves. For when self is the fixed point, the centripetal force is balanced with the centrifugal. Whereas when duty, a cause, etc., is the fixed point, the latter force is paramount, and only accident can balance it.

TO HON. ARTHUR HOLMWOOD

25 May.

My dear Art,

We've told yarns by the camp-fire in the prairies; and dressed one another's wounds after trying a landing at the Marquesas; and drunk healths on the shore of Titicaca. There are more yarns to be told, and other wounds to be healed, and another health to be drunk. Won't you let this be at my camp-fire tomorrow night?

I have no hesitation in asking you, as I know a certain lady is engaged to a certain dinner-party, and that you are free. There will only be one other, our old pal at the Korea, Jack Seward. He's coming, too, and we both want to mingle our weeps over the wine-cup, and to drink a health with all our hearts to the happiest man in all the wide world, who has won the purest heart that God has made and the best worth winning.

We promise you a hearty welcome, and a loving greeting, and a health as true as your own right hand. We shall both swear to leave you at home if you drink too deep to a certain pair of eyes. Come!

Ever and always,

Quincey P. Morris.

TELEGRAM TO MORRIS

26 May.

Count me in every time. I bear messages to make your ears tingle.

ART.

6

Diaries, Etc

MINA MURRAY

24 July. Whitby.

Lucy met me at the station, looking sweeter and lovelier than ever, and we drove up to their house in the Crescent. This is a lovely place. The little river, the Esk, runs through a deep valley, which broadens out as it comes near the harbour. A great viaduct runs across, with high piers, through which the view seems, somehow, farther away than it really is. The valley is beautifully green, and so steep that, when you are on the high land on either side, you look right across it.

The houses of the old town – the side away from us – are all red-roofed, and seem piled up anyhow, like the pictures we see of Nuremberg. Right over the town is the ruin of Whitby Abbey, which was sacked by the Danes, and which is the scene of part of *Marmion* where the girl was built up in the wall. It is a ruin of immense size, and full of beauty and romance.

(Legend has it that a white lady is sometimes seen in one of the windows.)

Between the Abbey and the town is the parish church, round which is a big graveyard, all full of tombstones. This is, to my mind, the nicest spot in Whitby, for it lies right over the town, and has a perfect view of the harbour and all up the bay to where the headland called Kettleness stretches out into the sea. It descends so steeply over the harbour that part of the bank has fallen away, and some of the graves have been destroyed. In one place part of the stonework of the graves stretches out over the sandy pathway far below. There are walks, with seats beside them, through the churchyard; and people go and sit there all day long, to admire the view and enjoy the breeze.

I shall come and sit here very often myself – to work. Indeed, I am writing now; with my book on my knee, and listening to three old men beside me. They seem to do nothing all day but sit up here and talk.

The harbour lies below me. On the far side a long granite wall stretches out into the sea. There is a curve outwards at the end of the wall, and in the middle of the curve stands a lighthouse. On the near side, the sea-wall makes an elbow, and at its end stands a second lighthouse. Between the two piers there is a narrow opening into the harbour, which then suddenly widens.

It is nice at high tide; but when the tide is out it shoals away to nothing, and there is merely the stream of the Esk, running between banks of sand, with rocks here and there. Outside the harbour on this side there rises for about half a mile a great reef, the sharp edge of which runs straight out from behind the south lighthouse. At its end is a buoy with a bell, which swings in bad weather, and sends in a mournful sound on the wind.

(They have a legend here that when a ship is lost, bells are heard out at sea. Must ask Old Gnarly about this . . .)

He is a funny old chap, and must truly be quite ancient, for his face is all gnarled and twisted like the bark of a tree. He says he is nearly a hundred, and was a sailor in the Greenland fishing fleet when Waterloo was fought. But he is, I am afraid, a very sceptical person, for when I asked him about the bells at sea and the White Lady at the Abbey he said very brusquely:

'I wouldn't fash masel' about them, miss. Them things be all wore out. Mind, I don't say they never was, but I do say that they wasn't in my time. They be all very well for trippers an' the like, but not for a nice young lady like you. Them feet-folks from York and Leeds that be always eatin' cured herrin's an' drinkin' tea an' lookin' out to buy cheap jet would creed aught. I wonder masel' who'd be bothered tellin' lies to them — even the newspapers, which is full of fool-talk.'

I thought he would be a good person to learn interesting things from, so I asked him about whale-fishing in the old days. He was just settling himself to begin when the clock struck six, whereupon he laboured up, and said:

'I must gang ageeanwards home now, miss. My granddaughter doesn't like to be kept waitin' when the tea is ready.' He hobbled away, hurrying, as well as he could, down the steps.

The steps, from the town up to the church, are a great feature. There are hundreds of them, and they wind up in a delicate curve, so gently that a horse could easily manage them. I think they must originally have had something to do with the Abbey. But now I must go home too. Lucy went out visiting with her mother, and as they were only duty calls, they will surely be home by now.

1st August.

I came up here an hour ago with Lucy, and we had a most interesting talk with Old Gnarly and his two companions. He is evidently their Oracle and must in his time have been a most dictatorial person. He will not admit anything, and downfaces everybody. If he can't out-argue them he bullies them, then takes their silence for agreement.

Lucy was so pretty in her white lawn frock – she has got beautiful colour since she has been here – that the old men lost no time in coming up and sitting near us. She is so sweet with old people, too. I think they all fell in love with her on the spot. Even Old Gnarly succumbed and did not contradict her, but gave me double share instead. I got him on the subject of the legends, and he went off at once into a sort of sermon:

'It be all fool-talk,' he thundered. 'Fool-talk. These bans an' wafts an' bob-ghosts an' bar-guests and bogles an' all anent them is only fit to set bairns an' dizzy women a-belderin'. They be nowt but air-blebs! They, an' all grims an' signs an' warnin's, be all invented by parsons an' illsome beuk-bodies an' railway touters to skeer an' scunner hafflin's, an' to get folks to do somethin' that they don't other incline to.

'It makes me ireful to think o' them.

'Why, it's them that, not content with all thar printin' lies on paper an' preachin' them out of pulpits, does want to be cuttin' them on the tombstones. Look here all around in what airt ye will; all them steans, holdin' up their heads as well as they can out of their pride is acant – simply tumblin' down with the weight o' the lies wrote on them:

'"Here lies the body" or "Sacred to the memory" wrote on all of them, an' yet in nigh half of them there bean't bodies at all! An' the memories of them bean't cared a pinch snuff about, much less sacred. Lies! All of them. Nothin' but lies! My gog, but it'll be a quare scowderment at the Day of Judgment when they come tumblin' up here in their death-sarks, all jouped together an' tryin' to drag their tombsteans with them to prove how good they was. Some of them trimmlin' and ditherin', with their hands that dozzened an' slippy from lyin' in the sea that they can't even keep their grup o' them.'

I could see from the old fellow's self-satisfied air and the way in which he looked round for the approval of his cronies that he was 'showing off', so I put in a word to keep him going:

'Oh, Mr Swales, you can't be serious. Surely these tombstones are not *all* wrong?'

'Yabblins! There may be a poorish few not wrong, savin' where they make out the people too good; for there be folk that do think a balm-bowl be like the sea, if only it be their own. The whole thing be only lies. Now look you here; you come here a stranger, an' you see this kirk-garth.'

I nodded, for I thought it better to assent, though I did not quite understand his dialect. I knew it had something to do with the church.

He went on:

'And you consate that all these steans be aboon folk that be happed here, snod an' snog?'

I assented again.

'Then that be just where the lie comes in. Why, there be scores of these lay-beds that be toom as old Dun's bacca-box on Friday night.' He nudged one of his companions, and they all laughed. 'And my gog! How could they be otherwise? Look at that one, the aftest abaft the bier-bank. Read it!'

I went over and read:

'Edward Spencelagh, master mariner, murdered by pirates off the coast of Andres, April 1854.'

When I came back Old Gnarly went on:

'Who brought him home, I wonder, to hap him here? Murdered off the coast of Andres! An' you consated his body lay under! Why, I could name ye a dozen whose bones lie in the Greenland seas above' – he pointed northwards – 'or where the currents may have drifted them. There be the steans around ye. Ye can, with your young eyes, read the small print of the lies from here:

'Yon Braithwaite Lowrey? I knew his father – lost in the *Lively* off Greenland in '20. Or Andrew Woodhouse? Drowned in the same seas in 1777. Then John Paxton? Drowned off Cape Farewell a year later. And poor John Rawlings, whose grandfather sailed with me? Drowned in the Gulf of Finland in '50. Do ye think all these men will rush to Whitby when the trumpet sounds?

'I have me antherums aboot it!

'I tell ye that when they got here they'd be jommlin' an' jostlin' one another like a fight up on the ice in the old days, when we'd be at one another from daylight to dark, an tryin' to tie up our cuts by the light of the aurora borealis.'

This was evidently local pleasantry, for Old Gnarly cackled over it, and his cronies joined in with gusto.

'But', I said, 'surely you are not quite correct, for you assume that all the poor people, or their spirits, will have to take their tombstones with them on the Day of Judgment.'

'Well, what else be they tombsteans for? Answer me that, miss!'

'To please their relatives, I suppose.'

'To please their relatives, you suppose!' This he said with intense scorn. 'How will it pleasure their relatives to know that lies is wrote over them, and that everybody in the place knows that they be lies?' He pointed to a stone at our feet which had been laid down as a slab, on which the seat was rested, close to the edge of the cliff. 'Read the lines on that thruffstean,' he said. The letters were upside down to me from where I sat, but Lucy leant over and read:

'"Sacred to the memory of George Canon, who died, in the hope of a glorious resurrection, on July 20, 1873, falling from the rocks at Kettleness. This tomb is erected by his sorrowing mother to her dearly beloved son. He was the only son of his mother, and she was a widow."

'Really, Mr Swales, I see nothing funny in that,' Lucy commented somewhat severely.

'Ye don't see aught funny! Ha! But that's because ye don't gawm the sorrowin' mother was a hell-cat that hated him because he was acrewk'd — a regular lamiter he was — an' he hated her so that he committed suicide in order that she mightn't get an insurance she put on his life. He blew nigh the top his head off with an old musket they had for scarin' the crows. 'Twarn't for crows then, for it brought the clegs and the dowps to him.

'That's the way he fell off the rocks. And as to hopes of a glorious resurrection, I often heard him say he hoped he'd go to hell, for his mother was so pious that she'd be sure to go to heaven, an' he didn't want to addle where she was. Now isn't that stean at any rate' — he hammered it with his stick as he spoke — 'a pack of lies? And won't it make Gabriel keckle when Geordie comes pantin' up the grees with the tombstean balanced on his hump, and begs it to be took as evidence!'

I did not know what to say, but Lucy jumped up with some passion:

'Oh, why did you tell us all this? It was my favourite seat, and now I find I have been sitting over the grave of a suicide.'

'That won't harm ye, my pretty. An' it may make poor Geordie gladsome to have so trim a lass sittin' on his lap. That won't hurt ye. Why, I've sat here for nigh twenty years past, an' it hasn't done me no harm. Don't ye fash about them as lies under ye, or that doesn' lie there either! It'll be time for ye to be getting scart when ye see the tombsteans all run away with, and the place as bare as a stubble-field. But there's the clock, an' I must gang. My service to ye, ladies!' And off he hobbled.

Lucy and I sat awhile, and it was all so beautiful before us that we took hands as we sat, and she told me again about Arthur and their coming marriage. That made me just a little heartsick, for I haven't heard from Jonathan for a whole month.

The same day. Later.

I came up here alone, for I am very sad. There was no letter for me. I hope there cannot be anything the matter with Jonathan. The clock has just struck nine. I see the lights scattered all over the town, sometimes in rows where the streets are; sometimes singly. They run right up the Esk and die away in the curve of the valley. To my left the view is cut off by a black roof line of the old house next the Abbey. The sheep and lambs are bleating in the fields away behind me, while a donkey's hooves are clattering up the paved road below. The band on the pier is playing a harsh waltz in good time, and farther along the quay there is a Salvation Army meeting in a back street.

Neither of the bands can hear the other, but up here I hear and see them both. How I wonder where Jonathan is. And is he thinking of me? I wish so much that he were here.

DR SEWARD

5 June.

The case of Renfield grows more interesting. The man has certain qualities very largely developed: selfishness, secrecy, and purpose. But why? He seems to have some settled scheme of his own, but what? His redeeming quality is a love of animals, though this takes such strange forms that I sometimes imagine he is only abnormally cruel.

And his pets are of odd sorts. Just now his hobby is catching flies, of which he has accumulated such a quantity that I have had to expostulate.

To my astonishment, he did not break out into a fury, as I expected, but thought seriously for a moment, then said:

'May I have three days? I shall clear them away.'

Of course I said that would do. But I must watch him.

18 June.

He has turned his mind now to spiders, and has got several very big fellows in a box. He keeps feeding them with his flies, and the number of the latter is becoming sensibly diminished, although he has used half his food in attracting more flies into his room.

5 July.

His spiders are now becoming as great a nuisance as his flies, and today I told him to get rid of them. He looked very sad at this, so I said he must clear out *some* of them. He cheerfully acquiesced in this, then disgusted me horribly when a blow-fly, bloated with some carrion food, buzzed into the room. Renfield deftly caught it, held it exultingly for a moment between his finger and thumb, and, before I could protest, popped it into his mouth and ate it.

I scolded him for that, but he argued quietly that it was very good and wholesome; that it was life, strong life, and nourishing to him. This aroused my suspicions, and I must watch how he gets rid of his spiders. He has evidently some deep problem in his mind, for he keeps a little notebook in which whole pages are filled with masses of figures, generally single numbers added up in batches, and then the totals added in batches again – as though he were 'focusing' some account, as the auditors put it.

8 July.

There is a method in his madness, and though he has parted with some of his pets he has also got a new one. A sparrow, which he has already partially tamed, by dint of a diet of spiders. Meanwhile the remaining spiders are also well fed, as Renfield brings in flies from outside by tempting them with his own food.

19 July.

Renfield now has a whole colony of sparrows, and his flies and spiders are all but gone. When I came in he ran to me and said he wanted to ask me a very great favour. As he spoke he fawned on me like a dog.

'What favour?' I asked him.

With a sort of rapture in his voice and bearing, he said:

'A kitten. A nice little, sleek, playful kitten, that I can play with, and teach, and feed. And feed – and *feed!*' I was not unprepared for this request, for I had noticed how his pets went on increasing in size and vivacity. But I did not care that his pretty family of tame sparrows should be wiped out in the same manner as the flies and the spiders, so I said I would see about it, and asked him if he would not rather have a cat.

His eagerness betrayed him:

'Oh, yes. I would like a cat! I only asked for a kitten lest you should refuse me a cat. No-one would refuse me a kitten – would they?'

I shook my head, and said I feared it would not be possible, but that I would see about it.

His face fell, and I could see a warning of danger in it, for there was a sudden fierce, sidelong look which meant killing. The man is an undeveloped homicidal maniac. I shall test him with his present craving and see how it all works out.

10 p.m.

I have visited him again and found him sitting in a corner, brooding. When I went in he threw himself on his knees and *begged* for a cat; insisted that his salvation depended on it.

I was adamant, however, whereupon Renfield sat down without a word, gnawing his fingers, in the corner where I had found him. I shall see him in the morning.

20 July.

Visited Renfield very early, before the attendant went his rounds. Found him up and humming a tune. He was spreading out his sugar, which he had saved, in the window, and was manifestly beginning his fly-catching again; and seemed surprisingly cheerful. I looked around for his birds, and not seeing them, asked him where they were.

He replied, without turning round, that they had all flown away. There were a few feathers about the room and on his pillow a drop of blood. I said nothing, but went and told the keeper to inform me immediately if there were anything odd about Renfield during the day.

11 a.m.

The attendant has just reported that Renfield has been very sick and disgorged a whole lot of feathers. 'My belief is, doctor,' he said, 'that he has *eaten* his birds . . . raw!'

11 p.m.

I gave Renfield a strong opiate tonight, enough to make even him sleep, and took away his pocket-book to look at it. The thought that has been buzzing about my brain lately is complete, and the theory proved. My homicidal maniac is of a peculiar kind. I shall have to invent a new classification for him, and call his mania zoophagous, or life-eating. What he desires is to absorb as many lives as he can, and in a cumulative manner. He gave many flies to one spider and many spiders to one bird, and then wanted a cat to eat the many birds. What would have been his later steps?

I am almost tempted to let him complete the experiment. If only there were a sufficient cause. Men sneered at vivisection, yet look at its results today! Why not advance science in its most difficult and vital aspect – our knowledge of the brain?

And how well Renfield reasons! Lunatics always do, within their own scope. I wonder at how many lives he values a man. He has closed the account most accurately, and today begun a new record. How many of us begin a new record with each day of our lives?

Lives?

To me it seems only yesterday that my whole life ended. Oh, Lucy, Lucy. I cannot be angry with you. Nor angry with my friend, whose happiness is yours. And yet . . . but at least I have my work.

MINA MURRAY

26 July.

I am anxious, and it soothes me to express myself here. It is like whispering to one's self and listening at the same time. And there is also something about the shorthand symbols that makes it different from writing. I am unhappy about Lucy and about Jonathan. I had not heard from Jonathan for some time, and was very concerned; but yesterday dear Mr Hawkins – who is always so kind – sent me a letter from him. It is only a line dated from Castle Dracula, saying Jonathan was just starting for home.

But that is not like Jonathan. I do not understand it, and it makes me uneasy.

Then Lucy too. Although she is so well, she has lately resumed her old habit of walking in her sleep. Her mother has spoken to me about it, and we have decided that I am to lock the door of our room every night. Mrs Westenra has got an idea that sleepwalkers always go out on roofs of houses and along the edges of cliffs, and then get suddenly awakened and fall over with a despairing cry that echoes all over the place. Poor dear, she is naturally anxious about Lucy, and she tells me that Lucy's father had the same habit: would get up in the night, dress himself and go out; if he were not stopped.

Lucy is to be married in the autumn, and she is already planning out her dresses and how her house is to be arranged. I sympathize with her, for I do the same, only Jonathan and I will start life in a very simple way, and shall have to work to make ends meet. Mr Holmwood (he is the Hon. Arthur Holmwood, only son of Lord Godalming) is coming up here very shortly – as soon as he can leave town, for his father is not very well, and dear Lucy is counting the moments till he comes. She wants to take him up to the seat on the churchyard cliff and show him the beauty of Whitby. I daresay it is the waiting which disturbs her; she will be all right when he arrives.

27 July.

No news from Jonathan. I am getting quite uneasy about him, though why I do not know. But I do wish that he would write, if only a single line. Lucy walks more than ever, and each night I am awakened by her moving about the room. Fortunately, the weather is so hot that she cannot get cold; but still the anxiety and the perpetually being wakened is beginning to tell on me, and I am getting nervous and wakeful myself. Thank God Lucy's health keeps up.

Mr Holmwood has been suddenly called to Ring to see his father, who is now seriously ill. Lucy frets at the postponement of seeing him, but it does not touch her looks. She is a trifle stouter, and her cheeks are a lovely rose pink. She has lost that anaemic look. I pray it will all last.

3 August.

Another week gone, and no news from Jonathan, not even to Mr Hawkins. Oh, I do hope he is not ill. He surely would have written. I look at that last letter of his, but somehow it does not satisfy me. It does not read like him, and yet it is his writing. Lucy has not walked much in her sleep the last week, but there is an odd concentration about her which I do not understand. Even in her sleep she seems to be watching me. She tries the door, and finding it locked, goes about the room searching for the key.

6 August.

Still no news. This suspense is getting dreadful. If only I knew where to write to, I should feel easier; but no-one has heard a word of Jonathan since that last letter. I must pray to God for patience.

And Lucy . . . she is more excitable than ever, but otherwise well. Last night was awfully threatening, and the fishermen say we are in for a storm. I must try to watch it and learn the weather signs. Today is a grey day, and the sun is hidden in thick clouds, high over Kettleness. Everything is grey – except the green grass, which seems like pools of emerald between the grey earthy rocks and the grey clouds, tinged with the sunburst at the far edge, which hang over the grey sea, into which the sand-points stretch like grey fingers.

The sea is tumbling in over the shallows and the sandy flats, muffled in the drifting mists. The horizon is lost in grey. All is vastness. The clouds are piled up like giant rocks, and there is a 'brool' over the sea that sounds like some presage of doom. Dark figures on the beach here and there, sometimes half shrouded in the mist, seem 'men like trees walking'. The fishing-boats are racing for home, and rise and dip in the ground swell as they sweep into the harbour, bending to the scuppers.

Now here comes old Mr Swales, making straight for me, and I can see, by the way he lifts his hat, that he wants to talk.

I have been quite touched by the change in the poor old man. When he sat down beside me, he said in a very gentle way:

'I want to say something to you, miss.'

I could see he was not at ease, so I took his poor old wrinkled hand in mine and asked him to speak freely.

Leaving his hand in mine, he said:

'I'm afraid, my deary, that I must have shocked you by all the wicked things I've been sayin' about the dead, and suchlike, for weeks past. But I didn't mean them harmfully, and I want ye to remember that when I've gone. We aud folks that be daffled, and with one foot abaft the krok-hooal, don't altogether like to think of it, and we don't want to feel scary of it. That's why I've took to makin' light of it, to cheer up my own heart a bit.

'But, Lord love ye, miss, I ain't afraid of dyin' not a bit. Only I don't want to die if I can help it. My time must be nigh at hand now, for I be aud, and a hundred years is too much for any man to expect. And I'm so nigh it that the Aud Man is already whettin' his scythe. Ye see, I can't get out o' the habit of caffin' about it all at once. The chafts will wag as they be used to. Some day soon the Angel of Death will sound his trumpet for me. But don't ye dooal an' greet, my deary!'

For he saw that I was crying—

'If he should come this very night I'd not refuse to answer his call. For life be, after all, only a waitin' for somethin' else than what we're doin'. And death be all that we can rightly depend on. But I'm content, for it's comin' to me, my deary, and comin' quick. It may be comin' while we be lookin' and wonderin'. Maybe it's in that wind out over the sea that's bringin' with it loss and wreck, and sore distress, and sad hearts. Look! look!' he cried suddenly:

'There's something in that wind and in the hoast beyont that sounds, and looks, and tastes, and *smells* like death. It's in the air. I feel it comin'. Lord, make me answer cheerful when my call comes!' He held up his arms devoutly, and raised his hat. His mouth moved as though he were praying. After a few minutes' silence, he got up, shook hands with me, blessed me, said goodbye, and hobbled off.

It all touched me, and upset me very much. I was glad when the coastguard came along, with his spy-glass under his arm. He stopped to talk with me, as he always does, but all the time kept looking at a strange ship.

'I can't make her out,' he said. 'She's a Russian, by the look of her, but she's knocking about in the queerest way. She doesn't know her mind a bit. Seems to see the storm coming, but can't decide whether to run up north in the open, or to put in here. Look there again! She is steered mighty strangely, for she doesn't mind the hand on the wheel. Changes about with every puff of wind. We'll hear more of her before this time tomorrow.'

7

The Whitby Dailygraph

REPORT, 8 AUGUST
One of the greatest and suddenest storms on record has just been experienced here, with results both strange and unique. The weather had been somewhat sultry, but not to any degree uncommon in the month of August. Saturday evening was as fine as ever known, and the great body of holiday-makers set out yesterday for visits to Mulgrave Woods, Robin Hood's Bay, Rig Mill, and the various resorts in the neighbourhood of Whitby.

The steamers *Emma* and *Scarborough* made excursions along the coast, and there was an unusual amount of 'tripping' both to and from Whitby. The day was unusually fine till the afternoon, when some of the gossips who frequent the East Cliff churchyard, and from that commanding eminence watch the wide sweep of sea visible to the north and east, called attention to a sudden show of 'mares' tails' high in the sky to the north-west. The wind was then blowing from the south-west in the mild degree which in barometrical language is ranked:

'No. 2: light breeze.'

The coastguard on duty at once made report, and one old fisherman, who for more than half a century has kept watch on weather signs from the East Cliff, foretold emphatically the coming of a sudden storm. The approach of sunset was so very beautiful, so grand in its masses of splendidly-coloured clouds, that there was, on the churchyard walk along the cliff, quite a company assembled to enjoy the view. Before the sun dipped below the black mass of Kettleness, standing boldly athwart the western sky, its downward way was marked by myriad clouds of every sunset-colour — flame, purple, pink, green, violet, and all the tints of gold; with here and there masses not large, but of seemingly absolute blackness, in all sorts of shapes, as well outlined as colossal silhouettes. The experience was not lost on the painters, and doubtless some of the sketches of the 'Prelude to the Great Storm' will grace the Royal Academy walls next May.

More than one captain made up his mind then and there that his 'cobble' or his 'mule', as they term the different classes of boats, would remain in the harbour till the storm had passed. The wind fell away entirely during the evening, until there was a dead calm, a sultry heat, and that prevailing intensity which, on the approach of thunder, affects persons of a sensitive nature. There were but few lights in sight at sea, for even the coasting steamers, which usually 'hug' the shore so closely, kept well to seaward, and but few fishing-boats were in sight.

The only sail noticeable was a foreign schooner with all sails set, which was seemingly going westwards. The foolhardiness or ignorance of her officers was a prolific theme for comment while she remained in sight, and efforts were made to signal her to reduce sail in face of her danger. Before the night shut down she was seen with sails idly flapping as she gently rolled on the undulating swell of the sea:

'As idle as a painted ship upon a painted ocean.'

Shortly before ten o'clock the stillness of the air grew quite oppressive, and the silence was so marked that the bleating of a sheep inland or the barking of a dog in the town was distinctly heard, and the band on the pier, with its lively French air, was like a discord in the great harmony of nature's silence. A little after midnight came a strange sound from over the sea, and high overhead the air began to carry a strange, faint, hollow booming.

Then without warning the tempest broke.

With incredible rapidity the whole aspect of nature at once became convulsed. The waves rose in growing fury, each overtopping its fellow, till the lately glassy sea was like a roaring and devouring monster. White-crested waves beat madly on the level sands and rushed up the shelving cliffs. Others broke over the piers, and with their spume swept the lanthorns of the lighthouses which rise from the end of either pier of Whitby Harbour. The wind roared like thunder, and blew with such force that even strong men clung grimly to the iron stanchions. It was found necessary to clear the piers of the crowding onlookers, else the fatalities of the night would have been increased manyfold.

To add to the dangers, masses of sea-fog came drifting inland – white, wet clouds, which swept by in ghostly fashion, dank and cold like the spirits of those lost at sea come to touch their living brethren with the clammy hands of death.

And many were the shudders among us, as the wreaths of sea-mist swept by.

At times the mist cleared, and the sea for some distance could be seen in the glare of the lightning, which now came thick and fast, followed by such sudden peals of thunder that the whole sky overhead seemed trembling under the shock of the footsteps of the storm. Some of the scenes thus revealed were of immeasurable grandeur – the sea, running mountains high, threw skywards with each wave mighty masses of white foam, which the tempest seemed to snatch and whirl away into space. Here and there a fishing-boat, with a rag of sail, running madly for shelter before the blast. Now and again the white wings of a storm-tossed sea-bird.

From the summit of the East Cliff the new searchlight swept the surface of the sea. Once or twice its service was effective, as when a fishing-boat, its gunwale under water, rushed into the harbour, able, by the beaming light, to avoid being dashed against the piers. As each boat reached safety there came from the crowds ashore a shout of joy which for a moment cleaved the gale and then was swept away. Before long the searchlight discovered some distance away a schooner with all sails set, apparently the same vessel which had been noticed earlier in the evening. The wind had by this time backed to the east, and there was a groan amongst the watchers on the cliff as they realized that between the schooner and the port lay the great flat reef on which so many good ships have foundered, and that, with the wind blowing from its present quarter, she could never reach the harbour.

It was now nearly the hour of high tide, but the waves were so great that in their troughs the shallows of the shore were almost visible, and the schooner, with all sails set, was rushing with such speed that, in the words of one old salt, 'she must fetch up somewhere, be it only in hell'. Then came another rush of sea-fog, greater than any hitherto – a mountain of dank mist which enveloped all till only the sense of hearing remained – to register the ongoing roar of the tempest, the crashing thunder, and the mighty billows booming through the damp oblivion even louder than before.

The rays of the searchlight were kept trained on the harbour mouth across the East Pier, where the shock was expected, and all onlookers waited breathlessly. Then the wind suddenly shifted to the north-east, the remnant sea-fog quickly melted in the blast, and between the piers, leaping from wave to wave at headlong speed, swept the strange schooner with all sails set.

The searchlight followed her as she gained the safety of the harbour, and a gasp of horror rose up from all who saw her. For lashed to the helm was a corpse, its drooping head swinging horribly to and fro at each motion of the ship. No other form was visible on deck, and a great awe came over us all as we realized that the ship had gained the harbour unsteered – save by that dead man's hand. Next, more quickly than it takes to write these words, the schooner hurtled across the harbour and stranded on that accumulation of sand and gravel washed by many tides and storms into the south-east corner of the pier jutting under the East Cliff (known locally as Tate Hill Pier).

There was of course a considerable concussion as the vessel drove up on the sand-heap. Every spar, rope, and stay was strained, and some of the 'top-hammer' came crashing down. But, strangest of all, the very instant the shore was touched an immense dog sprang up on deck from below, as if shot up by the shock. From the bow it leapt down to the sand, then ran straight for the cliff where the churchyard hangs over the laneway to the East Pier so steeply that some of the flat tombstones – 'thruff-steans' or 'through-stones', as we call them in Whitby – actually project over where the sustaining cliff has fallen away. Thence the hound disappeared in the darkness, which somehow seemed intensified just beyond the searchlight's focus.

Now it so happened that there was no-one just then on Tate Hill Pier, as all who lived near were either in bed or out on the heights above. Thus the coastguard on duty on the eastern side of the harbour, who at once ran down to the little pier, was the first to climb on board. The men working the searchlight, after scouring the harbour entrance without seeing anything, then turned the light on the derelict vessel and kept it there. The coastguard ran aft, and when he came beside the wheel, bent over to examine it and recoiled at once as though under some sudden emotion. This seemed to pique the general curiosity, and quite a number of people began to run towards the schooner.

It is a good way round from the West Cliff by the Drawbridge to Tate Hill Pier, but your correspondent is a fairly good runner, and came well ahead of the crowd. When I arrived, however, I found already assembled on the pier quite a gaggle, whom the coastguard and police refused to allow on board. By the courtesy of the chief boatman, I was, as an official of the press, permitted to climb on deck, where I was one of a small group who actually saw how that dead seaman was lashed to the wheel. His hands were tied, one over the other, to a spoke of the wheel, and between the inner hand and the wood was a crucifix, the set of beads on which it was fastened being around both wrists and wheel, and all kept fast by binding cords.

The poor fellow may have been seated at one time, but the flapping and buffeting of the sails had worked through the rudder to the wheel and dragged him to and fro, so that the cords with which he was tied had cut his flesh to the bone. Accurate note was made of the state of things, and a doctor – Surgeon J. M. Caffyn, of 33, East Elliot Place – who came immediately after me, declared, after making examination, that the man must have been dead for quite two days. In his pocket was a bottle, carefully corked, yet empty save for a little roll of paper, which proved to be an addendum to the log.

The coastguard said the man must have tied up his own hands, fastening the knots with his teeth. The fact that a coastguard was the first on board may save some complications, later on, in the Admiralty Court; for the coastguards cannot claim the salvage which is the right of the first civilian entering on a derelict. Already, however, the legal tongues are wagging, and one young law student is loudly asserting that the rights of the owner are already completely sacrificed, his property being held in contravention of the statutes of mortmain, since the tiller, as emblemship, if not proof, of delegated possession, is held by a dead hand – although, of course, the dead steersman has now been detached from his ghastly stormy watch, and placed in the mortuary to await inquest.

Already the sudden storm is passing. As its fierceness abates, the crowds are scattering homewards, and the sky begins to redden over the Yorkshire wolds. Our next issue, rest assured, will give further details of the derelict ship which found her way so miraculously into harbour in the storm.

REPORT, 9 AUGUST

The sequel to the strange schooner's arrival last night is almost more startling than the events of the storm itself. It appears that this is a Russian craft sailing out of Varna, called the *Demeter*. She is almost entirely in ballast of silver sand, with, relatively, only a very small cargo – a number of large wooden boxes filled with mould. This cargo was consigned to a Whitby solicitor, Mr Samuel Billington, of 7, The Crescent, who this morning went aboard and formally took possession of the goods.

The Russian Consul, too, acting for the charter-party, took formal possession of the ship, and paid all harbour dues and other costs. Nothing is talked about here today except these strange goings-on. The officials of the Board of Trade have insisted on strict compliance with regulations. As the matter is to be a 'nine-day wonder', they are determined that there shall be no cause for retrospective complaint.

A good deal of interest was also shown in the dog which landed when the ship struck, and several members of the S.P.C. (which is very strong in Whitby) have tried to befriend the animal. To the general disappointment, however, it seems to have disappeared entirely from the town and may – understandably frightened – have made its way on to the moors, where it is still hiding in terror. There are some who look with dread on such a possibility, lest later on it should in itself become a danger, for it is evidently a fierce brute. Early this morning a large dog, a half-bred mastiff, belonging to a coal merchant, was found dead in the roadway opposite its master's yard near Tate Hill Pier. It had been fighting, manifestly with a savage opponent, for its throat was torn away and its belly slit open as if by a ferocious claw.

Later.

By the kindness of the Board of Trade inspector, I have been permitted to examine the logbook of the *Demeter*, which was in order up to three days ago, but contains nothing of special interest except as to details of missing men. Much more important, it seems, is the paper found in the bottle, which was today produced at the inquest. Certainly, a more bizarre history than the log and the paper between them unfold it has never been my lot to encounter. As there is no motive for concealment I am permitted to use them, and accordingly send you a rescript (omitting only technical details of seamanship and supercargo) which to me suggests that the Captain must have been possessed by some mania near the outset, and that his condition deteriorated persistently throughout the voyage. Of course, my interpretation must be taken *cum grano*, being based on the dictation of a clerk of the Russian Consul, who kindly translated for me, time being short.

FROM THE DEMETER'S LOGBOOK

Written 18 July, things so strange happening, that I shall keep accurate note henceforth till we land.

On 6 July we finished taking in cargo, silver sand and boxes of earth. At noon set sail. East wind, fresh. Crew, five hands . . . two mates, cook, and myself (Captain).

On 11 July at dawn entered Bosphorus. Boarded by Turkish Customs officers. Backsheesh. All correct. Under way at 4 p.m.

On 12 July through Dardanelles. More Customs officers and flagboat of guarding squadron. Backsheesh again. Work of officers thorough, but quick. Want us off soon. At dark passed into Archipelago.

On 13 July passed Cape Matapan. Crew dissatisfied about something. Seemed scared, but would not speak out.

On 14 July was somewhat anxious about crew. Men all steady fellows, who have sailed with me before. Mate could not make out what was wrong. They only told him there was *something*, and crossed themselves. Mate lost temper with one of them that day and struck him. Expected fierce quarrel, but all was quiet.

On 16 July mate reported in the morning that one of crew, Petrofsky, was missing. Could not account for it. Took larboard watch, eight bells last night. Was relieved by Abramoff, but did not go to bunk. Men more downcast than ever. All said they expected something of the kind, but would not say more than that there was *something* aboard. Mate getting very impatient with them.

I feared some trouble ahead.

On 17 July, yesterday, one of the men, Olgaren, came to my cabin. In an awestruck way he claimed there was a strange man aboard the ship. Said that in his watch he had been sheltering behind the deck-house, as there was a rain-storm, when he saw a tall, thin man, not like any of the crew, come up the companion way, go along the deck forward, and disappear. Olgaren followed cautiously, he says, but when he got to bows found no-one, and the hatchways were all closed.

He was in a panic of superstitious fear, and I am afraid the panic may spread. To allay it, I shall today search entire ship carefully from stem to stern.

Later.

With whole crew, made thorough search. All keeping abreast, with lanterns, we left no corner unturned. As there were only the big wooden boxes, there were no odd corners where a man could hide. Men much relieved, and went back to work cheerfully. First mate scowled, but said nothing.

22 July.

Rough weather last three days, and all hands busy with sails – no time to be frightened. Men seem to have forgotten their dread. Mate cheerful again, and all on good terms. Praised men for work in bad weather. Passed Gibraltar and out through Straits. All well.

24 July.

There seems some doom over this ship. Already a hand short, and entering on the Bay of Biscay with wild weather ahead. Yet last night another man lost – disappeared. Like the first, he came off his watch and was not seen again. Men, all in a funk, sent a round robin asking to have double watch, as they fear to be alone.

Mate violent.

I fear there will be some trouble, as either he or the men will do some violence.

28 July.

Four days in hell, knocking about in a sort of maelstrom, and the wind a tempest. No sleep for anyone. Men all worn out. Hardly know how to set a watch since no-one fit to go on. Second mate volunteered to steer and watch and let men snatch a few hours' sleep.

Wind abating. Seas still terrific, but feel them less, as ship is steadier.

29 July.

Another tragedy. Had single watch tonight, as crew too tired to double. When morning watch came on deck, could find no-one but steersman. Raised outcry, and all came on deck. Thorough search, but no-one found. Are now without second mate, and crew in a panic. Mate and I agreed to go armed henceforth and wait for any sign of cause.

30 July.

Last night. Rejoiced we are nearing England. Weather fine, all sails set. Retired worn out. Slept soundly. Awaked by mate telling me that both watch and steersman missing. Only self, mate and two hands left to work ship.

1 August.

Two days of fog. Not a sail sighted. Had hoped when in the English Channel to signal for help or get in somewhere. Not having power to work sails, have to run before wind. Dare not lower – could not raise them again. We seem to be drifting to some terrible doom. Mate now more demoralized than either of the hands. His stronger nature seems to have worked inwardly against himself. The men are beyond fear, working stolidly and patiently, with minds made up to worst.

They are Russian, he Romanian.

2 August. Midnight.

Woken from a few minutes' sleep by hearing a cry, seemingly outside my port. Could see nothing in fog. Rushed on deck, and ran against mate. Tells me he heard cry and ran, but no sign of man on watch. One more gone.

Lord help us.

Mate says we must be past Straits of Dover, as in a moment of fog lifting he saw North Foreland just as he heard the man cry out. If so, we are now off in the North Sea, and only God can guide us in the fog, which seems to move with us.

And God seems to have deserted us.

3 August.

At midnight I went to relieve the man at the wheel, but when I got to it found no-one there. The wind was steady, and as we ran before it there was no yawing. I dared not leave the wheel, so shouted for the mate. After a few seconds he rushed up on deck in his flannels. He looked wild-eyed and haggard, and I fear his reason has given way. He came close to me and whispered hoarsely, with his mouth to my ear, as though fearing the very air might hear:

'*It* is here. I know it, now. On the watch last night I saw It. Like a man, very tall and thin, and ghastly pale. It was in the bows, looking out. I crept behind It, and gave It my knife. But the knife went through It, empty as the air.' He stabbed his knife savagely into space, then went on:

'But It is here, and I'll find It. In the hold, perhaps, in one of those boxes. I'll unscrew them one by one and see. You work the helm.' And, with a warning look and his finger on his lip, he went below. There was springing up a choppy wind, and I could not leave the helm. I saw him come out on deck again with a tool-chest and a lantern, and go down the forward hatchway. He is mad. Stark, raving mad. No use my trying to stop him. He can't hurt those big boxes anyway. They are invoiced as 'clay', and to pull them about may keep him from worse harm.

So here I stay, and mind the helm, and scribble down these notes. I can only trust in God and wait till the fog clears. Then, if I can't steer to any harbour with the wind that is, I shall cut down sails and lie by, and signal for help . . .

It is nearly all over now. Just as I was beginning to hope the mate would come out calmer – for I heard him knocking away at something in the hold – there came up the hatchway a sudden, startled scream, which made my blood run cold. And up on the deck he came as if shot from a gun – a raging madman. Eyes rolling and his face convulsed with fear.

'Save me! Save me!' he cried, and then looked round on the blanket of fog. His horror turned to despair, and in a steady voice he said:

'You better come too, Captain, before too late. *He* is there. I know the secret now. The sea shall save me from Him!'

Before I could say a word, or move to seize him, he sprang on the bulwark and hurled himself into the sea. I suppose I know the secret too, now. It was this madman who got rid of my men, one by one. And now he has followed them himself. God help me! How am I to account for all these horrors when I get to port? *When* . . . will that ever be?

4 August.

Still fog, which the sunrise cannot pierce. I know there is sunrise because I am a sailor. Why else, I know not. I dared not go below, and I dared not leave the helm. So here all night I stayed, and in the dimness of the night I saw It – *Him*. God forgive me, but the mate was right to jump overboard. Better to die like a man. To die in blue water – no sailor can complain. But I am Captain, and I must not leave my ship.

But I shall baffle this monster, for I shall tie my hands to the wheel when my strength begins to fail, and along with them I shall tie that which . . . *It* dare not touch. Thus, come good wind or foul, I shall save my soul. And my honour as Captain.

Now I grow weaker.

The night comes on.

If *He* can look me in the face again, I may not have time to act . . .

If we are wrecked, mayhap this bottle will be found, and those who find it may understand. If not, pray God and the Blessed Virgin won't spurn a poor ignorant soul . . . only trying to do . . . his duty . . .

EDITORIAL

Of course the verdict was an open one. There is no clear evidence, so might not the Captain himself have committed the murders? Who now can say? In any case the folk here hold almost universally that the

Captain must be given a hero's funeral, his body to be sailed with great ceremony up the Esk a way, then back to Tate Hill Pier and up the Abbey steps — for he is to be buried in the churchyard on the cliff. The owners of more than a hundred boats have already volunteered to be part of this funerary fleet.

As to the vanished great dog, still there is no further trace. At this there is much mourning, for, with public opinion in its present state, he would, I believe, be adopted by the town.

Tomorrow will see the funeral.

And so will end this one more 'mystery of the sea'.

8

Mina Murray's Journal

8 August.

Lucy was very restless all night, and I too could not sleep. The storm was fearful, and as it boomed loudly among the chimney-pots, it made me shudder. When a sharp puff came, it seemed like a distant gun. Strangely enough, Lucy did not wake; but she got up twice and dressed herself. Fortunately, each time I awoke in time, and managed to undress her without waking her, and got her back to bed.

It is a very strange thing, this sleep-walking, for as soon as her will is thwarted in any physical way, her intention seems to wither, and she yields placidly to the requirements of normal life.

Early in the morning we got up and went down to the harbour to see what had happened in the night. There were few people about, and though the sun was bright, and the air clear and fresh, the big, grim-looking waves, that seemed dark themselves because the foam that topped them was like snow, forced in through the narrow harbour mouth like a bully going through a crowd. Somehow I felt glad that Jonathan was not on the sea last night, but really . . . how do I know? Oh, where *is* he?

10 August.

The funeral of the poor sea-captain today was most touching. Every boat in the harbour was there, and the coffin was carried by captains all the way from Tate Hill Pier up to the churchyard. Lucy and I went early to our old seat, while the cortège of boats went up the river to the Viaduct and came down again. We had a lovely view of the procession, and the poor fellow was laid to rest quite near our seat, so, standing on it, we saw everything.

Poor Lucy seemed much upset. She was restless and uneasy all the time, and I cannot but think that her dreaming at night is telling on her. She is quite odd in one thing: refusing to admit she has any cause for restlessness. Whatever it be, I fear she does not understand it herself.

There is an additional cause in that poor old Mr Swales was found dead this morning on our seat, his neck being broken. He had evidently, as the doctor said, fallen back in the seat in some sort of fright, for there was a look of fear and horror on his face that the men said made their flesh creep.

Poor dear old man! Perhaps he had seen Death with his dying eyes!

Lucy is so sweet and sensitive that she feels influences very acutely. Just now she was quite upset by a little thing which I did not much heed, though I am myself very fond of animals. One of the men who come up here often to look for the boats was followed by his dog. The dog is always with him, and I had never seen the man angry, nor once heard the dog bark. During the service, however, the dog would not come to its master, who was on the seat with us, but kept a few yards off, barking and howling. Its master spoke to it gently, then harshly, then angrily.

But the dog would neither come nor cease its noise. It was in a sort of fury, eyes savage, and all its hairs bristling out like a cat's tail on the war-path. Finally the owner became furious, jumped down and kicked the dog, took it by the scruff of the neck and dumped it down on the tombstone to which our seat is fixed. The moment it touched the stone the poor dog became quiet and fell into a tremble. It did not try to get away, but cowered down, quivering, in such a pitiable state of terror that I tried, though without effect, to comfort it.

Lucy was full of pity, too, but she did not attempt to touch the dog, merely looking at it in an agonized sort of way. I greatly fear that she is of too super-sensitive a nature to go through the world without trouble. She will be dreaming of this tonight, I am sure. The whole agglomeration of things – the ship steered into port by a dead man; his attitude, tied to the wheel with a crucifix and beads; the touching funeral; the dog, now furious and now in terror – will all affect her dreams.

I think it best for her to go to bed tired out physically, so I shall take her for a long walk by the cliffs, to Robin Hood's Bay and back. She ought not to have much inclination for sleep-walking then.

Same day, 11 p.m.

Oh, but I am tired!

Had I not made my diary a duty, I should not open it tonight. But we had a lovely walk. Lucy, after a while, was in gay spirits; owing, I think, to some dear cows who came nosing towards us in a field close to the lighthouse, and frightened the wits out of us. I believe we forgot everything, except, of course, personal fear, and it seemed to wipe the slate clean and give us a fresh start. We had a capital 'severe tea' at Robin Hood's Bay, in a sweet little old-fashioned inn, with a bow-window right over the seaweed-covered rocks of the strand.

I believe our boyish appetites would have deeply shocked the 'New Woman'. Men are so much more tolerant.

(Bless them!)

Then we walked home, with several stoppages to rest, and with our hearts in terror of wild bulls. Lucy was really tired, and we intended to creep off to bed as soon as we could. The young curate came in, however, and Mrs Westenra asked him to stay for supper. Lucy and I had quite a battle with Morpheus, and really I feel the time has come for the bishops to breed up a new class of curates – who won't take supper, no matter how warmly pressed, and who will know when girls are tired.

Now Lucy is asleep and breathing softly. She has more colour in her cheeks than usual, and looks . . . divine. If Mr Holmwood fell in love with her seeing her only in the drawing-room, how would he behave if he could only see her here, in bed!

'New Woman' writers will doubtless soon insist that men and women should be allowed to see each other 'asleep' before proposing or accepting. But will the New Woman of the future deign to accept? Or will she do the proposing herself?

And a nice job she would make of it!

I am so happy tonight, because dear Lucy seems better. I really believe she has turned the corner, and that we are over her troubles with dreaming. I should be *completely* happy, if only Jonathan . . . God bless and keep him.

11 August, 3 a.m.

Diary again. I am too agitated to sleep, so may as well write. We have had such an adventure, such an agonizing experience. I fell asleep as soon as I had closed my diary. Then suddenly I became broad awake, and sat up, with a horrible sense of fear upon me, and of emptiness around me. The room was dark, and I could not see Lucy's bed, so I stole across and felt for her. The bed was empty. I lit a match, and found she was not in the room. The door was shut, but not locked, as I had left it. I feared to wake her mother, whose health has been poor of late, so threw on some clothes and got ready to look for her.

As I was leaving the room it struck me that the clothes Lucy wore might suggest her dreaming intention. Dressing gown would mean house; dress, outside. Dressing gown and dress were both in their places. 'Thank God,' I said to myself. 'She cannot be far, as she is only in her nightdress.'

I ran downstairs and looked in the sitting room. Not there! Then I looked in all the other open rooms of the house, with a growing fear chilling my heart. Finally I came to the hall door and found it shut but unlocked. The Westenras are careful to lock up every night, so I feared that Lucy must have gone out as she was, undressed.

Leaving no time to think of what might happen – a vague overmastering fear obscuring all details – I threw on a warm shawl and ran out. The clock struck one as I was in the Crescent, and there was not a soul in sight. I ran along the North Terrace but could see no sign of the white figure I expected. At the edge of the West Cliff above the pier I looked across the harbour to the East Cliff, in the hope – or fear; I don't know which – of seeing Lucy in our favourite seat. There was a bright full moon, with driving dark clouds throwing the whole scene into a fleeting diorama of light and shade as they sailed across the sky.

For a moment I could see nothing: shadows obscured St Mary's Church and all around it. Then, as the cloud passed, the ruins of the Abbey came into view. Sharp as a sword-cut, a narrow edge of light combed the scene, and the churchyard became gradually visible. And there! There on our favourite seat was a half-reclining figure, snowy white in the silver moonlight.

Incoming clouds overshadowed the scene too quickly for me to see clearly, but my impression was of something dark behind the seat where the white figure shone, and bending over it. What it was, whether man or beast, I pondered frantically as I flew down the steps to the pier and along by the fish-market to the bridge – the only way to reach the East Cliff. Not a soul did I see, and at this I rejoiced, for I wanted no witness of poor Lucy's condition.

After a seeming age my knees trembled and my breath came laboured as I toiled up the endless steps to the Abbey, feeling as if my feet were weighted with lead, and as though every joint in my body were choked with rust. When I neared the top I glimpsed the white figure through the shadows. And there . . . undoubtedly something – long and black, bending over the passive white form. To whom I called in fright:

'Lucy! Lucy!'

Something raised a head, and I glimpsed a white face and a pair of red-gleaming eyes. Lucy did not answer, and I ran on to the churchyard. As I entered, the church was between me and the seat, and for a moment I lost sight of her. When I rounded the church the cloud had passed, and the moonlight shone brilliantly on Lucy's white nightdress. Her head was propped skywards, resting on the back of the seat, and she was quite alone.

Perching beside her, I saw she was still asleep. Her lips were parted, and she was breathing in long, heavy gasps, as though with unusual difficulty. As I reached to feel her brow, her sleeping hand pulled the collar of her nightdress close round her throat, and a shiver rippled through her body, as though suddenly she felt the cold. Fearing lest she catch a chill, I flung my warm shawl over her and drew the edges tight round her neck, for I dreaded lest she should get some deadly chill from the night air, unclad as she was. I fastened the shawl at her throat with a big safety-pin, but I must have been clumsy in my anxiety and pinched or pricked her with it, for when her breathing became quieter she put her hand to her throat again and moaned. When I had her carefully wrapped up I put my shoes on her feet, and then began very gently to wake her. At first she did not respond, but gradually she became more and more uneasy in her sleep, sighing and occasionally moaning. Feeling it vital to get her home at once, I shook her more forcibly, till finally she opened her eyes.

She did not seem surprised to see me, as, of course, she did not realize at first where she was. Lucy always wakes prettily, and even at such a time, her body chilled with cold, and her mind bemused at waking unclad in a churchyard at night, she did not lose her grace. She trembled a little, and clung tightly to me. When I told her she must come home she rose without a word, obedient as a sleepy child.

As we walked together the gravel hurt my feet, and Lucy noticed me wince. She stopped and wanted me to take back my shoes, but I would not. However, when we got to the pathway outside the churchyard, where there was a puddle of water remaining from the storm, I daubed my feet with mud, so that no-one might notice my pale bare feet.

Fortune favoured us, and we got home without meeting a soul. Once we saw a man who seemed not quite sober, passing along a street in front of us. But we hid in a doorway till he disappeared up a steep little close, or 'wynd' – as they call them in Scotland. My heart beat so loud all the while that sometimes I thought I should faint. I was filled with anxiety about Lucy, not only for her health, lest she should suffer from the exposure, but for her reputation, if the story got out.

When we got in, and had washed our feet, and said a prayer of thankfulness together, I tucked her into bed. Before falling asleep she asked – even implored – me to say not a word to anyone, not even her mother, about her sleepwalking adventure.

I hesitated at first, but on thinking of her mother's poor health, and how such a thing would fret her, and thinking, too, of how such a story must become distorted if it should leak out, I finally promised what Lucy asked.

I hope I did right.

Now I have locked the door, and the key is tied to my wrist. Pray God I shall not be disturbed again. Lucy is sleeping soundly, and the dawn is rising, far over the sea.

Same Day. Noon.

All goes well. Lucy slept deeply till I woke her. The adventure of the night seems not to have harmed her. On the contrary, she looks better this morning than she has for weeks. I was sorry, though, to notice that my clumsiness with the safety-pin had pierced Lucy's throat. In the dark I must have pinched up and penetrated a little fold of her skin, and fastened it along with the shawl – for there are two little red points like pin-pricks, and on the band of her nightdress is the stain of a drop of blood. When I apologized Lucy merely laughed, patted me, and said she did not feel it.

Fortunately she should not be scarred, as the mark is so tiny.

Same day. Night.

We passed a happy day. The air was clear, the sun bright, and there was a cool breeze. We took our lunch to Mulgrave Woods, Mrs Westenra driving by the road, while Lucy and I walked by the path along the cliff. I felt a little sad myself, unable not to wish that Jonathan were here. But there! I must be patient.

In the evening we strolled in the Casino Terrace, and heard some good music by Spohr and Mackenzie. Then we went to bed early. Lucy, seeming more restful than for some time, fell asleep at once. I shall lock the door and secure the key as before, though I do not expect any trouble tonight.

12 August.

It seems I was mistaken. Twice during the night I was awakened by Lucy trying to get out. She seemed, even in her sleep, to be impatient at finding the door shut, and was led back to bed under protest. I awoke with the dawn, and heard the birds chirping outside. Lucy woke, too, and I was glad to see her even brighter than yesterday. All her old gaiety apparently revived, she snuggled into bed beside me, and told me all about Arthur. I told her how anxious I was about Jonathan, and Lucy tried to comfort me. Comfort? Yes, a little. For though sympathy can't alter facts, it can help to make them more bearable.

13 August.

Another quiet day. To bed with the key on my wrist, as before. Again I awoke in the night – to find Lucy sitting up in bed, still asleep, pointing to the window. I got up quietly, pulled aside the blind, and looked out. It was brilliant moonlight, and the soft effect of the light over the sea and sky – merged together in one vast, silent mystery – was beautiful beyond words. But then between me and the moonlight there swooped an enormous bat, whirling round in dizzying circles. Once or twice it came quite close, but was, I suppose, frightened at seeing me, and flitted away across the harbour towards the Abbey. When I turned round from the window Lucy had lain down again, and was sleeping peacefully.

Nor did she stir again all night.

14 August.

On the East Cliff, reading and writing all day. Lucy seems as much in love with the spot as I am. More so, perhaps. For it is hard to get her away, even for tea. Today she made a funny remark as we were coming home for dinner. At the top of the West Pier steps we stopped to look at the setting sun. Already low in the sky, it was just dropping behind Kettleness, thus bathing all the East Cliff and the old Abbey in a beautiful rosy glow. We were silent for a minute, then Lucy murmured, as if to herself:

'His red eyes again! They are just the same.'

It was such an odd expression, coming apropos of nothing, that it quite startled me.

Lucy seemed in a half-dreamy state, but with a peculiar look on her face. I said nothing, but followed her eyes. She appeared to be gazing over at our seat, whereon a dark figure was seated, alone. And yes, it seemed for an instant that the stranger had eyes like great crimson flames.

But a second look dispelled the illusion, which had been created by the red sunlight shining on the windows of St Mary's Church, behind our seat. As the sun sank below the horizon, Lucy came to with a start, but still she looked sad. Could she be dimly remembering that terrible chilly night up there? We never refer to it, so I said nothing, and we went home to dinner.

Lucy had a headache and went early to bed. I saw her asleep, then went out for a final stroll. I walked along the cliffs to the westward, and was full of sweet sadness, for I was thinking of Jonathan. As I was coming home a trick of the moonlight drew my attention to our window, where I saw Lucy's head leaning out. I thought she must be looking out for me, so I waved my handkerchief in the moonbeams. She did not notice or make any movement whatever. As I neared the house I drew breath to call to her but just then I saw to my amazement that she was fast asleep and that perched beside her on the windowsill, in a posture at once protective yet strangely menacing, was a huge black bird – like an overgrown owl, though I could not see its eyes.

Fearing Lucy must catch a chill, I ran upstairs to lead her away from the window. But I found her already moving back to her bed, fast asleep. She was breathing heavily, and holding her hand to her throat, as though to protect it from cold. I tucked her up warmly, managing not to wake her, and have ensured that the door is locked and the window securely fastened.

By candlelight.

Lucy looks so sweet as she sleeps. Yet she is paler than is her wont, and there is a drawn, haggard look under her eyes which I do not like. I fear she is fretting about something, but what?

15 August.

Rose later than usual. Lucy was languid and tired, and slept on after we had been called. We had a happy surprise at breakfast, however. Arthur's father is better, and wants the marriage to take place soon. Lucy is full of quiet joy, and her mother is at once glad and sorry. Later in the day she told me why: the poor, dear lady has got her death-warrant. She has not told Lucy, and swore me to secrecy, but her doctor has told her that her heart is weakening fast. Any sudden shock, henceforth, is almost sure to kill her.

How wise we were to keep from Mrs Westenra the details of that dreadful night, when Lucy sleep-walked up to the churchyard.

17 August.

No diary for two whole days. I have not had the heart to write. Some awful pall is hovering over our happiness. No news from Jonathan, and Lucy seems weaker again, while her mother's hours are numbering to a close. I do not understand Lucy's condition. She eats and sleeps well, and enjoys the fresh air, yet all the time the roses in her cheeks are fading, and at night I hear her gasping as if for air. I keep the key of our door always fastened to my wrist at night, but she gets up and walks about the room, and sits at the open window. Last night I found her leaning out when I woke up, and when I tried to wake her I could not: she was in a faint.

When I managed to restore her she was weak as water, and cried silently between long, painful struggles for breath. When I asked her how she came to be at the window she shook her head and turned away. I hope her feeling ill is not due to that unlucky prick of the safety-pin. I looked at her throat just now as she lay asleep, and the tiny wounds seem not to have healed. They are still open, and seem larger than before, with edges turned faintly white – and little red centres. Unless they heal within a day or two, I shall insist on the doctor seeing them.

18 August.

Today as I write, sitting on our churchyard seat, I am *happy*. Lucy is ever so much better. Last night she slept well, and did not disturb me once. There were hints of pale roses in her cheeks this morning, and yet . . . she is still sadly wan-looking. If she had a history of anaemia I could understand it, but she has not. Still, she is in gay spirits and full of life. All her morbid reticence seems to have passed, and she has just reminded me, as if I needed reminding, of *that* night – when on this very seat I found her so strangely asleep. As she told me, she tapped playfully with the heel of her boot on the stone slab, and said:

'My poor little feet didn't make much noise then! I dare say poor old Mr Swales would have said it was because I didn't want to wake up Geordie!'

Seeing her in such a communicative humour, I asked if she had dreamed during the night. Before she answered, that sweet, puckered look came over her forehead, which Arthur – I call him Arthur from her habit – says he loves so much. Then she went on in a faraway voice, as if trying to recall it herself:

'I didn't quite *dream*, for it all seemed awfully real. I only wanted to be here in this spot – I don't know why, for I was afraid of something. Yet I don't know what. I remember, though I suppose I was asleep, passing through the streets and over the bridge. A fish leaped as I went by, and I leaned over to look at it. Then I heard a lot of dogs howling – the whole town seemed suddenly full of dogs all howling at once – as I went up the steps. Next, I have a vague memory of something long and dark, with red eyes, just as we saw in the sunset, and something very sweet and very bitter all around me all at once. Then . . .

'I seemed to be sinking into deep green water. There was a singing in my ears, as is said to be heard by drowning men, and . . . my soul appeared to rise up from my body and float about the air. I have a vivid impression of the West Lighthouse right under me, and a sort of agonizing feeling, as if I were in an earthquake. When I returned to earth, I found you shaking my body, yet I *saw* you do it before I felt you.'

Then she began to laugh.

It seemed a little uncanny to me, and I listened to her breathlessly. I did not quite like it, and thought it better not to dwell on the subject. So we drifted on to other matters, and Lucy was like her old self again. When we got home the fresh breeze had braced her up, and her pale cheeks were really quite rosy. Her mother rejoiced when she saw her, and we all spent a very happy evening together.

19 August.

Joy, joy! At last, news of Jonathan. Not all joy, though. The dear fellow has been ill, which is why he did not write. Mr Hawkins sent me on the letter, and wrote himself; oh, so kindly. I am to leave in the morning for Budapest, to nurse Jonathan back to full health, and to bring him home. Mr Hawkins suggests we might marry while out there.

Oh, how I have cried over the good Sister's letter. Even now I feel it moist against my bosom – next my heart, to remind me of Jonathan. My journey is all mapped out, and my luggage ready. I am only taking one change of clothes with me, as Lucy will take my trunk to London and send it on, if I . . . if Jonathan, for it may be that . . . but I must write no more. The rest is a precious secret, which only . . . my husband must share. God guard Jonathan till then.

9

Several Communications

LETTER FROM ST JOSEPH'S HOSPITAL, BUDAPEST
12 August.
Dear Miss Murray,

I write by desire of Mr Jonathan Harker, who is himself not strong enough to write, though progressing well, thanks to God and St Joseph. He has been under our care for nearly six weeks, suffering from a violent brain fever. He wishes me to convey his love, and to say that by this post I write for him to Mr Peter Hawkins, Exeter, to say, with dutiful respects, that he is sorry to have been delayed, but that all his work is completed. He will require some few weeks' rest in our sanatorium in the hills, but will then return. He wishes me to say that he has not sufficient money with him, and that he would like to pay for his staying here, so that others who need shall not be wanting for help.

Believe me,

Yours, with sympathy and all blessings,

Sister Agatha.

P.S. My patient being asleep, I open this to let you know something more. He has told me all about you, and that you are shortly to be his wife. All blessings to you both! He has had some fearful shock – so says our doctor – and in his delirium his ravings have been dreadful: of wolves and poison and blood; of ghosts and demons; and phantasies too horrible to describe. Be careful that nothing should excite him to imaginings of this nature for many a month to come. The traces of such an illness do not lightly die away. We should have written long ago, but we knew nothing of his friends, and there was on him nothing that anyone could understand. He came in the train from Klausenburg, and the guard was told by the station-master there that he rushed into the station demanding a ticket for home. Seeing from his violent demeanour that he was English, they gave him a ticket for the farthest station on the way.

Be assured that he is well cared for here. He has won all hearts by his

98

gentle kindness and truly he is getting on well, and I have no doubt will in a few weeks be all himself. I pray God and St Joseph for many, many happy years for you both together to come.

LETTER TO CARTER, PATERSON & CO, LONDON

17 August.

Dear Sirs,

Herewith please receive invoice of goods sent by Great Northern Railway. Same are to be delivered at Carfax, near Purfleet, immediately on receipt at goods station King's Cross. The house is at present empty, but enclosed please find keys, all labelled.

You will please deposit the boxes, fifty in number, which form the consignment, in the partially ruined building marked 'A' on diagram enclosed. Your agent will easily recognize this building, as it is the ancient chapel of the mansion. The goods leave by the 9.30 tonight, and are due at King's Cross at 4.30 tomorrow afternoon. As our client wishes the delivery made as soon as possible, we shall be obliged by your having teams ready at King's Cross to forthwith convey goods to destination. On coming away your men are to leave all keys in the main hall of the house.

Pray do not take us as exceeding business courtesy in pressing you in all ways to exercise the utmost expedition.

Faithfully yours,

Samule F. Billington & Son.

TO BILLINGTON & SON, WHITBY

19 August.

Dear Sirs,

Goods delivered to Carfax yesterday in exact accordance with your instructions and keys left in parcel in main hall, as directed.

Yours respectfully,

Carter, Paterson & Co.

DR SEWARD'S DIARY

19 August.

Strange and sudden change in Renfield last night. About eight o'clock he got all excited and began to sniff about like a game dog on a scent. The attendant, knowing my interest in him, encouraged him to talk. He is usually respectful to the attendant – at times even servile – but tonight, the man tells me, he would only say, and in a condescending manner:

'I don't want to talk to you. You don't count now. Now the Master is at hand.'

The attendant thinks it some religious mania which has seized him. If so, we must look out for squalls. Homicidal and religious manias at once might make a dreadful combination, especially in a physically powerful man. At nine o'clock I visited him myself, and he behaved to me as to the attendant. In his self-regarding serenity the difference between myself and the attendant seemed to him as nothing. It certainly looks like religious mania, and if so he will doubtless soon be declaring himself Almighty.

Meanwhile, for the next hour, Renfield kept getting more and more excited, till all at once that shifty look came into his eyes which we always see when a madman has seized an idea. He became quite quiet, sat on the edge of his bed resignedly, and looked into space with lack-lustre eyes. Thinking to find out if his apathy were real, or merely assumed, I attempted to talk of his pets, a theme which had never before failed.

Renfield at first made no reply, but at length said testily:

'Bother them all! I don't care a pin about them.'

'What?' I said. 'Not even about spiders?' (Spiders are his special hobby at present, and his note-book is filling up with columns of small figures.) To this he answered enigmatically:

'The bride-maidens rejoice the eyes that await the coming of the bride. But when the bride draweth nigh, then the maidens shine not to the eyes that are filled.'

He would not explain himself, but remained obstinately seated on his bed all the time I remained with him.

I am weary tonight and low in spirits. I cannot but think of Lucy, and how different things might have been. If I don't sleep at once, chloral, the modern Morpheus . . . but I must not to let it grow into a habit. No, I shall take none tonight! I have thought of Lucy, and I shall not dishonour her by mixing the two. If need be, tonight shall be sleepless . . .

Glad I made the resolution – gladder I kept to it. I had lain tossing about, and heard the clock strike two, when the night-watchman came to me, sent up from the ward, to say Renfield had escaped. I threw on my clothes and ran down at once. My patient is too dangerous to be roaming about, and how might he act with strangers?

The attendant was waiting for me. Said that ten minutes before he had looked through the observation trap in Renfield's door, and seen the man seemingly asleep in his bed. Then his attention was alerted by the sound of the window being wrenched out. The attendant ran back and saw Renfield's feet disappear through the window. He was only in his night-gear, and cannot be far off. The attendant thought it best to watch where he should go, rather than try to follow him, as he – the attendant – is a bulky man, and could not get through the window. I am less large, so, with his aid, I squeezed out, and, as we were only a few feet above ground, I landed unhurt. The attendant told me the patient had made for the belt of trees to the left, and I followed as fast as I could run. As I emerged from the trees I saw a white figure scale the high wall which separates our grounds from those of the deserted house.

I ran back at once, and told the watchman to get three or four men immediately and follow me into the grounds of Carfax, in case Renfield might turn violent. I got a ladder myself, crossed over the wall, and dropped down on the other side. I could see Renfield's figure just disappearing behind the angle of the house, so I ran after him. On the far side of the house I found him pressed close against the old iron-bound oak door of the chapel. He was talking, apparently to someone, but I was wary of approaching near enough to hear what he was saying, lest I might scare him into further flight.

Chasing a swarm of errant bees is nothing to following a naked lunatic when the fit of escaping is upon him!

After a few minutes, however, I realized he was oblivious to all around him, and so ventured closer – then closer still when I saw that my men had now crossed the wall and were hemming Renfield in.

Then I heard him say:

'I am here to do Your bidding, Master. I am Your slave, and You will reward me, for I shall be faithful. I have worshipped You long from afar. Now You are near I await Your commands, and You will not pass me by, will You, Master, in Your distribution of good things?'

He *is* a selfish old beggar, is our Renfield. Thinks of the loaves and fishes even when he believes he is in a Real Presence. His manias make a startling combination. When we surprised him he fought like a tiger. He is immensely strong, and struggled more like a wild beast than a man.

Never before have I seen a lunatic in such a paroxysm of rage, and I hope I shall not again. But he is safely caged again now, thank goodness. Jack Sheppard himself couldn't wriggle free from the strait-waistcoat that keeps Renfield restrained, and he's chained to the wall in the padded room. His cries are at times awful, but the silences that follow are more appalling still, for his ever-rasping breath wishes murder upon us.

A moment ago I heard his first coherent words:

'I shall be patient, Master. It is coming – coming – *coming!*'

After all that I was too excited to sleep, but this diary has quieted me, and perhaps now, at last, I shall get some sleep tonight.

LETTER FROM WHITBY

21 August.

My dearest Mina,

Oceans of love and millions of kisses, and may you soon be in your own home with your husband. I wish you could be coming home soon enough to stay with us here. This strong air would soon restore Jonathan, as it has quite restored me. I have an appetite like a cormorant, am full of life, and sleep like a baby. You will be glad to know I no longer go walking in my sleep. I think I have not stirred out of my bed for a week – during the night, I mean!

Arthur says I am getting fat!

By the way, I forgot to tell you that Arthur is here. We have such walks and drives, and rides, and rowing, and tennis, and fishing together – and I love him more than ever. He says *he* loves *me* more . . . but this is nonsense. There he is, calling to me. So no more just at present from your loving,

Lucy.

P.S. Mamma sends her love. She seems a little better, poor dear.

P.P.S. We are to be married on 28 September.

FROM BUDAPEST

24 August.

My dearest Lucy,

I know you will be anxious to hear all that has happened since we parted at Whitby station. Well, my dear, I got to Hull all right, and caught the boat to Hamburg, and then the train on here. I feel I can hardly recall anything of the journey, except that I knew I was coming to Jonathan, and that, as I should have to nurse him, I had better get all the sleep I could . . .

I found my dear one, oh, so thin and pale and weak-looking. All the resolution has gone out of his dear eyes, and that quiet dignity which I told you was in his face has vanished. He is a wreck of his former self, and remembers nothing that has happened to him for a long time past. Or at least . . . that is what he wants me to believe, and I feel it would be wrong to quiz him. He has had some terrible shock, and I fear it might overtax his poor brain to recall it.

Sister Agatha, who is a good creature and a born nurse, tells me that Jonathan raved of *dreadful* things while he was off his head. I urged her to be precise, but she would only cross herself, and refuse me. The ravings of the sick, she argued, are the secrets of God, and if a nurse through her vocation should overhear them, she must respect her trust. She is a kindly soul, however, and the next day, seeing me troubled, she said:

'I can tell you this much, my dear: he himself has done nothing wrong, and you, as his wife to be, have no cause for concern. He has neither forgotten you nor ceased to love you. His dread was of terrible, unnatural things – things too ghastly for mortals to imagine.'

I believe dear Sister Agatha feared I was jealous lest my poor darling might have fallen in love with some other girl. The idea of *my* being jealous about Jonathan! And yet – oh, Lucy, let me whisper – I felt a stab of joy thrill through me when I *knew* no other woman was behind it.

And now I am sitting by Jonathan's bedside, where I can see his face while he sleeps. He is waking!

Later.

Having rubbed his eyes, and smiled at me weakly, he asked me to get his coat, as he wanted something from the pocket. I called Sister Agatha, and she brought all his things. Amongst them was Jonathan's notebook, and I was going to ask to look at it – for any clue to his trouble – but he must have seen my wish in my eyes, for he placed his poor thin hand over the notebook, and said to me very solemnly:

'Wilhelmina,' – and never, since our engagement, had he addressed me so formally, so seriously – 'I know, my dearest, that we agreed there should be no secrets, no concealments, between us. And yet . . . I have had a great shock, you know, and still my head spins round and round, and I do not know if it was all real, or but the dreaming of a madman. I have had brain fever, they say, and that is . . . to be mad. The secret, the truth, is written here,' – weakly his fingers tapped the journal – 'yet somehow, I cannot say why, I do not want to know it. Rather do I want to start my life afresh, here, with our marriage.'

For you see, Lucy, we have decided to be married in Budapest, just as soon as the formalities are complete!

'Are you willing, Wilhelmina, to share my ignorance? Here is the book. Take it. Keep it. Read it if you will, but never let me know. Unless . . . unless – and pray God it will not – some sacred duty commands my return to those nightmare hours, sane or mad, which are recorded here.'

He fell back, exhausted.

I put the book under his pillow, and kissed him. I have asked Sister Agatha to beg the Superior to let our wedding be this afternoon, and am awaiting her reply . . .

The Anglican chaplain has been sent for! We are to be married in an hour, or as soon as Jonathan awakes . . .

Lucy, the time has come and gone. I feel very solemn, but very, very happy. Jonathan woke a little after the hour, and all was ready. He sat up in bed, propped up with pillows, and uttered his 'I do' in a faint but firm voice. As for me, I could hardly speak! My heart was so full that even two words seemed to choke me! And the Sisters were so kind. Pray God I never forget them. Nor the grave yet wonderful responsibilities I have taken upon me.

I must tell you of my wedding present. When the chaplain and the Sisters had left me alone with my husband – oh, Lucy! – I took the journal from under his pillow, wrapped it in white paper, tied it with a pale blue ribbon from around my neck, sealed the knot with wax, and for my seal used my wedding ring. Then I kissed it, showed it to my husband, and told him I would keep it so, as a lifelong token of our trust.

Then Jonathan took my hand – *his wife's* hand – and said it was the dearest hand in all the wide world, and that to win it again if need be he would go through all those horrors again. And then – oh, Lucy! – when he kissed me, and drew me to him with his poor weak hands, and . . . it was like a solemnization in heaven of the eternal pledge between us.

I tell you all this, dear Lucy, because, since it was my privilege to be your guide and friend when you came from the schoolroom to prepare for the world of life, I want you to see now, as with the eyes of a very happy wife, whither duty has led me — so that your own married life may be equally as happy. My dear, please Almighty God, your life shall be all it promises: a long day of glorious sunshine, with no harsh winds or rain. Goodbye, dear Lucy. I shall post this at once, and write you again very soon. For now I must stop, as Jonathan is waking, and I must attend to my husband!

Your ever-loving,

Mina.

DR SEWARD'S DIARY

24 August.

The case of Renfield grows even more interesting. He has now so far quieted that there are spells of cessation from his passion. In the first days after his attack he was perpetually violent. Then one night, just as the moon rose, he grew quiet, and kept murmuring to himself:

'Now I can wait. *Now* I can wait.'

He was still in the strait-waistcoat, and in the padded room, but the suffused look had gone from his face, and his eyes had something of their old pleading — I might almost say, 'cringing' — softness. I was satisfied with his present condition, and directed that he be untied. The attendants hesitated but did not protest. It was a strange thing, that. For Renfield had humour enough to see their distrust, and, coming close to me, all the while looking furtively at them, he whispered:

'They think I could hurt you! Fancy! *Me* hurting *you*! The fools!'

It was somehow soothing to the feelings to find myself dissociated, even in the mind of this poor madman, from the others; but all the same I do not follow his thought. Am I to take it that I have anything in common with him, so that we are, as it were, to stand together? Or has he to gain from me some good so stupendous that my well-being is needful to him? I must find out later on. Tonight he will not speak. Even the offer of a kitten will not tempt him. He will only say:

'I don't take any stock in cats. I have more to think of now, and I can wait. I can wait.'

After a while I left him. The attendant tells me that he was quiet until just before dawn, and then he began to get uneasy, and at length violent, until at last he fell into a paroxysm which so exhausted that he swooned into a sort of coma.

. . . Three nights has the same thing happened – violent all day, then quiet from moonrise to sunrise. I wish I could get some clue to the cause. It could almost seem as if there was some influence which came and went. Happy thought! We shall tonight play sane wits against mad ones. He escaped before without our help; tonight he shall escape with it. We shall give him a chance, and have the men ready to follow in case they are required.

25 August.

'The unexpected always happens.'

How well Disraeli knew life! Our bird when he found the cage open would not fly, so all our subtle arrangements went for naught. At any rate, we have proved one thing: that the spells of quietness last a reasonable time. We shall in future be able to ease his bonds for a few hours each day. I have given orders to the night attendant merely to shut him in the padded room, when once he is quiet, until an hour before sunrise. The poor soul's body will enjoy the relief even if his mind cannot appreciate it. Hark! The unexpected again! I am called; the patient has once more escaped.

Later.

Another night adventure. Renfield artfully waited until the attendant was entering the room to inspect. Then he dashed out past him and flew down the passage. I sent word for the attendants to follow. Again we went into the ground of the deserted house, and we found him in the same place, pressed against the old chapel door. When he saw me he became furious, and had not the attendants seized him in time, he would have tried to kill me. As we were holding him a strange thing happened.

He suddenly redoubled his efforts, and then as suddenly grew calm. I looked round instinctively, but could see nothing. Then I caught the patient's eye and followed it, but could trace nothing as it looked into the moonlit sky except a big bat, which was flapping its silent and ghostly way to the west. Bats usually wheel and flit about, but this one seemed to go straight on, as if it knew where it was bound for or had some intention of its own. The patient grew calmer every instant, and presently said:

'You needn't tie me. I shall go quietly!'

Without trouble we came back to the house.

I feel . . . there is something ominous in his calm, and shall not forget this night . . .

LUCY WESTENRA'S DIARY

LUCY WESTENRA'S DIARY

26 August. Hillingham.

I must imitate Mina, and keep writing things down. Then we can have long talks when we do meet. I wonder when it will be. I wish she were with me again, for I feel so unhappy. Last night I seemed to be dreaming again, just as I was at Whitby. Perhaps it is the change of air, or getting home again. It is all dark and horrid to me, for I can remember nothing; but I am full of vague fear, and I feel so weak and worn out. When Arthur came to lunch he looked quite grieved when he saw me, and I hadn't the spirit to be cheerful. I wonder if I could sleep in Mamma's room tonight. I shall make an excuse and try.

27 August.

Another bad night. Mamma did not seem to take to my proposal. She seems not too well herself, and doubtless she fears to worry me. I tried to keep awake, and succeeded for a while; but when the clock struck twelve it waked me from a doze, so I must have been falling asleep. There was a sort of scratching or flapping at the window, but I did not mind it, and as I remember no more, I suppose I must then have fallen asleep.

More bad dreams.

I wish I could remember them. This morning I am horribly weak. My face is ghastly pale, and my throat pains me. It must be something wrong with my lungs, for I don't seem ever to get enough air. I shall try to cheer up when Arthur comes, else he will be miserable to see me so.

10

Enter the Professor

LETTER TO DR SEWARD

Albemarle Hotel,

31 August.

My dear Jack,

I want you to do me a favour. Lucy is ill – that is, she has no special disease, but she looks awful, and is getting worse every day. As to the cause, I dare not ask her mother, for to disturb the poor lady, in the present state of her own health, would be fatal. She, Mrs Westenra, has terminal disease of the heart, and though Lucy does not know this yet, I am sure there is *something* preying on my dear girl's mind. I told her I would ask you to see her, and though she demurred at first – I know why, old fellow – she finally consented.

It will be a painful task for you, I know, but it is for *her* sake. If you will come to lunch at Hillingham tomorrow – so as not to arouse any suspicion in Mrs Westenra, then after lunch Lucy will contrive an hour alone with you. I shall come in for tea, and we can go away together. I am filled with anxiety, and want to consult with you alone immediately you have seen her. Please do not fail me.

Arthur.

TELEGRAM TO SEWARD

1 September.

Am summoned to see my father, who is worse. Write me fully by tonight's post to Ring. Wire me if necessary.

Arthur.

LETTER TO ARTHUR HOLMWOOD

2 September.

My dear old fellow,

With regard to Miss Westenra's health, I hasten to let you know at once that in my opinion there is no functional disturbance or malady. At the same time, her appearance is certainly disquieting, and she is woefully different from when I saw her last. Of course you must realize I could not examine her quite as fully as pure objectivity would wish. We are still close friends, after all, and — our relationship raises a certain barrier which not even medical science can bridge over. With those reservations, my report is as follows.

I found Miss Westenra in seemingly gay spirits. Her mother was present, and in a few seconds I made up my mind that Lucy was trying hard to mislead her mother and prevent her from being anxious. I have no doubt she guesses, if she does not know, the gravity of her mother's condition. At lunch we all exerted ourselves to be cheerful, then Mrs Westenra went to lie down, and Lucy was left with me. We went into her boudoir, where, the moment the door was closed, the mask fell from the poor girl's face, and she sank down into a chair with a great sigh, hiding her eyes behind her hand. I at once took advantage of her reaction to suggest an examination, whereupon Lucy said to me very sweetly:

'I cannot tell you how I loathe talking about myself.'

I reminded her that a doctor's confidence was sacred, but that you were grievously anxious about her. She caught on to my meaning at once, and settled that matter in a word:

'Tell Arthur everything you choose. I do not care for myself, but all for him!'

So I am quite free.

As to details, she is clearly somewhat bloodless, but without the other usual anaemic signs. Luckily I was actually able to test the quality of her blood, for as she was opening her bedroom window a cord gave way, and her hand was slightly cut by broken glass. The wound was not serious, and in dressing it I was able to collect a few drops of Lucy's blood for analysis. Qualitatively it seems quite normal and in itself would imply vigorous health. In other purely physical respects I found nothing amiss — but, as there must be a cause somewhere, I believe it must be mental.

Lucy complains of difficulty in breathing satisfactorily at times, and of heavy, lethargic sleep during which she dreams dreams that frighten her, but regarding which she can remember nothing. She says that as a child she used to walk in her sleep, and that recently in Whitby the habit came back, and that once in the night she sleepwalked out to the East

Cliff, where Miss Murray later found her. Though Lucy assures me her nocturnal restlessness has not followed her south, I am in doubts myself and so have written to my old friend and master, Professor Van Helsing, of Amsterdam, who knows as much about obscure diseases as anyone in the world.

All things being at your charge, I have asked the Professor to come over to give us his diagnosis, so that dear Lucy may have the benefit of his unparalleled erudition. Van Helsing, I may say, is at once a philosopher and probably the most advanced scientist of our age. He has an absolutely open mind, an iron nerve, indomitable resolution, and yet the kindliest and truest heart that ever beat. I tell you these facts that you may know why I have such confidence in him.

Professor Van Helsing, I have no doubt, will be with us very shortly. Meanwhile I shall myself examine Miss Westenra again tomorrow.

Yours always,

John Seward.

LETTER FROM PROF. BRAM VAN HELSING, M.D., D.PHIL., ETC

2 September.

My dear good John,

When I have received your letter I am already coming to you. By good fortune I can leave just at once, without wrong to any trust. Tell your friend that when that time you suck from my wound so swiftly the poison of the gangrene from that knife that our other friend, too nervous, let slip, you did more for him when he wants my aids than all his great fortune could. But it is pleasure added to do for him, your friend. Have then rooms for me at Great Eastern Hotel, and please it so arrange that we see the young lady same day. Till soon goodbye, dear John.

Van Helsing.

LETTER TO ARTHUR HOLMWOOD

4 September.

My dear Art,

Van Helsing has been and gone. He came on with me to Hillingham, and found that, by Lucy's discretion, her mother was lunching out. Van Helsing made a very thorough examination of the patient. He is to report to me within three days (for of course I was not present all the time), and I shall advise you of his findings. He is, I fear, much concerned. When I told him of your engagement to Lucy, he said:

'You must tell him all you think. Tell him what I think too, if you can guess it – nay, I am not jesting. This is no jest, but life and death, perhaps more.'

I asked what he meant by that, for he seemed supremely serious. This was back in London, as we had tea before the Professor started on his return to Amsterdam. I pressed him, but he would not elaborate. Please do not feel angry with him, Art. His very reticence means his mind is working furiously on Lucy's case. He will speak plainly enough when the time comes, be sure. As we parted I told him I would simply write you a layman's account of our visit to Lucy. The Professor seemed not to notice, but remarked that the smuts in London had improved since his student days.

As to our visit, Lucy seemed more cheerful than last week, and certainly looked better. She had lost something of the ghastly look that so upset you, and her breathing was normal. She was very sweet (as ever) to the Professor, and tried to make him feel at ease – but I could see the effort it was costing her. I believe Van Helsing saw it, too, for he quickly began to chat of all things except ourselves and diseases, and with such infinite geniality that poor Lucy's pretence of animation soon merged into reality. Then, gradually and gently, he brought the conversation round to his visit, and suavely said:

'My dear young miss, I have the so great pleasure because you are much belove. They tell me you are in the spirit, and that you were of a ghastly pale. To them I say:

'"Pouf!"'

And he snapped his fingers at me and went on:

'But you and I shall show how wrong they are. How can *he*' – pointing at me as once he pointed me out to his class, when I had dropped a classic clanger – 'how can *he* know anything of young ladies? He has his madmans to play with, to bring them back to happiness, and to those that love them. It is much to do, and rightly he got rewards.

'But the young ladies!

'Dear Doctor John have no wife nor daughter, see, and the young do not tell themselves to the young, but to the old, like me, who have known so many sorrows and the causes of them. So, my dear, we will send him away to smoke the cigarette in the garden, whiles you and I have little talk alone.'

I took the hint, and strolled about the apple trees till the Professor came to the window and called me in. He looked grave, but said:

'I have made careful examination, but there is no functional cause. Yet with you I am agree there is much blood lost. However the conditions of her are no way anaemic. Though I musts go home to Amsterdam I there will think the cause, for cause there always is. You, friend John, shall send me the telegram every day, and if needs I shall come again.'

So now, Art, you know all I know. I hope most fervently your poor dear father is rallying, and meanwhile I shall mount the most vigilant watch over Lucy. Should the slightest necessity arise I shall send you word to come at once, so do not be over-anxious unless you hear from me.

John Seward.

DR SEWARD'S DIARY

6 September.

Zoophagous patient had an outburst yesterday at an unusual time. Just before noon he began to grow restless. The attendant knew the symptoms, and at once summoned aid. Just in time, too, for on the stroke of noon he became so violent that it took all their strength to hold him. In about five minutes, however, he began to subside and rapidly sank into a sort of melancholy, in which state he has remained ever since. The attendant tells me his screams while in paroxysm were really appalling. Certainly I found my hands full when I got in, having to calm some of the other patients whom Renfield's howls had frightened.

It is now after dinner – asylum time – and yet my patient sits in a corner brooding, with a dull, sullen, woebegone look on his face. I cannot quite understand it.

Later.

Another change in my patient.

At five o'clock I looked in, and found him seemingly as placid and contented as he used to be. He was catching flies and eating them, and noting his captures by making nail-marks on the edge of the door between ridges of the padding. When he saw me he came over and apologized for his bad conduct, and asked me in a very humble, cringing way to be returned to his own room and to have his note-book back again. I thought it well to humour him, so he is back in his room, with the window open. He has his tea sugar sprinkled on the windowsill, and is reaping quite a harvest of flies. He is not now eating them, but putting them in a box, as of old, and periodically scours the corners of his room for a spider. I tried to get him to talk about the past few days, for any clue to his thoughts would be of immense help to me.

For a moment Renfield looked very sad, and said in a far-away voice, as though rather to himself than me:

'All over! All over! He has deserted me. No hope for me now. Unless I do it for *myself!*' Then with sudden resolution he turned to me and said:

'Doctor, won't you let me have a little more sugar? I think it would be good for me.'

'And the flies?' I said.

'Yes! The flies like it, too, and I like the flies. Therefore I like the sugar.'

And still there are people who believe madmen cannot argue!

As to the sugar, I procured him a double supply, and left him apparently as happy as any free man in the world. How I wish I could fathom his mind.

Midnight.

Another change in Renfield. I had been to see Miss Westenra, whom I found much better, and had just returned and was standing at our own gate looking at the sunset, when once more I heard him yelling. What a nasty shock it was to be torn thus from the wonderful smoky beauty of a sunset over London, with its lurid lights and inky shadows and all the marvellous tints that come on foul clouds even as on foul water, and to realize all the grim sternness of my own cold stone building, with its wealth of breathing misery, and my own desolate heart to endure it all.

I reached him just as the sun was going down, and from his window I saw the red disc sink. As it vanished Renfield became less frenzied and finally slid from the hands that held him and collapsed, an inert mass, on the floor. It is wonderful, however, what recuperative power lunatics have, for within minutes he stood up and looked quite calmly around him. I signalled to the attendants not to hold him, for I was anxious to see what he would do. He went straight over to the window and brushed out the grains of sugar. Then he took his fly-box and emptied it outside, and threw away the box. Next he shut the window, crossed the room, and sat down on his bed. Fascinated, I asked him:

'Are you not going to keep flies any more?'

'No,' said he. 'I am sick of all that rubbish!'

He certainly is a complex case, but I sense we may be on to something: if we can find why today his paroxysms came on at high noon and at sunset. Could there be a malign influence of the sun at these times, which affects certain susceptible natures – as the full moon influences others?

We shall see.

TELEGRAMS FROM SEWARD IN LONDON TO VAN HELSING IN AMSTERDAM

6 September.

Miss Westenra still better today.

7 September.

Patient greatly improved. Good appetite; sleeps naturally; good spirits. Colour coming back.

8 September.

Terrible change for the worse. Come at once – pray do not lose an hour.

LETTER TO ARTHUR HOLMWOOD

9 September.

My dear Art,

My news today is not so good. Lucy this morning had relapsed a bit. There is, however, one good thing which has arisen from it: Mrs Westenra was naturally anxious concerning Lucy, and has consulted me professionally about her. I took advantage of the opportunity, and told her that my old master Van Helsing, the great specialist, was coming to stay with me – he will be here tomorrow morning – and that I would put her in his charge. So now we can tend Lucy without alarming her mother unduly, for a shock to Mrs Westenra now would spell instant death, and this, in Lucy's weak condition, might be disastrous to *her*.

We are hedged in with difficulties, all of us, my poor old fellow. However, please God, we shall come through them all right. If any emergency, I shall of course wire. Otherwise, you shall hear from me the moment I have the Professor's diagnosis.

In haste.

Yours ever,

John Seward.

11

Dr Seward's Diary

7 September.

The first thing Van Helsing said to me when we met at Liverpool Street was:

'Have you said anything to our young friend the lover of her?'

'No,' I said. 'I waited till I had seen you, as I said in my telegram. I wrote him a letter simply telling him that you were coming, as Miss Westenra was not so well, and that I should let him know if need be.'

'Right, my friend John,' he said. 'You and I shall keep as yet what we know here, and here.' He touched me on the heart and on the forehead, and then touched himself the same way. 'I have for myself thoughts at the present. Later I shall unfold to you.'

'Why not now?' I asked.

Van Helsing looked at me, and said:

'When the corn is grown, even before it has ripened – while the milk of its mother-earth is in him, and the sunshine has not yet begun to paint him with his gold, the husbandman he pull the ear and rub him between his rough hands, and blow away the green chaff, and say to you:

'"Look! He's good corn; he will make good crop when the time comes."'

I did not see the application, and told him so. For reply he reached over and took my ear in his hand and pulled it playfully, as he used long ago to do at lectures, and said:

'The good husbandman tell you so then because he knows, but not till then. But you do not find the good husbandman dig up his planted corn to see if he grow; that is for the children who play at husbandry, and not for those who take it as of the work of their life. See you now, friend John? I have sown my corn, and nature has her work to do. If he sprout at all, there's some promise; and I wait till the ear begin to swell.'

When I described Lucy's symptoms – which were as before, but more marked – he looked very grave, but said nothing. He took with him a bag in which were many instruments and drugs, 'the ghastly paraphernalia of our beneficial trade', he once had called them, in a lecture.

We were shown in, and Mrs Westenra met us. She was alarmed, of course, but less so than I had expected – nature ordaining that even death has some antidote to its own terrors. Van Helsing and I were shown up to Lucy's room, and if I was shocked when I saw her yesterday, today I was absolutely horrified. She was ghastly, chalkily pale; the red seemed to have gone even from her lips and gums, and the bones of her face stood out prominently; her breathing was painful to see or hear. Van Helsing's face grew set as marble, and his eyebrows converged over his nose.

Lucy lay motionless and did not seem to have strength to speak, so for a while we were all silent. Then Van Helsing beckoned to me, and we went gently out of the room. The instant we had closed the door he stepped quickly along the passage to the next door, which was open. Then he pulled me quickly in with him and closed the door.

'My God!' he said. 'This is dreadful. There is no time be lost. She will die for sheer want of blood. There must be transfusion at once. Is it you or me?'

'I am younger and stronger, Professor. It must be me.'

'Then get ready at once. I will bring up my bag. I am prepared.'

I went downstairs with him, and as we reached the hall the maid had just opened the front door.

In stepped Arthur, who rushed up to me, whispering:

'Jack, I was so anxious. I read between the lines of the letter, and have been in an agony. My father seemed better, so I have hastened here as fast as I could. Is not that gentleman Van Helsing? I am so thankful to you, sir, for coming.'

Seeing Arthur's stalwart proportions and the strong young manhood emanating from him, the Professor's eyes gleamed. As he held out his hand, he said gravely:

'Sir, you have come in time. You are the lover of our dear miss. She is in very bad—'

But Arthur had suddenly grown pale and sat down in a chair almost fainting.

'Nay, but you are to help her,' the Professor urged comfortingly. 'You can do more than any that live, and your courage is your best help.'

'What can I do?' asked Arthur hoarsely. 'My life is hers, and I would give the last drop of blood in my body for her.'

The Professor has a humorous side, which hinted in his answer:

'Many drops, young sir! But never the last!'

'What shall I do?' There was fire in Arthur's eyes, and his nostrils quivered.

Van Helsing slapped him on the shoulder. 'Come!' he said. 'You are a man, and it is a man we want.'

Arthur looked bewildered, and the Professor went on by explaining in a kindly way:

'Young miss must have blood, or die. My friend John and I are about to perform transfusion – to transfer from full veins of one to the empty veins who pine. Friend John was to give his blood, as he is the more young and strong than me' – here Arthur took my hand and wrung it hard in silence – 'but now! You are more good than even he, who toil much in the world of thought, and have nerves less calm and blood less bright than yours!'

Arthur turned to him and said:

'How gladly I would *die* for her—' A sort of choke stopped his voice.

'God, boy!' said Van Helsing 'Soon you will be happy that you have done all for her you love. Come now and be silent. You shall kiss her once before it is done, but then you must go; and you must leave at my sign. Say no word to Madame; you know how it is with her! There must be no shock; any knowledge of this would kill off her. Come!'

We all went up to Lucy's room.

Arthur remained outside.

Lucy turned her head and looked at us. She was not asleep, but simply too weak to converse. Her eyes spoke to us; that was all. Van Helsing laid some things from his bag on a little table out of sight. Then he mixed a narcotic, and coming over to the bed, said cheerily:

'Now, little miss, here is your medicine. Drink it off, like a good child. See, I lift you so that to swallow is easy. Yes?'

Soon sleep began to flicker in Lucy's eyelids. When she had fallen into a deep slumber, the Professor called Arthur into the room, and bade him strip off his coat. Then he added:

'You may take that one little kiss whiles I bring over the table. Friend John, help to me!'

So neither of us looked while Arthur bent over her.

Van Helsing said to me:

'He is of so young and strong blood that you need not defibrillate.'

Then with swiftness, but with absolute method, Van Helsing performed the operation. As the transfusion went on, something like life returned to Lucy's poor cheeks, and Arthur's fond joy shone through his growing pallor. After a bit I began to grow anxious, for the loss of blood was telling on Arthur, strong man as he was. It gave me an idea of what a terrible strain Lucy's system must have undergone: that what weakened Arthur restored her only partially. But the Professor's face was set, and he stood watch in hand, with his eyes fixed on the patient.

I could bear my own heart beat.

Presently the Professor said softly:

'Enough. You attend him – I will look to her.'

Now I saw how much Arthur was weakened. I dressed the wound and took his arm to lead him away, when Van Helsing murmured:

'The brave lover I think deserve another kiss.' As he was adjusting the pillow to Lucy's head, the narrow black velvet band which she seemed always to wear round her throat, buckled with an old diamond buckle which her lover had given her, was dragged a little up, and showed a red mark on her throat.

Arthur did not notice it, but I heard a deep hiss of indrawn breath from Van Helsing. He said nothing at the moment, but turned to me, saying:

'Now take down our brave young lover. Give him of the port wine, and let him lie down a while. He must then go home, to rest and eat much: that he recruit back what he has so given to Miss Lucy. But he must not stay here – no!'

For Arthur was drawing breath to protest.

The Professor pre-empted him:

'But you are anxious of result? Then know you have saved her life. So now you go home and rest easy. I shall tell her all when she is well; she shall love you ever more. Goodbye.'

When Arthur had gone I went back to the room. Lucy was sleeping gently, but her breathing was stronger; I could see the counterpane move as her breast heaved. By the bedside sat Van Helsing, looking at her intently. The velvet band again covered the red mark. I asked the Professor in a whisper:

'That mark on her throat?'

'What of it?'

'I have not examined it yet,' I answered, and proceeded to loose the band.

Just over Lucy's jugular vein were two small but evil-looking punctures. There was no sign of disease, but the edges were white and worn-looking, as if by some trituration. It at once occurred to me that these wounds might be the means of Lucy's loss of blood. But no: the whole bed would have been drenched scarlet with the blood which the girl must have lost, to leave such a pallor as she had before the transfusion.

'Well?' said Van Helsing.

'I can make nothing of it.'

The Professor stood up.

'I must go back to Amsterdam tonight,' he said. 'There are books and things there which I want. You must remain here all the night, and you must not let your sight pass from her.'

'Shall I have a nurse?' I asked.

'We are the best nurses, you and I. You keep watch all night. See she is well fed, and that nothing disturbs her. Yourself you must not sleep – not all the night. Later we can sleep. I shall be back as soon as possible. And then we may begin.'

'Begin?' I said. 'What on earth do you mean?'

'We shall see!' he answered as he hurried out. A moment later he popped his head back inside the door, and said, with warning finger held up:

'Remember, she is your charge. If you leave her, and harm befall, you shall not sleep easy hereafter!'

8 September.

Lucy's opiate wore off towards dusk, and she waked looking a different being, full of a happy vivacity. Still, I could see evidences of the absolute prostration she had undergone. When I told Mrs Westenra of Dr Van Helsing's direction that I should sit up with Lucy, she pooh-poohed the idea, pointing out her daughter's renewed strength and excellent spirits.

I was firm, however, and made preparations for my long vigil. When Lucy's maid had prepared her for the night, I came in, having in the meantime had supper, and took a seat by the bedside.

She made no objection, and looked at me gratefully whenever I caught her eye. At length I felt she was sinking into sleep, but then with an effort she shook it off. When this was repeated, I asked:

'Do you not want to sleep?'

'No. I am afraid.'

'But why? Is not sleep the boon we all crave?'

'Not if – when – sleep is a presage of horror.'

'A presage of horror! What on earth do you mean?'

'I don't know. Oh, I don't *know*. And that is what is so terrible. All this weakness comes to me in sleep; until I dread the very thought.'

'But, my dear girl, you may sleep tonight. I am here watching you, and I can promise that nothing will happen.'

'Ah, I can trust you!'

I seized the opportunity, and promised:

'If I see you having bad dreams I will wake you at once.'

'Oh, how good you all are to me. Then I will sleep!' And with a deep sigh of relief, she sank back and fell asleep almost instantly.

All night long she lay quietly in a profound, tranquil, life-restoring sleep. Her lips were slightly parted, and her breast rose and fell with the regularity of a pendulum. There was a smile on her face, and it was evident that no bad dreams disturbed her.

In the early morning Lucy's maid came in to relieve me. Anxious about many things, I returned home and sent short wires to Van Helsing and Arthur, telling them of Lucy's continuing splendid recovery. My own work had got badly behind, and it was dark again before I found time to inquire after the zoophagous Renfield. The report was good: he had been quite quiet for the past day and night. While I was at dinner, a telegram came from Van Helsing: suggesting that I should stay at Hillingham again tonight, and stating that he was leaving Amsterdam by the night mail and would join me early in the morning.

9 September.

I was badly tired when I got to Hillingham. For two nights I had hardly slept a wink, and my brain was numb with exhaustion. Lucy was up and in cheerful spirits. When we shook hands she looked sharply in my face and said:

'No sitting up tonight for you. You are worn out. I am quite well again. Indeed I am, and if there is to be any sitting up, it is *I* who will sit up with *you*.'

That was at supper, so I did not argue the point. Enlivened by Lucy's charming presence, I enjoyed my meal, and had a couple of glasses of the Westenras' excellent port. Then Lucy took me upstairs and showed me a room next her own, where a cosy fire was burning.

'Now,' she said, 'you must stay here. I shall leave this door open and my door too. You can lie on the sofa, and if I want anything I shall call out, so you can come to me at once.'

I was dog-tired now, and could not have sat up had I tried. So, on Lucy's renewing her promise to call out if she should need me, I lay on the sofa, and forgot all about everything.

12

Only Common Garlic

9 September.

I feel so happy tonight.

Recently I have been so miserably weak, that to be able to think and move about is like sunshine after a long spell of east-wind rain. Somehow Arthur feels terribly close to me. I seem to feel his presence warm about me. Perhaps because, while sickness turns our inner eyes and sympathy on ourselves, health and strength give rein to Love. Certainly I know where my thoughts are. If only Arthur knew! His ears must tingle as mine do now.

Oh, blissful rest of last night! With dear Dr Seward watching me, how well I slept. Nor shall I fear to sleep again tonight, since he is close at hand. Thank everybody for being so good to me! Thank God! Goodnight, Arthur.

10 September.

I was conscious of the Professor's hand on my head, and started awake in a second.

'And how is our patient?'

'Well, when I left her,' I answered.

'Come, let us see,' he said.

Together we went into Lucy's room.

The blind was down, and I went over to raise it gently, while Van Helsing stepped, with his soft, catlike tread, over to the bed.

As morning sunlight flooded the room, I heard the Professor's low hiss, and a deadly fear gripped my heart.

'*God's Heavens!*' he exclaimed, and as he pointed to the bed, his iron face was drawn and ashen white.

I felt my knees tremble.

There on the bed, seemingly in a swoon, lay poor Lucy, more horribly white and wan-looking than ever. Even her lips were white, and the gums seemed to have shrunk back from her teeth, as we sometimes see in a corpse after a prolonged illness.

'Quick!' snapped the Professor. 'Brandy!'

I flew to the dining-room, and returned with the decanter. He wetted Lucy's poor white lips with it, and together we rubbed her palms and wrists. Van Helsing felt her heart, and after an agonizing pause he said:

'Not too late. It beats, though feebly. All our work is undone; we must begin again. There is no young Arthur here now; I have to call on you this time, friend John.' As he spoke, he was dipping into his bag for the instruments of transfusion.

I removed my jacket, rolled up my shirt sleeve, and the operation began.

After several minutes the draining away of one's blood, no matter how willingly given, is a terrible feeling.

Van Helsing held up a warning finger.

'Do not stir,' he said. 'I fear that with growing strength she may wake, and that would make much danger. But I shall precaution take. I shall give her injection of morphia.'

Lucy's faint seemed to merge subtly into a narcotic sleep, and – how can I deny a shudder of pride when I saw a faint tinge of colour steal back into those pallid cheeks and lips? To feel one's life'sblood pumping into the veins of the woman one loves?

The Professor watched me critically.

'That will do,' he said.

I remonstrated:

'You took a great deal more from Art.'

Van Helsing smiled sadly as he replied:

'Arthur is her lover, her *fiancé*. You, friend John are a doctor, and have much vital works to do for her, and others. So, for the present, enough.'

He attended to Lucy, while I applied digital pressure to my own incision. Then I lay down, for I felt faint and a little sick. By-and-by the Professor bound up my wound, and sent me downstairs to drink some wine. As I was leaving the room, he whispered after me:

'Mind, nothing must be said of this. If our young lover turn up unexpected, as before, no word to him. It would at once frighten him and enjealous him, too. So!'

When I came back he looked at me carefully, then said:

'You are not the much worse. Go and lie on your sofa awhile; then have much breakfast, and return here to me.'

I fell asleep on the sofa, wondering how Lucy could have lost so much blood, and my thoughts revolved round those little punctures in her throat, and their ragged – wasted – edges.

Lucy slept well into the day. When she woke she was fairly well, though less robust than the day before. When Van Helsing had seen her, he went out for a walk, leaving me in charge, under strict orders not to leave her for a moment. As he left, I could hear his voice in the hall: asking the way to the nearest telegraph office.

Lucy chatted with me freely, and seemed quite unconscious that anything had happened. I tried to keep her amused, and when her mother came up she too seemed not to notice any change. To me she said gratefully:

'We owe you so much, Dr Seward, but really you must not overwork yourself. You are looking pale yourself. You want a wife to look after you; that you do!'

As her mother spoke, Lucy turned crimson. Then – for her poor wasted veins could not support such an unwonted drain to the head – came a reaction of excessive pallor as she turned imploring eyes on me.

I smiled, nodded, and laid my finger on lips. With a sigh, she sank back amid her pillows.

Two hours later Van Helsing returned.

'Go home now,' he said to me. 'Eat and drink much. Make yourself strong. I tonight shall sit up with little miss myself, for we must have none other to know. I have grave reasons, but do not for the moment ask them. Goodnight.'

Home in time for a late supper; went my rounds – all well; set this down while waiting for sleep.

It is coming.

11 September.

This afternoon I went over to Hillingham. Found Van Helsing in excellent spirits, and Lucy much better. Shortly after my arrival a big parcel from abroad came for the Professor. He opened it theatrically, and withdrew a great bundle of white flowers.

'For you, Miss Lucy.'

'Oh, Dr Van Helsing! Really you are too good to me!'

'No, my dear. These are medicines.'

Lucy made a wry face.

'Medicinal but not nauseous,' the Professor reassured her. 'See! I put some in the window, then I make pretty wreath, and hang him round your neck, so that you sleep well. Oh yes! Like the lotus flower, he make your trouble all forgotten.'

Lucy obediently sniffed at the flowers but immediately pushed them away. In mock disgust she exclaimed:

'Professor, you must be joking! Why, these flowers are only common garlic.'

To my surprise, Van Helsing rose up and said sternly, his iron jaw set and his bushy eyebrows meeting:

'I do not jest, pretty miss. Take care for the sake of others, if not for your own.' Then, seeing poor Lucy scared, he went on more gently:

'Oh, Miss Lucy, do not fear me. I only do for your good, and there is much virtue in this so common flower. See? I shall make myself the wreath for you to wear, but first we must deck the room with my garlic, which is all the way from Haarlem, you know, Miss Lucy, where my friend Vanderpool raise herb in his glasshouses all the year.'

The Professor's procedure was certainly odd, and not to be found prescribed in any pharmacopoeia known to me. First he snibbed the windows securely; next, taking a handful of the flowers, he rubbed them all over the sashes, as though to ensure that every whiff of air must be pregnant with the garlic smell. Then he rubbed likewise all round the door and fireplace. It all seemed grotesque to me, and presently I said:

'It is perhaps well, Professor, that we have no sceptic present.'

'Why so, friend John?'

'He might accuse you of working white witchcraft, to keep evil spirits away.'

'Perhaps I am!' he answered quietly as he wove the wreath for Lucy's neck.

When Lucy had made her toilet for the night, and was tucked into bed, the Professor fixed the wreath of garlic round her neck.

'Take care you do not disturb it,' he warned her gravely. 'Even if the room feel close, do not tonight open the window or the door.'

'I promise,' said Lucy sleepily, 'and thank you both a thousand times for all your kindness!'

As we left the house in my fly, Van Helsing said:

'Tonight I can sleep in peace, and sleep I want — two nights of travel, much reading in the day between, much anxiety on the day to follow, and a night to sit up, without to wink. Tomorrow in the morning early you call for me, and we come together to see our pretty miss: so much more strong for my "spell" which I have work. Ho-ho!'

He seemed so confident that I — remembering my own confidence two nights before, and the baneful consequence — felt awe, and vague, incommunicable terror. Like unshed tears.

LUCY WESTENRA'S DIARY

12 September.

How good they all are to me! I quite love that dear Dr Van Helsing. But I wonder why he was so anxious about these flowers. He positively frightened me, he was so fierce. And yet he must have been right, for somehow I do not dread being alone tonight. I feel I shall sleep without fear, and not mind any flapping outside the window. Oh, the terrible pain of sleeplessness I have had of late. And the *fear* of sleep, with such unknown horrors. How blessed are those with no dreads; to whom sleep brings only sweet dreams. Well, here I lie tonight, hoping for sleep. A little like Ophelia, I suppose, with my 'maiden strewments'. I never liked garlic before, I must say, but tonight there is peace in its smell, and I feel sleep coming already.

DR SEWARD'S DIARY

13 September.

Called at the Berkeley for Van Helsing, and arrived at Hillingham at eight o'clock. It was a lovely morning; bright sunshine and all the fresh feeling of early autumn. The leaves are all kinds of beautiful colours, but have not yet begun to fall. When we entered we met Mrs Westenra — ever an early riser — coming out of the morning-room. She greeted us warmly, and said:

'You will be glad to know that Lucy is still sleeping deeply, and looks much better.'

The Professor smiled jubilantly. Rubbing his hands together, he said:

'Aha! My treatment is working.'

Mrs Westenra answered:

'You must not take all the credit, doctor. Lucy's state this morning is due in part to me.'

'How do you mean, madame?' asked the Professor.

'Well, I was anxious about the dear child in the night, and went into her room. She was sleeping soundly — so soundly that even my coming did not wake her. But the room was awfully stuffy. There were a lot of those horrible, strong-smelling flowers about everywhere, and she had actually a bunch of them round her neck. I feared that the heavy odour would be too much for her weak state, so I took them all away and opened the window to let in some fresh air. You will be delighted with her condition, I am sure.'

She moved off into her boudoir, where she took her breakfast. As she had spoken, I saw the Professor's face turn grey as ash. Now, the moment she disappeared from view, he pulled me into the dining-room and closed the door.

Then, to my horror, I saw Van Helsing break down. He raised his hands over his head, and beat his palms together in despair. Finally he sat down on a chair, and putting his hands before his face, began to sob. Loud, dry sobs that seemed to come from the very racking of his heart. Then he raised his arms again, as though appealing to:

'God! God!' he said. 'What have we done? What has this poor girl done, to be so sore beset? This miserable mother, all unknowing, and all for the best as she think, does such thing as lose her daughter body and soul. And we must not tell her, not even warn her, or she die. And then both die. Oh! How we are beset! All powers of devils against us!'

Suddenly he jumped to his feet. 'Come,' he said. 'We fight him all the same.' He went to the hall for his bag, and together we went up to Lucy's room. Once again I drew up the blind, while Van Helsing approached the bed. This time he did not start as he looked on the poor face with the same awful, waxen pallor as before. His face expressed infinite pity.

'As I expected,' he murmured. Without another word he locked the door, then set out on the little table the instruments for yet another transfusion of blood.

I began to take off my coat, but he stopped me with a warning hand.

'No!' he said. 'Today you must operate. *I* shall provide. You are weakened enough already.' As he spoke he took off his coat and rolled up his shirt sleeve.

Again the operation; again the narcotic; again some return of colour to the ashy cheeks, and the regular breathing of healthy sleep. This time I watched while Van Helsing rested.

Presently he took an opportunity of telling Mrs Westenra that she must not remove anything from Lucy's room without consulting him; that the flowers were of medicinal value, that the breathing of their odour was a part of the cure.

After another hour Lucy waked from her sleep, fresh, bright, and seemingly little the worse for her terrible ordeal.

But what does it all mean? Now, as I sink into weariness myself, I cannot but wonder if my prolonged contact with the insane is beginning to affect my own brain.

LUCY WESTENRA'S DIARY

17 September.

Four days and nights of peace. I feel so strong again that I hardly know myself; as if I had passed through some long nightmare, and now awaken to the beautiful sunshine and fresh air of the morning around me. I have a dim half-remembrance of long, anxious times in darkness; of no hope; long spells of oblivion, then a struggling back to life like a breathless diver rushing up through a great press of water.

But since Dr Van Helsing has been with me, all this bad dreaming seems to have passed away. The noises that used to frighten me out of my wits – the flapping against the windows, the distant voices which seemed to harshly command me to do I know not what – have all ceased. I go to bed now without fear. I do not strive to remain awake, and I have even grown quite fond of the garlic, of which a boxful arrives every day from Haarlem.

Tonight Dr Van Helsing is going away, as he has an appointment in Amsterdam. But I need not be watched; I am well enough to be left alone. Thank God for Mamma's sake, and dear Arthur's. I shall not even feel the change, I dare say, for last night, twice when I awoke, I found Dr Van Helsing fast asleep in his chair. And even then I did not fear to go back to sleep myself – although the owls, or bats, or whatever, were flapping against the window-panes . . . almost angrily, it seemed.

13

Wolves, Bats & Blood

NEWSPAPER INTERVIEW, 18 SEPTEMBER
With the words *Pall Mall Gazette* as his credentials, your reporter
was at last granted access to the Zoological Gardens' keeper of wolves.
Thomas Bilder lives in a cottage behind the elephant house, and was
just sitting down to his tea when I found him. Thomas and his wife are
hospitable folk, elderly, and without children.

The keeper would not enter on what he called 'business' until supper
was over. When the table was cleared, and he had lit his pipe, he said:

'Now, sir, arsk me all what you want. You'll excoose me refoosin'
to talk of perfeshunal subjects afore meals. I gives the wolves – and the
jackals, and the hyenarse – *their* tea afore I arsks *them* questions. So—'

'How do you mean, ask them questions?' I inquired at once.

''Ittin' of them over the 'ead with a pole is one way. Scratchin' of their
hears is another, when flush gents wants a show-orf for their gals.'

'And how do the wolves reply?' I responded politely.

'I know what yer a-comin' at,' Mr Bilder informed me abruptly.

'What am I a-comin' at?'

'That there wolf what's escaped.'

'Exactly,' I agreed, inspecting a handful of guineas. 'Just describe to
me exactly what happened.'

'All right, guv'nor. 'Eres the 'ole story. That there Bersicker was
one of three grey wolves that came from Norway to Jamrach's, which
we bought off him four year ago. He was a nice well-behaved wolf,
Bersicker. Never gave no trouble to talk of. I'm surprised at 'im wantin'
out, but there you are.'

'Where am I?'

'You can't trust wolves no more nor women.'

'Don't you mind him, sir!' broke in Mrs Bilder, with a cheery laugh.
''E's got just like a crusty old wolf 'isself, 'e 'as! But there ain't no 'arm
in 'im.'

'Quite so,' I assented gravely.

'Well, sir,' the keeper continued earnestly, as I toyed with more guineas, 'it were about two hour arter feedin' yesterday when I first 'eard any disturbance. I was makin' up a litter in the monkey-house, for a young puma what's got ill; but when I 'eard the yelpin' and 'owlin' I kem away straight. There was Bersicker a-tearin' like a mad thing at the bars. There weren't much people about yesterday, and close at hand was only a tall, thin gennleman, with a 'ook nose.'

'Any other identifying features?'

'A pointed beard, 'e 'ad, fair enuff, with few white hairs runnin' through it. 'ard, cold look, 'e 'ad about 'im. Red eyes too. I took agin 'im straight orf, I did, for it seemed it was 'im as was fashin' the wolf. 'e 'ad white kid gloves on 'is 'ands, and he pointed out Bersicker.

'"Keeper, this wolf seems upset," 'e says.

'"Maybe at you," says I.

''e didn't get angry, as I 'oped, but 'e smiled. Kind of insolent like, with a mouth full of white, sharp teeth.

'"Why me?" says e'.

'"They always likes a bone to clean their teeth, arter tea," I tells him, "orf which you 'as a bagful."

'Well bless me if – when the animiles seen us a-talkin' – they didn't lay down all quiet like. Even ole Bersicker there, 'e let me stroke 'is ears same as ever. That there man kem over, and blessed but if 'e didn't put in 'is 'and and stroke the wolf's ears too!

'"Tyke care," says I. "Bersicker is quick."

'"Never mind," the gent says. "I'm used to 'em!"

'"Is you in the business yourself?" I says, tyking off my 'at, for a man what trades in wolves, anceterer, is a good friend to keepers.

'"Not exactly in the business," says 'e, "but I 'ave made pets of several."

'And with that 'e lifts his 'at as perlite as a lord, and walks away. Old Bersicker kep' a-lookin' arter 'im till 'e was out of sight, and then went and lay down in a corner, and wouldn't come hout the 'ole hevening. Well, larst night, so soon as the moon was hup, the wolves all began a-'owling. There warn't nothing for 'em to 'owl at. There warn't no-one near, 'cept someone a-callin' a dog somewheres out the gardings in Park Road. Twice I gone out to see that all was right, and it was, and then the 'owling stopped. Just before twelve o'clock I took a last look round afore turnin' in, an', bust me, but when I kem opposite old Bersicker's cage I seen the rails all broken wide, and the cage hempty. An' 'at's all I knows for certing.'

'Did anyone else see anything?'

'One of our gardingers, a-comin' 'ome from a 'armony, seen a big grey dog comin' out through the 'edges. So 'e says.'

'But?'

'Well!' Mr Bilder drawled ominously.

'Well, what?'

'Don't give much for it meself.'

'Why not?' your reporter asked a little severely, making to pocket several guineas.

''e never said a word about it to his missis when 'e got 'ome,' Mr Bilder quickly explained, 'and it was only *arter* the escape of the wolf was made known, and us 'ad been up all night a-'untin' for Bersicker, that 'e remembered seein' anything. 'armony gone to 'is 'ead, more like, if you arsk me.'

'And those are all the facts, as known to you?'

Mr Bilder nodded at my guineas.

'What about theories?'

'Beg parding?'

'How do we *explain* the wolf's escape?'

'Well, sir,' he said, with a suspicious sort of modesty, 'I don't know as 'ow you'd burlieve me.'

'Why not? If a man who has known the wolf professionally cannot hazard a guess, why, who else should we ask?'

'Well then, sir,' said Mr Bilder proudly, 'it seems to me . . . '

'Yes?'

'That there Bersiker escaped . . . '

'Yes, yes?'

''cause 'e *wanted out.*'

From the hearty way that both Thomas and his wife laughed at the joke I could see the high value they placed upon his wit. So I said:

'Now, Mr Bilder, we'll consider this first guinea earned.'

'What about them others?' he protested anxiously, secreting the first.

'Waiting to be claimed, when I hear what you expect to happen next.'

'The ole wolf is ovyarsely a-'idin' somewheres. The gardinger, 'm of the 'armony, said 'e was a-gallopin' northward faster than a horse.'

'The gardener said that?'

Mr Bilder nodded, then frowned:

'But 'es nut to be burlieved.'

'Why not?'

'Wolves doesn't gallop! No more than dogs does. They's not built that way. This ole Bersicker, what's more, ain't even used to providin' for 'isself. Most like 'e's a-shiverin' darn some widder's coal-cellar, and wondrin' where 'e' to get his breakfast from. My eye, won't some cook get a rum start when she sees his green eyes a-shining at her out of the dark! Or some hinfant in 'is perhambulator – but Lor' bless us all!'

'What, what, Mr Bilder?' I asked, for he was staring out of the window, his face having doubled its natural length with surprise.

'Ole Bersicker!' he marvelled. 'Come back by 'isself!' He went to the door and opened it; a most unnecessary proceeding it seemed to me. I have always thought that a wild animal never looks so well as when some obstacle of pronounced durability is between us. But there is nothing like custom, it seems, for neither Bilder nor his wife thought any more of the wolf than I should of a dog.

What followed was all pathos relieved by comedy. The wicked wolf that for half a day had paralysed London, and set all the children squealing, was welcomed home and petted like a sort of penitent prodigal son. Old Bilder examined him with tender solicitude, then pronounced:

'There!'

'Where?'

'Poor ole feller's belly. Hall cut hopen, hit is, and full of broken glass. 'E's been a-gettin' over some bloomin' wall or other, 'e 'as. Cryin' shyme, is what I says, that folks is allowed to top their walls wiv bottles. This 'ere's the mischief what comes of it. Come along, Bersicker.'

He took the wolf to his cage, plucked the shards out of his flesh, and left him happily gnawing at a huge hunk of bleeding beef.

Then Mr Bilder went off to report to his superiors, and your reporter came away too, to publish this exclusive information regarding the strange escapade at the Zoo.

DR SEWARD'S DIARY

17 September.

After dinner I was in my study, posting up my books – which, due to the many visits to Lucy, had fallen sadly into arrears. Suddenly the door burst open and in rushed Renfield, his face distorted with passion. Thunderstruck, I exclaimed:

'Renfield, for goodness—'

Without an instant's pause he lunged at me, a dinner-knife in his hand. Seeing what a dangerous state he was in, I tried to keep the table between us, but before I could get my balance he had slashed my left wrist. He tensed for another stab, but this time I got in my right to his chin, and Renfield was knocked sprawling on his back on the floor.

My wound was bleeding copiously on to the carpet, so, seeing that my assailant was not intent on further mischief, I occupied myself with binding my wrist. A minute later the attendants rushed in, and we turned our attention to Renfield, who now was lying on his belly on the floor licking up, like a dog, the blood which had flowed from my wrist. He was easily secured and, to my surprise, went with the attendants quite placidly, simply repeating over and over again:

'The blood is the life!'

Really the idea of Renfield imbibing blood from me is thoroughly sickening, especially as I cannot afford to lose blood just at present. I have lost too much of late for my physical good, and the prolonged strain of Lucy's illness is telling on me. I need rest. *Rest.* Happily Van Helsing has not summoned me, so I need not forgo my sleep tonight.

TELEGRAM FROM AMSTERDAM

17 September.

Stay with Miss Lucy at Hillingham tonight, and frequently check her flowers to be in place. This most vital. Do not fail. I come to be with you again so soon as possible.

DR SEWARD'S DIARY

18 September.

Van Helsing's telegram, so late last night, filled me with dismay. A whole night lost, and I know by bitter experience what may happen in a night. Of course all may be well, but somehow I fear not. For it seems as if some horrible doom hangs over us, and we are thwarted at every turn.

But now I must go for the London train. Shall take this cylinder with me, and complete it on Lucy's phonograph.

17 September

Dead of night.

I feel I am dying of weakness, and have barely strength to write, and yet I must.

I went to bed as usual, taking care that the flowers were placed as Dr Van Helsing directed, and soon fell asleep.

Some time later I was waked by the flapping at the window, which had begun after that sleep-walking on the cliff at Whitby, when Mina saved me, and which now I know so well. I was not afraid, but I did wish that Dr Seward was in the next room – as Dr Van Helsing said he would be – so that I might have called him. I tried to go to sleep, but could not. Then there came to me the old fear of sleep, and I determined to keep awake. Perversely, sleep would try to come when I did not want it; so, as I feared to be alone, I opened my door and called out:

'Is anybody there?'

There was no answer.

I was afraid to wake Mamma, and so closed my door again. Then outside in the shrubbery I heard a sort of howl like a dog's, but more fierce; and deeper. I went to the window and looked out, but could see nothing, except a big bat, which had evidently been buffeting its wings against the window. So I went back to bed again, but determined not to sleep. Presently the door opened, and Mamma looked in. Seeing that I was not asleep, she came in and sat by me. Soothingly she said:

'I was uneasy about you, darling. Are you all right?'

Fearing she might catch cold sitting there, I urged her to get into bed with me. She lay down beside me, but did not take off her dressing-gown, for she said she would only stay a little while. As she lay there in my arms, and I in hers, the flapping and buffeting came to the window again. Startled, Mamma cried out:

'What is that?'

I tried to pacify her, and at last she lay quiet; but I could hear her poor weak heart still fluttering terribly. Then came again that low howl out in the shrubbery, immediately followed by a crash at my window, and a spray of broken glass on my floor. The window blind blew back as the wind rushed in, and there, framed amid the jagged panes, was the head of a great grey wolf.

Mamma sat up and cried out in terror. In her panic she clutched at the wreath of garlic flowers round my neck, and tore it away from me. For several seconds she sat rigid, pointing wordlessly at the wolf. Then there was a strange and horrible gurgling in her throat. She collapsed sideways, as if struck by lightning, and her falling head hit mine. Dizzied by the blow, I tried to fix my eyes on the window. Suddenly the grey wolf's head withdrew, and a myriad cloud of coloured specks blew in and whirled into the form of a pillar – like the dust that travellers describe when there is a simoon in the desert.

I tried to stir, but poor Mamma's body, already cold – for her dear heart had ceased to beat – weighed me down. I also felt some paralysing spell creep upon me, and . . . then I must have swooned.

When I recovered consciousness a nearby bell was tolling; the dogs all round the neighbourhood were howling; and in our shrubbery a nightingale was singing. I was dazed and stupid with pain and terror and weakness, but the sound of the nightingale seemed like the voice of my dead mother come back to comfort me. The din of the dogs appeared to have awakened the maids, too, for I could hear them whispering outside my door. I called to them, and they came in. When they saw what had happened, and Mamma's body lying over me on the bed, they screamed out. The wind rushed in through the broken window, and the door slammed to.

Trembling, the maids obeyed my instruction to lift Mamma off me, help me up, and cover her lifeless body with a sheet. The poor girls were so upset – hysterical, even – that I sent them to the dining-room for a glass of sherry wine. The door flew open for an instant and banged shut again. The maids shrieked in terror, then fled to the dining-room. As I laid some garlic flowers on Mamma's breast, I remembered what Dr Van Helsing had told me, but I didn't like to remove them again. Besides, now I would have some of the servants to sit with me. But where were they? Surprised that the maids had not returned, I called for them, but got no answer.

Next I struggled down to the dining-room, and how my heart sank when I saw what had happened. There they were – all four – lying helpless on the floor, breathing heavily. The decanter of sherry was on the table half full, but there was a queer, acrid smell in the air. My suspicions aroused, I examined the decanter, which smelt distinctly of laudanum. Then I looked for the bottle which Mamma's doctor uses for her – oh! – *did* use . . . and I found it on the sideboard, empty.

What am I to do?

What *am* I to do?

Now I am back in the room with Mamma. I cannot leave her, and I am alone, save for the sleeping servants, whom someone has drugged. Alone with the dead. Yet I dare not go out, for still the low howl of the wolf drifts through the broken window. The air seems full of specks, floating and circling in the draught from the window, and the lights burn blue and dim.

What am I to *do?* God help me. I shall hide this paper in my breast, where the doctors will surely find it – if . . . My dearest Mamma – gone. Perhaps, then, I must go too. Goodbye, dear Arthur, if I should not survive this night.

God keep you.

14

Dr Seward's Diary

18 September.

I drove at once to Hillingham and arrived early. Keeping my cab at the gate, I went up the avenue alone. I knocked gently and rang as quietly as possible, for I feared to disturb Lucy or her mother, and hoped to bring only a servant to the door. After a minute I knocked and rang again. Still no answer. I cursed the laziness of servants who could lie abed at such an hour – for it was now ten o'clock – and so rang and knocked again, more loudly.

But still without response.

And now a terrible fear assailed me: could this be a house of death to which I had come, too late? I knew that even seconds of delay might mean hours of danger to Lucy, should she suffer one of those frightful relapses. So round the house I ran, determined to effect an entry.

But every window was securely fastened, every door locked, and I returned baffled to the porch. There I heard the rapid clip-clop of a swiftly driven horse. A few seconds later I met Van Helsing running up the garden path. When he saw me, he gasped out:

'How is she? Are we too late? Did not you get my telegram?'

I answered that I had only got his telegram early in the morning and had not lost a minute in coming here, but that I could not make anyone in the house hear me.

The Professor raised his hat as he said solemnly:

'Then I fear we are too late. God's will be done!' With his usual recuperative energy, he went on:

'Come. Time is all in all to us now.'

We went round the house to the kitchen window. The Professor took a small surgical saw from his case, handed it to me, pointed to the iron bars which guarded the window. I attacked them at once and had very soon cut through three of them. Then with a long thin knife we pushed back the snib, and the window was open. I helped the Professor in and followed him. There was no-one in the kitchen or in the servants' rooms, which were close at hand. In the dining-room, dimly lit by rays of light through the shutters, we found four servant-women lying on the floor. Their stertorous breathing and the acrid smell of laudanum in the room left no doubt as to their condition.

Van Helsing and I looked at each other, and he said:

'Them we can attend to later.'

Up the stairs we rushed to Lucy's room. With white faces and trembling hands, we opened the door gently.

Oh, how shall I describe what we saw? On the bed lay two women, Lucy and her mother. The latter lay farthest in, and she was covered with a white sheet, the edge of which had been blown back by the draught through the broken window, showing the drawn, white face, with a look of terror fixed upon it. By her side lay Lucy, her face as white and yet more drawn. The flowers which had been round her neck we found upon her mother's bosom, and her throat was bare, showing that the two little wounds we had noticed before seemed somehow to have grown, both in diameter and depth.

Without a word the Professor bent over the bed, his head almost touching poor Lucy's breast; then a jubilant twitch of his head, as leaping to his feet he cried:

'It is not yet too late! Quick! Quick! The brandy!'

I flew downstairs and returned with it, taking care to smell and taste it, lest it, too, like the sherry, were drugged. The maids were still breathing, but more restlessly, and I fancied that the narcotic was wearing off. Back in Lucy's room, Van Helsing rubbed the brandy on her lips, gums, wrists, and the palms of her hands. Then he said:

'No more we can do at the present. You go wake those maids. Flick them in the face with wet towels, and flick them hard. Make them get heat and fire and a warm bath. This poor soul is nearly as cold as that beside her. She will need good heating before we can treat her more.'

I went at once, and found little difficulty in waking three of the women. The fourth was only a young girl, and the drug had evidently affected her more strongly, so I lifted her on to the sofa and left her to sleep. The others were dazed at first, but as their awareness returned they broke into hysterical weeping. I was stern, however, and told them that one life was bad enough to lose, and that if they delayed they would sacrifice Miss Lucy too. So, sobbing and crying, they went about their work, half-clad as they were.

Fortunately, the kitchen and boiler fires were still alive, and there was no lack of hot water. We got a bath, and carried Lucy out as she was and placed her in it. While we were busy chafing her limbs there was a knock at the hall-door. One of the maids ran off, hurried on some more clothes, and ran to the door. When she returned she whispered to us that there was a gentleman with a message from Mr Holmwood. I bade her tell him to wait, for we could see no-one now. She went away with the message, and, engrossed with Lucy, I clean forgot all about the messenger.

Never before had I seen the Professor work in such deadly earnest.

'It is a stand-up fight with death, is it not?' I murmured gravely.

With the sternest of looks over his shoulder he replied:

'If that were all, I would stop here and now, and let her fade away into peace, for I see no light in life over her horizon.' Then he returned to Lucy with renewed – almost frenzied – vigour.

Presently the heat of the bath water and the Professor's chafing seemed to take effect. Lucy's heart beat a shade more audibly through the stethoscope, and her lungs awoke with a flutter just perceptible to the naked eye. Van Helsing beamed and chortled with delight, and as we lifted her from the bath and rolled her in a hot sheet to dry her he said to me:

'Check to the king!'

We took Lucy into another room, which the maids had prepared, laid her in bed and forced a few drops of brandy down her throat. I noticed that Van Helsing tied a soft silk handkerchief round her throat. She was still unconscious and looked terribly vulnerable and weak.

Van Helsing instructed one of the women to stay with Lucy, and not to take her eyes off her till we returned. Beckoning me out of the room, he muttered:

'We must consult.'

From the hall he led me into the dining-room, closing the door carefully behind him. The shutters had been opened, but the blinds were already down, with that obedience to the etiquette of death which British women of the lower classes always rigidly observe. The room was, therefore, dimly dark, yet light enough for our purposes, and I noticed that Van Helsing's sternness was somewhat compounded by perplexity.

'What are we to do now?' he exclaimed at length. 'Where shall we turn for help? We must have another transfusion of blood, and soon, or that poor girl will not last an hour. You are exhausted already; I too. I fear to trust the women's blood, even if they would have courage to submit. What shall we find a good man to open his veins for her?'

'What's the matter with me, anyhow?' The voice came from the sofa across the room, and its drawling tones brought joy to my heart.

Van Helsing started angrily at the interruption, but gladness flooded his eyes as I cried out:

'Quincey Morris!' and rushed towards him with outstretched hands.

'What brought you here?' I cried as our hands met.

'I guess Art is the cause.' Quince handed me a telegram:

'Have not heard from Seward for three days, and am terribly anxious. Cannot leave. Father still in same condition. Send word how Lucy is. Do not delay. Holmwood.'

'Seems I came just in time,' Quincey added softly. 'Only tell me what to do.'

Van Helsing strode forward and took his hand, looking him straight in the eyes as he said:

'A brave man's blood is the best thing on this earth when a woman is in trouble. You're a man, and no mistake. Hard may the devil may work against us, yet God sends us men when we need him. Hallelujah.'

Once again we went through that ghastly operation. Lucy's system had been terribly shocked, and it told on her more than before, for though plenty of Quincey's blood went into her veins, her body did not respond as well as on the previous occasions. This time her struggle back into life was truly frightful to see and hear. However, eventually the action of both her heart and lungs improved, and Van Helsing made a subcutaneous injection of morphia, and her faint relaxed into a profound slumber.

The Professor stayed to watch over her while I went downstairs with Quincey Morris, and sent a maid to pay off one of the cabmen who were waiting. I left Quincey lying down after a large glass of wine, and told the cook to get ready a good breakfast. Then a thought struck me, and I went back upstairs.

Van Helsing had a sheet of notepaper in his hand. He had evidently read its content, and was thinking it over as he sat with his hand to his brow. With grim satisfaction on his face, as of a dreadful doubt dispelled, he handed me the paper; saying only:

'It dropped from Lucy's breast when we carried her to the bath.'

I read it feverishly, then, bewildered, demanded of the Professor:

'In God's name, what does it all mean? Was she, or is she, mad?'

Van Helsing took back the paper, saying:

'Forget it for the present. You shall understand all in good time. For now, what came you to me to say?'

This restored me to my purpose:

'The certificate of death, for Lucy's mother. If we are not careful, there may be an inquest.'

'And so?'

'The trauma of an inquest would surely kill poor Lucy.'

'Then what, friend John, do you propose?'

'I know, and you know, Professor, and the other doctor who attended her knows, that Mrs Westenra had disease of the heart, so let us certify that she died of it. Let us complete the certificate at once, in fact, and I shall take it myself to the registrar and go on to the undertaker.'

'So it be, friend John! Excellently bethought! Truly Miss Lucy, if she be sad in her foes, is happy in her lovers. One, two, three, all open their veins for her, besides one old man. Ah yes, I know, friend John; I am not blind! I love you all the more for it! Now go.'

In the hall I met Quincey Morris, with a telegram for Arthur telling him that Mrs Westenra was dead; that Lucy also had been ill, but now was rallying again; and that Van Helsing and I were with her. I told him where I was going, and he hurried me out, with the parting whisper:

'When you get back, Jack, can we have two words to ourselves?'

I nodded and went out. There was no objection to my registration of Mrs Westenra's death, and the local undertaker was happy to make all necessary arrangements for the funeral.

When I got back Quincey was impatient for our two words together, but I told him I must see Lucy first. She was still sleeping, and the Professor seemingly had not moved from his seat by her bedside. He put his finger to his lips, to order silence, so I went down to Quincey and took him into the breakfast room, which was a little less cheerless than the other rooms. When we were alone, he said:

'Jack Seward, I don't want to shove myself in anywhere I've no right to be; but this is no ordinary case. You know I loved that girl, and wanted to marry her. Okay, that's all past, but I care for her all the same. So won't you tell me what in hell's name is wrong with her? I heard the

Dutchman say she must have *another* transfusion of blood, and that both you and he were exhausted.'

'That's so,' I said, and he went on:

'I take it both you and Van Helsing had already given Lucy blood?'

'That's so.'

'And I guess Art was in it too. When I saw him four days ago down at his own place he looked queer. Ain't seen nothing pulled down so quick since I had a Pampas mare go to grass between dusk and dawn. One of them there big bats they call vampires got her in the night. With all he sucked, and her pore veins left open, by morning there wasn't enough blood left in her to let her stand, and I had to put a bullet through her as she lay. Lucy, now . . . '

As he spoke the poor fellow looked terribly anxious. He was in a torture of suspense regarding the woman he loved, and his utter ignorance of the terrible mystery which seemed to surround her intensified his pain. His very heart was bleeding, and it took all the manhood of him – and there was a royal lot of it – to keep him from breaking down. I paused before answering, for I felt I must not divulge any matter which the Professor wished kept secret.

'And how long has this been going on?' Quincey pressed me.

'About ten days.'

'Ten days! And that pore pretty creature that we all love has had put into her veins the blood of four strong men. Man alive, what kind of illness *is* this?' Seizing my shoulders, he whispered fiercely:

'What took it out?'

I shook my head. 'That', I said, 'is the crux. Van Helsing is simply frantic about it, and I am at my wits' end. I can't even hazard a guess. There has been a series of curious circumstances which have thrown out our calculations as to Lucy being properly watched. But these shall not occur again. Here we stay until all be well – or ill.'

Quincey held out his hand. 'Count me in,' he said. 'You and the Dutchman tell me what to do, and I'll do it.'

When she woke late in the afternoon, Lucy's first movement was to feel in her breast, and, to my surprise, she produced the paper which Van Helsing had given me to read. The careful Professor had replaced it, lest on waking she should be alarmed. Her eye then lit on Van Helsing and on me too, and gladdened. Next, she looked round the room, shuddered, gave a loud cry, and put her poor thin hands before her pale face.

We both understood what that meant – that she had recalled her mother's death. We tried to comfort her, and doubtless our sympathy eased her somewhat, but she was very low in thought and spirit, and for a long time wept silently to herself. We told her that one of us would now remain with her all the time, and that seemed to cheer her. Towards dusk she fell into a doze, and here a very odd thing occurred.

While still asleep she took the paper from her breast and tore it in two. Van Helsing stepped over and carefully teased the pieces from her. All the same, however, she went on with the action of tearing, as though the paper were still in her hands; finally she lifted her hands and opened them as though scattering the fragments.

Van Helsing seemed surprised, his great brows gathered, but he said nothing.

19 September.

All last night Lucy slept very poorly, being always afraid to sleep, and seemingly a little weaker each time she woke. The Professor and I took it in turns to watch, and we never left her for a moment unattended. Quincey Morris said nothing about his intention, but I knew that all night long he was patrolling round and round the house.

When day came, its searching light showed the ravages in poor Lucy's strength. She was hardly able to turn her head and the little nourishment she could take seemed to do her no good. At times she slept, and both Van Helsing and I noticed the difference in her, between sleeping and waking. While asleep she looked stronger, although more haggard, her breathing was softer; her open mouth showed the pale gums drawn back from the teeth, which looked strangely longer and sharper than before. When she woke, the softness of her eyes evidently changed the expression, for she looked her own self, although a dying one. In the afternoon she asked for Arthur. We telegraphed for him at once, and Quincey went off to meet him at the station.

When Arthur arrived it was nearly six o'clock. The sun was setting full and warm, and the red light streamed in through the window and gave more colour to Lucy's pale cheeks. When he saw her, Arthur choked with emotion, and none of us could speak. In the hours that had passed, Lucy's fits of almost comatose sleep had grown more frequent. Arthur's presence, however, seemed to act as a stimulant; she rallied a little, and spoke to him more brightly than she had to us. He too pulled himself together, and spoke as cheerily as he could.

It is now nearly one o'clock, and I am entering this on Lucy's phonograph. Arthur and Van Helsing are sitting with Lucy, and I am to relieve them on the hour. Until six o'clock they are to try to rest, and then . . . but I fear that tomorrow will end our watching. The shock to Lucy's system has been too great, and I feel she lacks the strength to recover again.

God help us all.

15

Three Letters

FROM MINA HARKER TO LUCY WESTENRA
17 September.

My dearest Lucy,

It seems *an age* since I heard from you, or indeed since last I wrote. You will pardon me, I know, when you have read all my news. Well, I got my husband back all right. When we arrived at Exeter there was a carriage waiting for us, and in it, though poorly with gout, was Mr Hawkins. He took us to his house, where there were rooms ready for us, all nice and comfortable, and we dined together. After dinner Mr Hawkins said:

'My dears, I drink to your health and prosperity. May every blessing attend you both. I have, with love and pride, seen you grow up. Now I want you to make your home here with me. I have remaining to me neither wife nor child. All are passed on, and hence, in my will, I leave everything to you.'

How I cried, Lucy dear, as Jonathan and the old man clasped hands. Our evening was so happy.

So here we are, installed in this beautiful old house, and from both my bedroom and drawing-room I can see the great elms of the cathedral close, with their huge dark trunks standing out against the old yellow stone of the cathedral, while the rooks caw overhead. I am fully occupied, I need hardly tell you, arranging things and housekeeping. As for Jonathan, he and Mr Hawkins are busy all day. Now that Jonathan is a partner, Mr Hawkins wants him to know everything about the clients.

How is your dear mother? I wish I could get up to town to see you, dear, but I dare not yet, with so much on my hands. Jonathan, you see, wants looking after still. His bones are fleshing out a bit again, but he really was terribly weakened by his illness. Even now he sometimes starts out of his sleep, all trembling until I calm him.

However, these occasions grow fewer as the days pass by, and soon will cease altogether, I trust.

But what about yourself? When are you to be married, and where, and who is to perform the ceremony? What are you to wear, and is it to be a public or a private wedding? Tell me all about it, Lucy dear. Tell me *everything*, for nothing which touches you is indifferent to me. Jonathan sends his 'respectful duty', but I do not think that is good enough from the junior partner of the important firm of Hawkins and Harker. And so, as you love me, and he loves me, and I love you with all the moods and tenses of the verb, I send you simply his 'love' instead.

Goodbye, my dearest Lucy. All blessings on you.

Mina.

FROM PATRICK HENNESSEY, M.D., M.R.C.S., L.K.Q.C.P.I, E.T.C.

20 September.

Dear Dr Seward,

In accordance with your wishes, I enclose report of the conditions of everything left in my charge. With regard to patient, Renfield, there is more to say. He has had another outbreak which might have had a dreadful ending, but which, as it fortunately happened, was unattended with any unhappy results. This afternoon a carrier's cart with two men made a call at the empty house whose grounds abut on ours – the house to which, you will remember, the patient twice ran away. The men stopped at our gate to ask the porter their way.

I was myself looking out of the study window, having a smoke after dinner, and saw one of them come up to the house. As he passed the window of Renfield's room, the patient began to rate him from within, and called him all manner of filthy names. The man, who seemed a decent fellow enough, contented himself by telling him to 'shut up, you foul-mouthed beggar', whereon our man accused him of robbing him and wanting to murder him and said that he would hinder him if he swung for it.

I opened the window and signed to the man not to notice, so he contented himself with:

'Lor' bless yer, sir, I wouldn't mind what was said to me in a bloomin' madhouse. I pity ye and the guv'nor for havin' to live with a wild beast like that.'

Then he asked the way civilly enough, and I told him where the gate of the empty house was. He went away, followed by revilings from Renfield.

I went down to investigate Renfield's anger, and found him, to my astonishment, quite composed and most genial. I tried to get him to talk about the incident, but he blandly asked me questions as to what I meant, and acted as if nothing had happened. This was, I am sorry to say, merely another instance of his cunning, for within half an hour he had broken out through his window, and was running down the avenue.

I called to the attendants to follow me, and ran after him, for I feared he was intent on some mischief. My fear was justified when I saw the same cart which had passed before coming down the road, having on it some great wooden boxes. The men were wiping their foreheads, and were flushed in the face, as if from violent exercise. Before I caught up with him the patient rushed at the carters, pulled one of them off the cart, and began to knock his head against the ground. If I had not seized him just at that moment I believe he would have killed the man. As I held Renfield, the other carter jumped down and struck him over the head with the butt of his heavy whip.

It was a terrible blow, but Renfield seemed hardly to heed it. On he struggled with all three of us, pulling us to and fro as if we were kittens. You know I am no lightweight, and the carters were both burly men. At first he was silent in his fighting, but when the attendants had helped us master him, and were putting the strait-waistcoat on him, he shouted:

'Not me! They shan't rob me! They shan't murder me by inches! I'll fight for my Lord and Master!' and all sorts of similar ravings.

It was with considerable difficulty that they got him back to the house and put him in the padded room, by which time one of the attendants, Hardy, had a broken finger. (I set it myself, by the way, and he will be all right.)

The two carriers were at first loud in their threats of actions for damages, and promised to rain all the penalties of the law upon us. Their threats were, however, mingled with a subtle whinge of apology for the defeat of the two of them by one feeble-headed madman. They said that if it had not been for the earlier great effort of lugging the heavy boxes to their cart they would have made short work of Renfield. As another reason for their defeat they cited the extraordinary dehydration to which they had been reduced by the dusty nature of their occupation.

I quite understood their drift, and after a stiff glass of grog, and with each a sovereign in hand, they made light of the attack, and swore that they would encounter a worse madman any day for the pleasure of meeting such a 'bloomin' good a bloke' as myself. (Their employers, should anyone ever require carters in London, are Harris & Sons, Moving and Shipment Company, Orange Master's Yard, Soho.)

That is all for the present. I shall of course wire you at once if anything of further importance occurs.

Faithfully yours,

Hennessey.

FROM MINA HARKER

18 September.

My dearest Lucy,

Such a sad blow has befallen us. Mr Hawkins has died very suddenly. Some may not think it so sad for us, but we loved him so much that it really seems as though we had lost a father. Jonathan is particularly distressed. He feels grief, of course, for the dear, good man who has befriended him all his life, and now left him a fortune which to people of our modest backgrounds is wealth beyond the dreams of avarice, but Jonathan also says the responsibility which it puts upon him makes him nervous. He begins to doubt himself. I try to cheer him up, and my belief in him helps, I have no doubt. But it is here that the grave shock that he experienced in Transylvania tells most. Oh, it is too hard that such a strong and noble nature as his should be so reduced.

Forgive me if I worry you with my troubles in the midst of your own happiness. But truly, Lucy dear, I must tell someone. For the strain of keeping up a brave and cheerful appearance to Jonathan tries me, and I have no-one here to confide in. I dread coming up to London, as we must the day after tomorrow; for poor Mr Hawkins is to be buried alongside his father. As there are no surviving relations, Jonathan will have to be chief mourner. It will be a grim day, but I shall try to run over to see you, dearest Lucy, if only for a few minutes.

Forgive me for troubling you.

With all blessings,

Mina.

16

Dr Seward's Diary

20 September.

Only resolution and habit make me write tonight. I am so miserable, low-spirited, so sick of the world, even of life itself, that I would not care if I were touched this moment by the wings of the angel of death. And has he not been flapping hard of late? Lucy's mother, Arthur's father, and . . .

But let me seek solace in detail.

I duly relieved Van Helsing from his watch over Lucy. We wanted Arthur to rest also, but at first he refused. Only when I told him he must help us during the following day too, and that we must not all break down for want of rest, lest Lucy should suffer, did he agree to go. Van Helsing was very kind to him.

'Come, my child,' he said. 'You are sick and weak, and have had much sorrow and mental pain, as well as the tax on your blood. As solitude is full of fears, come with me to the drawing-room, where there is a big fire and two sofas. You shall lie on one, I on the other, and our sympathy will comfort each other, even through our sleep.'

Arthur went off with him, looking back longingly at Lucy's face, which seemed whiter than the pillow beneath it. When the door had closed behind them, I checked round the room and found that the Professor had again been most liberal in his applications of the garlic. The window-sashes reeked of it, and round Lucy's neck, over the silk handkerchief which Van Helsing made her keep on, was a rough chaplet of the same odorous flowers.

Lucy was breathing somewhat stertorously, and her face did not best become her native beauty, for the open mouth showed the gums very pale, and her teeth, in the dim, uncertain light, seemed somehow longer and sharper than they had in the brightness of day. In particular, by some trick of the light, her canines appeared disproportionately large. I sat down by her, and presently she moved uneasily. At the same moment there came a sort of dull flapping or buffeting at the window. I went over to it softly, and peeped out round the edge of the blind.

The noise had been made by a great black bat which now was wheeling like a huge dark seagull in the moonlight, and every now and again struck the window with the tips of its wings. When I returned to my seat I found that Lucy had moved in her sleep and somehow torn away the garlic flowers from her throat. I replaced them as well as I could, and sat watching her. Presently she woke, and I gave her food, as Van Helsing had prescribed. She took but a little, and that languidly. Gone, it seemed, was the unconscious struggle for life and strength that hitherto she had shown.

It struck me as curious, however, that the moment she became conscious she pressed the garlic flowers close to her. And on reflection I discerned an unmistakable pattern: whenever she got into that lethargic state, with the laborious breathing, she put the flowers from her; but later, when she came closer to waking, she would clutch them close. Scrutinizing her carefully, during the long hours that followed, I saw my theory confirmed several times. But what did it imply?

At six o'clock Van Helsing came to relieve me. Arthur had at last fallen into deep slumber, so we let him sleep on.

When the Professor saw Lucy's face the breath fairly hissed between his teeth as to me he whispered sharply:

'Draw up the blind. I want *light*.' Then he bent down, and, with his face almost touching Lucy's, examined her carefully. He removed the flowers and lifted the silk handkerchief from her throat.

'Dear God, no!' he ejaculated hoarsely, starting back in horror.

I bent over and looked too, and a ghastly chill overcame me as I noticed:

The wounds on Lucy's throat: absolutely disappeared.

For fully five minutes Van Helsing stood staring at her. Then he turned to me and said calmly:

'She is dying. Soon. No saving her, alas, from that. But it makes much difference, mark me, whether she dies conscious or in her sleep. Wake that poor boy Arthur. Let him come and see the last.

I went to the dining-room and roused him. He was dazed for a moment, but when he saw the sunlight angling in between the shutters he jumped up in self-reproach at having overslept. I told him that was of no consequence since (as gently as I could) Van Helsing was convinced the end was nigh.

Arthur covered his face with his hands, and slid down on his knees by the sofa, where he remained for fully a minute, evidently praying, while his shoulders shook with grief.

I took him by the hand and raised him up.

'Come,' I said. 'Summon all your fortitude. For her sake.'

When we entered Lucy's room I saw that Van Helsing, with his usual forethought, had been making everything look as pleasing as possible. He had even brushed Lucy's hair.

As we approached her bed she opened her eyes. Seeing Arthur, she whispered softly:

'Oh, my love! I am so glad you have come!'

Arthur stooped to kiss her, but Van Helsing motioned him back:

'No,' he whispered. 'Not yet. Hold her hand. It will comfort her more.'

So Arthur took her hand and knelt beside her, and she looked her former beautiful best, with all the soft lines matching the angelic beauty of her eyes. Then, gradually, her eyes closed, and she sank into sleep. For a while her breast heaved softly, and her breath came and went like that of a tired child.

But then, insensibly, there came the strange change I had noticed in the night. Her breathing grew harsher, the mouth opened, and the pale gums, drawn back, made the teeth seem more sabre-like than ever. In a sort of sleep-waking, vague, unconscious way she opened her eyes, now gone dull and hard, and said in an alien, sultry, voluptuous voice:

'Arthur! Oh, my love! Come kiss me!'

Arthur bent over her eagerly, but at that instant Van Helsing, who, like me, had been startled by her voice, swooped upon him. He caught Arthur by the neck with both hands and dragged him back with a fury of strength which I would never have thought he possessed, and actually almost hurled him across the room.

'No! For your life!' he said. 'As you value your living soul, and hers!' And he stood between them like a righteous lion.

Arthur was too dumbstruck to react, and a moment later we all saw a spasm as of rage flit like a shadow over Lucy's face. Her tongue flicked over those strange sharp teeth, then her mouth champed shut. Her eyes closed, and she breathed heavily, almost in a groan of despair.

Yet a minute later her eyes opened, soft with all their old kindness. She put out her poor pale, thin hand, took Van Helsing's great brown one, and with trembling weakness kissed it.

'My true friend,' she said, with faint but harrowing pathos. 'My true friend, and his! Oh, guard him, and give him peace!'

'I swear it!' said the Professor solemnly, kneeling beside her and holding up his hand, as one who registers an oath. Then he turned to Arthur:

'Come, my child, take her hand in yours, and kiss her on the forehead, but only once.'

Their eyes met before their lips, and – so they parted.

Lucy's eyes closed.

Van Helsing took Arthur's arm and drew him away.

Lucy's breathing became painful again.

Then suddenly it ceased.

'It is all over,' said Van Helsing. 'She is dead!'

I led Arthur away to the drawing-room. There he slumped down and covered his face with his hands, sobbing in a depth of private despair I could do nothing to alleviate.

I went back to Lucy's room, and found Van Helsing staring sternly at her corpse – for some curious change had come over her body. Death, it seemed, had restored a part of her beauty, for her brow and cheeks had recovered some of their lines and colour. Even the lips had lost their deadly pallor. It was as if the blood, no longer needed by the heart, had returned in death to animate her flesh.

> *We thought her dying while she slept*
> *And sleeping when she died.*

I stood beside Van Helsing, and said:

'Ah, well. Poor girl. Peace at last.'

He frowned gravely:

'Not so. Alas. This is but the beginning.'

Of course I asked what he meant, but the Professor only shook his head, and said:

'We can do nothing as yet. Wait and see.'

The funeral was arranged so that Lucy and her mother might be buried

together. I attended to all the ghastly formalities, made ever more ghastly
by the obsequious suavity of the undertaker and his staff. Even the
woman who performed the last offices remarked to me confidentially,
when she emerged from the death-chamber:

'She makes a very beautiful corpse, sir, and will do credit to our
establishment.'

I noticed that Van Helsing never kept far away. This was made
possible by the disordered state of the household. There were no relatives
at hand, and as Arthur had to attend his own father's funeral the following
day, Van Helsing and I took it upon ourselves to examine papers, etc. He
insisted upon examining Lucy's papers himself. I asked him why, for I
feared that he, being a foreigner, ignorant of English legal requirements,
might inadvertently cause some unnecessary complication.

He answered:

'You forget that I am lawyer as well as doctor. But this is not a matter
for the law. You know that too, when you avoid the coroner. Yes? But I
have more than him to avoid, and I seek for other papers such as this.' He
took from his pocketbook the memorandum which had been in Lucy's
breast, and which she had torn in her sleep. Then he said:

'When you locate the solicitor of Mrs Westenra, seal all her papers,
and write him tonight. For me, I must look here in Miss Lucy's room.'

I left the Professor browsing through Lucy's papers, and within the
hour I found the name and address of Mrs Westenra's solicitor. Hardly
had I finished writing to him, when, to my surprise, Van Helsing walked
into the room, saying:

'Can I assist you, friend John?'

'Have you got what you were looking for?' I asked.

The Professor replied:

'I did not look for any thing specific. Only what I have: some letters,
a few memoranda, and a diary new begun. Think you nothing of
them – for the present. And now, friend John, I think we may to bed.
We want both rest to recuperate. Tomorrow we have much to do, but for
the tonight there is no more need of us. Alas.'

Before turning in we went to look at poor Lucy. The undertaker had
certainly done his work well, for the room was turned into a small
chapelle ardente. There was a wilderness of beautiful white flowers,
and death was made as little repulsive as might be. The end of the
winding-sheet was laid over the face, and when the Professor turned it

gently back, we wistfully admired, by the light of those tall wax candles, the sad dead beauty that was Lucy. All her loveliness seemed restored in death, and it was almost impossible to believe that we were gazing upon a corpse.

The Professor looked sternly grave. He had not loved her as I had, and there were fewer tears in his eyes.

'Remain till I return,' he said, and left the room. Soon he was back with a handful of wild garlic from a new box in the hall. The fresh flowers he placed amongst the others on and around the bed. Then he took from his neck, inside his collar, a little golden crucifix, and placed it over Lucy's mouth. He drew the sheet over her head once more, and we left the room.

Weary beyond words, I was soon undressing in my own room. Before I could get into bed there came a peremptory rap on the door, and the Professor entered with an aspect of urgency.

'What is it?' I asked him.

'Tomorrow I want that you bring me, before night, a set of postmortem knives.'

'Must we make an autopsy?' I asked.

'Yes, and no. I want to operate, but not as you think. Let me tell you now, but to absolute secrecy you must swear. Do you swear?'

'As you wish,' I agreed, a little impatient at being kept longer from my sleep. 'But why?'

'I have to cut off her head and take out her heart.'

'You – *what?*'

'Ah!' he almost chortled. 'You a surgeon, and so shocked! You, who with no tremble do operations of the body that make the rest shudder. Oh, but I forget, friend John, how you love her. Loved her. But no matter. It is I that shall operate and you must only help. I would like to do it tonight, but for Arthur I must not. After his father's funeral tomorrow he will want to see her. After then, when she is coffined ready for the next day, you and I shall come when all sleep. We shall unscrew the coffin lid, and perform our operation. At last we replace all, so that none know, save we.'

'But why do it at all? The girl is dead. Why mutilate her poor body? Where is the gain to us? To science? To *anyone?*'

The Professor put his hand on my shoulder. With great tenderness he said:

'Friend John, I pity your poor bleeding heart. But there are things that you know not. Not yet. Things . . . not pleasant. Was it not for these causes that you send for me when the great trouble came? Yes! There are strange and terrible days before us. Let us then work as one, to achieve the end of our good. Friend John? Will you not have faith in me?'

I took his hand, and promised him. Without another word he left, and after, through my door held ajar, I had watched him disappear into his own room, I saw one of the maids pass silently along the passage and enter the room where Lucy lay. Somehow the sight touched me deeply: this poor girl, putting aside her terrors of death, to watch alone by the bier of the mistress she loved. If only . . .

I must have slept soundly, for it was broad daylight when Van Helsing waked me. Hovering by my bedside he said:

'You need not trouble about the knives.'

'Why not?'

'We shall not do it.'

'Why not?' I asked. For his solemnity of the night before had greatly impressed me.

'Because', he said sternly, 'it is too late – or too early. See!' He held up the little golden crucifix. 'This was stolen in the night.'

'How stolen,' I asked in wonder, 'since you have it now?'

'Because I get it back from the worthless wretch who stole it, from the woman who robbed the dead. Her punishment will surely come, but not through me. She knew not altogether what she did, and thus unknowing, she only stole. Now we must wait.'

He stormed away angrily, leaving me with a new mystery to grapple with.

The morning was a dreary time, but at noon the solicitor came: Mr Marquand, of Wholeman, Sons, Marquand & Lidderdale. He was very genial, appreciative of what we had done, and took all further details off our hands. During lunch he disclosed that Mrs Westenra had long expected a sudden death from her heart, and, accordingly, had left her affairs in excellent order. With the exception of a certain entailed property of Lucy's father's, which now, in default of direct issue, went back to a distant branch of family, the whole estate, real and personal, was left entirely to Arthur Holmwood.

'Frankly,' Mr Marquand told us over his dessert, 'we did our best

to prevent such a testament disposition, and pointed out certain con-
tingencies that might leave her daughter either penniless or unable to
act freely with regard to matrimony. Indeed, we pressed the matter so
far that we almost came into collision, for Mrs Westenra asked if we
were not prepared to carry out her wishes. Of course, we had then no
alternative. We were right in principle, however, and ninety-nine times
out of a hundred should have proved, by the logic of events, the accuracy
of our judgment.

'Frankly, however,' he continued over his cheese, 'I must admit that,
in this tragic case, any other disposition would have thwarted the carrying
out of Mrs Westenra's wishes.

'Why so?' I asked him politely, seeing the Professor smothering
a yawn.

'Oh, because by her predeceasing her daughter the latter would have
come into the property, and, even had she only survived her mother by
five minutes, her property would, given the case of no will on Miss
Westenra's part, have been treated at her decease as under intestacy.
In which case, Lord Godalming, though so dear a friend, would have
had no claim in the world, and the inheritors, being remote, would not
be likely to abandon their just rights for sentimental reasons regarding
an entire stranger. I assure you, my dear sirs, I am rejoiced at the result.
Perfectly rejoiced.'

He was a good fellow, but his rejoicing at the one little part – in which
he was officially interested – of so great a calamity was an object-lesson
in the limitations of sympathetic understanding.

He did not remain long after lunch, but said he would look in later
to see Lord Godalming. Arthur was expected at five o'clock, so a
little before that time we visited the death chamber, where mother and
daughter now lay side by side. The undertaker, true to his cosmetic craft,
had made the best display he could, but there remained a mortuary air
about the place that lowered our spirits at once.

Poor Arthur, when he arrived, looked desperately sad and broken.
Even his stalwart manhood seemed to have shrunk under the strain of his
much tried emotions. He had been unusually devoted to his father; and to
lose him, and at such a time, was a terribly bitter blow. With me he was
warm as ever, and to Van Helsing he was wholly courteous. Yet there
was a distance in his courtesy. The Professor was quick to notice this,
and by a nod he indicated that I alone should take Arthur upstairs. I left

him at the door of Lucy's room, feeling he would prefer to be alone with her, but he seized my wrist and pulled me in with him, saying huskily:

'You loved her too, old fellow. She told me all about it, and truly no friend had a warmer place in her heart than you. I don't know how to thank you for all . . . but I can't think yet . . . '

Here he suddenly broke down, threw his arms round my shoulders and laid his head on my breast, crying:

'Oh, Jack, Jack! What shall I do? The whole of life seems gone from me all at once, and I have nothing in the wide world to live for.'

I comforted him as well as I could. In such cases men do not need much expression. A grip of the hand, the tightening of an arm over the shoulder, a sob in unison, are expressions of sympathy dear to a man's heart. I stood still and silent till his sobs died away, and then I said softly:

'Come and look at her.'

Together we moved over to the bed, and I lifted the lawn from her face. God, how beautiful she was. Every hour seemed to enhance her loveliness. It amazed me – even frightened me somewhat. As for Arthur, he was trembling as with ague. After what seemed an age he whispered faintly:

'Jack, is she really dead?'

I assured him sadly that she was, and that it often happened, after death, that faces resolved back into a likeness of their youthful beauty; especially when death had been preceded by suffering.

Apparently comforted a little, Arthur knelt beside Lucy's body and gazed upon her lovingly and long. When at last he rose to his feet I intimated that this must be his last goodbye, since the coffin had to be prepared. So he took her dead hand in his and kissed it repeatedly.

'Come now, Arthur,' I suggested gently.

With a final sob he leaned down and pressed a fond kiss on her forehead. Then I led him away, he walking backwards, as in a hypnotic trance, until the door of that room was closed.

I left him in the drawing-room, and told Van Helsing that the lovers' leavetaking was complete. The Professor went to the kitchen to tell the undertaker's men to proceed, and to screw up the coffin. When that was done I repeated to the Professor, in low tones, the question Arthur had asked me:

'Is she really dead?'

Van Helsing replied:

'I am not surprised. Just now, for a moment, I doubted it myself!'

We all dined together, all trying to put on brave faces. But Arthur was, naturally, too stricken to speak, and even the Professor fell silent during most of the meal. But when we had lit our cigars he turned to Arthur, and began:

'Lord—'

'No, no!' Arthur protested. 'Not "Lord", for God's sake! I mean . . . no, but forgive me, sir. I did not mean to speak offensively. Only, my loss is so recent.'

The Professor responded affectionately:

'But I must not call you "Mr", so what shall you prefer?'

Arthur held out his hand, and took the old man's warmly.

'Always call me "Arthur",' he insisted. 'As a token of how grateful I shall always be, for your kindness . . . to my poor dear . . . ' He paused for a moment, blew his nose, then went on:

'Lucy understood your goodness perfectly, and I – if I appeared in any way hostile, you know . . . '

The Professor nodded.

'Please forgive me.'

Van Helsing answered with a kindly gravity:

'I know it is hard for you to quite trust me – for you do not yet understand. But a time shall come—'

'Indeed, sir,' said Arthur warmly, 'I shall in all ways trust you. You are Jack's friend, and you were Lucy's. Of course I trust you.'

The Professor cleared his throat a couple of times, as though in hesitation, before finally saying to Arthur:

'May I ask you something now?'

'Certainly.'

'You know that Mrs Westenra left you all her property?'

'No. Poor dear. I never thought of it.'

'Well, it is yours. All. And so I ask your permission to read Miss Lucy's papers. Believe me, this is no idle curiosity. I have a motive which, be sure, she would approve. I have them all here. See? I took them before we knew that all was yours, so that no strange hand might touch them – no strange eye look through words into her soul. With your consent I ask that even you may not see them yet. I shall keep them safe, and in the good time give them back to you. For Miss Lucy's sake, friend Arthur?'

Right heartily, more like his old self, Arthur retorted:

'Dr Van Helsing, do whatever you think best.'

The old Professor stood up as he said solemnly:

'Good. There will be pain for us all still to come. We, and you most of all, my dear Arthur, must struggle through bitter waters yet, before we reach the sweet. But if we struggle bravely, with unselfish heart, and do our sacred duty, then all may still be well.'

That night I slept on a sofa in Arthur's room, and Van Helsing did not go to bed at all. He paced to and fro, as if on sentry patrol, and was never far from the room where Lucy lay in her coffin, strewn with the wild garlic flowers, which sent, through the odour of lily and rose, a heavy, overpowering smell into the night.

Part III

VAMPIRES ABROAD

England

17

Enter the Bloofer Lady

MINA HARKER'S JOURNAL
22 September.

In the train to Exeter. Jonathan sleeping.

It seems only yesterday that I was in Whitby with Lucy, Jonathan away and no news of him. And now here we are, married, Jonathan a solicitor, rich, master of his business, Mr Hawkins dead and buried, and Jonathan . . . with another strange attack. Some day he may talk to me about — about all that. I suppose. Goodness but my shorthand is rusty — see what unexpected prosperity does for us — anyway . . .

The service was very solemn, but simple. There were only ourselves and the servants there, one or two old friends of his from Exeter, his London agent, and a gentleman representing Sir John Paxton, the President of the Incorporated Law Society. Jonathan and I stood hand in hand, feeling deeply that our dearest friend was gone from us . . .

We came back to town quietly, taking a bus to Hyde Park Corner. Jonathan thought it might cheer me to go into the Row for a while, but it was sad-looking and desolate, and all the many empty chairs only reminded us of the empty chair at home. So we soon got up and instead walked together down Piccadilly, Jonathan holding me by the arm, the way he used to in the old days before I became a teacher.

I was looking admiringly at a very beautiful girl, in a big cart-wheel hat, sitting in a victoria outside Giuliano's, when I felt Jonathan clutch my arm so tight that he hurt me, and he said under his breath:

'My God!'

I am always anxious that some nervous fit may upset Jonathan again, so instantly I quizzed him:

'What is it?'

He was very pale, and his eyes seemed bulging out as, between terror and amazement, he gazed at a tall, thin man with a beaky nose, black moustache and pointed beard, who was also observing the pretty girl.

He was staring at her so hard that he did not see either of us, and so I had a good view of him. His face was hard, cruel, and sensual, and his big white teeth, that looked all the whiter because his lips were so red, were pointed like an animal's.

Jonathan kept gaping at this man till I was afraid he would notice and might take it ill; he looked so fierce and nasty. I asked Jonathan why he was disturbed, and he answered:

'Don't you know who that is?'

'No, dear,' I said, disturbed by Jonathan's manner, for he spoke as if to a stranger. 'Who is it?'

'It is . . . *him.*'

Poor Jonathan was evidently greatly terrified; I do believe that if he had not had me to lean on he would have collapsed. Meanwhile, as he kept staring at the large-toothed gentleman, a second man came out of the shop with a small parcel, and gave it to the pretty young lady, who then drove off. The dark man – the cause of Jonathan's distress – kept his eyes fixed on her, and when the carriage moved up Piccadilly he followed in the same direction, and hailed a hansom.

Looking after them, Jonathan said, as if to himself:

'I believe it *is* the Count, but . . . grown young. My God. If this be so. Oh, my God. If only I could be sure.'

He was so disturbed that I feared to keep his mind on the subject by asking him questions, so I remained silent. I drew him away quietly, and we walked a little further before going in to sit for a while in the Green Park. It was a hot evening for September, and there was a comfortable seat in a cool place. After a few minutes' staring at nothing, Jonathan's eyes closed, his head leaned on my shoulder, and he shuddered into a fitful sleep.

I thought it best to let him rest, and about twenty minutes later he woke up suddenly, and said to me almost cheerfully:

'Goodness, Mina, have I been asleep? Oh, how rude! Do forgive me. Now, what about a nice cup of tea?'

He had evidently forgotten all about the dark stranger, as in his illness he had forgotten all that this episode had reminded him of. I don't like this lapsing into forgetfulness; it may make or continue some injury to the brain. I suppose I dare not quiz him, for fear of doing more harm than good.

But I *must* somehow learn the facts of his journey abroad.

The time is come, I fear, when I must open that parcel and read whatever is in it. Forgive me, Jonathan, when the time comes, but it is for your own dear sake.

Later.

A sad home-coming in every way – the house empty of the dear soul who was so good to us; Jonathan still pale and dizzy from that relapse into his malady; and now a telegram from Van Helsing, whoever he may be:

'You will be grieved to hear that Mrs Westenra died five days ago, and that Lucy died the day before yesterday. They were both buried today.'

Oh, what a wealth of sorrow. Poor Mrs Westenra. Poor Lucy. Never to return. And poor, poor Arthur, to have lost such sweetness out of his life. God help us to bear our troubles.

DR SEWARD'S DIARY

2 September.

It is all over.

Arthur has gone back to Ring, and has taken Quincey Morris with him. What a fine fellow Quincey is. I believe he suffered as much over Lucy's death as any of us; but he bore himself through it like a moral Viking. If America can go on breeding men like that, she will indeed become a major power in the world.

Van Helsing is lying down, having a rest preparatory to his journey. He goes over to Amsterdam tonight, to attend to some pressing affairs, but says he will return almost immediately. He is to stop with me then; having work to do in London which may take him some time. Poor old fellow. I fear that the strain of the past week has dented even his iron strength. Throughout the funeral he was clearly in the grip of some terrible emotion. When it was all over, and we men were left together, Arthur, tears in his eyes, recalled the transfusing of his own blood into Lucy's veins.

Van Helsing's face grew white and purple by turns, but he said nothing.

Arthur then confessed that since that giving of his blood he had secretly felt that, in the sight of God, Lucy already *was* his wife.

None of us mentioned the other transfusions, and none of us ever shall.

Arthur and Quincey went away together to the station, and Van Helsing and I came on here. The moment we were alone in the carriage he burst into a fit of near hysterics. Later he denied that it was hysterics, and insisted it was only his sense of humour asserting itself *in extremis*. He laughed, indeed, till he cried, and I had to draw down the blinds lest anyone should see us and misjudge. Then he cried till he laughed again; and laughed and cried together, just like a woman. I tried to be stern with him, as one would to a woman in similar circumstances; but this had no effect. Men and women are so different, I suppose. At length when his face grew grave again I asked him:

'Why such mirth, Professor, at such a time?'

His reply was logical, forceful, and at once mysterious:

'Ah, you don't comprehend, friend John. Do not think that I am not sad, though I laugh. See, I have cried even when the laugh did choke me. But no more think that I am all sorry when I cry, for the laugh he come just the same. Keep it always with you that laughter who knock at your door and say "May I come in?" is not the true laughter. No! True Laughter He is a King, and he choose no time of suitability. Only He say:

'"I am here."'

'Behold, in example, I grieve my heart out for that so sweet young girl; I give my blood for her, though I am old and worn; I give my time, my skill, my sleep; I let my other sufferers want that she may have all. And yet I can laugh at her very grave; laugh when the clay from the spade of the sexton drop upon her coffin and say "thud, thud" to my heart, till it send back the blood from my cheek. My heart bleed for that poor boy Arthur – so of the age of mine own boy had I been so blessed that he live, and with his hair and eyes the same. There, you know now why I love him so. And yet when he say things that touch my husband-heart to the quick, and make my father-heart yearn – yet even at such moment King Laugh he suddenly bellow in my ear:

'"Here am I, here am I! . . . "'

'Till the blood dance back and bring some sunshine again to my cheek. Oh, friend John, it is a strange sad world full of miseries and yet: when King Laugh come, all dance to the tune he play. Bleeding hearts, and dry bones of the churchyard, and tears that burn as they fall – all dance together to the song he sing through that smileless mouth of him. And we poor souls like ropes drawn tight with strain that pull us different ways! When tears come like rain upon the ropes, they brace us up! Until perhaps the strain become too great, and then we break. But King Laugh like the sunshine come to ease our strain again; and we bear to go on with our burdens, whatever they may be.'

I did not like to wound him by any hint of dissent or censure, but merely inquired as to what precise detail had immediately preceded his laughter.

At once his face drew into grimmer lines, as he said in a serious tone:

'It was the horrible irony of it all – this so lovely lady garlanded with flowers, that looked so fair as life, till one by one we wondered if she were truly dead; she laid in that so fine marble house in that lonely churchyard, where rest so many of her kin, laid there with the mother who loved her, and whom she loved; and that sacred bell going *dong; dong; dong*, so sad and slow; and those holy men, with the white garments of the angel, pretending to read books, and yet all the time their eyes never on the page; and all us with the bowed head. And all for what?

'She is dead. So. Is it not?'

'Well, for the life of me, Professor,' I said, 'I can't see anything to laugh at there. And even if there were incongruities in the burial itself, why, what about poor Arthur's great distress? Why, his heart was simply breaking.'

'Just so. And said he not that the transfusion of his blood to her veins had made her truly his bride?'

'The idea was clearly of much comfort to him.'

'Quite so, friend John. But then what about the others? Ho, ho! Then this so sweet maid is polyandrist, and me, with my poor wife dead to me but alive by Church's law, though no wits, all gone – even I who am faithful husband to this now no-wife, am bigamist!'

'I don't see the joke there either,' I said with some severity.

The Professor laid his hand on my arm, and said:

'Friend John, I show not my feeling to others when it would wound, but only to you, my old friend whom I trust. If you could have look into my very heart then, and when . . . King Laugh pack up his crown and go far away from me, perhaps for very long, perhaps . . . '

Touched by the tenderness of his tone, and by the wealth of emotion betrayed by his slipping English, I asked him to forgive me if I had seemed to be criticising him.

'No, no,' he muttered back darkly. 'It is I who will needs be forgiven.'

And now we are all scattered.

While loneliness hangs like a leaking roof over me, dear Lucy lies in the tomb of her kin, a lordly death-house in a peaceful churchyard far removed from the teeming of London; where the air is fresh; and the sun rises over Hampstead Hill, and wild flowers freely grow.

A HAMPSTEAD MYSTERY

(FROM 'THE WESTMINSTER GAZETTE')

25 September.

The neighbourhood of Hampstead is at present exercised with a series of events not unlike the recent 'Kensington Horror', or 'The Stabbing Woman', or 'The Woman in Black'. During the past three days several cases have occurred of young children mysteriously not returning from their play upon the Heath.

All these children have been too young to give any properly intelligible account, but the consensus of blame is on what they call 'the Bloofer Lady'. It is always late evening before they are missed, and two children were not found until early the following morning. It is generally supposed in the neighbourhood that, as the first child missed gave as his excuse that 'the Bloofer Lady' had asked him to come for a walk, the others had picked up the chorus. Now, so our Hampstead correspondent writes, to see some of the tinier tots pretending to be 'the Bloofer Lady' is really supremely funny.

There is, however, a more serious side to the matter, for all the children who have been missed at night have been found to be slightly injured in the throat. The wounds seem such as might be made by a small dog, or perhaps a large rat, and the Hampstead police have now been instructed to keep a sharp lookout for young children unaccompanied on the Heath, and also for any stray dogs.

THE BLOOFER LADY

(SAME PAPER, SAME DAY, LATE FINAL EDITION)

We have just received intelligence that another child, missed last night, was only discovered late this morning under a furze bush at the Shooter's

Hill side of Hampstead Heath, which is, perhaps, less frequented than the other parts. This child had the same tiny tears in the throat as was remarked in other cases, and looked quite emaciated and really terribly weak. When the child's strength had been partially restored, it too had the same unlikely tale to tell: of being lured away by 'the Bloofer Lady'.

18

Mainly Mina

23 September.

Jonathan is better after a bad night. I am so glad he has plenty of work to do, for it keeps his mind off . . . the terrible things. He will be away all day till late — said he could not lunch at home so, my household work is done, I shall take his foreign journal, lock myself up in my room and read it to the end . . .

24 September.

I hadn't the heart to write last night; that appalling record of Jonathan's upset me so. Poor dear. How he must have suffered, even if it all be only imagination. *Could* there really be any truth in it all? Did he get his brain fever, and *then* write all those terrible things? Or was there indeed some dreadful reality behind it? I suppose I shall never know, for I dare not broach the subject with him . . . And yet, that man we saw yesterday. He seemed quite certain of him . . . Poor dear. I suppose the funeral upset him, and jogged his mind back to his bad experiences.

But whatever the truth of the matter, Jonathan certainly believes it all himself. I remember how on our wedding day he said:

'Unless some solemn duty command me back to those bitter hours, sane or mad.'

And there does seem to run through it all some thread of continuity . . . That fearful Count *was* coming to London . . . And if it *really were* as Jonathan wrote, and that monster came to London, with its teeming millions . . . There may indeed be a solemn duty to perform. If so, I too must be prepared.

But how to begin?

I know. While Jonathan is away I shall copy up his foreign journal with my typewriter. Then his story, if authentic, shall be ready for other eyes.

TO MINA HARKER

23 September.

Dear Madame,

Pray feel me so far your friend as that I sent to you sad news of Miss Lucy Westenra's death. By the kindness of Lord Godalming, I am empowered to read her papers, for I am deeply concerned about certain matters vitally important. In them I find letters which show how great friends you were. Oh, Madame Mina, by that love between you misses, I implore you help me. It is for others' good that I ask to redress great wrong, and to lift much terrible troubles.

May it be that I see you? You can trust me. I am a friend of Dr John Seward and of Lord Godalming (that was the Arthur of Miss Lucy). From all others I must for the present keep it private, and so I should come to Exeter at once if you tell me I am privilege to see you.

Again I implore your pardon, madame. From your letters to poor Miss Lucy, I know how your good husband suffer. So I pray you enlighten him not for the moment, lest it may harm.

Hoping for your favourably,

V. H.

TELEGRAM TO VAN HELSING

25 September. Come today by quarter-past ten train.

Wilhelmina Harker.

MINA HARKER'S JOURNAL

25 September.

I cannot help feeling terribly excited as Dr Van Helsing's visit approaches, for surely it must throw some light upon Jonathan's sad experience. And as the Professor attended poor dear Lucy in her last illness, he can tell me all about her. That is the reason of his coming; I must not forget. It is concerning Lucy and her sleepwalking, and not about Jonathan. Oh dear. That awful journal seizes hold of my imagination and tinges all other thoughts.

Yes, of course it is about Lucy that the Professor wishes to speak. That awful night on the cliff must have made her more gravely ill than we realized. I had almost forgotten. She must have told him of her sleepwalking, and now he wants to discuss the matter with me. Oh, but I do hope Dr Van Helsing will not hold me to blame for my part in it all. I have had so much trouble and anxiety of late that I could not bear any more just at present.

I suppose a cry does us all good at times – clears the air, like rain. Perhaps it was reading the journal yesterday that upset me, and then Jonathan went away this morning, for a whole day and night – the first time we have been parted since our marriage. I do hope nothing will occur to upset him.

Well, now it is two o'clock, and the Professor will be here soon. I shall say nothing of Jonathan's journal unless he asks me. I am so glad I have typewritten out my own journal, so that, if he needs to know more about Lucy, I can give it to him to read.

Later.

He has come and gone. Oh, what a strange meeting! And how my head whirls round! I feel as if in a dream. Can it all be possible? Real? If I had not read Jonathan's journal first, I should never have believed a word of the Professor's story. How poor Jonathan must have *suffered*. And how I pray all this may not upset him again. I shall try to save him from it. And yet . . . ghastly though it all surely is, might it not comfort him to know, for certain, that his eyes and ears and brain did not deceive him? That it is all too horribly true? May it not be a lingering *doubt* which haunts him worst? So that when the doubt is removed . . .

Dr Van Helsing *must* be a good man, as well as a clever one, if he is Arthur's friend. And Dr Seward's. And if they brought him all the way from Holland to look after Lucy. I feel now, having seen him, that he is not only good and kind, but a noble nature. When he comes again tomorrow I shall ask him about Jonathan, and then, please God, all this sorrow and anxiety may cease. As to our interview today . . .

It was half-past two o'clock when the knock came. I took my courage *à deux mains* and waited. In a few minutes Mary opened the door, and announced:

'Dr Van Helsing.'

I rose to welcome him.

He came towards me. A man of medium height, strongly built, with his shoulders set back over a broad, deep chest. His poise strikes one at once as indicative of thought and power, and his head is nobly sized, broad, and large behind the ears. His face, clean-shaven, shows a hard, square chin, a large, resolute mouth, a good-sized nose, rather straight, but with quick, sensitive nostrils, that seem to broaden as the big, bushy eyebrows come down and the mouth tightens. His forehead rises at first almost straight but then slopes back above two ridges wide apart – such a forehead that his reddish hair cannot possibly tumble over it, but falls naturally back and to the sides. Big, dark blue eyes are set widely apart, and are quick and tender, or stern, as the man's moods change.

'Madame Harker?' he greeted me.

'I am she.'

'That was Miss Mina Murray?'

Again I assented.

'It is Mina Murray that I came to see, that was friend of that poor dear child Lucy Westenra. Madame Mina, it is on account of the dead I come.'

'Sir,' I said, 'you could have no better claim on me than that you gave succour to Lucy Westenra.' And I held out my hand.

The Professor took it and said tenderly:

'Oh, Madame Mina, I knew that the friend of that poor lily girl must be good, but I had yet to learn – ' He finished his speech with a courtly bow.

I asked him what, specifically, he wanted to see me about.

At once he began:

'I have read your letters to Miss Lucy. Forgive me, but I had to begin somewhere, and there was none to ask. I know that you were with her at Whitby. She sometimes kept a diary – you need not look surprised, Madame Mina. It was begun after you had left, and was made in imitation of you. And in that diary she traces by inference certain things to a sleepwalking in which she puts down that you saved her. In great perplexity then I ask you out of your so much kindness to tell it to me – all that you remember.'

'I can tell you, Dr Van Helsing, *all* about it.'

'Ah, then you have a good memory for facts? It is not always so with young ladies!'

'Not only do I remember perfectly, Professor, but I wrote it all down at the time. I can show it to you if you like.'

'Oh, Madame Mina, I will be so much grateful.'

I could not resist an urge to mystify him a bit – I suppose some taste of the original apple must linger still in our mouths – so I handed him the shorthand diary.

He took it eagerly, sat down, opened it, and for a moment his face looked really quite tragical. Then he jumped up and bowed:

'Oh, you so clever woman!' he exclaimed. 'And Mr Jonathan is a much thankful man to have his wife with such good things. And will she too so much honour me to read aloud what I cannot? For you see, alas, I know not the shortest hand.'

My little joke over, I took the typewritten copy from my work-basket and handed it to him.

'Somehow I knew it was of dear Lucy you wished to speak,' I explained, 'and so – as a doctor's time is precious – I have typed it all out for you.'

His eyes glistened:

'And may I read it now?'

'By all means,' I said, 'read it over while I order lunch. Then you can ask me questions while we eat.'

He settled himself in a chair with his back to the light, and became absorbed in the papers. When I came back I found him walking hurriedly up and down the room, his face all ablaze with excitement. He rushed up to me and took me by both hands.

'Oh, Madame Mina,' he said, 'how can I say what I owe to you? This paper is as sunshine. It opens the gate to me. I am daze, I am dazzle, with so much light. And yet clouds roll in behind the light every time. But that you comprehend. Oh, but I thank you, thank you, you so clever woman. Madame' – he said this very solemnly – 'if ever Abraham Van Helsing can do anything in return for yours, I trust you must let me know. It will be delight to service you truly. Indeed there are darknesses in life, and there are lights. You are one of the lights. You will have happy life and good, and your husband is blessed to possess you.'

'Professor, you praise me too much,' I protested, feeling my blush spreading. 'And really . . . you hardly know me.'

'Not know you! I, who am old? Who have studded men and women all my life? Who have made my specialty the brain and anyways have read your diary so goodly written for me, and which breathes out truth in every line! Of your love for poor Miss Lucy of course your letters speak, and nobly now I know you love your husband too—'

'Yes, indeed,' I interrupted him eagerly, seeing here an opening to quiz him about Jonathan. 'My husband is a wonderful man. He was almost recovered, you know. But then – he has been greatly upset by Mr Hawkins' death.'

'I know, I know,' the Professor sympathized gravely. 'I have read your last two letters.'

I went on:

'It – all – must have upset him more than I had realized.'

'What make you say that?'

'When we were in town on Thursday last he had a sort of shock.'

'A shock? And after brain fever so soon! That was not good. What kind of shock?'

'He thought he saw someone who recalled something terrible, something which led to his brain fever.' And here the whole thing seemed to overwhelm me in a rush. The pity for Jonathan, the horror which he experienced, the whole fearful mystery of his diary, and the fear that has been brooding over me ever since, all erupted in what I suppose I must admit was hysteria, for I threw myself on my knees, and held up my hands to the Professor, and implored him to make my husband well again.

He raised me up, pulled me to the sofa, and sat by me. There, holding my hands in his, he said – with, oh, such infinite sweetness:

'My life is so full of work that I have not much time for friendships. But since here to tend Miss Lucy I know so many good people that I feel more than ever – and how it grows with the years – the loneliness of my life. Believe me, then, that I come here full of respect for you. And you have given me hope. Hope that there are good women still left to make life happy. Good women, whose lives make lesson for the children that are to be.

'But now you must eat. You are overwrought, and husband Jonathan would not like to see you so pale. And what he like not where he love, is not to his health. Therefore for his sake you must eat and smile.'

After lunch, when we went back to the drawing-room, the Professor said:

'Now tell me about your husband's trouble.'

When it came to speaking to this great, learned man, I began to fear that he would think me a weak fool, and Jonathan a madman – that journal is all so strange – and I hesitated to go on. But he was so sweet and kind, and he had promised to help, and I trusted him, so I said:

'Dr Van Helsing, what I have to tell is so queer that you must promise not to laugh. I have been since yesterday in a fever of doubt. So you must be kind to me, and not think me foolish when I recount some very strange things.'

He reassured me both by his manner and words:

'Oh, my dear, if you only knew how strange is the matter regarding which I am here, it is *you* who would laugh. I think not little of *anyone's* belief, no matter how peculiar.'

'Thank you a thousand times! You have taken a great weight off my mind. Now let me give you to read what I have typewritten out. It will inform you of Jonathan's trouble.'

'What is it?' asked the Professor eagerly.

'A copy of Jonathan's journal when abroad, and all that happened. I dare not say anything about it. You must judge for yourself. And when I see you again, perhaps you will be very kind and tell me what you think.'

'I promise,' he said as I gave him the papers. 'And in the morning I come to see you and your husband together. If I may. For tonight I have in Exeter a hotel.'

'Jonathan will be here by twelve. Come again to lunch, and meet him then.'

So Dr Van Helsing took the papers away with him, and I sit here thinking – thinking I don't know what.

LETTER DELIVERED BY HAND

25 September; 6 o'clock.

Dear Madame Mina,

I have read your husband's so wonderful diary. You may sleep without doubt. Strange and terrible, yes, but it is true. I will pledge my life on it. It may be worse for others; but for him and you there is no dread. He is a noble fellow; and let me tell you from experience of men, that one who would do as he did in going down that wall and to that room – ay, and going a second time – is not one to be injured in permanence by a shock. His brain and his heart are sound. This I swear, before I have even seen him. So be at rest. I shall have much to ask him of other things. I am blessed that today I come to see you, for I have learn all at once so much that again I am dazzle – dazzle more than ever, and I must think.

Yours the most faithful,

Bram Van Helsing.

IMMEDIATE REPLY

25 September.

My dear Dr Van Helsing,

Countless thanks for your kind letter, which has taken such a weight off my mind. And yet, if it be true, what terrible things there are in the world, and what an awful thing if that *monster* be really in London. I fear to think. I have this moment, while writing, had a wire from Jonathan, saying that he leaves by the 6.25 tonight from Launceston and will be here at 10.18. So I need have no fears tonight. Will you therefore, instead of lunching with us, please come to breakfast, at eight o'clock, if this be not too early for you? You can get away, if you are in a hurry, by the 10.30 train, which will bring you to Paddington by 2.35. Do not answer this, as I shall take it that, if I do not hear, you will come to breakfast.

Your grateful friend,

Mina Harker.

JONATHAN HARKER'S JOURNAL

26 September.

I thought never to write in this diary again, but the time has come. When I got home last night Mina had supper ready, and later she told me of Van Helsing's visit, and of her having given him the two diaries copied out, and of how anxious she had been about me. She showed me in the doctor's wire that all I wrote down was true. It seems to have made a new man of me. It was the doubt as to the reality of the whole thing that knocked me over. I felt impotent, and in the dark, and distrustful. But now that I *know*, I am not afraid; not even of the Count. He has succeeded after all, then, in his design in getting to London, and it *was* him I saw. He *has* got younger, but how? Van Helsing is the man to unmask him and hunt him out, if he is truly as Mina says. We sat late, and talked it all over. Mina is dressing, and I shall call at the hotel in a few minutes and bring him over . . .

The Professor was, I think, surprised to see me. When I introduced myself, he took me by the shoulder, turned my face round to the light, and exclaimed:

'But Madame Mina told me you were ill. That you had had a shock?'

It was so funny to hear my wife called 'Madame Mina' by this kindly, strong-faced old man. I smiled, and said:

'I *was* ill, I *have* had a shock. But you have cured me already.'

'And how?'

'By your wire to Mina last night. I was in doubt, and then everything took on a hue of unreality, and I did not know what to trust, even the evidence of my own senses. Not knowing what to trust, I did not know what to do. All that seemed left was to keep on working in the groove of my life hitherto. But the groove ceased to avail me, and I mistrusted myself. Doctor, you don't know what it is to doubt *everything*, even oneself. No, you don't. You couldn't with eyebrows like yours.'

He seemed pleased, and laughed:

'So! You are physiognomist. Bumpologist, by the Jove! I learn more here with each hour. I am with so much pleasure coming to your breakfast. And – pardon such envious praise from an old lonely man – but you are blessed very much in your wife.'

Of course I did not disagree, but perhaps I looked taken aback, for the Professor went on:

'She is one of God's women fashioned by His own hand to show us men and other women that there is a heaven where we can enter, and that its light can be here on earth. So true, so sweet, so noble, so little an egoist – and that, let me tell you, is much in this age – so sceptical and selfish. And you, sir – I have read all Madame Mina's letters to poor Miss Lucy. Since some of them speak of you, I know you already a little before. But now then your true self I have witnessed in your journal just last night. You will give me your hand, will you not? And let us be friends all our lives.'

We shook hands and he was so earnest and so kind that it made me quite choky.

'And now,' he said, 'I have a great task to do, and need to know what went *before* your Transylvania trip.'

I replied:

'Does what you have to do concern the Count?'

'It does,' replied the Professor solemnly.

'Then I am with you heart and soul. As you go by the 10.30, I shall give you all the papers, and you can read them on the train.'

After breakfast I saw him to the station. When we were parting he said:

'Perhaps you will come to town if I send? And bring Madame Mina too?'

'Immediately you need us.'

I had got him the morning papers and the London papers from the previous evening, and while we were talking at the carriage window, waiting for the train to start, his eye suddenly seemed to catch something in the *Westminster Gazette* – I knew it by the colour – and he grew quite white. He read something intently, groaning to himself:

'*Mine God, mine God!* So soon!'

Just then the whistle blew, and the train moved off. This recalled him to himself, and he leaned out of the window and waved his hand, calling out:

'Mighty love to Madame Mina. I shall write so soon as I can.'

19

Dr Seward's Diary

26 September.

Until this afternoon Renfield had become, to all intents, as sane as he
ever was. He was already well ahead with his fly business; and he had
just started in the spider line also; so he had not been any trouble to me. I
had a letter from Arthur, written on Sunday, and from it I gather that he is
bearing up wonderfully well. Quincey Morris is with him, and from him I
hear that Arthur is beginning to recover something of his old buoyancy;
so, as to them, my mind is at rest. As for myself, I was settling down to
work with some enthusiasm — as if the wound which poor Lucy left on
me was becoming cicatrized — but . . . everything is now reopened; and
what will be the outcome?

God only knows.

I have an idea that Van Helsing thinks he knows too, but he will only
let on enough to whet my curiosity. He went to Exeter yesterday, and
stayed there all night. Today he almost bounded into my room at about
five o'clock, and thrust last night's *Westminster Gazette* into my hand.

'What do you think of that?' he asked as he stood back and folded
his arms.

I looked over the paper, for I really did not know what he meant;
but he took it from me and pointed out a paragraph about children
being decoyed away at Hampstead. It did not convey much to me,
until I reached a passage which described small punctured wounds on
their throats.

'Well?' asked the Professor.

I looked up:

'Like poor Lucy's?'

'And?'

'Do you believe whatever injured her has injured these children too?'

'Not directly.'

'How do you mean, Professor?' I asked. I was a little inclined to take his seriousness lightly – but when I saw his face it sobered me. Never, even in the midst of our despair about poor Lucy, had he looked more stern.

'Tell me!' I pressed him.

'Dear friend John, have you no suspicion as to of what poor Lucy died? Really not?'

'Of nervous prostration following on great loss of blood.'

'And how the blood lost?'

I shook my head.

He stepped over, sat down beside me, and went on:

'You are clever man, friend John, but do you not think that there are things which you cannot understand, and yet which are? That some people see things that others cannot? Ah, but. It is the fault of our science that it wants to explain all. And if it explain not, then it say there is nothing to explain! But yet we see around us every day in growth beliefs which think themselves new and yet be supremely old – which pretend to be young, like the fine ladies at the opera. I suppose now you do not believe in corporeal transference. No? Nor in materialization. No? Nor in astral bodies. No? Nor in the reading of thought. No? Nor in hypnotism—'

'Why, yes,' I protested. 'Charcot has proved that pretty well, has he not?'

The Professor smiled as he went on:

'Then you be satisfied! Yes? And can follow the mind of the great Charcot – alas that he is no more – into the very soul of his patient. No? Oh, friend John, what mysteries there are in life! Why was it that Methuselah lived nine hundred years, and 'Old Parr' one hundred and sixty-nine, and yet that poor Lucy, with four men's blood in her poor veins, could not live even one day! For, had she live one more day, we could have save her. Do you know all the mystery of life and death? Can you tell me why, when other spiders die small and soon, that one great spider lived for centuries in the tower of the old Spanish church and grew and grew, till, on descending, he could drink the oil of all the church lamps? Can you tell me why in the Pampas, ay and elsewhere, there are bats that come at night and open the veins of cattle and horses and suck dry their veins? How in some islands of the western seas there are bats which hang on the trees all day, that those who have seen describe as like giant nuts or pods, and that when the sailors sleep on the deck, because that it is hot, flit down on them, and then – and then in the morning are found dead men – white as even Miss Lucy was?'

'Good God, Professor!' I said, starting up. 'Do you imply that Lucy was bitten by such a bat? And that such a thing is here? In London in the nineteenth century?'

He waved me silent, then went on:

'Why the tortoise he live more long than generations of men? Why the elephant he outlive dynasties? And friend the parrot? Why he die ever only of bite of cat or dog, or other? And men? Why ever always be belief that some men – and women too – *can never die?*'

I had a dim idea that he was teaching me some lesson, as long ago he used to do in his study at Amsterdam; so I said:

'Professor, tell me the *thesis*. At present I feel like a novice blundering through a bog in a mist, jumping from one tussock to another in the mere blind effort to move on – without knowing where I am going.'

'That is good image,' he said. 'Well, I shall tell you. My thesis is this: I want you to believe.'

'Believe what?'

'In things that you cannot. Let me illustrate. I heard once of an American who so defined faith: "that which enables us to believe things which we know to be untrue." For one, I follow that man. He mean we shall have an open mind, and not let a little bit of truth check the rush of a Big Truth, like a small rock derail most heavy goods truck. We get the small truth first. Good! We keep him, and we value him; but all the same we must not let him think himself all the truth in the universe.'

'Then you want me not to let some previous conviction injure the receptivity of my mind with regard to some strange matter. Do I read your lesson aright?'

'Ah! My favourite pupil still! Now *willing* to understand, you take the *first step* to understand. You think then those so small holes in the children's throats to be made by the same beast that so hole Miss Lucy?'

'I can only suppose so.'

He stood up and said solemnly:

'Oh, would it were so! But alas! No. It is far, far worse.'

'In God's name, Professor, what do you mean?' I cried.

He threw himself with a despairing gesture into a chair, and placed his elbows on the table, covering his face with his hands as he spoke:

'They were made by Miss Lucy!'

Sheer anger mastered me – it was as if he had during her life struck Lucy on the face – and I smote the table hard and rose up as I said to him:

'Dr Van Helsing, are you mad?'

He raised his head and looked at me, and somehow the tenderness of his face calmed me at once. 'Would I were!' he said. 'Madness were easy to bear compared with truth like this. Oh, my friend, why, think you, did I take so long to tell you so simple thing? Was it because I wished to give you pain? In revenge for that time when you saved my life, and from a fearful death? Ah no!'

'Forgive me,' said I.

He went on:

'My friend, it was because I wished to be gentle in the breaking to you, for I know that you have loved that so sweet lady. But even yet I do not expect you to believe. It is so hard to accept at once any abstract truth, that we may doubt such to be possible when we have always believed the 'no' of it. And it is more hard still to accept so sad a concrete truth, and of such a one as Miss Lucy. Tonight I go to prove it. Dare you come with me?'

This staggered me.

The Professor saw my hesitation.

'The logic is simple,' he assured me. 'No madman logic this time, jumping from tussock to tussock in a misty fog. If it be not true, then proof will be relief; at worst it will not harm. If it be true! Ah, there is the dread. So. Come.'

'Where?'

'First we go to see that child in the hospital. Dr Vincent of the North Hospital, where the papers say is the child. He is good friend to me. We shall tell him nothing, mind, but only that we wish to learn.'

'And then?'

He took a key from his pocket and held it up:

'We spend the night, you and I, in the churchyard where Lucy lies. This is the key that lock the tomb. I had it from the coffin-man to give to Arthur.'

My heart sank within me then, for I felt that there was some fearful ordeal before us.

In the North Hospital we found the child awake. It had had a sleep, taken some food, and seemed to be making progress. Dr Vincent took the bandage from its throat, and showed us the punctures. There was no mistaking the similarity to those which had been on Lucy's throat. They were smaller, and the edges looked fresher: that was all.

We asked Vincent to what he attributed them, and he replied that it might have been a bite of some animal, perhaps a rat – but, for his own part, he was inclined to think that it was one of the bats which are so numerous on the northern heights of London.

'Out of so many harmless ones,' he said, 'there may be some wild specimen from the South of a more malignant species. Some sailor may have brought one home, and it managed to escape; or even from the Zoological Gardens: a young one may have got loose, or one be bred there from a vampire. These things do occur, you know. Only ten days ago a wolf got out, and was, I believe, traced up in this direction. For a week after, the children were playing nothing but Red Riding Hood on the Heath, and in every alley in the place, until this "bloofer lady" scare came along. Since then it has been quite a gala-time with the children, and even this poor little mite, when he woke up today, asked the nurse if he might go home. When she asked him why, he said he wanted to play with the "bloofer lady".'

'I hope,' said Van Helsing, 'that when you are sending the child home you do caution its parents to keep strict watch over it. These fancies to stray are most dangerous; and if the child were to remain out another night, it would probably be fatal.'

Our visit to the hospital took longer than we had reckoned on, and the sun had dipped before we came out. When Van Helsing saw how dark it was, he said:

'Come, let us eat, and then we shall be ready.'

We dined at Jack Straw's Castle along with a little crowd of bicyclists and others who were genially noisy. About ten o'clock we started from the inn. It was then very dark, and the scattered lamps made the darkness greater when we were once outside their radius. The Professor had evidently noted the road we were to go, for he went on unhesitatingly. As we went further, we met fewer people, and finally only the night patrol of the horse police.

At last we reached the wall of the churchyard, which we climbed over. With some little difficulty – for it was very dark, and the whole place strange – we found the Westenra tomb. The Professor took the key, opened the creaky door, stood back politely, and motioned me to precede him.

My companion followed me in quickly and cautiously drew the door to, after carefully ascertaining that the lock was a falling, and not a spring one. In the latter case we should have been in a bad plight. Then he fumbled in his bag for a matchbox and a piece of candle and proceeded to make a light. The tomb in the daytime, wreathed with fresh flowers, had looked grim and gruesome enough; but now, some days afterwards, when the flowers hung lank and dead, their whites turning to rust and their greens to browns; when the spider and the beetle had resumed their accustomed dominance; when time-discoloured stone, and dust-encrusted mortar, and rusty, dank iron, and tarnished brass, and clouded silver-plating gave back the feeble glimmer of a candle, the effect was more miserable and sordid than could have been imagined.

Van Helsing went about his work systematically. Holding his candle so that he could read the coffin plates, and so holding it that the sperm dropped in white patches which congealed as they touched the metal, he located Lucy's coffin. Another search in his bag, and he took out a turnscrew.

'What are you going to do?' I asked.

'Open the coffin. You shall yet be convinced.' Straightaway he began taking out the screws, and finally lifted off the lid, showing the casing of lead beneath. The sight was almost too much for me. It seemed as much an affront to the dead as to have stripped off her clothing in her sleep while she lived, and I actually took hold of his hand to stop him.

He only said:

'You shall see.' Next from his bag he produced a tiny fret-saw. Striking the turnscrew through the lead with a swift downward stab, which made me wince, he made a small hole, which was, however, big enough to admit the point of the saw. I expected a rush of gas from the week-old corpse, and I drew back towards the door. But the Professor never stopped for a moment; he sawed down a couple of feet along one side of the lead coffin, and then across, and down the other side. Taking the edge of the loose flange, he bent it back towards the foot of the coffin, held the candle into the aperture, and motioned to forward.

I looked.

The coffin was empty.

This gave me a considerable shock, but Van Helsing was unmoved.

'Are you satisfied now, friend John?' he asked.

I felt all the dogged argumentativeness of my nature awake within me as I answered:

'I am satisfied that Lucy's body is not in that coffin; but that only proves one thing.'

'What is that, friend John?'

'That it is not there.'

'That is good logic,' he said, 'so far as it go. But how do you *account* for it not being there?'

'Perhaps a body-snatcher,' I suggested. 'Some of the undertaker's people may have stolen it.'

The Professor sighed. 'Ah well,' he said, 'we must have more proof. Come with me.'

He put on the coffin lid again, gathered up all his things and placed them in the bag, blew out the light, and placed the candle also in the bag. We opened the door, and went out. Behind us he locked the door, then put the key in his pocket. Myself he directed to watch at one side of the churchyard while he would monitor the other. I took up my place behind a yew tree, and I saw his dark figure move until the intervening headstones and trees hid it from my sight.

It was a lonely vigil. Soon after I had taken my place I heard a distant clock strike twelve, and in time came one and two. I was chilled and unnerved, and angry with the Professor for taking me on such an errand, and with myself for coming. I was too cold and too sleepy to be keenly observant, and not sleepy enough to betray my trust; so altogether I had a dreary, miserable time.

Suddenly, a little after two, I thought I saw something like a white streak, moving between two dark yew trees at the side of the churchyard farthest from the tomb; at the same time a dark mass moved from the Professor's side of the ground, and hurriedly went towards it. Then I too moved; but I had to go round headstones and railed-off tombs, and I stumbled over graves. The sky was overcast, and somewhere far off an early cock crew. A little way off, beyond the line of scattered juniper trees which marked the pathway to the church, a white, dim figure flitted in the direction of the tomb. The tomb itself was hidden by trees, and I could not see where the figure disappeared. I heard a rustle of movement where I had first seen the white figure, and coming over, found the

Professor holding in his arms a tiny child. When he saw me he held it out to me, and said:

'Are you satisfied now?'

'No,' I said aggressively.

'Do you not see the child?'

'Yes, it is a child, but who brought it here? And is it wounded?' I asked.

'We shall see,' said the Professor, who then led the way out of the churchyard, carrying the sleeping child.

When we had got some distance away we went into a clump of trees, struck a match, and looked at the child's throat.

It was without a scar or scratch of any kind.

'Well?' I asked triumphantly.

'We were just in time,' said the Professor thankfully.

However, we had now to decide what to do with the child. If we took it to a police station we should have to give some account of our movements during the night, so we decided that we would take it to the Heath, and when we heard a policeman coming, could leave it where he could not fail to find it.

All fell out well.

At the edge of Hampstead Heath we heard a policeman's heavy tramp, and laying the child on the pathway, we waited and watched until he saw it as he flashed his lantern to and fro. We heard his exclamation of astonishment, and then we went away silently. By good chance we got a cab near The Spaniards, and drove to town.

I cannot sleep, so I make this entry. But I must *try* to get a few hours' sleep, as Van Helsing is to call for me at noon. He insists that I shall go with him on another expedition.

27 September.

It was two o'clock before we found a suitable opportunity. The noon funeral was all completed, and the last stragglers of the mourners had taken themselves lazily away, when, looking carefully from behind a clump of alders, we saw the sexton lock the gate after him. We knew then that we were safe till morning did we desire it; but the Professor told me we should not want more than an hour. Again I felt that horrid sense of the the perils of the law which we were incurring in our unhallowed work.

Besides, I felt it was all so useless.

Outrageous as it was to open a leaden coffin, to see if a woman dead nearly a week were really dead, it now seemed the height of folly to open the tomb again, when we knew, from the evidence of our own eyesight, that the coffin was empty. I shrugged my shoulders, however, and rested silent, for Van Helsing had a way of going on his own road, no matter who remonstrated. He took the key, opened the vault, and again courteously motioned me to precede.

The place was not so gruesome as last night, but oh, how unutterably mean-looking when the sunshine streamed in. Van Helsing walked over to Lucy's coffin, and I followed. He bent over and again forced back the leaden flange; and then a shock of dismay shot through me.

There lay Lucy, seemingly just as we had seen her the night before her funeral. She was, if possible, more radiantly beautiful than ever; and I could not believe that she was dead. The lips were red – much redder than before – and on her cheeks was a delicate bloom.

'Is this a juggle?' I said to him.

'Are you convinced now?' the Professor responded, and in a manner which made my flesh crawl he reached to Lucy's mouth, and pulled back the dead lips for her long white teeth.

'See,' he went on. 'They are even sharper than before. With these – he touched one canine and the tooth below it – 'the little children can be bitten. Are you of belief now, friend John?'

Once more hostility woke within me. I could not accept such an overwhelming idea as he suggested; so I argued:

'She may have been placed here since last night.'

'By whom?'

'*Someone* has done it.'

'And yet she has been dead one week. Whose normal dead bodies in that time look so?'

I had no answer.

Van Helsing did not seem to notice my silence; at any rate, he showed neither chagrin nor triumph. He was looking intently at the face of the dead woman, raising the eyelids and looking at the eyes; once more opening the lips and examining the teeth. Then he turned to me and said:

'Here, there is one thing different from all recorded: here is some dual life that is not as the common. She was bitten by the Vampire when she was in a trance, sleepwalking – oh, you start; you do not know that, friend John, but you shall know it all later – and in her trance could he best come to take more blood. In trance she died, and in trance she is Un-Dead, too. So it is that she differ from all other. Usually when the Un-Dead sleep at home' – a comprehensive sweep of his arm suggested what to a vampire was home – 'their face show what they are, but this so-sweet-that-was when she not Un–Dead she go back to the nothings of the common dead. There is no malign there, see, and so it make hard that I must kill her in her sleep.'

This turned my blood cold, and it struck me that I was beginning to accept Van Helsing's theories. But then again: if she were really dead, what terror was there in the idea of killing her?

The Professor evidently saw the change in my face, for he said almost joyously:

'You believe now?'

I answered:

'How will you do this bloody work?'

'I shall cut off her head and fill her mouth with garlic, and I shall drive a stake through her body.'

It made me shudder to think of so mutilating the body of the woman I had loved. Yet the feeling was not so strong as I had expected. I was, in fact, beginning to loathe the very presence of this being, this Un-Dead, as Van Helsing called it. Is it possible that love is entirely subjective after all?

I waited a considerable time for Van Helsing to begin, but he stood as if wrapt in thought. Presently he closed the catch of his bag with a snap, and said:

'If you, who saw the wounds on Lucy's throat, and saw the wounds so similar on the child's at the hospital – if you, who saw the coffin empty last night and full today with a woman who have not change only to be more rose and more beautiful in a whole week after she die – if you know of this and know of the white figure last night that brought the child to the churchyard, and yet of your own senses you did not believe . . . how, then, can I expect Arthur, who know none of those things, to believe?

'He doubted me when I took him from her kiss when she dying. I know he has forgiven me because in some mistaken idea I have done things that prevent him say goodbye as he ought; and he may think that in some more mistaken idea this woman was buried alive; and that in most mistake of all we have killed her. He will then argue back that it is we, mistaken ones, that have killed her by our ideas; and so he will be much unhappy always. Yet he never can be sure . . . '

'Uncertainty is worst of all,' I agreed.

'And he will sometimes think', continued the Professor, evidently distressed at the thought, 'that she he loved was buried alive, and that will paint his dreams with horrors of what she suffer; and, again, he will think that we may be right, and that his so beloved was, after all, an Un-Dead. No! Arthur too must pass through the bitter waters to reach the sweet. He, poor fellow, must have one hour that will make the very face of heaven grow black to him; then we can act for good all round and send him peace. My mind he make up. Let us go. You return home for tonight to your asylum, and see that all be well. As for me, I shall spend the night here in this churchyard in mine own way. Tomorrow night you will come to the Berkeley Hotel at ten. I shall send for Arthur too, and also that so fine young man of America that gave his blood. Later we shall all have work to do. I come with you so far as Piccadilly and there dine, for I must be back here before the sun set.'

So we locked the tomb, climbed over the wall of the churchyard, and drove back to Piccadilly.

20

Note from the Berkeley

(never delivered)

27 September.

Friend John,

I write this in case anything should happen. I go alone to watch in that churchyard. It please me that the Un-Dead, Miss Lucy, shall not leave tonight, that so on the morrow night she may be more eager. Therefore I shall fix some things she like not − garlic and a crucifix − and so seal up the door of the tomb. She is young as Un-Dead, and will heed. Moreover, these only deter her coming out; they will not prevent her getting in; for then the Un-Dead is desperate. I shall be at hand all the night from sunset till after sunrise, and if there be aught to learn, I shall learn it.

For Miss Lucy, or from her, I have no fear: but that Other, for whom she is Un-Dead, he have now the power to seek her tomb and find shelter. He is cunning, as I know from Mr Jonathan. Also from his play with us for Miss Lucy's life, which we lost.

In many ways, you must know, the Un-Dead is fearsome strong. He have always the strength in his hand of twenty men. We four, remember, who gave our strength to Miss Lucy − through her it go all to him. Besides, he can summon his wolf, and I know not what else. So if he come thither this night he shall find me, and then − but equally he may not attempt the place. His hunting ground for game is wider far than the churchyard where the Un-Dead woman sleep, and one old man watch. But I write this in case . . .

Take the papers herewith, the diaries of Harker and the rest. Read them, then find out this great Un-Dead, and cut off his head and burn his heart or drive a stake through it, so that from him the world may rest.

If it be so, farewell.

V.H.

21

Dr Seward's Diary

28 September.

It is wonderful what a good night's sleep will do.

Yesterday I was almost willing to accept Van Helsing's monstrous ideas; now they outrage my sense. I have no doubt, though, that he believes it all. I wonder if his mind can have become unhinged. Surely there must be some rational explanation of all these mysterious things.

Is it possible that the Professor can have done it himself?

He is so abnormally clever that if he did go off his head . . .

I am loth to think it, and indeed it would be almost as great a marvel: to find that Van Helsing was mad. Still, I must watch him carefully.

29 September; morning.

Last night, a little before ten o'clock, Arthur and Quincey came into Van Helsing's room. He told us all what he wanted us to do, but especially addressing himself to Arthur, as if all our wills were centred in his. He began by saying that he hoped we would all come with him too. 'For', he said, 'there is a great duty to be done there. You were doubtless surprised at my letter?' This query was directly addressed to Lord Godalming.

'I was,' replied Arthur. 'It rather upset me for a bit. There has been so much trouble around my house of late that I could do without any more. I have been curious, too, as to what you mean. Quincey and I talked it over; but the more we talked, the more puzzled I got—'

'Me too,' said Quincey Morris laconically.

'Well,' said the Professor, particularly to Arthur. 'I want your permission to do what I think good this night. It is, I know, much to ask. Therefore may I ask that you promise me in the dark, so that afterwards, though you may be angry with me for a time, you shall not blame yourselves.'

Arthur replied:

'Dr Van Helsing, I don't like to buy a "pig in a poke", as they say in Scotland, and if it be anything in which my honour as a gentleman or my faith as a Christian is concerned, I cannot make such a promise. But if you can assure me that what you intend does not violate either value, then I give my consent at once. Though, for the life of me, I cannot understand what you are driving at.'

'I accept your limitation,' said Van Helsing.

'Thank you,' said Arthur. 'And now that the *pour parlers* are over, may I ask what we are to do?'

'I want you to come with me, in secret, to the churchyard at Kingstead.'

Arthur's face fell as he said:

'Where poor Lucy is buried?'

The Professor nodded.

Arthur went on:

'And when there?'

'To enter the tomb!'

Arthur stood up:

'Professor, is this some devilish joke? Pardon me, I see that you are in earnest.' He sat down again, but stiffly, as one who is on his dignity. There was silence until, reluctantly, he asked:

'And when in the tomb?'

'To open the coffin.'

'This is too much!' said Arthur, angrily rising again. 'I am willing to be patient in all things that are reasonable; but in this – this desecration of the grave – of one who—' He fairly choked with indignation.

The Professor looked pityingly at him.

'If I could spare you one pang, my poor friend,' he said, 'God knows I would. But this night our feet must tread in thorny paths; or later, and for ever, the feet you loved must walk in paths of flame!'

Arthur looked up with set, white face and said:

'Take care, sir.'

'Hear what I have to say,' pleaded Van Helsing. 'And then you will at least know my purpose.'

'That's fair enough,' broke in Morris.

Van Helsing went on, evidently with effort:

'Miss Lucy is dead, say. Then can I do no wrong to her. But if she be not dead—'

Arthur jumped to his feet. 'Good God!' he cried. 'What do you mean? Has there been a mistake? Surely she has not been buried alive?' He groaned in an anguish that no hope could soften.

'I go no further', murmured the Professor, 'than to say she may be . . . Un-Dead.'

'Un-Dead! What do you mean? Is this all a ghastly nightmare, or what?'

'There are mysteries which men can only guess at, which age by age they may solve only in part. Believe me, we are now on the verge of one. But I have not done.' With a deep breath the Professor asked:

'May I cut off the head of dead Miss Lucy?'

'Heavens and earth, no!' cried Arthur in a storm of passion. 'Not for the wide world will I consent to any mutilation of her dead body. Dr Van Helsing, you try me too far. What have I done to you, that you should torture me so? What did that poor, sweet girl do that you should so dishonour her grave? Are you mad? Or am I mad that listen to you? Do not, in any case, dare to think further of such a desecration.'

Van Helsing rose up sternly:

'My Lord Godalming, I, too, have duty. To others, to you; to the dead. And by God it shall be done! All I ask you now is that you come with me, that we look and listen. If when later I make the same request you do not be more eager for its fulfilment – even than I am, then . . . ' His voice broke a little, and he went on, full of pity:

'But do not go forth in anger with me. In long life of acts which were often not pleasant to do, and which sometimes did wring my heart, I never had so heavy task as now. Just think. For why should I give myself so much of labour and sorrow? I come here from my own land to do what I can of good. At the first to please my friend John, and then to help a sweet young lady – whom I too came to love.

'For her I gave what you gave: the blood of my veins. I, who was not like you her lover, but only her physician and her friend. I gave to her my nights and days – before death, after death; and if my death can do her good even now, when she is Un-Dead, then she shall have it freely.'

Arthur was much affected by the Professor's quiet sincerity. Pressing the old man's hand, he said with a faltering voice:

'I do not understand, Dr Van Helsing. But let us at least go with you, and observe.'

It was just a quarter before twelve o'clock when we got into the churchyard over the low wall. The night was dark, with occasional gleams of moonlight between rents of heavy cloud. We all kept close together, with Van Helsing leading the way. When we had come close to the tomb I looked well at Arthur, for I feared that the proximity to a place laden with so sorrowful a memory would upset him; but he bore himself well. I took it that the very mystery of the proceeding tended in some way to counteract his grief.

The Professor unlocked the door, closed it behind us, lit a dark lantern, and pointed to the coffin.

Arthur stepped forward hesitatingly.

Van Helsing said to me:

'You were with me yesterday. Was the body of Miss Lucy in that coffin?'

'It was.'

The Professor turned to the rest, saying:

'Yet one of you does not believe me.' He took his screwdriver and again approached Lucy's coffin.

Arthur looked on, very pale but silent. When the lid was removed and he saw the rent in the lead, the blood rushed to his face – but just as quickly it drained away again, so that he remained of a ghastly white; still silent. Van Helsing forced back the leaden flange, and we all looked in.

With various gasps we – all but the Professor – recoiled aghast.

For the coffin was empty.

Throughout a seeming age no-one spoke. The silence was broken by Quincey Morris:

'Professor, is this your doing?'

Van Helsing replied emphatically:

'I swear to you by all I hold sacred that I have not touched her. What happened was this: Two nights ago my friend Seward and I came here – with good purpose, believe me. I open that coffin, which then was sealed up, and we find it, as now, empty. We then wait, and see something white come through the trees. The next day we come here in daytime, and she lie there. Not so, friend John?'

'Yes.'

'That night we just in time. One more small child missing, and we find it, thank God, unharm amongst the graves. Yesterday I come here before sundown, for at sundown the Un-Dead can move. I wait here all the night till the sun rise, but I see nothing – most probably because over the clamps of those doors I have some garlic laid, which the Un-Dead cannot bear, and other things which they shun. Last night no exodus, so tonight before the sundown I take away my garlic and other stuff. And so it is we find this coffin empty. But bear with me. So far there is much strange. Wait you with me outside, unseen and unheard, and things much stranger are yet to be. So' – he shut the dark slide of his lantern – 'now to the outside.' He opened the door, and we filed out, he coming last and locking the door behind him.

Oh, but how fresh and pure it seemed in the night air, after the terror of that vault! How sweet to see the clouds race by, and the brief gleams of moonlight between . . . like the sorrow and gladness of life. To breathe the fresh air, that had no taint of death and decay; to see the red lighting of the sky beyond the hill; and to hear far away the muffled roar of city life.

Each of us, in his own way, was deeply moved.

Arthur, I could see, was struggling to comprehend the mystery of the empty coffin. Myself, I was now more inclined to accept Van Helsing's conclusions. Quincey Morris was phlegmatic in the way of a man who accepts all things, in the spirit of cool courage. Not being able to smoke, he cut himself a good-sized plug of tobacco, and began to chew.

As to Van Helsing, first he took from his bag a mass of what looked like thin, wafer-like biscuit, which was carefully rolled up in a white napkin. Next he produced a double-handful of some whitish stuff, like dough or putty. He crumbled the wafer up fine and worked it into the mass between his hands. This he then rolled into thin strips and began to lay them into the crevices between the door and its setting in the tomb.

Puzzled, I asked him what he was doing.

The Professor answered:

'I am closing the tomb, so that the Un-Dead may not enter.

'And is *that* stuff going to do it?' asked Quincey sceptically. 'Great Scott!'

'What is that stuff you are using?' This time the question was from Arthur.

Van Helsing reverently lifted his hat as he answered:

'The Host. Which I bring from Amsterdam. For I have Indulgence.'

Stunned into respectful silence, we others took the places assigned to us – close round the tomb, but concealed from anyone approaching.

Poor Arthur, I thought, for never did tombs loom so deathly white. Never did cypress, or yew, or juniper so seem the embodiment of funereal gloom; did trees so ominously rustle; or boughs so menacingly creak. While the discordant howling of distant dogs sent a woeful presage through the night.

Then a long spell of silence, an aching void of sound, until suddenly from the Professor we heard a keen:

'*S-s-s-s!*'

He pointed.

We looked.

And far down the avenue of yews we saw a white figure advance – with something dark held at its breast. The figure stopped, and a momentary ray of moonlight fell between the driving clouds to show in startling prominence a dark-haired woman, dressed in the cerements of the grave. We could not see the face, for it was bent over what we saw to be a fair-haired child.

There followed a sharp little cry, such as a child gives in sleep, or a dog as it dreams before the fire. We would have started forward, but the Professor behind his yew tree waved us back.

In a moment the white figure moved closer.

My heart grew cold as ice, and I could hear the gasp of Arthur as we recognized the features of Lucy Westenra. But yet how changed. The sweetness was turned to adamantine, heartless cruelty, and the purity to voluptuous wantonness.

Van Helsing stepped out, and, obedient to his gesture, we all advanced too. The four of us ranged in a line before the tomb. Van Helsing raised his lantern and drew the slide. By the concentrated light that fell on Lucy's face we saw lips glistening crimson with fresh blood, whose stream had trickled over her chin and stained her lawn death-robe. We shivered with horror, and I could see by the tremulous light that even Van Helsing's iron nerve was shaken. Arthur was next to me, and if I had not seized his arm he would have fallen.

When Lucy – I call the thing Lucy because it bore her shape – saw us she drew back with an angry snarl – like a cat taken unawares – and her eyes ranged over us. Lucy's eyes in form and colour; but Lucy's eyes unclean, and full of hellfire.

In that instant the remnant of my love passed into loathing, and had she then to be killed, I could have done it with savage delight. Her eyes blazed with unholy light, and the face became wreathed in a rapacious grin. With a careless motion, she flung to the ground the child she had clutched strenuously to her breast, growling over it as a dog with a succulent bone.

The child gave a short sharp cry, then lay there moaning.

The coldbloodedness of her action wrung a groan from Arthur which broke into sobs as she now approached him with outstretched arms and a wanton smile.

Falling back before her advance, he hid his face in his hands.

She, gliding ever closer, appealed to him with a suggestive grace:

'Come to me, Arthur. Leave these others. My arms are hungry for *you*. Come, my husband, come!'

There was something diabolically tempting in her tone – something of tinkling glass – which rang through the brains even of we others. As for Arthur, he seemed utterly entranced. Moving his hands from his face, he opened wide his arms. She – it – tensed lustfully to embrace him but just then Van Helsing sprang forward and held between them his little golden crucifix. The Lucy-thing recoiled from it, and, with a suddenly distorted face, full of rage, dashed past him as to the tomb.

Within two feet of the door, however, she halted as if thunderstruck. Then she turned, and never did I see such baffled moonlit malice on a face. The beautiful colour become livid, the eyes sparking hellfire, the brows wrinkled as though the folds of the flesh were the coils of Medusa's snakes, and that once lovely, blood-stained mouth snarling wide in a gaping square, like the passion masks of the Greeks.

If ever a face intended death, we saw it at that moment.

And so for moments which seemed an eternity, she remained between the lifted crucifix and the Host-sealed vault. Van Helsing broke the silence by asking Arthur:

'Answer me now, my friend! Am I to proceed?'

Arthur sank to his knees, hid his face in his hands, and wailed in harrowing despair:

'Do as you will, Professor. Oh, do – for no . . . horror . . . ' he groaned as he slumped, and Quincey and I leapt towards him together, to take his arms and pull him away.

Behind us we heard the click of the closing lantern as Van Helsing laid it down. Then we watched him circle the circling Lucy-thing to remove from the chinks round the vault door some of the sacred emblem which earlier he had placed there. Then to our inexpressible horror we saw, when the Professor stood back, this female apparition, whose body had seemed every inch as physical as ours, pass into the tomb through an interstice which scarce a scalpel could penetrate. What sense of weak – faintly sick – but definitely glad relief we felt, when we saw the Professor calmly restoring the strings of putty to the edges of the door.

That done, he lifted the child and said:

'Come, my friends. No more can we do till tomorrow. There is a funeral at noon, so here shall we come soon after. The friends of the dead will be gone by two, and when the sexton lock the gate then shall *we* remain. Then there is much more to do, but not like this of tonight. As for this little one, he is not much harm, and by tomorrow night will be well. We shall leave him where the police will find him, as before. Then to home.' Patting Arthur's shoulder, he added gently:

'Friend Arthur he is now in the bitter waters, poor child. But by this time tomorrow, you will, please God, have passed them, and have drunk of the sweet. So do not overmuch mourn tonight.'

Arthur and Quincey came home with me, and we tried to cheer each other on the way. We had left the child in safety, and were terribly tired; so I think we all slept a little.

29 September, night.

A little before twelve o'clock we three – Arthur, Quincey Morris, and myself – called for the Professor. It was odd to notice that by tacit consent we had all put on black clothes. We got to the churchyard by half-past one, and strolled about in the furthest leafy corners until the gravediggers had completed their task, and the sexton, believing everyone had gone, had locked the gate – leaving us with the place to ourselves.

Van Helsing, instead of his little black bag, had with him a long leather one – something like a cricketing bag, and manifestly heavy.

When we heard the last of the footsteps fade up the road, we silently followed the Professor into the tomb. There he took from his bag the lantern, which he lit, and also two wax candles, which, when lighted, he stuck, by their own melting ends, on other coffins nearby. When he again lifted the lid off Lucy's coffin we all looked – Arthur trembling like an aspen – and saw the body lying there, in all its death-beauty.

But there was no love in my heart, nothing but loathing for the foul Thing which had taken Lucy's shape without her soul. I could see even Arthur's face grow hard as he looked. Presently he said to Van Helsing:

'Is this really Lucy's body? Or a demon in her shape?'

'It *is* her body, and yet *not*. But wait a while, and you shall see her as she was – and is.'

She seemed like a Nightmare Lucy to me as she lay there: the pointed teeth, the bloodstained, vulpine mouth – the whole figure, so carnally unspiritual, like a devilish mockery of Lucy's sweet purity in life.

Van Helsing, in his methodical manner, began taking various items from his bag and placing them ready for use. First, a soldering iron and some plumbing solder. Then a small oil-lamp, which gave out, when lit in a corner of the tomb, a gas which burned at fierce heat with a blue flame. Next, his operating knives, and a round wooden stake some two inches thick and three feet long. One end of it was hardened by charring, and it was sharpened to a fine point. With this stake came a heavy hammer, of the sort used in coal-cellars for breaking up the lumps. To me, a doctor's preparations for work are always stimulating, but the effect on Arthur and Quincey was clearly consternation. They both, however, kept their courage, and remained quiet.

When all was ready, Van Helsing said:

'Before we do anything, let me tell you this – it is out of the lore of the ancients who have study the Un-Dead. When they become such, there comes the curse of immortality. They cannot die, but must go on age after age adding new victims and multiplying the evils of the world. For all that die from their preying become themselves Un-Dead, and prey likewise. So the circle ever widens, like ripples from a stone thrown in the water.

'You, friend Arthur, if you had met that kiss before poor Lucy die – or again, last night when you open your arms to her – you would in time, when you have die, become *nosferatu*, as they say in Eastern Europe, and all time for ever would *you too* make more of those Un-Deads that so fill us with horror.'

Arthur took a deep breath, but said nothing.

The Professor went on:

'The career of this so unhappy dear lady is but just begun. Those children whose blood she suck are not as yet so much the worse. But if she live on, Un-Dead, more and more they lose their blood, and by her power they come to her. And so she draw their blood with that so wicked mouth. But if she die in truth, then all cease. The tiny wounds of the throats disappear, and they go back to their plays, unknowing ever. But what of *her*?

'When this now Un-Dead be made to rest as *true dead*, then the soul of the poor lady whom we love again shall be free. Instead of working wickedness by night, and debasing more by day, she shall take her place with the Angels. So that, my friend, it will be a blessed hand for her that strike the blow to set her free. To this I am willing, yes. But is there no man with a better right? To the joy to think hereafter in silent night when sleep is not:

'"It was *my* hand that sent her to the stars. The hand of him that loved her *best*. The hand that she would herself have choose, if only . . . "'?

'Is there no such one amongst us?'

We all looked at Arthur.

Seeing the infinite kindness which suggested that his should be the hand to restore Lucy to us — as the holiest of memories — Arthur stepped forward and said bravely, though his hand trembled, and his face was as pale as snow:

'From the bottom of my broken heart I thank you. Tell me what I must do.'

Van Helsing laid a hand on his shoulder, and said:

'A moment's courage, and it is done. This stake must be driven through her. It will be terrible ordeal, but then you will rejoice more than your pain was great; and from this grim tomb you will emerge as though you tread on air. But you must not falter when once begun. Only think that we, your true friends, are round you.'

'Go on,' said Arthur hoarsely. 'Tell me.'

'Take this stake in your left hand, place the point over her heart, and the hammer in your right. When we begin our prayer for the dead — that I shall read him — *strike hard in God's name*. That so all may be well with the dead that we love, and the Un-Dead pass away.'

Arthur took the stake and the hammer, his mind made up and his hands barely trembling.

Van Helsing opened his missal and began to read.

Quincey and I followed as well as we could.

Arthur placed the pointed stake over Lucy's coffined heart, and as I saw it dint her milky flesh — how I winced.

Then he struck with all his might.

The Thing in the coffin writhed hideously and a bloodcurdling screech rose out of the wide red lips. The body shook and quivered and twisted in wild contortions, the sharp white teeth champed together till the lips and mouth were awash with crimson foam.

But Arthur never faltered.

He looked like a figure of Thor as his untrembling arm rose and fell, driving deeper and deeper the mercy-bearing stake, while the blood from the piercèd heart welled up and spurted round it. His face was set, high duty shining through it, and the sight of his gallant resolution gave courage to our voices, as our prayers rang through the vault.

Slowly the writhing of the body waned, the teeth ceased to champ, and the face to quiver. Finally it lay still.

The terrible task was over.

The hammer fell from Arthur's hand. He reeled and would have fallen had we not caught him. Great drops of sweat bubbled out on his forehead, and his breath came in broken gasps. It had been an awful strain on him; and had he not been forced to his task by more than human considerations he could never have gone through with it. For a few minutes we were so taken up with him that we did not look towards the coffin. When we did, however, a murmur of startled surprise escaped both Quincey and myself.

We rushed to the coffin and must have gazed in so eagerly that Arthur too rose – for he had been seated on the ground – and came over to look too.

And what he saw caused a strange glad light to banish the agony from his eyes.

For there in the coffin lay no longer the foul Thing we had so dreaded and grown to hate, but Lucy as truly in life, with her face of unequalled sweet purity. True, there were there, as latterly in her life, the traces of care and pain; but these were all dear to us, for they proclaimed her truly Lucy. One and all we felt the holy calm that lay like sunshine over her wasted face and form was only an earthly symbol of that Calm she would enjoy for ever.

Embracing Arthur, Van Helsing said:

'And now, dear lad, forgive me?'

Arthur's reaction to the terrible strain came as he pressed the old man's hand to his lips, and exclaimed:

'Forgive you? God bless you that you have given my dear one her soul again, and me peace.' He laid his head on the Professor's breast and cried for a while silently, while we stood unmoving. When he raised his head Van Helsing said:

'Now, my child, you may kiss *her*. Kiss her dead lips if you will, as she would have you to, if only. For she is no longer the devil's Un-Dead. She is God's true dead, whose soul is with Him!'

Arthur bent down and kissed her lovingly.

Then we sent him and Quincey out of the tomb. The Professor and I sawed the top off the stake, leaving the point of it in the body. Then we cut off the head and filled the mouth with garlic. We soldered up the leaden coffin, screwed on the coffin lid, gathered up our belongings, and came away. When the Professor had locked the door he gave the key to Arthur.

Outside the air was sweet, the sun shone, the birds sang, and it seemed as if all nature were tuned to a different pitch. There was gladness and mirth and peace everywhere, and we were glad, albeit with a tempered joy.

Before we moved away Van Helsing said:

'Now, my friends, one step of our work is done – one the most harrowing to ourselves. But there remains a greater task: to hunt out the author of all this our sorrow, and to stamp him out. I have clues which we can follow; but it is a long and difficult task, with danger in it, and pain. Who then shall help me?'

Each of us took his hand, and the promise was made. Then said the Professor, as we started home:

'Two nights hence shall we dine together at seven of the clock with friend John. I shall entreat two others – two that you know not yet – and I shall then our plans unfold. Friend John, you come with me home, for I have much to consult about. Tonight I leave for Amsterdam, but shall return tomorrow night. And then our great quest begin.'

When we arrived at the Berkeley Hotel, Van Helsing found a telegram waiting for him:

Am coming up by train. Jonathan at Whitby.
Important news. *Mina Harker.*

The Professor was delighted.

'That wonderful Madame Mina,' he said. 'Pearl among women! She arrive, but I cannot stay. She must go to your house, friend John. You must meet her at the station. Telegraph her *en route*, so that she prepare.'

When the wire was despatched he had a cup of tea. Over it he told me of a diary kept by Jonathan Harker when abroad – and gave me a typewritten copy of it, as also of Mrs Harker's diary at Whitby.

'Study these well,' he said. 'When I am return you will be master of the facts, so to better our inquisition. Keep them safe, for there is in them much treasure. What is here told', he laid his hand gravely on the packet of papers, 'may be the beginning of the end of you, and me, and many another. Or it may sound the knell for the Un-Dead who walk the earth. Read all with the open mind.' He then made ready for his departure, and shortly after drove off to Liverpool Street.

I made my way to Paddington, where I arrived about fifteen minutes before the train came in.

The crowd melted away after the bustling fashion common to arrival platforms, and I was beginning to feel uneasy, lest I had missed my guest, when a tallish and very handsome young woman stepped up to me.

'Dr Seward?' she inquired.

'And you are Mrs Harker!' I answered at once, whereupon she held out her hand.

'I knew you from . . . poor dear Lucy's description. But—' She stopped suddenly, and a blush overspread her cheeks.

The flush that inflamed my own cheeks somehow set us both at ease, for it sympathetically echoed her own. I got her luggage, which included a typewriter, and, after I had sent a wire to my housekeeper to have a sitting-room and bedroom prepared at once for Mrs Harker, we took the Underground to Fenchurch Street.

She knew, of course, that my home was a lunatic asylum, but I noticed she was unable to repress a slight shiver when we entered.

She told me that, if she might, she would come presently to my study, as she had much to say. So here I am finishing this entry in my phonograph diary while I await her. As yet I have had no time to peruse the papers the Professor left with me, though they lie open before me.

Hmn.

I must get Mrs Harker interested in something, to make some reading time. Yes. Of course she does not yet know how precious time is, or what an undertaking lies before us. Above all, though, I must be careful not to frighten her.

But here she is.

22

Journals

MINA HARKER
29 September.

After I had tidied myself I went down to Dr Seward's study. I thought I heard him talking, but as he had pressed me to be quick, I knocked on the door.

'Come in,' he called out, and I entered.

To my surprise, he was quite alone, but on the table opposite him was what I knew at once by description to be a phonograph.

'I hope I did not keep you waiting,' I said. 'I . . . thought there was someone with you.'

With a smile he replied:

'I was only entering my diary.'

'Your diary?'

'I keep it in this.' He pointed to the phonograph.

I felt quite excited by such an idea, and blurted out:

'Why, this beats even shorthand! May I hear it say something?'

'Certainly,' he replied with alacrity, and reached to set it going. Then a troubled look overspread his face.

'The fact is,' he began awkwardly, 'I only keep my diary in it. And as it is – almost entirely – about my cases, it may be awkward – I mean . . . ' He stopped, and I tried to help him out of his embarrassment:

'You helped to attend poor Lucy at the end. Let me hear how she died. For, you know, she was very, very dear to me.'

To my amazement he answered with horror:

'Tell you of her death? Not for the wide world!'

'Why not?' I asked, but with a vague yet terrible feeling creeping over me.

Again Dr Seward paused, and I could see he was trying to invent an excuse. At length he stammered:

'You see, I do not know how to pick out *any particular part* of the diary.'

'Really?'

'Upon my honour,' he blushed.

I could not but smile, at which he grimaced. 'I gave myself away that time!' he confessed. 'But in fact it is true that, although I have been keeping the diary for months, it never once struck me how I might locate any particular section of it, before the lot is transcribed.'

By this time my mind was made up that the diary of a doctor who attended Lucy might have something to add to our knowledge of that terrible Being, and I said boldly:

'Then, Dr Seward, you had better let me copy it all out for you – on my typewriter.'

He grew to a positively deathly pallor as he cried:

'No, no! For all the world, I wouldn't let you hear that terrible story!'

Then it *was* terrible! My intuition had been correct! As my wondering eyes ranged the room, they could not but light on a bundle of familiar-looking typewriting on his desk. His eyes caught mine, and his kindly face flushed as with guilt.

Forgivingly I said:

'When you have read those diaries – my own, and my husband's also, which I have typed – you will know us . . . intimately. May we not know you as well?'

He is certainly of a noble nature, Dr Seward – poor dear Lucy was right about that. In response to my frankness he stood up and opened a large drawer, in which were several hollow cylinders of metal covered with dark wax. Shyly he said:

'Take the cylinders and listen to them in your bedroom. The first few are personal to me, and not too dreadful. Meanwhile I shall read through your diaries, and . . . by dinner we shall know each other well.'

He carried the phonograph upstairs himself and adjusted it for me. Now I shall learn something pleasant, I am sure. For it will tell me the other side of a true-love episode of which I know one side already . . .

DR SEWARD

29 September.

I was so absorbed in the astonishing tale told by Jonathan Harker that

I lost track of time. Mrs Harker was not down when the maid came to announce dinner, so I said:

'Probably she is tired. Let dinner wait an hour.' And I went on with my work. I had just finished Mrs Harker's diary when the lady herself came in. She looked desperately pretty – beautiful, even – but very sad, and her eyes were flushed with crying. This somehow moved me much. Of late I have had cause for tears myself, God knows! But the relief of weeping is denied a man; and now . . . the sight of Mrs Harker's bright eyes, moist with recent tears, went straight to my heart. So I said very gently;

'I fear I have distressed you.'

'Not distressed,' she replied, 'but I have been more touched than I can say by your grief. That is a wonderful machine, your phonograph, but cruel. The anguish of your heart, in your voice – no-one else must hear that ever again! There. I have copied out your words on my typewriter, and none other need now hear your heart beat, as I did.'

'No-one else shall ever even *know*,' I muttered.

She laid her hand on mine and said seriously:

'But they must!'

'But why?'

'Because your very suffering is a part of the whole dreadful story. A part of poor dead Lucy's death, and all that led to it. And because, in the struggle which we have before us, to rid the earth of this terrible monster, we must share all the knowledge we can.'

'How much else do you know already?'

'Jonathan and I have been working day and night since Professor Van Helsing saw us. He – Jonathan – is gone to Whitby to get more information. Tomorrow he will be back here to help us. You see, between ourselves we must keep no secrets. Working together, in absolute trust, we will be stronger in our fight.' She looked at me so appealingly, yet with such courage and resolution, that I gave in at once.

'Come,' I said. 'Dinner is ready. When we have eaten you shall learn everything else I know, and I will answer all your questions.'

MINA HARKER

29 September

After dinner Dr Seward took me back to his study. He fetched the phonograph from my room, and I took my typewriter. He placed me in a comfortable chair, and arranged the phonograph so that I could stop it without getting up. Then he very thoughtfully took a chair with his back to me, so that I might feel more at ease, and began to read. I put the forked metal to my ears and listened to the later cylinders.

When the terrible story of Lucy's death – and all that followed – was done, I lay back in my chair powerless. Fortunately I am not of a fainting disposition, but when Dr Seward saw me he jumped up in alarm, produced a case-bottle from a cupboard, and gave me some brandy, which soon restored me somewhat. My brain was all a whirl, and but for the grateful belief that dearest Lucy was now, at last, at peace, I do not think I could have borne it without hysterics. It is all so dreadful that, had I not known of Jonathan's experience in Transylvania, I simply could not have believed it.

As it was, to allay my distress, by engaging in some useful activity, I took the cover off my typewriter, and said to Dr Seward:

'Let me copy this out. It should be ready for Dr Van Helsing to read.'

Dr Seward protested:

'The Professor already knows everything.'

But I insisted:

'Your diary may remind him of some vital details or dates. And the others must read it too. Jonathan, Lord Godalming, and Mr Morris.'

Dr Seward accordingly set the phonograph to slow, and I began transcribing from the seventh cylinder. I used manifold, and so made three copies at once. Meanwhile Dr Seward went about the nightly round of his patients.

When he had finished he came back and sat near me, reading, so that I did not feel too lonely while I worked. How thoughtful he is – the world seems full of good men, even if there are monsters in it too. Before I left him I remembered what Jonathan said about the Professor's perturbation at reading something in an evening paper at Exeter. So, seeing that Dr Seward keeps his newspapers, I have borrowed piles of the *Westminster Gazette* and the *Pall Mall Gazette*, and brought them to my room.

The *Dailygraph* helped us somewhat to understand the terrible events at Whitby, when Count Dracula landed, so . . . since I am not sleepy . . .

DR SEWARD

30 September.

Mr Harker arrived at nine. He is uncommonly clever, to judge from his face, and full of energy. Also a man of great nerve, it appears. That going down to the vault a second time was a remarkable piece of daring. After reading his account of it I was prepared to meet a good specimen of manhood, but hardly the quiet, business-like gentleman who arrived this morning.

Later.

After lunch Harker and his wife went back to their room, and as I passed a while ago I heard the click of her typewriter. They are hard at it. Mrs Harker says they are knitting together in chronological order every scrap of evidence they have. Harker has the letters between the consignee of the boxes at Whitby and the carriers in London who took charge of them. He is now reading his wife's typescript of my diary. I wonder what they will make of it. Ah, here he is. . .

Later.

Strange that it never struck me that the very next house to here might be the Count's hiding-place. Goodness knows, in hindsight, we have had enough clues from Renfield! If only – but no. Stop. That way lies madness.

Harker has gone back to collate more material. He says that by dinner they should have a whole connected narrative. He thinks that in the meantime I should see Renfield, as hitherto he has been a sort of index to the movements of the Count. I hardly see this yet, but when I get at the dates perhaps I shall. How useful that Mrs Harker has turned my cylinders into type. Otherwise . . .

Renfield I found sitting placidly in his room, hands folded, smiling benignly, seemingly sane as a judge. I sat down and talked with him, and he spoke seriously of going home, a subject he has never before mentioned during his sojourn here. Indeed, he talked so sensibly, and so confidently about getting his discharge, that I believe that, had I not had the chat with Harker and read the letters, and the dates of his outbursts, I should have been close to signing him out.

As it is, I am darkly suspicious.

All those outbreaks were in some way linked with the proximity of the

Count. What then does his present calm mean? Is it his serene conviction as to the Vampire's ultimate triumph?

Remember, too, how zoophagous he has shown himself. And how, in his ravings outside the chapel door of the deserted house he spoke of 'Master'.

So I came away mistrustful of his mood, and I have warned the attendant to watch him closely, and to have a strait-waistcoat ready.

JONATHAN HARKER

29 September; in train to London.

When I received Mr Billington's courteous message that he would give me any information in his power, I thought it best to visit Whitby at once. It was now my object to trace that hideous cargo of the Count's to its destination in London. Billington junior, a nice lad, met me at the station, and took me to his father's house, where they insisted that I stay the night.

They are hospitable, with true Yorkshire hospitality: give a guest everything, and leave him free to do as he likes. They all knew I was busy, and that my stay was short, and Mr Billington had ready in his office all the papers concerning the boxes. It gave me quite a turn to see again one of the letters I had seen on the Count's table before I knew of his diabolical plans. Everything had been planned with systematical precision. Witness the invoice, which detailed:

'Fifty cases of common earth, for experimental use.'

Also the letter to Carter Paterson, and their reply; both of which I got copied. This was all the information Mr Billington could give me, so I went down to the port and saw the coastguards, the Customs officers, and the harbour-master. They all had something to say about the strange forsaken ship, which is already secure in local tradition, yet no-one could add to the simple description:

'Fifty cases of common earth.'

I then saw the station-master, who kindly put me in communication with the men who received the boxes. Their tally was exact with the list, and they had nothing to add except that the boxes were 'main and mortal heavy', and that shifting them was dry work. One of them added that it was hard lines that there wasn't any gentleman 'such-like as yourself, squire' to show appreciation of their efforts in a liquid form — which hint of course I took.

30 September.

The station-master was good enough to put me on to his old compan-ion at King's Cross, who in turn, when I arrived there in the morning, put me at once in communication with the proper officials, and I saw that their tally was correct with the original invoice.

From there I went on to Carter Paterson's central office, where I met with the utmost courtesy. They looked up the transaction in their day-book and letter-book, and at once telephoned to their King's Cross office for further details. The men who had done the teaming were at once sent over, and with them the way-bill for the delivery of the boxes to Carfax.

Here again I found the tally agreeing exactly, and the carriers' men well able to supplement the written facts with verbal details on the dusty nature of the job and the consequent thirst engendered in the operators. On my affording an opportunity, through the medium of the currency of the realm, of the allaying at a later period this occupational evil, one of the men remarked:

'That 'ere 'ouse, guv'nor, is the rummiest I ever was in. Blyme, but it ain't been touched sence a hundred year! There was dust that thick in the place that you might have slep' on it without 'urtin' of yer bones. An' the place was that neglected that yer might 'ave smelled ole Jerusalem in it. But the ole chapel – that took the kike, that did! Me and me mate, we thort we wouldn't never git aht quick enough. Lor', I wouldn't take less nor a quid a moment to stay there arter dark.'

Having been in the house, I could well believe him, and if he knew what I know, he would, I think, have raised his terms a hundredfold.

Of one thing I am now satisfied: that all the boxes which arrived at Whitby from Varna in the *Demeter* were safely deposited in the old chapel of Carfax. There should be fifty of them there, unless any have since been removed – as from Dr Seward's diary I fear.

I shall try to see the carter who took away the boxes from Carfax when Renfield attacked them. By following up this clue we may learn a good deal.

Later.

Mina and I have worked all day, and all the papers are now in order.

MINA HARKER
30 September.

I am so glad that I hardly know how to contain myself. It is, I suppose, a reaction from my haunting fear that this terrible affair, and the re-opening of his old wound, might act detrimentally on Jonathan. I saw him off for Whitby with as brave a face as I could, but I was sick with apprehension. The effort has, however, done him good. He was never so resolute, so strong, so full of volcanic energy, as at present. It is just as Professor Van Helsing said: Jonathan really is true grit, and he improves under strain that would kill a weaker nature. He came back full of determination, even hope, and we have got everything in order for tonight.

I feel myself quite wild with excitement.

I suppose one ought to pity anything so hunted as the Count; but that is just it: this Thing is not human — nor even beast. To read Dr Seward's account of Lucy's death, and what followed, is enough to dry up all the springs of pity in anyone's heart.

Later.

Lord Godalming and Mr Morris arrived earlier than we expected. Dr Seward was out on business and had taken Jonathan with him, so I had to greet them. It was for me a painful meeting for it brought back all poor Lucy's hopes of only a few months ago. Of course they had heard Lucy speak of me, and it seemed that Dr Van Helsing, too, had been quite 'blowing my trumpet', as Mr Morris expressed it.

Poor fellows — neither is aware that I know all about the proposals they made to Lucy.

I also knew, from Dr Seward's diary, that they had been in at Lucy's death — her real death — so I told them that I had read all the papers and diaries, and now had typewritten them up. I then gave them each a collated copy to read in the library.

Lord Godalming thanked me quietly, and said:

'Mrs Harker, I know you loved my Lucy . . . ' Here he turned away and covered his face with his hands.

I could hear the tears in his silence.

Mr Morris, with instinctive delicacy, just laid a hand for a moment on his friend's shoulder, and then walked quietly out of the room.

I suppose there is something in woman's nature that encourages a man to break down before her and express his tender emotions, without feeling it derogatory to his manhood. At any rate, when Lord Godalming found himself alone with me, he sat down on the sofa and gave way utterly. I sat beside him, took his hand – I hope he didn't think it forward of me – and said to him, for I could see that his heart was breaking:

'I loved dear Lucy, and I know what you and she were to each other. She and I – we were like sisters. Well, now she is gone, will you not let me be like a sister to you too? Let my sympathy be of some little service, for Lucy's sake?'

In an instant Lord Goldaming grew quite hysterical with grief. Raising his open hands, he beat his palms together in a perfect agony of despair. He stood up, then sat down again, and the tears rained down his cheeks. I felt an infinite pity for him, and opened my arms unthinkingly. With a sob he laid his head on my shoulder and cried like a wearied child, while he shook with helpless emotion.

I felt this big, sorrowing man's head resting on me, like that of the baby that some day may lie on my bosom, and I stroked his hair as though he were my own child.

And I never thought, at the time, how strange it all was.

Shortly his sobs ceased. Sitting upright apologetically, he confessed that for weeks past – weeks of weary days and sleepless nights – he had been unable to speak with anyone, as even a man must speak in his sorrow.

'Now all that has changed,' he said, as he dried his eyes, 'now you and I shall be as brother and sister, shall we not, all our lives – for our darling Lucy's sake?'

'For Lucy,' I said, as we clasped hands.

A short while later, as I walked along the corridor I found Mr Morris staring out of a window. Turning, as he heard my footsteps, he asked:

'How is Art?' Then, noticing my red eyes, he went on:

'Ah, I see you have been comforting him. Some guys get all the luck!'

Beneath his levity Mr Morris was bearing his own troubles so bravely that my heart bled for him. Seeing my typescript in his hand, I knew that, having read it, he must realize how much I knew; so I urged him:

'Will you, too, be not ashamed to come to me for comfort?'

Mr Morris took my hand, raised it to his lips, and kissed it with grateful decorum. Somehow this seemed such scant consolation for so brave and unselfish a soul that impulsively I embraced him, and kissed him full upon the lips. Tears rose in his eyes, and there was a momentary choking in his throat before he swore – quite calmly, but with such a radiant smile:

'Little girl, that's one kiss you won't never regret!' Then he went into the study to his friend.

'Little girl!' The very words he had used to Lucy.

23

Before and After Dinner

30 September.

I got home at five o'clock, and found that Godalming and Morris had already studied the transcript of the various diaries and letters which Harker's wonderful wife had made. Harker had not yet returned from his visit to the carriers' men, of whom Dr Hennessey had written to me. Mrs Harker gave us a cup of tea, and I can honestly say that, for the first time since I have lived in it, this old house seemed like *home*. When we had finished, Mrs Harker said:

'Dr Seward, may I ask a favour? I want to see your patient, Mr Renfield. Do let me see him. What you have said of him in your diary interests me so much!'

She looked so appealing and so pretty that I could not refuse her, so I took her with me. When I told Renfield that a lady would like to see him, he answered curtly:

'Why?'

'She wants to see everyone in our house.'

'Oh, very well,' he said. 'But just wait a minute till I tidy up.' His method of tidying was typically peculiar:

First he emptied all the flies and spiders from all his little boxes into a single pile. Then, before I had time to prevent him, he scooped up the pile, stuffed all the insects into his mouth, and swallowed them. Having completed his disgusting task, he said cheerfully:

'Now let the lady come in.' Then he sat on the edge of his bed, head down, but with his eyelids raised, to inspect her as she entered. For a moment I thought that he might have some homicidal intent – I remembered how quiet he had been just before he attacked me in my study – so I stood where I could seize him at once if he attempted to assault her.

Mrs Harker came into the room with an easy gracefulness which would at once command the respect of any lunatic – easiness being a quality most mad people can respect. She walked over to him, smiling pleasantly, and held out her hand.

'Good evening, Mr Renfield,' she greeted him warmly.

He eyed her all over intently, with a set frown on his face. This soon gave way to wonder, which rapidly merged into doubt. Then, to my astonishment, he said:

'You're not the girl the doctor wanted to marry, are you? You can't be, you know, for she's dead!'

Mrs Harker smiled sweetly as she replied:

'Oh no! I have a husband of my own, Mr Renfield, to whom I was married before I ever saw Dr Seward, or he me. I am Mrs Harker.'

'What are you doing here?'

'My husband and I are visiting Dr Seward.'

'Then don't stay.'

'But why not?'

I thought that this style of conversation might not please Mrs Harker any more than it did me, so I joined in:

'How did you know, Renfield, that I wanted to marry anyone?'

His reply was witheringly contemptuous. Hardly taking his eye off Mrs Harker, he scoffed:

'What an asinine question!'

'I don't see why, Mr Renfield,' said Mrs Harker, at once championing me.

Renfield replied to her with as much courtesy as he had shown contempt for me:

'You will, of course, understand, Mrs Harker, that when a man is honoured – nay, loved! – as is our medical host here, everything about him becomes of intense interest to the little flock he herds. Dr Seward is loved not only by his household and his friends, but even by his patients, who, being some of them hardly in mental equilibrium, are apt to confuse cause and effect.

'Since I myself have been an inmate of a lunatic asylum, I have not infrequently remarked that the sophistic traits of certain inmates are not above *non cause*, nor even *ignoratio elenchi*.'

My eyes opened wide at this new development: my own pet luna-tic – the most intractable of his type that ever I met with – talking elemental philosophy, and with the polished air of a gentleman. I wonder if Mrs Harker's presence can have touched some chord in his memory. Certainly, if this new aspect of Renfield was due to her unconscious influence, she must have some very rare power.

We continued to talk. Renfield seeming reasonable, Mrs Harker ventured, looking at me questioningly as she began, to lead him to his favourite topic. I was again astonished, for he addressed himself to the question with the impartiality of utter sanity – even concerning himself:

'Why,' he reflected, 'I myself once embraced a strange belief. No wonder my friends were alarmed, and insisted on my being restrained. I used to fancy, you know, that life was a positive and perpetual entity, and that by consuming a multitude of live things, no matter how low in the scale of creation, one's own life might be indefinitely prolonged. On one occasion – and Dr Seward here will bear me out – I even attempted to kill him personally: for the purpose of strengthening my own vital powers – by the assimilation into my body of his life, through the medium of his blood. Sanctioned, of course, by the Scriptural wisdom:

'"For the blood is the life."

'Isn't that true, doctor?'

I nodded warily, temporarily dumbfounded by such urbane eloquence from a madman who, not ten minutes before, had gobbled up all those spiders and flies. Looking at my watch, I saw that I should go to the station to meet Van Helsing, so I told Mrs Harker we must leave. To Renfield she said:

'Good bye, and I hope I may see you again, under auspices pleasanter to yourself.'

Renfield, to my further astonishment, replied:

'Good bye, my dear. I pray God I never see your sweet face again. May He bless and keep you!'

At the station Van Helsing jumped down from his carriage with the eager nimbleness of a boy. Rushing up to me, he cried:

'Ah, friend John, how goes all? Well? So! I have been busy for I come here to stay if need be. All affairs are settled with me and I have much to tell. Madame Mina is with you? Yes. And her so fine husband? And Arthur? And my friend Quincey? All with you too? Good, good.'

As we drove to the house I told the Professor how even my own diary had proved of service:

'All through Mrs Harker's—'

'Ah, that wonderful Madame Mina!' the Professor interrupted me.

'She has man's brain – brain of a man much gifted, too! – and woman's heart. The good God fashion her for a goodly purpose, yes, when He make that so good union. However, friend John, up to now our fortune she make that woman of great help to us. But after tonight she must nothing do in this so terrible affair. We men we pledge to destroy this evil ghoul; but there no part in it is for a woman. No, no.'

'But why not?'

'Even if she be not harm, her heart may fail in so much ghastly horrors. Then hereafter she dreadfully suffer – both in waking, from her nerves, and in sleep, from her dreams. Besides she is young, beautiful, and not so long marry! There be *other things* to think!'

'What to do you mean, Professor?'

Brushing aside my query, he hurried on:

'You say she have wrote up all? Good, good. Then must she consult with us tonight. But tomorrow', the Professor emphasized sternly, 'Madame Mina she say byebye to this work, and we men go alone.'

I heartily agreed, then told the Professor what we had found in his absence: that the house Dracula had bought was immediately next to my own.

For a moment the Professor looked as if poleaxed. Then a terrible concern overclouded his countenance:

'Oh, that we have know before!' he lamented. 'We might have catch him in time to save poor Lucy. However, the spilt milk cries not after, as you English say. We shall not think behind us, then, but go forward to our end.'

Then from his great excitement he fell into a silence that lasted till we entered my gateway. Before we went up to dress for dinner, he said to Mrs Harker:

'Friend John, he tell me, Madame Mina, that you have all things that have been typed, up to this moment now.'

'Not quite now, Professor,' she replied conscientiously. 'Everything up to this morning.'

'But why not up to *now*?' he rebuked her with good-humoured zeal.

Mrs Harker broke out in a most becoming blush. Taking a paper from her pocket, she said:

'Dr Van Helsing, this is my record of today. There is little in it except what is . . . extremely personal. Must it go on record?'

The Professor read over her paper gravely. Handing it back, he said:

'It only should make your husband lover you the more. And all we, your friends, more honour you.'

Mrs Harker re-pocketed her paper with another blush and a strangely brilliant smile.

So now, up to this very hour, all our pooled information is complete. The Professor took away one copy of the documents to read after dinner, and before our meeting, which is fixed for nine o'clock. The rest of us already know everything. When we meet in the study we shall all be fully equipped to plan our battle with this terrible enemy.

MINA HARKER'S JOURNAL

When we met in Dr Seward's study after dinner, we unconsciously formed into a committee. Professor Van Helsing took the head of the table, to which Dr Seward motioned him as he came into the room. He made me sit next to him on his right, and asked me to act as secretary. Jonathan sat near me, and opposite us were Lord Godalming, Dr Seward, and Mr Morris – Lord Godalming being next the Professor, and Dr Seward in the centre.

When we were all sitting comfortably, the Professor said:

'It were good I tell you of the *kind* of enemy we face. I then make know what of the history of this *individual Dracula* has been ascertain for me. After, we discuss how to *act*.

'Now there are, you know, such beings as *vampires*' – here he nodded with very grave emphasis. 'Even had we not the proofs of unhappy experience, the teachings of past ages give conclusive. I admit I too was sceptic – too long, alas – and only could believe such horror when it thunder on my ear:

'"See, see! I prove!"

'Alas, poor Lucy. If only – but that is past, Lucy at peace, and we now must so work that *other* souls not perish, whiles we can save. *Nosferatu*, you see, do not die like the bee, when he sting once. *Nosferatu* is only *stronger*, and have *yet more power to work evil*. This Vampire Dracula is of himself so strong as *twenty mortal men*. And of cunning he is more than mortal, for his cunning have the growth of down the age. *And* he have all the aids of necromancy which is, as his entomology imply, the divination by the dead – and all the dead nigh he are for him at command.'

As the Professor paused to sip from a glass of water, Mr Morris seized his opportunity to comment:

'I ain't no medicine man myself, but it seems to me this Dracula guy sure is *vermin* – yeah? And I ain't never yet met no vermin that a Winchester could not cure.'

The Professor frowned reprovingly:

'Count Dracula is brute, yet more than brute. He is devil in callous, and his heart is not. He can appear at will in any forms that are to him. He can, within his range, direct the elements: the storm, the fog, the thunder. He command all meaner things: as the rat, the owl, and the bat – the moth, the fox, and the wolf. He can grow big and shrink small. Even at times he can vanish all away. How then are we to conquer him? How find his where, and him at last destroy?'

I think that, round the table, our faces must have betrayed our consternation bordering on despair, for the Professor continued:

'Indeed, my friends. It is terrible task we undertake, for if we lose, then he must surely win! And where end we? Life – life of me – is nothings, yes. I heed him not. But to fail here is not mere life or death, but that *we* become as *him* – henceforward foul things of the night, like him, without heart or conscience, preying on the bodies *and the souls* of even those we love so very best. To us then for ever are the gates of heaven shut – for who should open them again to us? We strand for ever, abhorred by all. A blot on the face of God's sunshine. An arrow in His side.

'So should we shrink? Between our duty and this dreadful?

'For me I say no, but then I am old and life's bird song and music love lie far away behind. You others, you are young. Some have sorrow seen, but all can hope for fairer days not yet. What say?'

When the Professor concluded, my husband looked in my eyes, and I in his. Between us there was no doubt, and:

'I answer for Mina and myself,' said Jonathan.

'Count me in, Professor,' said Mr Morris, laconical as ever.

'I am with you,' said Lord Godalming. 'For Lucy's sake.'

Dr Seward simply nodded.

The Professor stood up, laid his golden crucifix on the table, and held out his hands on either side. I took his right hand, and Lord Godalming his left. Jonathan held my right with his left and stretched across to Mr Morris. Thus was our solemn compact sworn. My heart felt icy cold, but never for a moment did it occur to me to draw back. We resumed our places, and Professor Van Helsing went on with a grave cheerfulness which showed that the serious work had begun.

'Well,' he reflected encouragingly, 'you know what dreadful enemy we contend against, however we too are not without our strengths. We have on our side *power of combination* — a power denied to the vampire kind. Also we have resources of *science*. Plus we are *free*, and the hours of the day are ours equally with the night. Moreover all we have self-devotion in a cause not selfish. These things are much. Now let us consider the limitations of vampire in general, yes?'

With nods we all agreed.

'In old Greece,' Professor Van Helsing continued, 'in old Rome, the vampire he flourish terrific. In Germany all over, in France, in India, even in the China, so far from us in all ways, there even is he, and the peoples fear him still. He have follow the wake of the berserker Icelander, the devil-begotten Hun, Slav, Saxon, and Magyar. Thus the vampire live on experience. The vampire live on, and cannot be kill by merely passing of the time. He flourish whenever he can fatten on the blood of the living true. Even more, as already we have see, *he even can grow younger* — then his vital faculties grow strenuouser and marvellous refresh — when his special pabulum is plenty. But he cannot flourish without this diet: he eat not normal as we. Even friend Jonathan, who live with the Count for weeks, did *never see him eat*. Yes, yes?'

'Not once,' agreed Jonathan. 'Always some story about having already dined.'

The Professor pursed his lips in grim satisfaction.

'And of this particular Dracula,' he inquired somewhat rhetorically, 'what else we know? That he throw no shadow. That he make in the mirror no reflect, as Jonathan again observe. That he have the strength of many in his hand — witness again Jonathan when he shutting door against the wolfs, and when he help him from the diligence too. That Count Dracula also can *transform himself to wolf*, as after ship reaching Whitby — when he tear open the dog. That also he may *fly as bat*, as Madame Mina saw him on the window at Whitby. Again as friend John saw him fly from this so near house he have taken, and friend Quincey at the window of Miss Lucy.'

'Is there not also', asked Dr Seward, clearing his throat, 'the bizarre phenomenon of the mist?'

'Yes, yes,' applauded the Professor. 'Sometimes he come in mist which he create – that noble ship's captain prove him of this. And yet it seem the distance he can make this mist is limit, to near around himself. Also, he come on moonlight rays as elemental dust – as Jonathan experiencing those awful beauty sisters in the Castle. Other time he become microscope small – as we ourselves saw Miss Lucy, ere at peace, slip through the breadth of one hair, through door into her tomb. This Dracula too he *see through the dark* – no small power this, in a world half shut from light.'

'Can't we press on, Professor,' asked Mr Morris, in his polite American way, 'with how to send this stinking varmint to the hell where he belongs?'

'Soon, soon,' beamed Professor Van Helsing. 'But first, for the better of our plans, please hear me through. Count Dracula, you see, he can do all these things, *yet he is not free.* Nay, even he is more prisoner than the galley slaves, or the madman in his cell. He cannot go *all* where he lust, for even he, not of nature, has yet to obey *some* of nature's laws – why, we know not. For instances of this:

'He may not enter anywhere at the first, unless someone of the household bid him to come. Though after he can come as he please. Even vitaller for our plans' – here the Professor flashed a glance of benevolent triumph at Mr Morris – 'the vampire's power cease suddenly with rising of the day. For fear of touching by the sun must he retreat to his earth-cell, his coffin-home, the place unhallowed – and there lie helpless until night come round afresh. It too is said that he only can pass running water at slack or flood of tide. Then there are things which so afflict him out of his power – as the garlic, that we know of. Also things sacred, as this symbol, my crucifix, from which presence the vampire must take his presence far off, and trembling with respect. Others, yes, like the branch of wild rose: on his coffin it keep him that he move not from it. Plus a sacred bullet fired into the coffin should kill him so he be true dead. As for the stake through the heart of him, we know already of its peace. Or the cut-off head that giveth rest. Praises be.'

As the Professor quietly crossed himself, Mr Morris leaned over and murmured to Lord Godalming:

'Sacred bullets will sure do me.'

'Thus,' the Professor explained, 'when we find the habitation of this man-that-was, we can confine him to his coffin and destroy him, if we play the cards we know. But we must be ware. This Dracula he is clever.

I have ask my friend Arminius, of University in Budapest, to make his record. From all he tell me the Count must indeed have been being that Voivode Dracula who won his name against the Turk, over the great river, on the very frontier of Turkey-land. If so, then was he no common man: for centuries famous as most clever, cunningest and brave of the 'land beyond the forest'. That mighty brain and that iron resolve went with him to his grave, and so now array against us.

'The Draculas were, say Arminius, a great and noble race though sometimes having scions rumoured to deal with the Evil One. They learn his secrets in the Scholomance, amongst the mountains, over Lake Hermanstadt, where the Devil he claim every tenth scholar as his due. In the records are words as *stregoica* – witch; *ordog* and *pokol* – Satan and hell. Also in one manuscript is this very Dracula describe as *wampyr*, which all we understand too well. There have been from the loins of this very one, great men and good women, whose graves' – here Professor Van Helsing shook his head and sighed – 'whose graves make sacreder the earth where alone this foulness can dwell.'

'I don't quite follow you there, Professor,' said Dr Seward politely.

'What I say', the Professor retorted emphatically, 'is precisely our greatest terror! That this evil thing is root deeply in all good – in soil all barren of holy memory, this Dracula he cannot rest.'

For some time Mr Morris had been staring abstractedly at the window. Now he got up quietly, and went out of the room. When the door closed behind him, the Professor went on:

'Next to settle what we do. We know from the inquiry of Jonathan that from the Castle to Whitby came fifty boxes of earth, all which deliver at Carfax. We also know that *some* of these boxes have been remove. It seem to me, so, our first step must find if all the rest of boxes remain in the house beyond that wall where we look today. Or have any more been move? If yes latter, we must trace—'

Here we were interrupted in a very startling way. Up from the garden came the sound of a pistol shot and the glass of Dr Seward's window was shattered by a bullet, which, ricocheting from the top of the embrasure, struck the far wall of the room. Involuntarily I shrieked out loudly as the men all jumped to their feet. Lord Godalming flew over to the window and threw up the sash. As he did so we heard Mr Morris's voice below:

'Sorry to alarm you folks. I'll be up in a minute to explain.' Back with us round the table, he said:

'I ask your pardon, Mrs Harker, most sincerely. I must have frightened you terribly. But the fact is that while the Professor was talking I saw a big bat flap silently to perch on the windowsill. I never liked the brutes, and following recent events I detest them absolutely. So, not wanting to shoot this one through Dr Seward's window, I went to have a pot at him from outside.'

'Did you *hit* it?' asked Professor Van Helsing eagerly.

'I fancy not, for it flew away into the wood.' Mr Morris lapsed into silence, evidently disgruntled by his failure to kill the bat, and the Professor continued:

'We must trace all fifty boxes, and then either kill this monster in his lair or sterilize the earth in his coffin, so no more he find safety in it. Thus we force him into form of man before sunset, to tackle him most weak.

'For you, Madame Mina, this night is the end – until all be well. You are too precious to have such risk. When we part tonight, you no more must question. We shall tell you all in good time. We others are men, so able to bear, and shall act the more free that you share not the danger as we.'

All the men, even Jonathan, agreed wholeheartedly with the Professor, and – though it was a bitter pill for me to swallow – I could not sensibly protest, and so accepted their chivalrous concern for me as graciously as I could.

Mr Morris broke his silence:

'I vote we search his house right now. Swift action may save another victim.'

So the meeting concluded, and the men have gone round to Carfax, armed, and with means to break into Count Dracula's house. Manlike, they advised me to go to bed and sleep – as if a woman could sleep, when those she loves are in such danger!

Midnight.

I shall lie down now and pretend to sleep, lest Jonathan be anxious about me when he returns.

24

Into October

DR SEWARD'S DIARY

1 October. 4 a.m.

Just as we were leaving the house, an urgent message was brought asking if I would see Renfield at once, as he had something of the utmost importance to say to me. I told the messenger I would attend to Renfield in the morning, since at the moment I was extremely busy.

The attendant remarked:

'I have never seen Renfield so eager, sir. I fear . . . well, that if you don't see him soon, he'll throw one of his violent fits.'

I knew the man would not venture such an opinion lightly, so I said:

'Very well,' and I asked the others to wait a few minutes for me, as I had to see my patient.

'Take me with you, friend John,' said the Professor. 'Renfield's case in your diary interest me much, and he may have bearing on our enemy. I should like to see him especially, your permitting, when his mind is disturbed as now.'

'May I come also?' asked Lord Godalming.

'Me too?' said Quincey Morris.

I nodded, apprehensive that otherwise my companions might proceed to Carfax without me, and we all went down the passage together.

Renfield we found in a state of considerable excitement, yet far more rational than I had ever known him before. There was an unusual understanding of himself, which was unlike anything I had ever met with in a lunatic, and he took it for granted that his reasoning would prevail with others entirely sane.

We all five went into the room, and Renfield's instant request, for the moment ignoring his other visitors, was that I should at once release him from the asylum and send him home. This he backed up with arguments regarding his complete recovery, and adduced his own present sanity.

'I appeal to your friends,' Renfield then said suddenly. 'Confident that they will not mind sitting in judgement on my case. By the way, you have not introduced me.'

I was so much astonished, and there was such a certain dignity in the man's manner, that I at once announced:

'Lord Godalming; Professor Van Helsing; Mr Jonathan Harker; Mr Quincey Morris, of Texas – gentlemen, Mr Renfield.'

He shook hands with each of them, amd particularly welcomed:

'Lord Godalming, I had the honour of seconding your father at the Windham – and I grieve to know, by your holding the title, that he is no more. He was a man loved and honoured by all who knew him, and in his youth was, I believe, the inventor of a burnt rum punch much patronized on Derby night. Mr Morris, you should be proud of your great state. Its reception into the Union was a precedent which may have far-reaching effects hereafter, when the Pole and Tropics swear allegiance to the Stars and Stripes.

'And what a pleasure to meet Van Helsing! Sir, I make no apology for omitting your conventional prefix. For when an individual has revolutionized therapeutics, by his discovery of the continuous evolution of brain matter, why limit him to one of a class? What fool would presume, I argue by well-deserved analogy, to address the great Plato as "Professor"?

'Well, gentlemen,' he addressed my companions ensemble, 'you who, by your communal possession of such superior natural gifts: to you I appeal for judgement: whether I am not at least as sane as most free men at large. As for Dr Seward, humanitarian and medico-jurist as well as scientist, I appeal with confidence to his renowned sense of moral duty: whether the moment has not now arrived, to restore me to my liberty?' Renfield made this last appeal with a courtly power of persuasion by which we were all taken aback – even I who knew him of old.

However, in view of his history of sudden changes, sometimes traumatic, I contented myself for the moment with a promise that, as he appeared to be improving rapidly, I would have a longer chat with him in the morning, and would then see what I could do to meet his wishes. This did not at all satisfy him, for he retorted sharply:

'Dr Seward, my desire is to go at once – now – this very moment. Time presses, and in our implicit contract with the relentless old scytheman it is the vital essence. So I beg you to let me go. Now.'

He looked at me keenly, and, seeing the negative in my eyes, appealed to my companions:

'Then must I shift the ground of my request to *the sake of others*. I am not at liberty to detail my reasons, but could you look into my heart, good sirs, you must applaud the sentiments of duty that spur me. More, you would count me amongst the truest of your friends.' Again he regarded us with eager entreaty.

I now was persuaded that this fluent switching of his method was but another phase of his madness, so I determined to let him go on a little longer, judging that he would, like all lunatics, give himself away in the end.

Van Helsing, meanwhile, was gazing at Renfield with the utmost intensity, his eyebrows united in concentration. In a tone as of one addressing an equal, he asked:

'Mr Renfield, can not you frankly tell to us your real reason for wishing to be free tonight? I will undertake that if you will, then Dr Seward will allow to you such privilege of freedom which you seek.'

Renfield shook his head sadly, poignant regret all over his face.

The Professor went on:

'Come, sir, bethink. You argue on strengths of your reason. Well, then. Be reasonable. Help us, that we may help you.'

Renfield shook his head again:

'Dr Van Helsing, if I were free to speak I should not hesitate. But I am not my own master in this matter. Consequently I can only plead with you to trust me. If you refuse me, the responsibility' – glancing sorrowfully at me – 'shall not be mine.'

'Come, my friends,' said I, a trifle impatiently. 'We have work to do. Goodnight, Renfield.'

As I moved to the door a new change came over the patient. He started towards me so swiftly that for an instant I tensed for another homicidal attack. My fears, however, were groundless, for he sank to his knees and held up two imploring hands in a manner really quite biblical.

'I'm sorry, Renfield,' I said gently.

This caused him to wring his hands in pitiful supplication, pour forth a torrent of repetitious entreaty, meanwhile drenching both his cheeks with emotional tears.

'Come, gentlemen,' I said uncomfortably, not wishing my friends to be embarrassed by the lunatic's lack of control – but at this Renfield again became less garbled:

'Oh, let me *implore* you, Dr Seward. Free me from this house at once. Send me away where you will. Send keepers with – keepers with whips and chains. Have them take me in a strait-waistcoat, manacled and leg-ironed. Put me in prison, if you will, oh but *let me out of here.*'

'Really, Renfield,' I began, but:

'Ooooh,' he ranted on. 'I pray you all *to save my soul* and LET ME GO,' he fairly bellowed.

I knew that the longer this went on the wilder he would get, and so would bring on a fit, so I took him by the hand and pulled him up.

'Come,' I said sternly, 'no more of this. Get to your bed and try to rest. In the morning—'

Suddenly Renfield broke free of my clasp and sat down calmly on the side of his bed, apparently oblivious to our presence. As I was leaving the room, last of our party, he remarked, in a quiet, well-bred voice:

'You will later have cause to recall, Dr Seward, that I did what I could to convince you – tonight.'

JONATHAN HARKER'S JOURNAL
5 a.m.

I joined the search party with an easy mind, for Mina seemed so well and strong. I am so glad she consented to let us men do the dangerous work henceforth, for really it was a dreadful worry to me that she was involved in this fearful business at all.

As to our search party, we were all, I think, a little upset by the scene with Mr Renfield. When we came away from his room we were silent till we got back to the study. Then Mr Morris said to Dr Seward:

'Say, Jack, that man sure seems about the sanest lunatic I ever saw.'

Lord Godalming and I were silent, but Dr Van Helsing added:

'Friend John he know more of lunatics than I, and in our present task we must take no chance, yes? So leave all best as he are.'

Dr Seward answered in a strangely dreamy way:

'I don't entirely disagree agree with you, and with an ordinary lunatic I would probably have taken a chance. But Renfield seems so mixed up with the Count, somehow, and . . . I can't forget how he prayed with almost equal fervour for a cat, and then tried to tear my throat out with his teeth. Besides, he called the Count 'Lord and Master', and since that diabolical monster already has wolves and rats and all his own kind to help him, he surely wouldn't be above making use of a poor lunatic like Renfield.'

'He certainly did seem in earnest, though,' I tentatively suggested, regarding Renfield.

'Yes,' admitted Dr Seward wearily. 'I only hope we have done what is best. These things . . . ' his voice faltered, 'together with . . . very trying on one's nerves.'

The Professor stepped over, laid a hand on Dr Seward's shoulder, and said with kind emotion:

'Friend John, have no fear. We doing duty in terrible case. So we do as we best, and trust to mercy of God!'

Lord Godalming had slipped away for a few minutes, but he now returned. Holding up a little silver whistle, he remarked:

'That old place may be full of rats. If so, I've got just the remedy.'

Minutes later, having passed the wall, we tiptoed to the house, taking care to keep in the lawn shadows of the moonlit trees. When we got to the porch the Professor opened his bag and took out a number of items, which he then laid on the step in four little groups, one for each of us others. Then he whispered:

'My friends, we enter utmost peril, so need arms of many kinds. Our enemy is not mere spiritual, remember. He have strength of twenty men, and his windpipes is not crushable. A body of men more strong in all than he may hold him, but yet they cannot hurt him physical as he us. So must we guard from his touch. Keep this near your heart' – he offered a little silver crucifix to me, I being nearest – 'put these flowers round your neck' – he handed to me a wreath of withered garlic – 'for other enemies more mundane, this revolver and this knife. And for aid in all, these so small electric lamps, which fasten to your breast. Above all, this – which we must not desecrate needless.'

That final weapon was a portion of sacred wafer, which the Professor put in an envelope and handed to me.

Each of the others was similarly equipped.

'Now,' he said, 'friend John, where are those thin-bone keys? If so can we open the door, we need not break house by window, as before at Miss Lucy's.'

Dr Seward tried one or two skeleton keys, his surgical dexterity serving well, and presently the rusty hinges creaked, and the heavy door slowly opened. I felt the scene was startlingly like the description in Dr Seward's diary of the opening of Miss Westenra's tomb, and I fancy the same idea seemed to strike the others, for with one accord they shrank back. Only the Professor moved forward. Stepping to the door:

'*In manus tuas, Domine!*' he intoned, crossing himself as he passed over the threshold.

Silently we followed, and soon the light from our tiny lamps revealed all sorts of odd forms as the rays crossed each other, and our moving bodies threw fantastic shadows round the walls. I could not for my life shrug off the feeling that someone else was there amongst us. I suppose it was partly an echo of my ghastly experiences in Transylvania, but others too seemed jumpy, as every slight sound and new shadow confirmed.

The whole place was thick with dust – the floor seemingly inches deep, except where some recent footsteps contained the marks of hobnails, where the dust was caked. The walls and corners were fluffy with grimy spiders' webs, and on a table in the hall was a large ring of keys, with a time-yellowed label on each. They had been used recently, to judge by several scuffs in the blanket of dust on the table.

Lifting the keys, the Professor turned to me and said:

'You know this place, friend Jonathan, having copied maps of it. Which way to the chapel?'

I recalled where the chapel should be, so I led the way, and after a few wrong turnings found myself opposite a low, arched oaken door, ribbed with iron bands.

'This is the spot,' said the Professor, as he turned his lamp on a small map of the house, copied from my original correspondence regarding the purchase. With a little trouble we found the key on the bunch and opened the door.

I was well prepared for some unpleasantness, for there was a faint malodour in the air outside the chapel, but no-one could have anticipated such a stench as we encountered. None of the others had met the Count at close quarters, and even I had only ever seen him in fasting mode, in his rooms, or – when he was glutted with fresh blood – in a ruined building open to the air. But here was a space rather small and closely confined, in which long disuse had already made the air stagnant and foul. The new foul smell on top . . . how shall I describe it? Pungent with the acridity of slaughterhouse blood, it stank as though corruption had itself become corrupt. Faugh! How it sickens me to think of it.

Every breath exhaled by that monster seemed to have impregnated the atmosphere.

In normal circumstances such a vile miasma would have brought our enterprise to a speedy end. But this was no ordinary affair, and so, after involuntarily shrinking from that first nauseous whiff, we stifled our revulsion, and set to work.

'First,' directed the Professor, 'we count the boxes.'

A rapid double-check disclosed that of the original fifty earth-laden chests, only twenty-nine remained.

In his own language the Professor muttered some expression of his frustration.

'What was that?' exclaimed Lord Godalming.

I followed his gaze — back through the vaulted door into the dark passage beyond — and for an instant my heart hung frozen. For looming in the shadows I seemed to glimpse, as it were all luminous, the highlights of the Count's evil face: the ridge of his nose, red eyes, crimson lips; and patches of the awful pallor of his cheeks. Or did I? It was only for a second and, as Lord Godalming said:

'For a moment I thought I saw a face back there, but it was only a trick of our lamplight.' And he resumed his examination of the chapel.

Less convinced, I quietly shone my lamp into the passage. There was no sign of anyone; and as there were neither corners nor doors, but only solid walls, there could be no hiding-place — not even for *him*. Concluding that apprehension had distorted my imagination, I said nothing and turned back to the chapel.

A minute later Quincey Morris stepped suddenly back from a corner he was investigating. All our eyes were instantly on him, for undoubtedly some communal nervousness was infecting us. For a moment we were blinded by a mass of phosphorescence which flashed like shooting stars. Then we all gasped as the stars fell writhing to the ground and the place came alive with rats.

Together we stood temporarily transfixed with horror, all save Lord Godalming. Rushing over to the great iron-bound oaken door, which Dr Seward had described from the outside, he drew the huge bolts, and swung the door open. Then he took that small silver whistle from his pocket and he blew a low, shrill call. It was answered from behind Dr Seward's house by a frenzied yelping, and moments later terriers came dashing round the house. By now the rats had vastly multiplied and swarmed all over the place till the lamplight on their dark bodies and glittering baleful eyes made the walls of the chapel seem like a seething bank of earth set with fireflies.

When Lord Godalming's dogs arrived at the threshold of the chapel to our surprise they suddenly stopped dead, snarled, then raised their snouts to the sky and began to howl most lugubriously.

Lord Godalming jumped out, lifted one of the dogs into the chapel and thew him at the rats. The instant the terrier's feet hit the ground he seemed to recover all his courage and hurled himself into the oncoming tide of rats with enormous gusto. They fled before him in such panic that, before he had worried the life out of a score, the other dogs, similarly hoisted in, found but small prey ere the whole mass of rodents had vanished.

With the passing of the rats it seemed as if some deeper evil had departed too, for the dogs frisked about and barked merrily as they tossed their prostrate victims into the air with vicious shakes.

We humans also felt our spirits rise.

Whether it was a purifying of the deadly atmosphere by the opening of the chapel door, or the relief of finding ourselves in the open, I know not. But most certainly the shadow of our dread slipped off us like a robe, and it was with lighter hearts that we re-locked the outer chapel door, and, bringing the dogs with us, resumed our search of the house. We found nothing throughout except dust in extraordinary proportions, and all untouched save for my own footprints from my former visit. Never once did the dogs appear uneasy, and when we emerged from the front of the Count's house – to find the morning quickening in the east – they frisked about as happily as after a rabbit hunt in a summer wood.

Dr Van Helsing had confiscated the main-door key from the hall-table bunch and now locked up the house in orthodox fashion, pocketing the key when he had done.

'Our night', he said, 'is being eminently successful. No harm to us, yet we ascertain how many boxes missing. Above all do I rejoice this dangerous step accomplished without troubling of our most sweet Madame Mina with such sights and sounds and smells of horror what a woman might never forget.

'One vital lesson, too, we have confirm: that the brutes in Count Dracula's command yet not amene to his spiritual power – for look! These rats! Just as from his castle top he summon the wolves against friend Jonathan's going and to that poor mother's cry! Though the rats they flock to him, they run pell-mell from the so little dogs of Lord Arthur. And that monster himself have lurk elsewhere. Good, good! It has give us some "check" in this chess game, which we play for human souls.

'And now let us go home. The dawn is close, and we have content with our first night's work.'

The house was silent when we got back, save for some poor creature screaming away in a distant ward, and a low, moaning sound from Renfield's room. The poor wretch was doubtless torturing himself, after the manner of the insane, with needless thoughts of pain.

Tiptoeing into our own room, I found Mina asleep, thank goodness, and breathing so softly that I had to bend my ear down to hear her. She looks paler than usual. I hope the meeting last night did not upset her. For truly it is best that she be excluded from our future work, and even our deliberations. It is all too severe a strain for a woman to bear. I did not think so at first, but I know better now.

Henceforth, then, our mission shall be a sealed book to her, till such time as all is over, and the good earth rid of Count Dracula for ever. I dare say it will be hard for me to keep silence after such marital confidence as ours; but I must be resolute.

And for now, I rest on the sofa, so as not to disturb my Mina.

1 October, late morning.

I suppose it was natural that we should all oversleep, after such a hectic night. Mina must have been exhausted too, for though I slept till the sun was high, I was awake before her, and had to call three times before she roused. Indeed, so sound asleep was she that for a few seconds she did not recognize me, but looked up with blank terror, as one stirring from a dreadful dream. She complained of being still tired, so I said she could rest till later.

Now we know of the twenty-one earth boxes having been removed, I shall look up Thomas Snelling today.

DR SEWARD'S DIARY

At nearly noon I was awakened by the Professor bustling into my room. He was extremely cheery, and after going over our adventure of the night he suddenly said:

'Your patient interests me much. May with you I visit him this morning? It is new experience to find a lunatic who talk philosophy, and reason so sound.'

I had some pressing work to finish, so I suggested the Professor might visit Renfield alone. Van Helsing seemed delighted, so I called an attendant and gave him the necessary instructions. Before the Professor left my room I cautioned him against getting any false impression from my Renfield.

'What I want', answered the Professor, 'is he talk of his delusion to consuming things alive. Why you smile, friend John?'

'Because', I explained, 'the answer is here.' I laid my hand on the pile of typewritten pages on my desk. 'When our learned lunatic related how he *used* to consume life, his mouth was actually nauseous with the flies and spiders *he had just eaten* immediately before Mrs Harker entered the room.'

Van Helsing smiled in turn.

'Good!' he exulted.

'Why good?'

'Good for this very obliquity of thought and memory make mental disease so fascinate. Perhaps I may gain more knowledge of this madman than from teachings of most wise. Who know?' And off he went.

I must have become very absorbed in my reports, for it seemed as though only moments had passed before the Professor was back in my study.

'I have see him!' complained Van Helsing, his eyebrows fairly knotting with frustration as he hurled himself into my armchair.

'And?' I prompted him politely.

'I fear he appraise me at little,' grumbled Van Helsing. 'Our interview most short. When I enter he sitting on a stool, elbows on knees, and his face all discontent.

'Most respectful I greet him.

'No reply whatever he make.

'"Don't you know me?" I ask.

'His not reassuring answer:

'"I know you well enough, old fool Van Helsing. And I wish your idiotic brain all to hell. Damn all thick-headed Dutchmen!"

'No word more he say, but sit sullen indifferent as though I less than empty air. Thus depart, for this being of time, my chance of much learning from this lunatic so clever. Ah, well. To cheer myself again I now go for some happy words with that sweetest Madame Mina, who it rejoice me unspeakable that she no more will be pained with our doings so terrible.'

'I most heartily agree,' said I emphatically, for I did not want the Professor to weaken on this point. 'Mrs Harker is much better out of it. Things are quite bad enough for us – all men of the world, with not a few tight spots behind us – but it is absolutely no place for a woman. Any more contact, with the sordid details of our war against the Count, would infallibly have wrecked her mind.'

So Van Helsing has gone to confer with Mrs Harker; possibly Harker too. Quincey and Art are both out following up the clues as to the earth-boxes. I must now go round my patients, and we shall meet tonight.

MINA HARKER'S JOURNAL

It is strange to be kept in the dark as I am today; after Jonathan's full confidence for so many years. This morning I slept late after the fatigues of yesterday, and though Jonathan was late too, he was the earlier. Before he went out he never mentioned a word of what happened in the Count's house. And yet he must have known how terribly anxious I was. Poor Jonathan. I suppose it must distress him even more than me. They all agreed I should proceed no further in this awful work, and I acquiesced. But to think he keeps things from me! And now I am crying like a silly fool, when I *know* it is all thanks to my husband's great love – and the kindest intentions of those other gallant gentlemen . . .

That has done me good.

Well, some day Jonathan will tell me all. Meanwhile I must keep my journal as usual, with every thought of my heart writ down, for his dear eye to read . . . when the time comes.

Oh dear. I feel strangely sad and low-spirited today. I suppose it is a reaction from all the terrible excitement.

Last night I only went to bed, when the men had gone, because they had told me to do so. I didn't feel at all sleepy; rather full of devouring anxiety. Everything one does in this affair, no matter how right, seems to bring on the very thing one most deplores. If I hadn't gone to Whitby, for example? Perhaps poor Lucy would be with us now. She hadn't taken to visiting the churchyard till I came, and if she hadn't come there in the day-time with me she wouldn't have walked there in her sleep. And if she hadn't gone there at night, and asleep? That monster couldn't have destroyed her as he did. Oh, why did I ever go to Whitby?

There now, crying again!

I wonder what has come over me today. I must hide it from Jonathan. If he knew I had been crying twice in one morning – I, who never cry on my own account, and whom he has never caused to shed a tear, the dear fellow would fret his heart out. So I shall put on a bold face, and if I do feel weepy, he shall never see it.

I can't quite remember how I fell asleep last night. I remember hearing the sudden barking of the dogs and a lot of queer sounds – like tumultuous praying – from Mr Renfield's room, which is somewhere under this. Then silence over everything. Silence so profound that it startled me, and I got up and looked out of the window. All was dark and silent, the black shadows thrown by the moonlight seeming full of silent mystery. Not a thing stirring. Until . . . a thin streak of white mist, that crept with almost imperceptible slowness across the grass towards the house.

When I returned to bed I felt a profound lethargy assail me. I lay motionless awhile but still could not sleep – so soon got up and looked out of the window again. The mist was spreading close up to the house; thick against the walls, and lapping up towards the windows. Poor Renfield was louder than ever, and though I could not distinguish the words he spoke, I discerned distinctly the tones of some passionate entreaty.

Then came the sound of a struggle, and I deduced the attendants were restraining him. Sad, and somehow uncontrollably frightened, I crept back into bed, pulled the bedclothes over my head, and put my fingers in my ears. Not a bit sleepy, so I thought; but I must have fallen asleep, for, excepting dreams, I remember nothing further until morning, when Jonathan roused me. Then it took me a considerable effort and some little time to realize where I was, and that it was truly Jonathan bending over me.

In my dreams too I had been waiting for Jonathan to come back. I was very anxious about him, yet powerless to act. My feet, hands and even my brain seemed weighted down as by anchors, and soon it began to dawn upon me that the air was heavy, dank, and chillingly cold. I pulled the bedclothes down from my face, and found to my surprise that all was dim around me. The gas-light which I had left lit for Jonathan, but left burning low, came only like a tiny red spark through the fog which now filled the room. Then, sluggishly, it occured to me that surely I had *shut* the window before coming to bed. Had I not?

I would have got up to check, but that leaden lethargy seemed to chain my limbs where I lay, and even my very will. Lying there, helpless, I closed my eyes, but found I could now see just as well through my eyelids. The mist grew ever thicker, yet now I could see how it came in: like smoke – or with the white energy of boiling water – pouring in, not through the window, but through the joinings of the door . . . thicker and thicker still, like a pillar of cloud in the room, through the top of which I could just see the light of the gas, like a red eye glowing dimly.

Things began to whirl through my brain just as the cloudy column was now whirling round the room, and through it all came the scriptural words 'of cloud by day and of fire by night'. Was this indeed some spiritual guidance, coming to aid me in my sleep? But the pillar was of both day and night confused, for the fire was in the red eye, which somehow now acquired a new fascination. As I looked, the fire divided and seemed to shine on me through the fog like two red eyes, such as Lucy told me of in her mental wandering when, on the cliff, the dying sunlight struck the windows of St Mary's Church.

Suddenly the horror burst upon me that it was thus that Jonathan had seen those awful women growing into reality through the whirling mist in the moonlight, and in my dream I must have fainted into darkness, for my last apparent memory is of a livid white face bending over me out of the mist. I must be wary of such dreams, which could unseat a weak soul's reason. I would get Professor Van Helsing or Dr Seward to prescribe something to make me sleep soundly, only . . . I fear to alarm them. Tonight I shall strive hard to sleep naturally. If I fail, I shall tomorrow try a dose of chloral; that cannot hurt me for once, and it will give me a good night's sleep. Last night – somehow it tired me more than if I had not slept at all.

2 October, 10 p.m.

Last night I *must* have slept soundly, for I was not woken by Jonathan coming to bed. It seems I did not dream, and yet the sleep has not refreshed me, for today I feel terribly weak and spiritless. I spent all yesterday trying to read, or lying down dozing. In the afternoon Mr Renfield asked if he might see me.

Poor man.

He was very gentle, and when I came away he kissed my hand and bade God bless me. It affected me greatly; and even now I am crying when I think of him. This is a new weakness of which I must be careful.

Jonathan would be miserable if he knew I had been crying.

He and the others were out until dinner, and they all came in tired. I did what I could to cheer them up, and I suppose the effort did me good, for I forgot how tired I was. After dinner they sent me to bed, and all went off to smoke together. So they said, but I could see from Jonathan's manner that something important was afoot. Before they went I asked Dr Seward to give me a sleeping draught, to counter my late waking that morning. He very kindly mixed me up a cordial of brandy and opiate, which he assured me would do me no harm, as it was very mild . . . I have drunk it all down, and now lie waiting for sleep; which still keeps aloof.

I hope I have not been foolish, for as sleep begins to flirt with me, a new fear comes: that I may have deprived myself of the power of waking. And what if – but here comes sleep.

Goodnight.

25

Jonathan Harker's Journal

1 October, evening.

I found Thomas Snelling in his house at Bethnal Green, but unhappily he was not in a condition to remember anything. The very prospect of beer which my expected coming had opened to him had proved too much, and he had begun too early on his expected debauch. I learned, however, from his wife, who seemed a decent soul, that Snelling's more sober mate, Joseph Smollet, lived at Walworth. So off I drove, and found Mr Smollet at home and in his shirt sleeves, taking a late tea out of a saucer.

He is an intelligent, reliable type of workman, remembered all about the incident of the boxes, and from a wonderful dog's-eared note-book – produced from some mysterious receptacle about the seat of his trousers – thick with hieroglyphical entries in half-obliterated pencil, he gave me the destinations of the boxes:

Six in the cartload taken from Carfax to 197 Chicksand Street, Mile End New Town, and another six deposited at Jamaica Lane, Bermondsey.

If, then, the Count means to scatter these ghastly refuges of his over London, surely he does not purpose to confine himself to only two sides of town. The north and west are surely never omitted from his diabolical scheme – let alone the City itself, and the very heart of fashionable London in the south-west and west. So of Smollet I inquired whether he knew if any other boxes had been taken from Carfax.

He replied:

'Well, guv'nor. You'se treated me wery 'an'some' – I had given him half a sovereign – 'an' I'll tell yer all I know. I heerd a man by the name of Bloxam say four nights ago in the 'Are an' 'Ounds, in Pincher's alley, as 'ow he an' his mate 'ad 'ad a rare dusty job in a old 'ouse at Purfleet. There ain't a-many such jobs as this 'ere, an' I'm finkin' that maybe Sam Bloxam could tell ye summut.'

I intimated that Bloxam's address might well inspire another half-sovereign.

Smollet gulped down the rest of his tea and stood up, saying that he would begin the search then and there. At the door he stopped, and said:

'Look 'ere, guv'nor, there ain't no sense in me a-keepin' you 'ere. I may find Sam soon. Or I mayn't. But anyhow he ain't like to be in a way to tell ye much tonight. Rare one on the booze, is Sam. If you can give me a envelope with a stamp on it, and put yer address on it, I'll post yer infurmashion tonight.'

This was all very practical, so one of the children went off with a penny to buy an envelope and a sheet of paper, and to keep the change. When she came back I addressed the envelope, stamped it, entrusted it to Smollet, and then made my way home.

We're on the track, at any rate.

I am tired tonight, and need sleep. Mina is fast asleep, and looks a little too pale. Her eyes seem as though she had been crying. Poor dear. No doubt it frets her to be kept in the dark. But it is for the best, and she herself has been reticent of late, and has not spoken of the Count at all since we excluded her from our proceedings.

2 October, evening.

A long and trying but exciting day. By the first post I got my directed envelope with a dirty scrap of paper enclosed, on which was written with a carpenter's pencil in a sprawling hand:

'Sam Bloxam. Korkrans, 4 Poters Cort, Bartel Street, Walworth. Arsk for the depite.'

I got the letter in bed, and rose without waking Mina. She looked heavy and pale, and far from well. I determined that, when I should return from this new search, I would arrange for her going back to Exeter. I think she would be happier in our own home, with her daily tasks to interest her, than in being here – amongst us, and yet in ignorance. I only saw Dr Seward for a moment, and told him where I was off to, and why.

I drove to Walworth and – with some difficulty, thanks to Mr Smollet's spelling – I found Potter's Court. However, once in the court I had no difficulty in discovering Corcoran's lodging-house. When I asked the man who came to the door for the 'depite', he shook his head, and said:

'Ain't no such person 'ere.'

I re-read Smollet's letter, and in view of the spelling I thought to ask: 'Who are you?'

'The depity,' he answered.

A half-crown tip put the deputy's knowledge at my disposal, and I learned that Mr Bloxam, who had slept off his previous night's beer at Corcoran's, had left for his work at Poplar at five o'clock that morning. The deputy could not tell me where Bloxam's work was situated, but he had a vague idea it was some 'new-fangled ware'us'. And with that slender clue I had to start for Poplar.

It was twelve o'clock before I got on the trail of any such building, and this in a coffee-shop, where some workmen were having their dinner. One suggested there was being erected at Cross Angel Street a new 'cold storage' building. As this might well relate to a 'new-fangled ware'us', I at once drove to it.

An interview with a surly gatekeeper and a surlier foreman, both agreeably appeasable by coin, put me on the track of Bloxam. He was sent for on my offering to pay his day's wages to his foreman for the privilege of asking him a few questions on a private matter.

He was a smart enough fellow, Bloxam, though rough of speech and bearing. When I had promised to pay for his information and given him an earnest, he told me he had made two journeys between Carfax and a house in Piccadilly, transporting to the latter nine great boxes – 'main heavy' – with a horse and cart hired for the purpose.

I asked him *which* house in Piccadilly.

He replied:

'Well, guv'nor. I forgits the number, but it was only a few doors from a big white church or somefink not long built. Dusty ole 'ouse, too. Though nothin' to the dust in the 'ouse we tooked the bloomin' boxes from.'

'How did you get into Carfax?'

'There was the old party what engaged me. He 'elped me lift the boxes too, and put them in the dray. Curse me, but he was the strongest old feller I ever struck. That thin, too – you'd fink he couldn't throw a shadder.'

'With a white moustache?'

'White as new snow, guv'nor.'

How this information thrilled through me!

'Why,' continued Bloxam, ''e took up 'is end o' the boxes like they was pounds of tea. And me a-puffin' an' a-blowin' afore I could up-end mine anyhow. An' I'm no chicken, neither.'

'How did you get into the house in Piccadilly?' I asked.

'He was there too! Must 'a' started off and got there afore me, for when I rung of the bell he kem an' oped the door 'isself. An' 'elped me carry the boxes into the 'all.'

'All nine?' I asked.

'Yus. Five in the first load. Four in the second. Main dry work, it was, an' I don't so well remember 'ow I got 'ome. Funny—'

Here I interrupted him:

'Were the boxes left in the hall?'

'Yus. Big 'all, an' 'all. Nofink else in it, neither.'

'You didn't have any key?'

'Never used no key nor nofink. The old gent, he oped the door 'isself, an' shut it again when I druv off. I don't remember the last time – but that was the beer.'

'And you can't remember the number of the house?'

'No, sir. But ye needn't have no difficulty about that. It's a 'igh 'un with a stone front. With a bow on it, and 'igh steps up to the door. I know them steps, 'avin' ad to carry the boxes up with three loafers what come round to earn a copper. The old gent give them shillin's, an' they seein' they got so much, they wanted more.'

'How did he react to that?'

'Took one of them by the shoulder and was like to throw 'im down the steps, till the lot of them went away cussin'.'

Seeing there was no more to be had, I paid my friend for his information, and started off for Piccadilly – very anxious.

The Count could, it seemed, handle the earth-boxes himself. If so, time was more desperately precious than ever.

At Piccadilly Circus I discharged my cab, and walked westward. Beyond the Junior Constitutional I came across the house described, and was satisfied that this was the next of the lairs arranged by Dracula. The house looked as though it had been long untenanted: windows encrusted with dust; shutters up; and from the ironwork the paint had mostly scaled away. It was evident that up to lately there had been a large notice-board in front of the balcony. It had, however, been roughly torn away – only the uprights which had supported it still remaining. Behind the rails of the balcony I saw there were some loose boards, whose raw edges looked white. I would have given a good deal for a look at the notice-board itself, as it would surely at least expedite contact with the previous owner of the house – and thence our access to it.

But there was at present nothing to be learned from the Piccadilly side, so I went round the back. The mews were active, the Piccadilly houses being mostly in occupation. I asked two of the grooms what they could tell me about the empty house. One said he believed it had lately been taken, but he couldn't say by whom. He told me, however, that up to very lately there had been a *For Sale* board up, and that perhaps Mitchell, Sons & Candy, the agents, could tell me something.

I did not wish to seem too eager, so, thanking him in the usual manner, I strolled away. The autumn night was now closing in, so I lost no time. Having learned the address of Mitchell, Sons & Candy from a directory at the Berkeley, I was soon at their office in Sackville Street.

The gentleman who saw me was excessively suave in manner, and uncommunicative in equal proportion. Having once told me that the Piccadilly house – which throughout he called a 'mansion' – was sold, he considered our business concluded. When I asked who had purchased it, he opened his eyes a thought wider, and replied:

'It is *sold*, sir.'

'Pardon me,' I said, with equal politeness, 'but I have a *special* reason for wishing to know who purchased it.'

Again he paused, his eyebrows raised.

'It is . . . sold, sir,' he stressed.

'Surely,' I said, 'you do not mind—'

'But I do mind,' he interrupted pompously. 'The affairs of their clients are absolutely safe in the hands of Mitchell, Sons & Candy.'

Here was manifestly a prig of the first water, so, to best him on his own ground, I said:

'Your clients, sir, are happy in having so resolute a guardian of their confidence. I am myself a professional man.' Here I handed him my card. 'In this instance I am not prompted by mere idle curiosity. Rather do I act on the part of Lord Godalming.'

The mention of aristocracy casting a different complexion on affairs, the prize prig hemmed, and said:

'I would like to oblige you, Mr Harker, and especially his lord-ship – for whom we once rented some chambers, I believe, when he was the Honourable Arthur Holmwood. Hmn. If you will let me have his lordship's address I will consult the House on the subject, and in any event shall communicate with his lordship by tonight's post. It will be a pleasure, to be sure, if we can so far modulate our rules as to give the required information to his lordship.'

I thanked the prig profusely, gave him Lord Godalming's address as care of Dr Seward, and came away. It was now dark, and I was tired and hungry. I got a cup of tea at the Aerated Bread Company and came down to Purfleet by the next train.

I found all the others at home. Mina looked tired and pale, but she made a gallant effort to be cheerful. Really it wrung my heart to think that perhaps the information we were keeping from her may have contributed to her disquietude. But still I could not tell the others of my day's discoveries till we were alone together. So after dinner – followed by a little token music – I took Mina to her room and left her to go to bed. The dear girl clung to me with great affection – almost as though . . . but there were urgent matters to discuss, so I kissed Mina a fond goodnight and went down again to the study, where I found the others all gathered round the fire. On the train I had written up my diary, so now simply read it out aloud, to bring them up to date.

When I had finished Van Helsing said:

'Splendid work, friend Jonathan. If we finding all missing boxes in that house, then our work near his end. If some be missing still for there, we search on until we find. Either way our final coup he approach, and we hunt the vile wretch to his eternal death.'

For a few minutes we sat smoking thoughtfully.

The silence was broken by Mr Morris:

'Say! How are we going to get *in* to that house?'

'We got into the other all right,' pointed out Lord Godalming.

'But, Art, this is different. We housebroke at Carfax all right, but we had night and a walled park to protect us. It will be a mighty different thing to commit burglary in Piccadilly – even at dead of night.'

Lord Godalming's brows contracted. Impatiently he stood up and walked round the room. Then he conceded:

'Quincey has a good point. But let us see what morning brings, when we hear from Mitchell & Sons. Who knows whether there may not yet be a set of keys we can commandeer?'

So we agreed to take no further action before breakfast. Claiming weariness, I left the others smoking, and retired to our room, determined to bring this diary right up to the moment before I sleep. Which now . . .

Just a line:

Mina sleeps soundly and her breathing is regular. Her forehead is puckered up into little wrinkles, as though she thinks even in her sleep. She is still too pale, but not so haggard as this morning. Tomorrow will, I hope, mend all this – she will be herself at home in Exeter.

God, how tired I am.

26

Puzzled about Renfield

DR SEWARD'S DIARY
1 October.

I am puzzled afresh about Renfield. His moods change so rapidly and always seem to focus on something more than his own well-being. This morning his manner was that of a man commanding destiny. He *was*, in fact, commanding destiny – subjectively. From his mental cloud he beamed benevolently down on all the weaknesses and wants of poor mortals such as I. Thinking to probe him a little, I asked:

'What about the flies?'

He smiled on me in a superior, Malvolio sort of way:

'The fly, my dear sir, has one striking feature: its wings are typical of the aerial powers of the psychic faculties. The ancients did well when they typified the soul as a butterfly!'

In a neutral voice I countered:

'So it's a soul you're after now, is it?'

Renfield's madness foiled his reason, and a puzzled look spread over his face. Shaking his head emphatically he cried:

'Oh no! No souls. *Life* is all I want.' Here he brightened up: 'Life is all right, you see. I have all I want. You must get a new patient, you know, doctor, if you wish to study zoophagy!'

This intrigued me, so I drew him on:

'Then you command life? You are a god, I suppose?'

Renfield smiled with an ineffably benign superiority:

'Indeed not! Far be it from me – to any deity. I am rather, regarding things purely terrestrial, in the position which Enoch occupied spiritually!'

'Why Enoch?' I asked guardedly.

'Because he walked with God.'

I could not see the point of Renfield's analogy, but thought it best not to admit the fact.

'So life's all right,' I recapped, 'but you don't care for souls. Why not?' I deliberately phrased my question somewhat sternly, to disconcert him. For an instant he relapsed into his old servile manner, bent low before me, and virtually fawned as he replied:

'Souls! I couldn't *use* them.'

'In what way?'

'I couldn't *eat* them. Or—'

'Yes?'

But the old cunning look had spread over Renfield's face, like wind across a pond. 'As to life, what is it after all? When you've got good friends – like you, Doctor Seward,' he said with a leer of inexpressible cunning. 'I know I shall never lack life!'

I think through the cloudiness of his insanity he glimpsed some antagonism in me, for he at once took refuge in a dogged silence. Seeing it would be useless to persist, I left him.

But later in the day he sent for me.

Ordinarily I would not have gone without special reason, but just at present I am so interested in him that . . . besides, I am glad of anything to help pass the time. Harker is out, following up clues; and so are Lord Godalming and Quincey. Meanwhile Van Helsing sits in my study poring over the record prepared by the Harkers. He seems to think that by ruthless sifting of all details he will unearth some vital link, and he does not wish to be disturbed.

Renfield I found sitting out in the middle of the floor on his stool, a pose generally indicative of heightened mental activity on his part. When I entered he said at once, as though the question had been hovering on his lips:

'What about *souls*?'

Evidently my surmise had been correct. Unconscious cerebration was having its effect, even on the lunatic. Determining to have the matter out:

'What about them?' I retorted.

He did not reply for a moment, but looked all round him, and up and down, as though searching for some inspiration.

'I don't want . . . any . . . souls!' he then said in a feeble, apologetic way. The subject seemed to be preying on him. So, being cruel only to be kind, I said:

'You *like* life, and you *want* life?'

'Yes, yes!'

'But how are we to get the *life* without getting the *soul* also?'

That seemed to affect his imagination more than I had intended, for Renfield put his fingers to his ears and shut his eyes, screwing them up tightly, like a small boy whose face is being soaped – though here the features were worn, and the stubble on the jaws was white.

A little chagrined to have upset him, I suggested kindly:

'Would you like some sugar? To get your flies round again?'

Renfield seemed to wake up all at once. Shaking his head vigorously, with a laugh he replied:

'No thanks! Flies are poor things, after all!' After a pause he added:

'But I don't want their souls buzzing round me, all the same.'

'Or spiders?' I went on.

'Blow spiders! What's the use of spiders? There isn't anything in them to eat or—' He stopped suddenly, as though reminded of a forbidden topic.

'So!' I thought to myself. 'This is the second time he has suddenly stopped at the word "drink". What does it mean?'

Renfield himself seemed aware of having slipped, for he hurried on, clearly hoping to distract me:

'"Rats and mice and such small deer" – as Shakespeare has it. "Chicken-feed of the larder", they might be called. I'm past all that sort of nonsense. You might as well ask a man to eat molecules with a pair of chop-sticks, as try to interest me in the lesser carnivora – when I know what lies before me.'

'I see,' I said. 'You want big things that you can get your teeth into? How would you like to breakfast on elephant?'

'What ridiculous nonsense you are talking!'

'I wonder', I pressed him reflectively, 'what an elephant's soul is like!'

At once Renfield tumbled down from his high-horse and became as a child again.

'I don't want an elephant's soul. Nor any soul at all!' he mumbled sulkily. For a few moments he sat despondently. Then suddenly he jumped to his feet, eyes blazing with cerebral excitement. 'To hell with you and your souls!' he shouted. 'Why do you plague me about souls? Haven't I got enough to worry me, and pain sufficient to distract me already, without all your nonsense about *souls*?' He looked so hostile that I thought he was in for another homicidal fit, so I blew my whistle. The instant, however, that I did so he became calm, and said apologetically:

'Forgive me, Doctor. I forgot myself. You do not need any help. It's just that I am so worried. If you only knew the problem I have to face, you would pity me. Pray do not put me in a strait-waistcoat. I want to think, and I cannot think freely when my body is confined. I'm sure you will understand!' He seemed in control of himself again, so when the attendants came I told them to withdraw.

Renfield watched them go. When the door was closed he said, with considerable dignity:

'Dr Seward, you have been so considerate. I am very, very grateful.'

I thought it well to leave him in this mood, and so I came away.

Points to ponder over in Renfield's case:

* Will not mention *drinking*.

* Fears being burdened with the soul of anything.

* Has no dread of lacking *life* in the future.

* Despises the meaner forms of life altogether, though he dreads being haunted by their souls.

Logically these things surely imply he feels assured of some higher life to come. Yet he dreads the consequence – the burden of a soul. Then – it is a *human* life he looks to!

And the assurance – ?

Merciful God, has the Count been at him? And have we here some terrible new scheme of evil afoot?

Later.

After my round I went to tell Van Helsing of my suspicion. He grew very grave. Having thought the matter over for a while, he asked me to take him to Renfield. I did so. As we approached Renfield's door we heard the lunatic within singing gaily, as he used to.

When we entered we saw with amazement that he had spread out his sugar – also as of old. The flies, lethargic with the autumn, were beginning to buzz into the room. We tried to make him talk, as during his previous conversation with me, but he would not attend – just carried on singing, as though we did not exist. His eyes were glued to a grubby scrap of paper which he was folding into a note-book.

We had to come away as ignorant as we went in.

Renfield's is a curious case indeed. We must watch him tonight.

27

Letter to Lord Godalming

2 October.

My Lord,

At all times delighted to gratify your wishes, we beg, with regard to the desire of your Lordship, expressed by Mr Harker, to supply the following information concerning the sale of No. 347 Piccadilly.

The vendors were the executors of the late Mr Archibald Winter-Suffield, deceased. The purchaser is a foreign nobleman, Count de Ville, who effected the transaction himself, paying the sum due in notes 'over the counter', if your Lordship will pardon so vulgar an locution. Beyond this we know nothing whatever of him.

Ever your Lordship's most humblest of servants,

Mitchell, Sons & Candy.

28

The Count Strikes Twice

2 October.

I placed a man in the corridor last night, and told him to note any sound from Renfield's room. After dinner we all gathered round the fire in the study – Mrs Harker having gone to bed – to discuss the events of the day. Harker was the only one to report real progress, and we are in great hopes that his findings may lead us to the Count.

Before going to bed I went round by Renfield's room and looked in through the observation trap. He was sleeping soundly and his chest rose and fell with regular respiration.

This morning the man on duty reported that a little after midnight Renfield had been restless and kept saying his prayers somewhat loudly. 'Was that *all*?' I asked the man sternly.

He replied that it was all he heard. There was something about his manner so suspicious that I asked him point-blank if he had been asleep. He denied sleep, but admitted having 'dozed' for a while. Really it is too bad that employees these days cannot be trusted in this way.

Today Harker is out following up his clue, and Art and Quincey are looking for horses. Godalming feels we must have horses in constant readiness, for when we get the information we seek there will be no time to lose. We must sterilize all the imported earth between sunrise and sunset – thus catching the Count at his weakest, and with no refuge to fly to. Van Helsing is off to the British Museum, looking up some authorities on ancient medicine. The old physicians took account of things which their present-day followers do not accept, and the Professor is searching for witch and demon cures which may be useful later.

I sometimes think we must be all mad, and that we shall wake to sanity in strait-waistcoats.

Later.

We have met again, and it seems our work tomorrow may be the beginning of the end. I wonder if Renfield's relative quiet recently may be significant here. His moods have so followed the doings of the Count, that the coming destruction of the monster may be conveyed to him in some subtle way. If we could only guess what went on in his mind between my argument with him yesterday and his resumption of fly-catching – what might that tell us? He is now seemingly quiet for a spell . . . or is he? – that wild yell seemed to come from his room.

A moment ago the attendant burst into my room with the news that Renfield has somehow met with an accident. He heard him yell, and when he rushed in he found him lying on his face on the floor – all covered with blood. I must go at once . . .

3 October.

Renfield I found lying on his left side, in a ghastly pool of blood. When I essayed to move him, it was immediately apparent that he had received some terrible injuries. His face was horribly bruised, as though it had been beaten against the floor – indeed, it was from his face wounds that the blood had poured. The attendant, who was kneeling beside the body, said to me as we turned him over:

'I think, sir, his back is broken. See. His right arm and leg – and the whole side of his face is paralysed.'

How such a thing could have happened puzzled the attendant beyond measure. His brows were furrowed in bewilderment as he said:

'I can't understand the *two* things. He could mark his face like that by beating his head on the ground. I saw a young woman do it once at the Eversfield Asylum before anyone could lay hands on her. And I suppose he might have broke his back by falling out of bed, if he got in an awkward kink. But for the life of me I can't imagine how the *two* things occurred. If his back was broke, he couldn't beat his head; and if his face was like that before he fell out of bed, there would be marks of it.'

I said to him:

'Go to Dr Van Helsing. And ask him to kindly come here at once.'

The man ran off.

Within two minutes the Professor, in his dressing gown and slippers, appeared. When he saw Renfield on the ground he looked keenly at him a moment and then turned to me. I think he recognized my thought in my eyes, for he said very quietly – manifestly for the ears of the attendant:

'A sad accident! He will need *very* careful watching and *much* attention. I must first dress myself, but shall rejoin you in the twin-kling.'

Renfield was now breathing as with terrible subconscious pain.

Van Helsing returned with extraordinary celerity, bearing with him a surgical case. Almost before he looked at the patient, he whispered to me:

'Send the attendant away. We must be alone with him when he becomes conscious – after the operation.'

So I said:

'Thank you, Simmons. You had better go your round, and Dr Van Helsing will operate. Let me know instantly if there be anything unusual elsewhere in the asylum.'

The man withdrew, and Van Helsing and I focused on Renfield. His face wounds, though gory, were comparatively superficial. The real injury was a depressed fracture of the skull, extending right up through the motor area. The Professor said:

'We must reduce the pressure, else suffusion of the brain increase too fast. We must trephine *at once*, indeed, or – too late.'

Then came a soft tapping at the door. I opened it to find, in the corridor without, Arthur and Quincey in pyjamas and slippers.

'I heard your man call Professor Van Helsing,' said Arthur, 'and tell him of an accident. So I woke Quincey. May we come in?' I nodded, and closed the door behind them.

When Quincey saw the state of the patient, and pool of congealing blood, he said softly:

'My God! Poor devil!'

I told them briefly what had happened, and added that we expected Renfield would recover consciousness after the operation – at least for a time.

'We must better wait,' said Van Helsing, 'just long enough to fix the best spot for trephining, so most perfectly remove the bloody clot. For the haemorrhage he increasing.'

Poor Renfield's breathing was coming now in uncertain, desperate gasps. Every few moments it seemed he would open his eyes and speak, but then would follow a prolonged stertorous groan, and he would relapse back into deeper insensibility. Inured as I am to sickbeds and death, this suspense grew heavy upon me. I could hear the loud beating of my own heart, and the blood surging through my temples like the thuds of a carpenter's mallet.

Soon the void of words became unbearable, and I saw from my companions' flushed faces and damp brows that they were enduring equal torture.

Finally it became apparent, at least to we two doctors, that the patient was sinking fast, and might die at any moment. The Professor's features were sternly resigned as he pronounced:

'Alas, but – even his dying words may be worth many lives. We shall operate just above the ear.'

Without another word he made the incision. For several moments Renfield's breathing continued as before, difficult and rasping. Then came a rattling inhalation, terribly prolonged, as though it must burst his poor chest open. With a start his eyes opened wide in a wild, helpless stare – then softened into a strange, glad surprise. From his lips came a sigh of relief. But his body jerked convulsively as his weak voice wheezed:

'I'll be quiet, Doctor. Please take off the strait-waistcoat. I have had a terrible dream, you know. It has left me so weak that I cannot move. What's wrong with my face? It feels all swollen, and it—' He tried to turn his head but with the effort his eyes grew glassy again, and his neck went limp.

The Professor said gravely:

'Tell to us your dream, Mr Renfield.'

Renfield's face brightened through its mutilation, and he murmured:

'Dr Van Helsing? How good of you to be here. Some water, please. My lips are dry. And I shall try to tell you . . . I dreamed—' he seemed about to faint.

I called quietly to Quincey:

'Brandy. From my study.'

Quincey rushed off and returned moments later with a glass, the decanter of brandy and a carafe of water. We moistened Renfield's poor parched lips, and instantly his wits seemed to rally. Looking at me with an agonized confusion I shall never forget, he said:

'I must not deceive myself, no. It was no dream – but all a nightmare reality.' Then his eyes roved round the room. As he caught sight of the two figures sitting patiently on the edge of the bed, he went on:

'If I were not sure already, I should know by them.' For an instant his eyes closed – not with pain or sleep but voluntarily, as though he were bringing all his faculties to bear. When he opened his eyes again he begged with failing urgency:

'Quick, doctor, quick. I am dying. I feel I have but minutes before my death – or . . . Wet my lips with brandy again. I have something I must say before I die – before my poor crushed brain dies, anyhow. Thank you, doctor. It was that night after you left me, when I implored you to let me leave here. I couldn't speak then – my tongue was tied – but I was as sane then as I am now. I was in an agony of despair after you left me. For hours, it seemed. Then came a sudden peace. My brain felt cool again, and I realized where I was. I heard the dogs bark behind our house, but not where He was!'

As Renfield spoke, Van Helsing's eyes never blinked. But his hand reached out for mine and gripped it hard.

'He came up to the window in the mist,' Renfield continued dreamily, 'as I had seen Him often before. But He was solid then – not a ghost, and His eyes were fierce and furious. Yet He was laughing. His fearsome red mouth was laughing. The sharp white teeth glinted brightly in the moonlight when He turned to look back over the belt of trees, to where the dogs were barking. I wouldn't ask Him to come in at first, though I knew He wanted to. Then He began promising me things. Not in words, but . . . '

'How?' the Professor prompted him softly.

'By making those things happen. Just as He used to send in the flies when the sun was shining. Great big fat ones, with steel and sapphire on their wings. And big moths, in the night, with skull and cross-bones on their backs.'

Van Helsing nodded sympathetically at Renfield as to me he muttered:

'The *Acherontia atropos of the Sphinges* – what you call the Dead-head moth.'

Renfield went on:

'Then he began to whisper:

'"Rat, rats, rats! Hundreds, thousands, millions of them, and every one a life! And dogs to eat them, and cats too. All lives! All red blood, with years of life in it – not merely buzzing flies!"'

'I laughed at Him, but then the dogs howled, away beyond the dark trees, in His house. He beckoned me to the window. I got up and looked out. He raised His hands, and seemed to call out without words. A dark mass spread over the grass, coming on like a flame of fire. Then He moved the mist to the right, to the left, and the mist was . . . '

'The mist was what?' I murmured encouragingly.

'*Rats.* Thousands and thousands of rats. With their eyes blazing red – like His, only smaller. He held up His hand, and they all stopped dead. I thought He seemed to be saying:

'"All these lives will I give you, ay. And many more, and greater, through countless ages, if you kneel down now and worship me."

'And then a red cloud the colour of blood seemed to close over my eyes. Before I knew what I was doing I found myself opening the sash and saying to Him:

'"Come in, Lord and Master."

'The rats were all gone, but He slid into the room through the sash, though it was only open an inch. Just as the Moon herself has often slipped in through the tiniest crack, and stood before me in all her splendour.' Renfield's voice was weaker, so I moistened his lips with brandy again, and he continued speaking. But it seemed his memory had skipped several stages. I was about to call him back to the point where he had paused, but Van Helsing whispered to me:

'Do not interrupt. He cannot go back, and will never recover, if once he lose his thread.'

'All day I waited to hear from Him,' Renfield was saying, 'but He sent me nothing – not even a blow-fly. And when the Moon got up I was pretty angry with Him. When He slid in through the window – though it was shut – and did not even knock, I got *mad* with Him. He sneered at me. His white face loomed out of the mist, with His red eyes gleaming, and He went on as though He owned the whole world, and I was no one. He didn't even smell the same as He went by me. I couldn't hold Him. And I felt that, somehow, it was as if Mrs Harker had come into the room.'

The two men sitting on the bed stood up and came over to stand behind Renfield, so they could hear him better. They were both silent, but the Professor was quivering with shock, and his face grew fearfully grim.

Renfield went on without noticing:

'When Mrs Harker came in to see me this afternoon she wasn't the same, you know. She seemed to me like tea after the teapot has been watered.'

I think we all trembled with outrage to hear this, but managed to remain silent as Renfield continued to address his ramblings to the ceiling.

'I didn't know', he recalled, 'that she was here, until she spoke. And *she didn't look the same*. I don't care for pale people. Women particularly I like to have lots of blood in them, and hers had all run thin. When she left me I began to think, and it made me mad to know that He had been taking the life out of her.'

Our lips were tight and our knuckles white with rage at this, but we let Renfield carry on:

'So when He came tonight I was ready for Him. I saw the mist stealing in, and I grabbed it tight – with all my madman's strength. And He felt it too, for He had to come out of the mist to struggle with me. I fought hard as I could to win, for I didn't want Him to suck away any more of the lady's life. Oh, till I saw His eyes. They burned into me deep, and my strength became like water. He raised me up like a doll and flung me down. There was a red cloud before me, and a noise like thunder, and the mist seemed to steal away under . . . the door.' Renfield's voice was fading.

Van Helsing jumped up with a plosive tut.

'We know the worst now,' he said. 'Count Dracula he be here, and we know his purpose. It may not be too late. Let us be armed – as we were the other night. But *now*. There is not an instant to spare.'

Leaving Simmons with Renfield, we all hurried to fetch from our rooms the equipment we had when we entered the Count's house. As we assembled in the corridor, the Professor fairly moaned:

'Alas. That my dear Madame Mina should so suffer too – this . . . ' He broke off with an angry sob, and meanwhile rage and trepidation did battle royal within my own breast.

Outside the Harkers' door we paused.

Quincey said doubtfully:

'Should we disturb her?'

'We must,' said Van Helsing sternly. 'If the door be locked, we needs break it in.'

'May it not frighten her terribly?' protested Arthur. 'I mean, to break into a lady's bedroom?'

Van Helsing said solemnly:

'This is life against death. Anyways all chambers is one to the doctor.

Friend John, when I turn the handle, do you put your shoulder down and shove. You others two too. Now!'

He turned the handle as he spoke. As the door did not yield, we younger three men hurled ourselves against it. With a crash it burst open, and we were in the Harkers' room. The Professor fell in front of me and what I saw across his body caused the hair to rise like bristles on the back of my neck, while my heart missed several beats.

The moonlight, bright through the thick yellow blind, shone upon Jonathan Harker: lying inert on the bed beside the window, his face flushed, his breathing like the snore of a stupor. Kneeling on the near edge of the bed the white-clad figure of his wife. Stooping over her was a tall, thin man, cloaked in black.

The Count.

The scar on his forehead was pulsing with lust as his left hand held both Mrs Harker's wrists captive and his right hand gripped the back of her neck and forced her face down on his bosom. The poor lady's white nightdress was smeared with blood, and a thin stream trickled down the Count's bare breast, revealed by his torn-open shirt. Their posture together bore a truly gruesome resemblance to a child forcing a kitten's nose into a saucer of milk to compel it to drink.

As we burst into the room the Count's head turned to us and his eyes flamed hellish with hate. The great nostrils of the white beak nose flared wide as a stallion's, while the sharp white teeth protruded down in a catlike snarl, silhouetted hideously against his blood-dripping lower lip. Tossing his victim like the corpse of a rat on the bed, he turned and sprang at us. But the Professor had regained his feet and now stepped forward, holding up towards the Count his little packet of Sacred Wafer.

The Count stopped dead as if poleaxed – just as poor Lucy had done outside the tomb – and cowered back, hissing. Hatefully the beast retreated as we three others, holding high our crucifixes, advanced in a line with the Professor.

Just then the moonlight suddenly failed, as a great black cloud sailed across the blinded sky. By the time the gaslight sprang up under Quincey's match, we saw, where the Count had stood, nothing left but a wisp of vapour which trailed from there to under the door, which Quincey had closed, and out into the passage.

Van Helsing and I rushed forward to tend Mrs Harker, who had begun to scream a scream so wild, so ear-piercing, so despairing that it seems to me now that it will echo in my memory till the moment of my death. As she lay screaming in helpless disarray, her face looked indescribably ghastly, with a pallor obscenely accentuated by all the blood that smeared her lips, and cheeks, and chin. From her throat oozed twin threads of blood, and her eyes were mad with terror. Perhaps sensing how appalled we were by her appearance, she now tried to hide her face behind her poor crushed hands, wealed scarlet from the Count's terrible grip. Meanwhile from deep within her throat, as from a separate voice than screamed the incessant scream, came the low desolate wail of endless grief.

Van Helsing bent over her and drew the coverlet decently over her almost naked body, while Arthur, overcome by emotion, ran groaning from the room.

To me Van Helsing whispered:

'Jonathan is in the trance we know the Vampire he produce. We can do nothing with Madame Mina till she subside. But Jonathan I must wake him.' He dipped the end of a towel in the cold-water jug and with it began to flick Harker's face, his wife all sobbing and yelling in a really quite heart-rending fashion.

As the Professor saw to Harker, I raised the blind, looked out of the window, and saw by the resurgent moonlight that Quincey Morris was running across the lawn and now hid himself in the shadow of a large and very dense yew tree. While I puzzled as to why Quincey was doing this I heard the bewildered sounds of Harker's return to partial consciousness, so I turned back to the bed. On his face, as well there might be, was a look of hysterical amazement. He seemed dazed as if slugged by a prizefighter, but then full consciousness burst upon him all at once, and he started up. His wife was aroused by his revival and turned to him with her arms outstretched – as though to embrace him. Instantly, however, she shrank back from him again, pressed her elbows together, held her hands to her face, and shuddered till the bed shook beneath her.

'In God's name, what does this mean?' cried out Harker. 'Professor Van Helsing, what has happened? Mina? My dear, what is that blood? My God, my God! Has it really come to this?' Rising to his knees, he beat his hands wildly together. 'Good God help us!' he wailed. 'Help her! Oh, help – ' Distractedly he jumped from the bed and began to pull on his nightrobe – all the man in him awake in this crisis.

'What has happened? *Tell me*,' he harangued us before we had time to respond. 'Professor Van Helsing, you love Mina, I know. Please save her. Things cannot yet have gone too far. Guard her, at least, while I look for *him*.'

Mrs Harker, through her own terror, now sensed some sure danger to her husband. Forgetting her own distress, she seized hold of him and protested:

'No, Jonathan. You must not leave me. I have suffered enough tonight, God knows, without the additional dread of his harming you. You must stay with me. And with these friends who will watch over you.' Her expression became utterly frantic as she spoke.

Reluctantly Harker yielded to her.

Mrs Harker pulled him down beside her on the bed, and clung to him fiercely.

Trying to calm them, the Professor held up his little golden crucifix, and said serenely:

'Do not fear, my dear. *We* are here. And with this sacred cross close to you, his foul being cannot approach. You are safe for tonight, and we must all be calm and take counsel together.'

Mrs Harker shuddered and was silent, pressing her head to her husband's breast. When she looked up, Harker's white nightrobe was stained with blood from her lips, and from the oozing wounds in her neck. When she saw how her blood had marked her husband she shrank away from him and sobbed:

'Unclean, unclean. I must touch him – kiss him – no more. Oh, how horrible. That *I* should become his enemy, whom he may have most cause to fear.'

Harker retorted fondly:

'Nonsense, Mina. I refuse to listen to such words from you. Hush now.' Forcefully he embraced her, folded her to his breast, and for a while she lay there sobbing. Harker looked up at us over her bowed head, with eyes damply blank. When Mrs Harker's sobs began to abate, Harker said to me, with heavily studied calm:

'And now, Dr Seward, please tell me all about it.'

I described what had happened.

Harker listened with determined impassiveness, but his nostrils betrayed his agony when I told how the ruthless hands of the Count had held his wife in that terrible position, her mouth forcibly pressed to the bleeding wound in his breast. It fascinated me to note, though, that, despite the torment wracking him, Harker's hands all the while stroked lovingly Mrs Harker's ruffled hair. Just as I was finishing, Quincey and Arthur knocked at the door, then entered in obedience to our summons.

Van Helsing looked at me significantly.

I nodded in terse agreement.

The Professor then, to divert the thoughts of the unhappy husband and wife from each other's misery, breezily inquired of the newcomers what they had discovered.

Lord Godalming answered:

'I looked in the study. Though he had clearly been there, he was now . . . gone. He had, however—' He stopped suddenly, looking anxiously at the stricken couple on the bed.

Van Helsing said gravely:

'Go on, friend Arthur. No more concealments. Our hope now is in knowing *all*. Tell freely!'

So Arthur went on:

'I suppose it could only have been there for a few seconds, yet all the manuscripts had been burned, and waxy blue flames were flickering amongst the white ashes – the cylinders of your phonograph, too, had been piled on the fire.

'Thank God there are still the other copies in the safe!' I ejaculated.

Arthur's face lit up for a moment, but fell again as he recalled:

'I ran downstairs then, but could see no sign of the Count. I looked into Renfield's room. Nothing there . . . except—'

'Go on,' insisted Harker hoarsely.

Arthur bowed his head sadly. Moistening his lips with his tongue, he continued:

'Except that the poor fellow is dead.'

Mrs Harker raised her head. With despondent weariness she murmured:

'God's will be done!'

I could not but feel that Arthur was keeping back something, but, respecting his discretion, I said nothing.

Van Helsing turned to Morris and asked:

'And you, friend Quincey? What to tell?'

He replied:

'I thought it well to know where the Count would go when he left the house. I did not see *him*, but I did see a large bat rise up from Renfield's window, and flap westward. I expected to see him, in whatever shape, head back to Carfax, but he evidently has fixed on some other lair. And he will not be back tonight again – will he, Professor? For the dawn is too close.'

After a minute's brooding silence, Van Helsing said, laying a fatherly palm on Mrs Harker's head:

'And now, Madame Mina – poor dearest. Tell us all what happened to you. God knows your pain, but it is need we know.'

Mrs Harker shivered as she clung tightly to her husband. Then she raised her head proudly, and held out one hand to Van Helsing, who stooped to kiss it reverently, then held it fast.

'I took my sleeping draught,' she began slowly, 'but for a long time it had no effect. I seemed to become more wakeful, and horrible fancies crowded round my mind – all about vampires and death; blood, and pain.'

Harker groaned to hear her anguish.

Mrs Harker reproved him lovingly:

'You must not fret, Jonathan. Be brave and strong, and help me through this hell. Now, where was I?'

'Sleeping draught,' the Professor prompted her keenly.

'Oh yes. Well, surely enough, sleep must soon have come. Nor can Jonathan's coming in have waked me, for he was already lying by me when next I remember. There was in the room the same thin white mist that I had noticed before. Now I felt the same vague terror again – the same gripping sense of some *presence*. I turned to wake Jonathan, but found he was sleeping so soundly that it might have been *he* who had taken the sleeping draught. I tried, but could not wake him. This caused me great fear, and I looked around – terrified . . . '

'Then?' nodded the Professor sympathetically.

'Indeed my heart felt dreadful shock when there, beside the bed, as if stepped out of the mist – or rather as if the mist had coalesced into him – for it had entirely disappeared – stood a tall, thin man, all in black. I knew him at once by description, of course. The waxen face. The high aquiline nose. The parted red lips, with those long white teeth pointing whitely down. Above all the red eyes I had seemed to see in the sunset on the windows of St Mary's Church at Whitby. I knew too the red scar on his forehead – where Jonathan had struck him. Oh, how I would have screamed, if only my voice were not paralysed. As my lips strained to move, the Count – pointing to Jonathan – admonished me in a merciless whisper:

"'Silence! If you make any sound I shall dash out his brains before your very eyes."

'Still too appalled to speak, I could do nothing but lie there, helpless. With a mocking smile the Count placed one hand upon my shoulder, held me tight, bared my throat with the icy fingers of his other hand, and said:

"'First, a little refreshment to reward my exertions. Be still, woman. This is not the first time, nor the second, that your veins have appeased my thirst!"

'I was bewildered, petrified, and yet – shameful but true – I did not *want* to hinder him. I suppose that is a part of the awful curse of his power . . . '

'What next?' insisted the Professor, patting Mrs Harker kindly.

'Then he – he – oh, God pity me. He thrust his reeking lips hard upon my throat!'

Her husband groaned piteously again.

She squeezed his hand harder, and looked at him with naught but compassion, as if *he* were the injured one. Then she went on:

'I felt my strength fading away. In a moment I was lost in a shallow but seemingly endless swoon. How long his horrible leeching must have lasted I do not know. Looking back, it feels as if hours must have passed before he removed his dribbling fangs from my throat. And I saw my own blood—'

The remembrance overpowered her and she would have collapsed but for her husband's sustaining arm. Several deep breaths restored to her sufficient strength to go on:

'Then he mocked me:

"'And so you, like your menfolk, would pit your little brains against mine? To help those foolish men to hunt, to frustrate my grand design? Ha! Well will you know, ere long, what it is to cross my path. While they played schoolboy wits against me – who commanded nations for hundreds of years before their birth – I was countermining them all the while. And you, their best beloved, are now become flesh of *my* flesh; blood of *my* blood. My bountiful pretty wine-press for a while," he chuckled obscenely, "who soon shall become my aide and companion too. When Dracula's brain cries 'Come!' to Mina she shall cross land or sea to do my bidding at any cost. And to that end, this!"

'He pulled open his shirt and with his long sharp nails tore open a vein in his breast. As the blood spurted forth he seized my neck and pressed my mouth to the wound, so that I must either suffocate or swallow down some of the – oh, my God, what have I done to deserve such a fate? Pity, pity . . .'

In heartrending distress Mrs Harker rubbed hard at her lips, as though hoping to purge them of pollution.

As she was telling her terrible story, the eastern sky had been quickening behind the blinds. Harker, as the diabolical narrative progressed, took on an ever darker hue, which deepened in the morning light till the first red streak of dawn showed his flesh almost black against the whitening of his hair.

God pity the poor Harkers.

We have arranged that one of us shall remain within constant call of the unhappy couple until our next move is ripe for execution. Meanwhile – of this I am sure – the sun rises today, all round the world, on no more miserable house than mine.

Part IV

THE HUNTER HUNTED

England

29

Jonathan Harker's Journal

3 October.

It is six o'clock, and we are to meet in the study in half an hour. Till then, as I must do something, or go mad, I write. All details, big and little, must go down — for in the end the little things may teach us most. God knows, though . . . what error, or even knowledge, could have landed Mina and me in more misery than today? However, we must trust — trust and hope. Poor Mina. Only moments ago she told me, the tears running down her dear cheeks, that only in trouble is our faith truly tested — that if we keep on trusting, God will aid us in the end. The end? Dear God, what end?

But let me take refuge in facts.

Earlier Professor Van Helsing and Dr Seward reported that in the room below they had found Renfield lying on the floor, all in a heap. His face was dreadfully bruised and crushed in, and the bones of the neck were broken.

Dr Seward asked the attendant on duty in the passage if he had heard anything. He said he had been sitting down — he confessed to 'half dozing' — when he heard loud voices in the room, followed by Renfield's calling out loudly several times:

'God! God! God!'

After that there was a sound of falling, and when the attendant entered the room he found Renfield lying on the floor, face down, just as the doctors described him later. Professor Van Helsing asked the attendant if he had heard voices, plural, or 'a voice'. The man said he could not say — that at first it had seemed to him there were two, but as he had discovered no-one else in the room, it followed that the voice could only have been singular. What he swore he could definitely swear to was that the word 'God' was spoken by the patient.

Dr Seward told us later, when we were alone, of the undesirability of an inquest — since it would never do to put forward the truth, as no-one would believe it. As it was, he thought that on the attendant's evidence he could give a certificate of death by misadventure: caused by Renfield's falling from his bed.

When the question arose as to our next best step, the first thing we decided was that Mina should now be kept in our fullest confidence, so that nothing – no matter how painful – should be kept from her. She herself agreed the wisdom of this, and it was pitiful to see her remain so brave in the teeth of her ghastly despair.

'There must be no more concealment,' she said. 'Alas, we have had too much already. Besides, there is nothing in all the world that can cause me more pain than I have already endured – *than I suffer now.*'

Van Helsing, looking at her fixedly, asked quietly:

'But, dear Madame Mina, are you not afraid – not *for* yourself, but for others *from* yourself? After what has happened?'

Mina's eyes shone with the devotion of a martyr as she answered:

'Ah, no! For my mind is made up!'

'To what?' the Professor asked gently, while we others sat deathly still, paralysed with horror in anticipation of Mina's reply:

'Because', she explained simply, 'if I find in myself – and I shall watch keenly for it – any sign of peril to anyone I love, I shall die.'

'You would not . . . kill yourself?' the Professor quizzed her hoarsely.

'I would,' she nodded emphatically, 'if there were no kind friend who would save me such a pain, and so desperate an effort.' Mina looked at Van Helsing meaningfully as she spoke.

The Professor jumped up and pressed his hand to Mina's head as solemnly he promised:

'My child, if for your good, there *is* such an one. But first, nay—' For a moment the Professor seemed to choke: a great sob rose in his throat, which he gulped down to say:

'But you must not die. Not by any hand, and most of least by your own. Not until—'

'Not until what, Professor?' interrupted Dr Seward suspiciously.

'Until that enemy – who has foul your sweet life – is true dead, you must not die.'

'Oh, Professor,' murmured Mina weakly, 'what do you mean?'

'If he be still with the quick Un-dead, *your* death would make *you* even as *he*. No! You must live! Struggle and strive to *live*, despite death seem a boon unspeakable. On your living soul I charge you not die – nor *think* of death – till this great evil pass.'

Poor Mina grew white as death, and shivered like a quicksand beneath the incoming tide.

We men were all silent; we could do nothing.

At length Mina's calm returned. Sweetly, but oh so sorrowfully, she held out her hand to the Professor:

'My dear friend, if God will let me live, I shall strive to do so.'

Fired by her courage, we began to discuss practicalities. I told Mina she was to have all the papers in the safe, and all diary or phonograph records that we may hereafter make; and that she was again to organize our intelligence as she had done before – she expressed pleasure at the prospect of something so useful to do.

Van Helsing, as usual, had thought ahead:

'It is well', he said, 'that after our visit to Carfax we decide not to trouble the earth-boxes there. Have we done so, the Count he must guess our purposes, and take measure to frustrate us against all the others, but now he know not our intentions. Nay, more – in all probable he know not such power exist to us can sterilize his lairs! Also today, when we have examine the house in Piccadilly, we may track the lastest box. Today, then, is ours; and until the sun set tonight that monster must retain whatever form he now have. Confined within his earthly envelope, he cannot melt into the air, no. Nor disappear through chinks. If he go through a doorway, he must open the door like a mortal. And so we have this day to hunt out all his lairs and sterilize them. So shall we drive him to bay in some place where the destroying shall be sure.'

Here I started up impatiently, indignant to feel that the seconds so preciously laden with Mina's life were flying from us while the Professor discoursed at such length.

But Van Helsing held up his hand warningly:

'Nay, friend Jonathan,' he said. 'In this the quickest home is the longest way, so your proverb say. We shall all act with desperate quick when the time he come. But think. In all probable our key there is lying in that house in Piccadilly. The Count he may have many houses bought. Of them he have deeds of purchasing, keys and other things. He have paper that he write on, books of his cheques, and so forthing. Many belongings he must have somewhere – why not in this place so central, yet quiet, where he come and go by front or back at all hour, when in the very vast of the traffic there is none to notice?

'Well! There shall we go and search that house. And when we learn what it holds, then do we what friend Arthur call, in his phrases of hunt, "stop the earth", and so we run down our old fox – so? Is it not?'

'Then let us go at once,' I cried. 'We are wasting priceless time.'

The Professor did not move, but simply said:

'And how we get *in* that house in Piccadilly?'

We shall *break* in if need be,' I told him, my blood boiling.

'And your so London police? What they say?'

Clearly the Professor was prevaricating deliberately. Sure he must have good reasons, I muttered quietly:

'Please let us not delay more than need be. You know what torture I am in.'

'Indeed, my child. And there is no wish of me to add your anguish. But just a moment *think*, shall we all?'

I nodded.

'We wish to get in that house, but we have no key. Yes?'

I nodded again.

'Now suppose you was, in truth, the *owner* of that house, and could not get in. What should you do?'

'Hire a respectable locksmith, to pick the lock for me.'

'But your police they not interfere?'

'Not in England. Not if they believed the man to be legitimately employed.'

'Then', the Professor looked keenly, 'all we need is not go so early that the policeman who have then little good to think of think it bad. So shall we go after ten o'clock – when there be many abroad, and when such things *would* be done, was we indeed *owners* of the house.'

I must have smiled with relief when I realized how right the Professor was, and even the terrible despair all over Mina's face relaxed a shade: with hope from such good counsel.

Van Helsing went on:

'Within that house we find much clues. Anyways some of us remain there while the rest find the more earth-boxes – at Bermondsey and Mile End.'

Lord Godalming stood up and said decisively:

'I shall wire my people to have horses and carriage ready.'

'Say there, Art,' said Quincey Morris politely. 'Don't you think that your snappy carriage, with its heraldic adornments, in a byway of Walworth or Mile End, would attract too much attention? Seems to me we should all take cabs, and even leave them someways from the place we aim to case.'

'Friend Quincey is right!' exclaimed the Professor. 'His head is in plane with horizon!'

Mina was following all this with growing interest, and I rejoiced to see her forget for a time her terrible experience of the night. She was very pale, almost ghastly, and so thin seemed her lips that they made her teeth appear unnaturally prominent. I did not mention this last, lest it cause her needless pain, but it made the blood run cold in my veins to think of what had occurred to her, and poor Lucy too – when the Count had sucked their blood. As yet there was no sign of Mina's teeth growing sharper, and yet . . . whose side was time on?

Next we discussed how best to sequence our efforts, and finally it was agreed that before starting for Piccadilly we should destroy the Count's lair close at hand. As to our disposal of forces, it was suggested by the Professor that, after our visit to Carfax, we should *all* enter the house in Piccadilly; that the two doctors and I should remain there, while Lord Godalming and Quincey found the lairs at Walworth and Mile End, and destroyed them. To this plan I objected strenuously: that my place was to stay and protect Mina.

Mina, however, would not hear of it. She insisted that amongst the Count's papers might lurk some clue which only I could understand – in the light of my experiences in Transylvania – and that all the strength we could muster was required: to cope with the Count's extraordinary power. In the end I had to give in, for Mina's resolution was absolute.

'As for me,' she said, 'I have no fear. Things have been as bad already as ever they could be. So go, dear husband. God can, if He wishes, guard me as well alone as with any mortal present.'

So again I leapt up, crying out:

'Then in God's name let us start at once, for we are losing time. The Count may visit Piccadilly before we think.'

'Not so!' said Van Helsing, holding up his hand.

'But why?' I asked.

'Do you forget', he inquired with a pregnant smile, 'that last night he banqueted heavily, and will sleep late?'

Did I forget? Shall I ever? *Can* I ever? Can any of us . . .

Mina struggled hard to maintain her brave countenance, but the pain overmastered her. Burying her face in her hands, she shuddered as she moaned.

Van Helsing, of course, preoccupied, had not intended to recall her frightful ordeal. Horrified at his thoughtlessness, he swooped down to comfort her:

'Oh, Madame Mina,' he apologized, 'dear Mina, alas. That I, of all who so reverence you, should speak so shocking forgetful. These stupid old lips of mine – this foolish head – do not deserve so, but you will forget it, will you not?' He bent low beside her as he spoke.

Mina took his hands, smiled weakly at him through her tears, and said hoarsely:

'No. I shall not forget, for it is well that I remember. But forgive – yes, yes. Now . . . you must all be going soon. Breakfast is ready, and you must eat to make you strong.'

Breakfast was a strange meal. We tried to be cheerful, to encourage Mina; yet, strangely, she seemed the brightest of us all. When the meal was over, Van Helsing stood up and said:

'Dear friends, we go forth to our terrible enterprise. Are we all armed? As on that first night when we visit our enemy's lair? Armed against ghostly attack as well as carnal?'

We assured him we were.

'Good-good,' said the Professor. 'Now, Madame Mina, let me see *you* armed against personal attack. I have myself, since you came down, made garland of your chamber with *the thing we know*, so that *he* may not enter. Now let me guard yourself. On your forehead I touch this Sacred Wafer . . . in the name of the Father, the Son, and—'

Now came a fearful scream which shocked our hearts to hear. As the Professor had brushed the Wafer against Mina's forehead, it seared it – burned her skin through to the bone – as if it were white-hot metal. My poor darling's brain told her the significance of the fact as quickly as her nerves felt the pain, and her overwrought nature found its voice in that dreadful scream. Its echo had not ceased to rend the air when Mina slumped to her knees in a perfect agony of abasement. Pulling her beautiful hair over her face, like a leper of old his mantle, she wailed:

'Unclean! Unclean! Even the Almighty shuns my polluted flesh! And I must bear this shame upon my forehead until the Judgment Day.'

In a rage of helpless grief I threw myself down beside her, put my arms around her, and hugged her tight against me. For a minute our sorrowful hearts beat together, while the friends around us averted eyes brimming with silent tears of sympathy.

Then, in tones of inspired gravity, Professor Van Helsing pronounced:

'It may that you must bear that mark till God Himself see fit, as He most surely shall – on the Judgment Day – to redress all wrongs of Earth, and of His children thereon. And oh, Madame Mina, may we who love you be there to see, when that scarlet scar, the carnal sign of God's knowledge of what has been, shall fade away to leave your brows as pure as the heart below we know. For surely as we live that wound shall lift, when God see right to lift our burden from hard on us. Till then we bear our Cross, as His Son did, obedient to His will.'

There was hope in the Professor's words, and the comfort of sublime resignation. Mina and I, simultaneously, each took one of the old man's hands, bent over, and kissed it. Then without a word we men all knelt in a circle together. All holding hands, we pledged a most solemn oath: to raise the veil of sorrow from the head of her whom, each in his own way, we loved so dearly. And in unison we prayed for guidance and help in the terrible task before us.

It was then high time to start. So I said farewell to Mina, a parting which neither of us shall forget to our dying day, and we men set out.

(To one thing I have privately made up my mind: if it should emerge that Mina MUST be a vampire in the end, she shall not fall from human grace alone. I suppose it is thus that, in old times, one vampire meant many. Just as their hideous bodies could only rest in sacred earth, so the recruiting sergeant for their ghastly ranks was the holiest of loves.)

We entered Carfax without trouble and found everything as before. Really it was hard to believe that amongst such prosaic surroundings of neglect and dust and decay were any grounds for fear. Were our minds not made up, and without scourging memories to spur us on, we could hardly have proceeded. But proceed we did, and in due course found no papers, nor any sign of recent occupation in the house. In the old chapel the heavy wooden boxes looked just as we had seen them last. As we stood before them, the Professor announced:

'My friends, we have duty here to do. To sterilize this earth, so sacred of holy memories, that *he* has brought from distant land, for such evil use. He has chose this earth because it have been holy. Thus with his own weapon we defeat him, for we make it more holy still. As it was sanctified to *man*, it now we sanctify to *God!*' As he spoke he took from his bag a screw-driver and wrench, and in moments the lid of one of the crates was prised off. The earth within smelled musty and fetid but we others did not mind, for our attention was concentrated on the Professor. Taking from his bag a piece of the Sacred Wafer he laid it reverently on the earth, then, shutting down the lid, he began to screw it fast; we aiding him.

Thus we treated every one of Dracula's boxes in the Carfax chapel, and left them, to all appearances, as we had found them – though in each was a portion of the Host.

When the door was closed behind us, the Professor said gravely:

'So much, so good. If with all the others we can do so successful, then sunset tonight he may shine on Madame Mina's forehead all white as ivory again, and with no stain!'

As we passed across the lawn, on our way to the station to catch our train, we could see the front of the asylum. In the window of our room I glimpsed Mina. Eagerly I waved to indicate that our work at Carfax had been successfully accomplished. She nodded to show she understood, then waved a gentle farewell. It was with a heavy heart that we sought the station and just caught the train, which was steaming in as we reached the platform.

I have written this on the train.

Piccadilly, half past noon.

Just before we reached Fenchurch Street, Lord Godalming said to me:

'Quincey and I will find a locksmith. You had better not come with us.'

'Why on earth not?' I protested.

'You are a solicitor. If you were to be caught breaking into an empty house, the Incorporated Law Society might not like it. Besides, it will attract less attention if there are not too many of us. My title will make it all right with the locksmith, and with any policeman that may come along. You had better go with Jack and the Professor and stay in the Green Park – somewhere in sight of the house. When you see the door open, and the smith gone away, then do you all come across.'

'Good-good advice!' agreed Van Helsing, so that was all decided.

Godalming and Morris hurried off in a cab, we following in another. At the corner of Arlington Street our contingent got out and strolled into the Green Park. My heart beat angrily as the house on which our hopes were centred loomed up grim and silent between its more inhabited and spruce-looking neighbours. We sat down on a bench within good view, and, so as not to attract attention by seeming without a purpose, began to smoke cigars. The following minutes seemed to pass on feet of lead as we waited for the others.

At length a four-wheeler drove up. Out of it, in leisurely fashion, got Lord Godalming and Morris; and down from the box descended a thick-set working man with a rush-woven basket of tools. Morris paid the cabman, who touched his hat and drove away. Together they ascended the steps, and Lord Godalming pointed at the lock. The workman took off his coat and hung it on a railing spike, saying something to a policeman who just then sauntered past. The policeman nodded acquiescence, and the man knelt down beside his tools. Next he peered into the keyhole, blew into it, and made some remark over his shoulder. Lord Godalming smiled, and the man began to probe the lock with a hefty bunch of keys. In response to the third key he tried, the door opened easily and Lord Godalming and Quincey Morris entered the hall.

We in the park sat still. My own cigar burnt furiously, as in suspense I sucked it, but Van Helsing's had gone out altogether. We continued to wait as the locksmith handed over the successful key to Lord Godalming, who put it in his pocket and gave the man some money. The locksmith touched his cap with great respect, gathered up his tools, put on his coat and departed.

Lord Godalming closed the door after him.

Not a soul had taken the slightest notice of the whole transaction.

When the man had rounded the corner, we three left the Park, crossed the street and knocked at the door. It was immediately opened by Quincey Morris, beside whom stood Lord Godalming, lighting a cigar.

'The place smells so vilely,' explained the latter as we came in.

And goodness yes how noxious it did indeed smell — just like the old chapel at Carfax — so plainly the Count had been using the place pretty freely, and recently too. Without delay we explored the house, all keeping closely together, not sure what we might find. In the dining-room, at the back of the hall, we discovered eight boxes of earth. *Eight* boxes out of the *nine* we sought. Here, certainly, was progress, and yet our mission could never be over till we found that missing box.

To deal with the present eight boxes we first opened the shutters of a window which looked out, across a narrow stone-flagged yard, to the blank face of a stable. It was pointed like the front of a miniature house, but there were no windows in it, so we had no fear of being observed. With the Professor's tools we opened the boxes, one by one, and planted fragments of Wafer in them, just as in the Carfax chapel.

Next, confident that the Count was not at present in the house, we proceeded to search for any of his effects. These too we found to be concentrated in the dining-room, on whose table lay: confirmation of purchase and outright ownership of the Piccadilly house; likewise in respect of the houses at Mile End and Bermondsey; notepaper, envelopes, pens and ink. All were covered up in thin wrapping paper to keep them from the dust. There were also a clothes brush, a brush and comb, and a jug and basin – the latter containing dirty water which was reddened as if by blood. Finally a heap of keys of all shapes and sizes, presumably those belonging to the other houses. When we had examined this last find, Lord Godalming and Quincey Morris, having noted the addresses in the East and South, scooped up all the keys and set off to deal with any boxes they might find in those places.

The Professor, Dr Seward and I are presently, with such patience as we can muster, awaiting their return – or the coming of the Count.

30

The Battle of Piccadilly

3 October.

It seemed an age that we waited for the return of Godalming and Quincey Morris. Meanwhile . . . God, what misery. Last night Harker was a frank, happy-looking man, with strong youthful face, full of energy, and with dark brown hair. Today he is a drawn, haggard old man, whose white hair matches well the hollow burning eyes and grief-written lines of his face. His energy, however, is still intact. Indeed, he is like a living flame. This may yet be his salvation, medically speaking, if it tides him through the worst despair. Poor Harker. I thought my own troubles were bad enough.

The Professor, perceptive as ever, went out of his way to keep Harker's mind active, saying:

'I have study all the papers relating to this monster. And the more I study, the greater seem necessity to utterly stamp him. All through recent centuries are signs of his advance. Not only of his power, but of his knowledge of it too. As I learn from researches of mine friend Arminius of Buda-Pest, this Dracula was in life a most wonderful soldier, statesman, *and alchemist* – which latter being the highest develop of the science-knowledge of his time. He had a mighty brain, a learning beyond compare, and a heart without fear nor remorse. He dared even attend the Scholomance, and no knowledge of his day did he not essay.

'Well, in Dracula the brain powers survive the physical death, though it seem his memory was not all complete. In some faculties of mind he become only a child, but growing, and some things childish at the first are now of man's stature. He is experimenting, you see, and doing it well. And if not we cross his path he would now be – and will yet, if we fail! – the further-master of new-order beings, whose road lead not through Life, but Death.'

Harker groaned:

'All this arrayed against my darling? Oh why, oh why? But in what way is he experimenting, Professor? Surely to know that will help us defeat him.'

Van Helsing smiled approvingly:

'He have been trying his power – like muscle – slow but sure. That big child-brain of his is working. Well for us, too, it is yet *child*-brain. For had he dare at the first certain things, he would long ago have go beyond our power. However, he means still to succeed, and a devil with centuries before him can afford to slowly go. *Festina lente* his motto.'

'I fail to understand,' complained Harker wearily.

The Professor laid his hand tenderly on Harker's shoulder.

'My child,' he urged, 'think how, of late, this monster creep into knowledge experimental. How he use the zoophagous patient, to penetrate friend John's asylum. For your Vampire, though in all afterwards he come how and when he will, must first make entry *only* when he have invitation. But these are not his best experiments. See? How at the first those so great boxes being moved by *others*. Then soon the growing child-brain consider whether *he himself* can move the box. Alone. So he progress to scatter these graves of him, none other knowing where he have them hid. He may have intend to bury them deep in the ground. So he only use them in the night, or when he change his form – they do him equal well, and none may know these are his hiding place!

'But let us not despair. His knowledge come to Dracula too late! Already all his lairs but one be sterilize. If before the sun set this night we find that other, then he have *no place* to take him rest. By my clock it is one hour, and already, if all well, friends Arthur and Quincey come returning—'

While the Professor was speaking we were startled by a knock at the hall door: the double postman's knock of the telegraph boy. We all moved out to the hall on a single impulse, and Van Helsing, holding up his hand for silence, stepped to open the door.

The boy handed in a despatch.

The Professor closed the door again and read aloud:

'Look out for D. He has just now, 12.45, left Carfax hurriedly and hastened South. He seems to be going the round and may want to see you – MINA.'

There was a pause, broken by Harker:

'Now, God be thanked, we shall have him soon!'

Van Helsing turned to him quickly and said:

'God will act in His own time. Do not rejoice as yet, for hasty wishes may bring terrible undoings.'

'I care for nothing now', Harker retorted hotly, 'except to wipe this brute from the face of creation. I would sell my soul to do it.'

'Hush, hush,' Van Helsing scolded him kindly. 'God does not purchase souls this wise. And the Devil, though he purchase, he not keep faith. But God is merciful, and just. He know your pain, and your devotion to dear Madame Mina. Think you how her pain double, did she hear your wild words. Do not fear however. Today this Vampire is limit to the powers of man, and till sunset he may not change. It will take him time to arrive here − see, it is twenty after one − and there are yet some times before he can come hither, be he so quick never. Hope we hard that my Lord Arthur and Quincey return back first.'

Half an hour after we received Mrs Harker's telegram, there came a quiet resolute knock at the hall door. It was just an ordinary knock, such as is given hourly by thousands of gentlemen, but it made even the Professor's heart and very mind beat loudly. We looked at each other, and together moved out to the hall, all ready with various armaments − spiritual in the left hand, moral in the right. Van Helsing unlocked the door and jumped backwards ready for action.

The gladness of our hearts must have lit our faces up like beacons when, there on the step, we beheld Lord Godalming and Quincey Morris. They came quickly in and closed the door behind them. Morris locked it and withdrew the key as Lord Godalming said:

'It is all right. We found both places. Six boxes in each, and we destroyed them all.'

'Destroyed?' asked the Professor.

'As refuges for *him*.'

We were silent for a minute, then Quincey said:

'If he doesn't turn up by five o'clock, we must get back. For it will not do to leave Mrs Harker alone after sunset.'

'He *will* be here *soon*,' murmured Van Helsing, consulting his pocket-book. '*Nota bene*, in Madame's telegram he go *south* from Carfax. That mean he cross the river − only possible at slack tide, a roundabout one o'clock. That he go south is meaning for us. He is yet only suspicious, and he go from Carfax first where he suspect interference least. You must have being at Bermondsey only short before him. That he is not here already show he go to Mile End next. This take some time, for then he have to cross the river some way. But now he cannot be long. Ready? Have all your arms!' the Professor hissed, brandishing his warning hand, as, in frozen fascination, we all heard a key being softly inserted into the main front-door lock.

I could not but admire, even at such a moment, the spontaneous strength of a dominant spirit. In our hunting parties, and adventures all over the world, Quincey Morris had always been our leader. Now, with a swift glance round the dining-room, he at once planned out our attack and, without a word, placed us each in position. Van Helsing, Harker, and I were posted behind the door, so that when it opened the Professor could guard it while we younger men stepped forward to accost the incomer. Godalming behind and Quincey in front stood out of sight behind the curtains – ready to block the window.

Then we waited in nightmare suspense as we listened to firm, deliberate footsteps proceeding along the uncarpeted hall.

Suddenly with a single bound the Count leaped into the room, scything past us before anyone could lift a hand to stay him. There was something so panther-like in the movement – so sinuously *unhuman* – that for a moment we were too stunned to respond. The first to recover was Harker, who threw himself before the door connecting with the front parlour. As the Count saw this a horrible snarl enlarged his face, showing the eye-teeth hugely long and pointed, but the evil rage as quickly cooled into a lion-like stare of disdain, as in a circle we advanced upon him.

I had no idea how things would develop next, when Harker without warning swung from behind his back a great Gurkha knife and slashed fiercely at the Count.

Only the diabolical speed of our enemy's reaction saved him: one instant more before he dodged, and the kukri had surely laid bare his vampire heart. As it was, the point flashed through the cloth of his coat, leaving a rent whence a bundle of bank-notes and stream of gold poured out. The renewed fury in the Count's eyes was so hellish that I feared the worst for Harker, despite his great gleaming knife being raised for another slash. On a protective impulse, I darted forward holding up my crucifix and wafer in either hand. Instantly I felt a strange but mighty power surge along my arms, and somehow I was not surprised to see the monster cower back. As each of my companions now threatened the Count with the same holy weapons, it would be impossible to describe the intensity of baffled malignity – of truly satanic fury – which inflamed Count Dracula's face. His waxen hue shone greenish-yellow round the red of his burning eyes, and the scarlet scar on his forehead pulsed in the pallid skin like a palpitating wound. The next instant, with a sinuous dive he swept under Harker's arm ere his kukri could strike. Grabbing a handful of money from the floor, he flew across the room and hurled himself into the window. Amid the crash and glitter of the splintered frames and shattered glass he somersaulted into the paved area below. Through the shivering sounds of glass shards landing, I heard a definite *ting* of gold, as some sovereigns fell on the flagging.

We ran to the shattered window and saw the Count spring unhurt from the ground, rush up several steps, cross the flagged yard, and push open the stable door. There he turned and mocked us:

'You think to thwart me? You! With your pale faces all in a row, like sheep in a butcher's shop! Well shall you pay dearly for your presumption. You think to leave me no place to rest? But I have more! And note you well that my revenge is just begun! I spread it over centuries, and time is on my side. Your girls that you all love, as sheep love, are mine already! Through them you, and others, shall be mine too. My creatures, to do my bidding. And to be my jackals, when I feed. Bah!' With a contemptuous sneer, he glided through the stable door, and we heard an unoiled bolt rasp behind him. Moments later we heard the faint sounds of another door beyond being opened and slammed shut.

Realizing the immediate futility of pursuing the Count through the stable, the Professor led us back to the hall.

'We have learn much!' he crowed in tones of triumph.

'What, exactly?' queried Quincey Morris, fuming with indignation at having missed his prey.

The Professor explained:

'For all the Count's brave words, yet he fear us. He fear time; he fear want! If not, why he so hurry? His very tone betray him, or my ears deceive. And why he take that money? See? Now – you young ones follow him quick. You are hunters of wild beasts, and understand it so. For me, I make sure nothing here service him, if so he return.' As he spoke the Professor swept the remaining money into his pocket, took the conveyancy papers in the bundle as Harker had left them, and heaped the remaining things into the open fireplace, where he set fire to them with a match from a box in his bag.

By now Godalming and Morris had rushed out into the yard, and Harker was lowering himself from the shattered window. Predictably, however, the Count had bolted the stable door, and by the time they had forced it open there was no sign of him. Van Helsing and I looked round the back of the house, but the mews was deserted and no-one had seen our fugitive depart.

It was now late afternoon – sunset not far off. We had to confess that our game for today was up, and with heavy hearts we agreed with the Professor when he said:

'Let us go back to Madame Mina. Dear lady. All here we can do just now is done. *There*, at least, we can protect *her*. But never despair. There is but *one* more earth-box. When that we find . . . ho-hum!'

I could see the Professor's bravado was largely to comfort Harker, who now and again could not suppress a low groan – clearly thinking of his wife.

With sad hearts we retreated to my house, where Mrs Harker awaited us with an appearance of cheerfulness which did great honour to her unselfish courage. But when she saw our faces her own became as pale as death. For a second her eyes closed as if in secret prayer. Then she said brightly:

'I can never thank you all enough. Oh, my darling!' She pulled her husband's grey head against her bosom and kissed it. 'Lay your tired head here. All may yet be well, you know. God shall protect us, if He will, in His good intent.'

Poor Harker could only groan, his misery too sublime for words.

We had a perfunctory supper together, and I think it revived us somewhat – none of us having eaten anything since breakfast. True to our promise, we told Mrs Harker everything which had passed, and although she turned snowy white at times (when danger had seemed to threaten her husband) and becomingly pink at others (when his devotion to her was manifest), she listened bravely and with calmness. When we came to Harker's reckless knife assault on the Count she clung to her husband's arm as though her clinging could protect him backwards. She said nothing, however, till the narration was over. Then, without releasing her husband's hand, she stood up to address us.

Oh, how I wish I could do justice to that scene: to that sweet, good woman in all the radiant beauty of her youth, marred only by the red scar on her forehead, which we saw with grinding teeth – remembering whence it came. And her loving kindness, against our grim hate. Her tender faith, against all our fears and doubting. And cruellest of all: our knowing that she, with all her goodness and purity, her love and her faith, was now outcast from God.

'Jonathan,' she said, the word like music on her lips, full of tender devotion, 'and you, my dear, true friends. I know that you must fight – that you must labour to destroy Dracula – even as you destroyed the false Lucy, so that the true Lucy might live hereafter. But let this not be a work of hate. That poor soul who has wrought all our misery is surely the saddest case of all. Imagine, then, *his* joy, when he too is destroyed in his worser part – that his spirit may live for ever. So must you be merciful to him too, though it may not hold your hands from destroying him.'

As Mrs Harker spoke I could see her husband's face darken and contract, as though the intolerable heat of his passion were shrivelling up his marrow. Involuntarily his grip on Mrs Harker's hand grew tighter and tighter till his knuckles showed sorely white. She did not flinch from the pain which, medically, I knew she must be suffering, but rather she gazed fondly upon him with eyes more appealing than ever. As she stopped speaking he leapt to his feet, snatched his hand from hers, and declaimed:

'May God give him into my hand just for long enough to cut the earthly life out of him. If beyond that I have the chance to send his soul for ever and ever to flaming hell, I gladly shall!'

'Hush!' she protested in horror. 'In the name of the good God, hush.'

'I shall not hush!' cried Harker.

'You *must*,' his wife insisted. 'Oh, Jonathan, do not say such awful things, or you will crush *me too*, with dread of your revenge. Just think, my dear – as I have thought all through these long hours past – that . . . perhaps . . . some day . . . *I too* may need such pity. And that some other, like you – and with equal cause for anger – might deny it to me . . . oh, Jonathan, how I pray that God will take your wild words as the wail of stricken love. Oh, yes. Dear God, let these poor white hairs proclaim what my husband has suffered, who all his life has done no wrong, nor ever deserved such sorrow. Forgive, forgive . . . '

We men were all in tears now. There was no resisting them, and we wept openly.

Mrs Harker wept too, but with gladness: to see that her angelic counsel had prevailed. Her husband flung himself on his knees beside her, embraced her passionately, and hid his face in the folds of her dress.

Van Helsing beckoned to we others and we stole out of the room, leaving those two loving hearts alone together with God.

Before they retired for the night the Professor fixed up their room against any attempted intrusion by the Vampire, and assured Mrs Harker that she might rest in peace. She, manifestly for her husband's sake, tried to seem at ease. Van Helsing placed on their bedside table a handbell, to be rung in case of emergency. When they had gone to bed, Quincey, Godalming, and I arranged to divide the night between us: to guard the stricken lady.

The first watch falls to Quincey, so we others must now rest.

Watching Mina's Teeth

JONATHAN HARKER'S JOURNAL
4 October.

A little after midnight.

I thought yesterday would never end. There was consuming me a yearning for sleep, in a blind belief that to wake would be to find things changed, and that any change must be better. Before we parted for the night we discussed what our next step should be, but nothing was decided. All we know for sure is that one earth-box remains, and the Count alone knows where. If he chooses to lie low, he could evade us for years; and in the meantime . . . the thought is too horrible. I dare not think it even now.

But this I know: that if ever a woman was all perfection, that one is my Mina. And I love her a thousand times more for her selfless compassion of last night, a compassion that made my own great hatred of the monster seem almost despicable. Surely God will not permit the world to be robbed of such a jewel as Mina is. Here lies hope.

We are all drifting reefwards, it seems to me, and faith is our only anchor.

Thankfully Mina is sleeping now, and sleeping without dreams. I cannot but dread what her dreams might be like, for she has such terrible memories to ground them in. Strange, though. She has not been so calm since sunset. Then, for a few moments, there came over her face a repose like the softness of April, after the last wintry blasts of March. I thought at the time it was merely a red touch of sunset brushing her cheek, but somehow now I feel it must have had a deeper meaning.

I am not sleepy myself, though terribly weary – weary to death. However, I must try to sleep; for there is tomorrow to think of, and there is no rest for me until . . .

Later.

I must have fallen asleep, for I was awakened by Mina, who was sitting up in bed, as if startled and afraid. She had placed a warning hand over my mouth, and now whispered in my ear:

'There is someone in the corridor!'

I got up quietly to investigate and discovered, just outside our bedroom door, stretched on a madman's mattress, Mr Morris – wide awake, and reading by candlelight.

'Go back to bed,' he hissed reassuringly. 'One of us will be here all night. We mean to take no chances!'

His manner forbade dissension, so I came back to bed and told Mina. She sighed. Then the shadow of a smile ghosted over her face as she wrapped her arms round me, and said softly:

'Thank God for good brave men!' With a sigh she sank back again to sleep.

I write this as I am again not sleepy, though I must try . . .

4 October. Morning.

Once more during the night I was wakened by Mina. This time the grey of coming dawn was seeping into our room round the shutters, making the windows into sharply defined oblongs, and the gas flame was no longer necessary.

Mina said to me hurriedly:

'Go call the Professor. I must see him at once.'

'Why?' I asked.

'I have an idea. I suppose it must have come to me in the night, and matured without my knowing.'

'What is it?'

'You shall hear when I tell the Professor. Go quick, dearest. There is no time to lose.'

I went to the door.

Outside in the corridor, Dr Seward was resting on the mattress. Seeing me, he sprang to his feet.

'Is anything wrong?' he asked in alarm.

'No,' I replied. 'But Mina wants Van Helsing, urgently.'

'I will go,' said Dr Seward, who hurried off to the Professor's room.

Three minutes later Van Helsing was with us in his dressing-gown. Mr Morris and Lord Godalming arrived soon after with Dr Seward. When the Professor saw Mina, a smile – a beam of positive delight – ousted the anxiety from his face. Rubbing his hands enthusiastically he said:

'This is most welcome change – see! Friend Jonathan, we have your Madame Mina as of old.' To her he said airily: 'And what I do to you? Not nothings at this hour, heh?'

'I want you to hypnotize me!' said Mina excitedly. 'Do it before the sun rises, while still I can speak freely.'

Without a word the Professor motioned her to sit up in bed. Staring hard into her eyes, he commenced to make sweeping passes from over the top of her head, downward, with each hand in turn. Mina gazed at him fixedly for several minutes, during which my heart beat like a trip-hammer, for I felt some crisis was at hand. Gradually her eyes closed. Soon she sat motionless – only the gentle heaving of her bosom proclaiming her still alive. The Professor made a few more passes, then stopped. His forehead was heavily beaded with perspiration.

When Mina's eyes opened she seemed hardly the same woman. There was a faraway look in her gaze, a sad dreaminess entirely new to me. Raising his hand to impose silence, the Professor motioned the others to come closer round the bed. They came on tip-toe. Mina appeared not to see them. The stillness was broken by Van Helsing, who, in a low, level tone which would not break the current of Mina's thoughts, asked her:

'Where are you?'

Her answer came in a neutral monotone:

'I do not know. Sleep has no place it can call its own.'

For several minutes there was silence. Mina sat rigid; the Professor stood staring at her fixedly; the rest of us hardly dared to breathe. The room was growing appreciably lighter now. Without taking his eyes from Mina's face, the Professor waved me to pull up the blind. I did so, and the day poured in upon us. A red streak shot across the sky, and a rosy light seemed to diffuse itself through the room.

'Where are you now?' the Professor asked again.

Mina's answer came dreamily:

'I do not know. It is all strange.'

'What do you *see*?'

'Nothing. All is dark.'

'What do you *hear*?' The Professor's patient voice betrayed some strain.

'The lapping of water. It is gurgling by, and little waves leap. I can hear them on the outside.'

'Then you are on a ship?'

We all looked at each other, excited by this possibility, yet laden with foreboding.

'Yes, yes!' exclaimed Mina.

'What else do you hear?'

'Men stamping about on the deck, overhead. There is the creaking of a chain, and a loud tinkle as the capstan falls into the ratchet.'

'What are you doing?'

'I am still – oh, so still. It is like . . . death.' Mina's voice faded away into a deep breath, as of one sleeping, and her eyes closed again.

By this time the sun had risen, and we were all in the full light of day. Professor Van Helsing placed his hands on Mina's shoulders, and laid her head softly down on her pillow. For a few moments she lay like a sleeping child. Then with a long sigh she awoke and stared in wonder to see us all gathered around her.

'Have I been talking in my sleep?' she asked. 'Oh, tell me: what did I say?'

The Professor told her, and Mina commented:

'Then there is not a moment to lose. It may not be yet too late.'

Mr Morris and Lord Godalming started for the door, but the Professor's calm voice called them back:

'Stay, good friends. That ship, wherever, was weighing anchors while she speak. There are many ships weighing anchors in your so great Port of London. Yes? Which of them we seek? God be thanked we have a clue, though whither it lead we know not yet.'

'What clue?' demanded Quincey Morris impatiently.

'We know now why the Count seize that money, though Jonathan's so fierce knife put him in danger that even he dread. He meant escape. Hear me. *Escape!* He see that with one earth-box left only, and a pack of men who chasing him like fox dogs, this London is no safe place longer for him. So? He have take his last earth-box on board a ship, and he leave the land. He think to escape, but no! We follow him. Tally ho, as friend Arthur say when he wear red frock. Our old fox Vampire he is cunning but in meantime we may rest. For there are waters between us which he do not want to pass, and which he could not if he would – unless the ship touch the land, and then only at full tide or slack. See? And the sun is just rose. All day to sunset is to us. Let us take bath, dress, and have breakfast which we need.'

Mina looked at the Professor appealingly as she asked:

'But why need we seek the Count any further at all? If he has left these shores?'

He patted her hand as he replied:

'When we have breakfast, then I answer all questions.' He would say no more, and we separated to dress.

After breakfast Mina repeated her question.

The Professor looked at her gravely as sorrowfully he explained:

'Because, my dear, now more than ever must we find him — even if in the veriest jaws of Hell!'

Mina persisted faintly:

'But why?'

'Because', he answered solemnly, 'Dracula he can live for centuries, and you are but mortal woman. Time is now to be dreaded, see? Since once he bite that mark upon your throat.'

I was just in time to cushion poor Mina's head, as she slumped forward in a faint.

DR SEWARD'S PHONOGRAPH DIARY
(SPOKEN BY VAN HELSING)

This to Jonathan Harker.

You are to stay with your dear Madame Mina. We others go make our search — but do you take care of *her*. This is your best and most holiest office today, when nothing can find him here. Let me tell you now what we four know already: that He, our enemy, is go back to Transylvania. I know it as if a great hand of fire is writing on the wall. He have prepare for this, and the last earth-box he have all ready safe to ship. For this he take the money. For this he hurry at the last, lest we catch him before the night. It was his last hope here — save hiding in the tomb that, he think, poor Miss Lucy, keep open to him. But there was not of time. When that fail he make straight for his last resource — his last earthwork, I might say, was I wishing you *double entente*.

Dracula he is clever, ho-ho. He know his game here finish, so decide he go back home. He find ship going, so we four hunt now *what* ship, and whither bound. When that we discover, we come back to comfort Madame Mina with new hope. For all is not losing. This very monster we pursue, he take hundreds of years to get so little far as London! Yet in one day, when knowing of the disposal of him, we drive him out. Though powerful to do much harm, and suffer not as we, this Dracula he is finite. We, alone more finite, are together all more strong.

So take heart afresh, dear husbander of Mina. This battle, but begun, in the end we win – sure as God on high watch over His children. Therefore comfort her much till we return.

Van Helsing.

JONATHAN HARKER'S JOURNAL

4 October.

When Mina heard Van Helsing's phonograph message, the poor girl brightened up considerably. Already she is encouraged by certainty that the Count has left the country. For my own part, now that this horrible danger wanes, even my own terrible experiences in Castle Dracula seem like a dying dream. Here in the crisp autumn air, in the bright sunlight – alas. How *can* I disbelieve? Never while my eye is assaulted by that foul red scar on my poor darling's white brow. And afterwards . . .

Mina and I fear to be idle, so we have been through all the diaries again. Somehow, though the reality seems harsher each time, the pain and the fear seem less. There are hints of a guiding purpose throughout, and Mina suggests that perhaps we are the unknowing instruments of ultimate good.

How can that be?

But I must try to think as she does. Meanwhile . . . when will the Professor and the others return from their investigations?

It is now three o'clock.

MINA HARKER'S JOURNAL

5 October, 5 p.m.

Our meeting for report. Present: Professor Van Helsing, Lord Godalming, Dr Seward, Mr Quincey Morris, Jonathan Harker, Mina Harker.

Professor Van Helsing described what steps were taken during the day to discover on what boat and whither bound Count Dracula made his escape:

'I feel sure he go by the Danube mouth, or port inside the Black Sea, since by that way he come. But what a dreary blank to start. *Omne ignotum pro magnifico.* So with heavy hearts we begin to find what ships leave last night. Dracula is in sailing ship, since Madame Mina tell of sails being set. So, by suggestion of my Lord Godalming, we try your Lloyd's, where are note all ships that sail, however so small. There we find only one Black Sea bound ship go out with the tide. She is the *Czarina Catherine*, and sail from Doolittle's Wharf for Varna, thence other ports and on up the Danube.

'"Soh!" said I. "This is the ship whereon the Count."

'So off we go to Doolittle's Wharf, and there we find a man in an office of wood so small that the man look bigger than the office. From him we inquire of the *Czarina Catherine*. He swear much – red face, loud voice – but he good fellow all the same, and better still when Quincey give him something from his pocket which crackle as he roll it. Humble servant he become and lead us round to ask others, rough and hot, who say much of blood and bloom. But they make know how last afternoon about five comes hurry a tall man, thin and pale, high nose, teeth sharp, and eyes that seem like fires. That he be all in black, they tell, except a hat of straw which suit not him nor the time. That he scatter his money too, they tell, in ask what ship go for the Black Sea.

'Some take him to the office, then ship, where he will not go aboard but halt at shore end of gangplank, and order that the captain come to him. When told he get pay well, the captain come. Though swearing much at first, he agree to term. Then the thin man go for horse and cart to hire. Soon he come again, himself driving cart on which is a great box. This he himself lift down, though it then take several hands to load it up the ship. He give much talk to captain as to where this box must place.

'Now the captain like it not and swear in many tongues, all polyglot, that he do want no Frenchmen – with bloom upon them, and also blood – in his ship – with blood on her also. But the thin man did not be offend, and went down with the mate to see his box place, then came up to stand awhile on deck – in sudden fog!

'Soon the fog begin to melt away, and all clear again. My friends of the thirst and the language of bloom laugh loud as they tell how the captain's swears exceed picturesque when other mariners coming up the river shout that they don't see no fog at all, but only round this wharf.

'However the ship went out on the ebb. Doubtless by morning she was well down the river mouth and by the time they tell us out to sea.

'So? We have a little time to rest, for our enemy is on the sea, and to sail a ship take time, go she never so quick. When we start on land we go more quick, and we meet him there.'

'What then?' inquired Quincey Morris aggressively.

'Our best hope is coming on him in his box, between sunrise and sunset – for then he can make no struggle, and we deal with him as need be. We know all where he go, for we have see the shipping papers. The box we seek shall unload at Varna: to an agent, one Ristics, who will there present his credentials. Then after . . . what is to do is not for police or customs.'

I asked the Professor if it were certain that the Count had remained on board the ship. He replied:

'We have best proof of that! Your own evidence, Madame Mina, in hypnotic trance this morning.'

I asked him again if it were really necessary to pursue the Count, for oh! I dread Jonathan leaving me, and I know that he would surely go, if the others went.

The Professor answered with great passion:

'Necessary? Quite absolutely.'

'But why?'

'For your sake in the first, and then for all humanity. This monster is doing harm untold already, in narrow scope and short time – when as yet he is only groping, as in darkness and not knowing. All this have I told these others. *You*, my dear, will learn it in the phonograph of my friend John, or in the pages of your Jonathan. I have tell how the Vampire's leaving of his own barren land, and coming to a new land – a land where men teem like standing corn, women too – was the work of centuries. Were another Un-Dead, like him, to try what Dracula has done, perhaps not all the centuries of the world could aid him. With this one, the Count, all the forces of nature's occulting must have wondrous work together. The very place where he have live, Un-Dead for untold years, is full of strange geologic. Deep fissures and caverns, reaching down none know whither. There be volcanoes still blowing out waters of strange properties. And gases: some that kill; others to make vivify. Doubtless something magnetic or electric in these forces work for physical life occulting. Certainly Dracula himself wear from the first some greatest qualities. In a hard and warlike time he was celebrate that he have more iron nerve, subtle brain, braver heart, than any mortal man. In him some vital principle have mysteriously find its uttermost. As his body keep strong, and thrive, so his brain grow too. All this *without* that diabolic aid which is surely to him.

'And still ask you why we cannot let him be?

'*Because he have infect youth.* Forgive, my dear, that I must say such. But it is for good of you that I speak. Count Dracula infect you in such wise that *even if He do no more to you,* you have only to live – live sweet like before – and yet your death shall make you *like to him.* Well! We men have swore together that this must not be. Thus are we ministers of God's own wish: that the world, and men for whom His Son die, women too, will not be give over to monsters, whose existence all defame Him. He allow us to redeem one soul already, and we go out – as the old Knights of the Cross – to redeem much more. Like them, we shall journey towards the sunrise. And like them, if we fall, we fall in good cause.'

As the Professor paused for breath, I asked:

'But will not the Count take his rebuff wisely? Since he has been driven from England, will he not avoid it in future? As a tiger shuns the village from which he has been hunted?'

'Aha!' cried the Professor. 'Your simile of the tiger good-good. I adopt him. Your man-eater, as India call the tiger who once is tasting human blood, care no more for other prey, but prowl unceasing till he get man. Woman too. Well! This Vampire we hunt from *our* village, he is man-eater too, and cease never to prowl. In his own living life, long ago, he go over the Turkey frontier and attack his enemy at home. He be beaten back, but does he yield? No, no. He come again; and again. Persistence. Endurance. Superhuman. His child-brain long since conceive his coming to a great city. What he do? He search and choose the city of all the world most of promise for him. Then he himself prepare. He find in patience his strength, and what his powers. He study new tongues. He learn new social life. New environment ways. The politic, law, finance; science. The habits of new people, come to be since he was. His glimpse whet his appetite only, and enkeen his desire. More: it help grow his brain, for it prove his first surmises.

'And he have done this alone! From a ruin tomb in a land forgot.

'Well! What more may he not do, when at loose in the greater world? He that smile at death, and flourish amid diseases that destroy whole peoples normal? Oh! If such an one could come from God, and not the Devil, what a glorious good for this sorry world of ours! But that is not, and so we few are pledge to set the world free. Our toil must be in silence, our efforts all secret. For in this enlighten age, when men believe not even what they see, women too, the doubting of the wise would be Count Dracula's greatest strength: at once his armour and his weapons – to destroy *us*, his enemies, who peril our own very souls, to salvate the one we love. For the good of mankind also, and for the honour and glory of God. Amen.'

The meeting was then, as it were, thrown open to the floor. As a result it was determined that, for tonight, nothing be definitely settled; that we should all sleep on the facts, and be decisive at breakfast tomorrow.

I feel a wonderful peace tonight, as if some haunting cancer were removed from me. Perhaps . . .

Then I caught sight in the mirror of the red mark on my forehead, and knew I was yet unclean.

DR SEWARD'S DIARY
5 October.

We all rose early, and I think much refreshed. At breakfast there was more general cheerfulness than any of us had expected to experience ever again.

It really is wonderful how much resilience is in human nature. Let any vexing obstruction be removed – even by death – and we fly back to enjoyment and hope.

More than once, as we sat around the table, my eyes widened in wonder: whether the horrific days past had not been all a dream. Only the red blotch on Mrs Harker's forehead brought me back to reality. Even now, in grave reflection, I find it hard to accept that the evil root of all our woes is still existent. Mrs Harker too seems to lose sight of her plight from time to time, only to be recalled to it by that terribly vivid scar.

We are to meet here in my study in half an hour and decide on our course of action. I see only one immediate difficulty, and that is my fear that, in some mysterious way, poor Mrs Harker's tongue is tied. I *know* she forms conclusions of her own, some quite likely brilliant, and yet she cannot – or will not – give them utterance. I have mentioned this to Van Helsing, and he and I are to talk it over privately.

Could it be some loathsome poison has got into her veins, and is now beginning to work? The Count surely had good reasons when he gave her what Van Helsing called 'the Vampire's baptism of blood'. How puzzling it all is. One thing I do know: that if my instinct be true, regarding poor Mrs Harker's silences, then there is a truly terrible danger still before us. For the same power that compels her silence may compel her speech. I dare not think further . . . lest my thoughts dishonour one of the noblest of women.

But perhaps Van Helsing will know. He is coming to my study a little before the others, so—

Later.

When the Professor came in, I could see he had something on his mind. After beating about the bush a little, he said suddenly:

'Friend John, there is something – later we may must tell the others, but now . . . '

I waited.

With obvious reluctance the Professor went on:

'Madame Mina. She is . . . changing.'

An icy shiver ran through me, to hear my worst fears echoed.

Van Helsing continued:

'With the sad experience of Miss Lucy, we must this time be not caught short. Our task is now more hard than ever, and I see characteristic of the Vampire come alive. Very slight, but there to see by eyes without prejudge.'

'What characteristics, excactly?' I pressed him.

'Her teeth are grow more sharper, and her eyes at times more hard. Also her longer silences, as so with Miss Lucy. But my worser fear is this: that if Madame Mina can, by *our* hypnotic trance, tell what the Count see and hear, is it not like that He, who hypnotize her first, and *drink of her very blood*, and make her drink of his, shall compel her mind stronger than we? To disclose to him what she know?'

I nodded reluctantly.

The Professor went on:

'Then what we must do? *Prevent.*'

'How?'

'Keep Madame Mina ignorant of our intent. So, she cannot tell. Not what she know not. This painful task heartbreak me to think of. But so we must. Today I announce she must no more be of our council, but only guarded by us.' The Professor wiped his forehead, which had broken out in profuse perspiration at the thought of inflicting such pain upon a poor soul. To comfort him a little I divulged that I too, independently, had come to the same conclusions.

Now it is time for us all to foregather. Van Helsing has gone off for a few minutes – he said to prepare for the meeting, but I suspect his real purpose is to say a prayer alone.

Later.

What a relief. Mrs Harker had asked her husband to say she would not join us, as she thought it best that we men should feel free to discuss our movements, without her presence to embarrass us. The Professor and I glanced at each other for an instant, as if reprieved from death, and we agreed, by silent nods, to keep our suspicions to ourselves – for the moment. This enabled us to proceed straight to our plan of campaign. As Van Helsing put it:

'The *Czarina Catherine* leave the Thames yesterday morning. It take her at least three weeks to reach Varna. We can travel overland in three days. If we reckon even two days less for the ship, for any magic on the weather that the Count can may be practise, and if we allow one full day and night for any delays to us, that give a margin of nearly two weeks. Thus, to be perfectly safe, we must leave here on the seventeenth at latest. Then we reach Varna a certain day before the ship – to preparate as necessary.

'And of course we all go armed. Armed against all evil: physical as well as spiritual.'

Here Quincey Morris added:

'I understand the Count comes from wolf country, so I propose we add Winchesters to our armament. Remember, Art, when we had that pack after us at Tobolsk? What wouldn't we have given then for a repeater apiece!'

'Good-good!' agreed Van Helsing. 'Winchesters for all. Quincey's head is most level when there is to hunt, though my metaphor more science dishonour than wolves endanger to man. Meantime, we can do nothing more here. So let us tonight and tomorrow get ready, and then we four embark.'

'What "we four"?' said Harker interrogatively.

'Of course!' answered the Professor quickly. 'You must remain to take care of your so sweet wife!'

Harker was silent for a minute. Then he said in a hollow voice:

'Let us talk about that in the morning. I want to consult with Mina.'

I felt now was the time for Van Helsing to warn Harker not to disclose our plans to his wife, so I looked at him significantly and coughed. For answer, he brushed his forefinger across his lips, then turned away.

JONATHAN HARKER'S JOURNAL
5 October, afternoon.

For some time after our meeting this morning I felt I was floundering in a state of passive wonder. Mina's determination to take no part in the discussion amazed me. The way the others received her decision was also most perplexing – since so recently they all agreed there must be no more concealments from Mina.

She is sleeping now. Calmly, like a contented child. Her lips curve with happiness. Thank God she still has such moments.

Later.

How bizarre it all is. I sat watching Mina's happy sleep, and came as close to happiness myself as I suppose I shall. As the evening drew on, and the earth gathered shadows from the sun sinking lower, the silence in our bedroom deepened. All at once Mina's eyes opened. Looking at me tenderly she said:

'Jonathan, I want you to promise me something.'

'What?'

'A promise made in God's holy hearing. Never to be broken, not even if I should later implore you on my knees with bitter tears.'

'But Mina,' I protested, 'a promise so momentous should not be made in haste.'

'Jonathan, dear,' she insisted intensely, her eyes like pole stars, 'it is *I* who wish it. Nor do I ask it for myself. Ask the Professor if I am not right. If he disagrees, you may consider the promise cancelled. Now, do you promise?'

'Very well,' I yielded, anxious as to the effect on Mina if I refused.

For a moment she looked radiant.

'But promise *what*?' I asked.

'To tell me nothing of the plan against the Count. Not even by implication. Never . . . while I bear – this.' She tapped her livid scar.

Seeing she was in earnest, I said solemnly:

'I promise!'

'On your honour?'

'On my honour as a gentleman.' And instantly I felt as if a heavy door had slammed between us.

Later. Midnight.

Mina has seemed in such good spirits all evening that we men have been infected by her gaiety. Even I felt the pall of my gloom somewhat lifted. We all retired early, and Mina is now sleeping peacefully again. Thank God at least her faculty of easy sleep remains. What would I not give for a dreamless sleep myself.

6 October. Morning.

Another surprise. Mina woke me early, as yesterday, and again asked to see Van Helsing. I thought it was another occasion for hypnotism, and without question went for the Professor. He was evidently expecting some such call, for I found him dressed, and ready to come at once.

'What is it?' he asked Mina kindly.

She replied firmly:

'You must take me with you on your journey.'

The Professor was as startled as I was. Recovering, he inquired:

'But why?'

'I am safer with you, and you shall be safer too.'

'But – but, dear Madame Mina! We go into danger – to which *you* may be most liable. From – from . . . ' He broke off in embarrassment.

'I know,' said Mina, pointing to her forehead. 'But look. This is why I must go. I can tell you now, before the sun is up. Later I may not be able. I know, you see, that when the Count's will commands me I must go. That if he bids me to him by wile, I must – by any device . . . hoodwinking even Jonathan.'

God surely saw the look that Mina turned on me as she spoke, and if there be indeed a Recording Angel that look is noted to her everlasting honour. I could only clasp her hand. I could not speak, and my emotion was too great for even the relief of tears.

Meanwhile Mina went on:

'You men are brave, strong, and numerous enough to protect me. Besides, I may be of service, may I not? Since you can hypnotize me, and so learn much that even I myself do not know.'

Nodding gently, the Professor murmured gravely:

'Madame Mina, most wise, you shall with us come indeed. Together shall we achieve.'

When I looked from him back to Mina I saw she had fallen back on her pillow, instantly fast asleep. Nor did she wake when I pulled up the blind and let sunlight flood the room. Van Helsing then quietly led me away to his room. Within a minute Lord Godalming, Dr Seward, and Mr Morris had joined us. The Professor told them what Mina had said, and added:

'In the morning we leave for Varna, yes. But we have now to deal with a new factor: Madame Mina. Oh, but her soul is true. See? It is to her such agony to tell us so much. But she is most right, and our warning is good. In Varna we must be ready to act the instant when that ship arrive.'

'What exactly shall we do?' asked Mr Morris laconically.

The Professor replied:

'We first board the ship, then find the earth-box, next fasten a branch of the wild rose hardly to it.'

'What in Heaven's name for?' objected Lord Godalming.

'For that no vampire can emerge,' explained the Professor. 'Then, when later we get the box alone, we open up him, and – all will be well.'

'No waiting for me,' said Morris grimly. 'When I find that box, I smash it open and destroy the monster forthwith – even though there were a thousand men looking on, to wipe me out next moment.'

Deeply moved, I grasped Quincey's hand instinctively and found it as firm as a chunk of steel. I think he understood my look; I hope he did.

'Brave boy,' applauded the Professor. 'Quincey is all American man. God bless it. Nor shall none of us be lag behind him. And yet consider . . .'

'Consider what?' drawled Quincey Morris, whose blood was very much up.

'We all may say what we *may*,' the Professor expounded dreamily, 'but we cannot know what we *shall* do. So many accidents – but that is philosophy. Anyways we go all armed, and no effort shall lack. Now:

'Let you young gentlemens today put all business in order. For old me, I arrange the tickets, yes? And tomorrow, let's go.'

There was nothing further to be said, and we parted. I shall now settle up all my worldly affairs, and leave ready for whatever.

Later.

All done, and my will is made. Mina, if she survive me, is my sole heir. If not, then the others, who have been so good to us, will share our all.

It is now late afternoon. Mina's uneasiness draws my attention to it. I am sure there is something on her mind, which sunset will reveal. But what? I write these things in my journal since my darling must not hear them now. Perhaps later—

But there she is calling.

Part V

THE UNHOLY GRAIL

Transylvania

32

Black Sea Bound

11 October. Evening.

Jonathan Harker has asked me to note this, as he feels unequal to the task, and he wants an exact record kept.

I think that none of us was surprised to be called to Mrs Harker a little before sunset. We have of late noted that sunrise and sunset are times of peculiar freedom for her, when her old self can be manifested without any controlling force subduing her. This condition begins some half-hour before actual sunrise or sunset, and lasts till either the sun is high or the last glow of the horizon fades into sunless dusk. At first it is as if some bonds were a little loosened. Then a more absolute freedom follows quickly. When, however, the twilight freedom ceases, Mrs Harker relapses rapidly, following a short spell of warning silence.

Tonight when we met she was somewhat constrained, and bore signs of an internal struggle. A few minutes of resolute effort gave her complete control of herself, and, motioning her husband to sit beside her on the sofa where she was reclining, she bade the rest of us bring chairs up close. Taking her husband's hand in hers, she began:

'We are all here together in freedom, for perhaps the last time. I know, my darling, that you will endeavour to be with me to the end.' This to her husband, whose hand had closed hers. Mrs Harker continued:

'In the morning we embark upon our mission, and God alone knows what lies in store. You good men have agreed to take me with you. I know everything brave men can do for a poor weak woman – whose soul perhaps is lost – you men will do for me. But you must remember that I am not as you. There is a poison in my blood, in my soul, which may destroy me. Oh, my friends, you know my soul is at stake. There is an easy way out, of course, but do you agree I must not take it?' She looked appealingly at us all in turn, beginning and ending with her husband.

'What easy way?' asked Van Helsing hoarsely.

'That I die *now*, by my own hand, or that of another, before the greater evil is wrought. We all know that, were I dead, you could set free my immortal spirit. Just as you did dear Lucy's. Were my death the only issue, I would certainly not shrink from dying, here, now, amid the friends who love me. But my death is not all. And when there is hope ahead, and a holy battle to be won, I cannot believe that for me to die thus now can be God's will. Therefore I forsake the certainty of eternal rest, and prefer to risk whatever awaits us out there in the darkness, and beyond.'

We men remained silent, for we felt this was only a prelude. The faces of the others were set, and Harker looked grey as ashes. Perhaps he guessed what was coming.

Mrs Harker continued:

'The staking of my soul. That is what I can give into our enterprise. Now, what will *you* give? Your lives, I know,' she went on quickly. 'That is easy for brave men. Your lives belong to God, and you can give them back to Him. But what will you give *me*?' She looked again at the rest of us, but this time avoided her husband's gaze.

Quincey seemed to understand. He nodded, and Mrs Harker's face lit up.

'Then I shall tell you plainly what I want,' she said. 'For there must be no doubt. You must promise me, one and all – even you, my beloved husband – that, should the time come, you will kill me.'

Harker's low moan was too agonized to describe.

'What is that time?' Even Quincey's voice was strained.

'When you become convinced I am so changed that I must die – die that I may live. When I am thus dead, in my flesh, then you will, without a moment's delay, drive a stake through my heart and cut off my head. With love, to give me rest.'

Quincey was first to stir. He knelt down before Mrs Harker, pressed her hand to his lips, and mumbled:

'I'm only a rough fellow, who hasn't lived as a man should, to win such an honour, but I swear by all sacred that, should the time come, I shall not flinch from what you ask.'

'My true friend,' was all she could say, amid her fast-falling tears, as, bending over, she kissed Quincey's hand.

'I swear the same, most dear Madame Mina!' cried Van Helsing.

'And I,' vowed Lord Godalming.

Each knelt by her to swear his oath, and I in turn followed. Harker himself, wan-eyed, and with a greenish pallor beneath his snow-white hair, beseeched her:

'And must I, too, make such a promise, oh, my wife?'

'You too, my dearest,' she insisted, and infinite yearning pity in her voice and eyes. 'You must not shrink, you from me – we, whose souls are knit into one, for all life and all time. Remember, if you must, the times and places in history when brave men would gladly kill their own wives, and all their womenkind, to save them from a hideous foe. *Their* hands did not falter when those they loved implored them for merciful death. It is, indeed, a man's positive duty to she he loves, in times of such sore trial. And if *I* must meet death at any hand, let it be his who loves me best. Professor Van Helsing, I have not forgotten your compassion in poor Lucy's case: to him who loved her – ' with a fleeting blush Mrs Harker changed her phrase – 'to him who had best right to give her peace. If that time comes to me, I look to you to make it a happy memory of my husband's life: that it was *his* loving hand which set me free from my awful thrall.'

'I swear! I swear!' boomed the Professor's resonant voice.

Mrs Harker smiled sublimely as, with a sigh of exhausted relief, she leaned back to say:

'And now a word of warning. My time, if it come, may come quickly. Unexpectedly. If so, you must act swiftly. For already I might – nay, *should* – be leagued with your enemy against you.

'One more request . . . ' Her voice dropped and she looked suddenly very young and shy. 'Not vital as the other, but I want – I would like you to read me the Burial Service—' Mrs Harker was interrupted by a ghastly groan from her husband. Taking his hand in hers, and holding it to her heart, she continued:

'You must read it over me some day—'

'But oh, my dear one,' pleaded Harker, 'your death is nowhere near you.'

'Alas,' she demurred, 'I am deeper in death at this moment than if my grave were filled in above me.'

'Oh, Mina, must I?' begged Harker.

'It would comfort me greatly,' was all she said.

With violently trembling hands Harker took the book from her and began to read.

How can I – how could anyone – describe that strange scene? Its solemn gloom, sad horror; and, withal, uplifting dignity? Even the bitterest sceptic must surely have been heart-melted to see that band of devoted friends kneeling round the stricken lady, and to hear the tender passion of her husband, as in tones so broken with grief that frequently he had to pause, he read the simple service.

Immediately it was concluded, however, Harker broke down and cried like an infant:

'I – I cannot go on – words – and . . . v-voice f-fail m-me . . . '

His wife was right in her instincts, though. Strange as it all was, bizarre as it may hereafter seem, even to us so involved at the time, this comforted us much, and the ensuing silence – which heralded Mrs Harker's coming relapse from her freedom of soul – was the silence of a despair at least not absolute.

JONATHAN HARKER'S JOURNAL

15 October. Varna.

We left Charing Cross on the morning of the 12th, got to Paris the same night, and took the places secured for us on the Orient Express. We travelled night and day, arriving here at about five o'clock. Lord Godalming went to the Consulate to see if any telegram had arrived for him, while the rest of us came on to this hotel – the Odessus. The journey was not without incident, but I was too eager to care. Until the *Czarina Catherine* comes into port I shall have no other interest in the whole wide world.

Mina, thank God, is well, and looks to be getting stronger. Her colour is coming back. She sleeps a great deal, however. Throughout our journey she slept nearly all the time. Only before sunrise and sunset is she very wakeful and alert, and it has become our routine for Van Helsing to hypnotize her at those times. At first he had some difficulty, and had to make many passes, but now she yields instantly. The Professor seems to have the power at these moments to simply *will*, and Mina's thoughts obey him. First he asks her what she can see.

She answers:

'Nothing. All is dark.'

'What can you *hear*?' he asks next.

'Waves. Lapping against the ship. And the water rushing by. Canvas and cordage straining. Masts and yards creaking. The wind is high – I can hear it in the shrouds – and the bow throws back the foam.'

Evidently the *Czarina Catherine* is still at sea, but hastening here to Varna.

Now Lord Godalming has just returned. He has had four telegrams, one each day since we started, from his agent in London, and all to the same effect: that the *Czarina Catherine* has not been reported to Lloyd's from anywhere.

We had dinner and went to bed early. Tomorrow we are to see the Vice-Consul, to arrange boarding the ship as soon as she docks. Van Helsing says our best chance is between sunrise and sunset. The Count, even if he assumes the form of a bat, cannot cross running water of his own volition, and so cannot leave the ship. As he dare not appear in human form without generating suspicion – which he evidently wishes to avoid – he must remain in his box. If, then, we board after sunrise, he is at our mercy: we can open the box and . . . deal with him – just as we did poor Lucy – before he wakes. Nor shall the mercy he receives of us count for much. We hope to have no trouble with officials or the seamen, for this is a country where bribery reigns supreme – thank God – and we are well supplied with money. We have only to ensure the ship cannot berth between sunset and sunrise without our being warned, and we shall be safe. Judge Moneybags will settle this case.

16 October.

Mina's report still the same: lapping waves, rushing water, darkness, and favouring winds. When the *Czarina Catherine* rounds the Dardanelles we should have some definite report.

17 October.

Everything is pretty well fixed now. Godalming told the shippers he fancies there is a box aboard containing valuables stolen from a friend of his. This has secured him permission to open the box, though at his own risk. The owner gave him a paper instructing the captain to give him every assistance. Also a similar authorization to his agent at Varna. We have seen the agent, who was much impressed with Godalming's kindly manner, and we are confident that whatever he can do to help shall be done.

And once we get the box open?

If the Count is therein, Van Helsing and Seward will at once cut off his head and drive a stake through his heart. Morris, Godalming and I shall prevent interference, by force of our firearms if necessary. The Professor says that if we can so treat the Count's body, it will rapidly disintegrate into harmless dust. Thus there should be no evidence against us, if any accusation of murder were to be voiced. In any case we should stand by our act, and who can say these very lines will not some day bolster our defence against the rope. For myself, I am absolutely resolved, and would willingly pay with my life.

24 October.

A whole week of waiting. Daily telegrams to Godalming, but always the same story:

'Not yet reported.'

Mina's hypnotic answer is unvaried:

'Lapping waves. Rushing water. Creaking masts.'

TELEGRAM

24 October.

Rufus Smith, Lloyd's London, to Lord Godalming, care of HBM Vice-Consul, Varna:

'Czarina Catherine' reported this morning from Dardanelles.

DR SEWARD'S DIARY

24 October.

How I miss my phonograph. To write with a pen has become irksome to me – but Van Helsing says I must. We were all wild with excitement today when Godalming got his telegram. I know now what soldiers feel when the battle trumpet sounds.

Mrs Harker, alone of our party, betrayed no emotion. In this and others ways she has greatly changed during the past three weeks. The lethargy grows upon her, and though she seems strong and well, recovering her colour, Van Helsing and I are not satisfied. We talk of her often, though never to the others. It would break poor Harker's heart – certainly his nerve – if he knew we had such suspicions. Twice daily, while she is in hypnosis, Van Helsing discreetly examines her teeth. He tells me that if the rate of lengthening and sharpening increases, then . . . it will be necessary to intervene. We both know what that would mean, though we do not verbalize our thoughts. Neither of us, of course, would shrink from the task – awful though it be to contemplate.

'Euthanasia' is an excellent and a comforting expression. I am grateful to whoever coined it.

It is only a day from the Dardanelles to here, at the rate the 'Czarina Catherine' has sailed from London. She should therefore arrive sometime tomorrow morning. As she cannot possibly get in before then, we are all to retire early. We shall rise again at one o'clock, so as to be ready before dawn.

25 October. Noon.

No news yet of the ship's arrival. Mrs Harker's hypnotic report this morning was the same as ever. We men are in a fever of excitement – all except Harker, who appears deadly calm. His hands are cold as ice, and an hour ago I found him whetting the great Gurkha knife which he now carries with him everywhere. It will be a bad look-out for the Count if that kukri reach his throat.

Van Helsing and I were a little alarmed about Mrs Harker today. About noon she got into a lethargy deeper than usual. She had been restless all morning, so we were at first glad to hear she was sleeping. When, however, her husband mentioned that she was sleeping too soundly for him to wake her, we went to her room to investigate. She was breathing naturally and looked so peaceful that, after conferring briefly, the Professor and I agreed that continued sleep would benefit her more than anything else.

Poor girl. She has so much to forget. No wonder the oblivion of sleep does her good.

Later.

It seems the Professor and I were right. When, after a refreshing sleep of several hours, Mrs Harker awoke, she seemed brighter than she has for days. At sunset she made the usual hypnotic report. Wherever he may be in the Black Sea, the Count is surely hurrying to his destination – and, let us pray, to his doom.

26 October.

Another day, and still no further tidings of the 'Czarina Catherine'. She ought to be here by now. That she is still journeying somewhere is apparent, for Mrs Harker's hypnotic report at sunrise was unchanged. It is possible, though, that the vessel may be delayed by fog, for some of the steamers which came in last evening reported patches of fog both north and south of the port.

27 October. Noon.

Most strange. *Still* no sign of the ship. Mrs Harker reported again this morning:

'Lapping waves and rushing water,' though she added that the waves were very faint.'

The telegrams from London have been the same:

'No further report.'

Van Helsing confided to me a few minutes ago that he now fears the Count may be escaping us. He added significantly:

'I am not liking this lethargy of Madame Mina. Memories and souls they can strange things do during trance.'

I was about to ask him to explain, but just then Harker came in, and the Professor changed the subject. Tonight, at sunset, when she achieves her hypnotic trance, we must probe Mrs Harker more fully.

TELEGRAM

28 October.

Rufus Smith, London, to Lord Godalming, care of HBM Vice-Consul, Varna:

'Czarina Catherine' reported entering Galatz at one o'clock today.

33

On to Galatz

28 October.

We all took it differently.

Van Helsing raised his hands over his head for a moment, as though in remonstrance with the Almighty. But he said not a word, and in a few seconds stood up with his face sternly set. Lord Godalming grew very pale, and sat breathing heavily. I myself felt stunned and looked in wonder round the room. Quincey Morris tightened his belt with that quick movement which I knew so well – in our old wandering days it meant *action*. Mrs Harker grew ghastly white, and her forehead scar seemed to burn more painfully than ever. But she folded her hands meekly and looked up in prayer. Harker smiled the dark bitter smile of one without hope. And yet his behaviour belied his looks, for his hands instinctively sought the hilt of his great kukri knife.

'When the next train for Galatz?' cried Van Helsing distractedly.

'Six-thirty tomorrow morning!'

We all started, for the answer had come from Mrs Harker.

'How on earth do you know?' said Art.

'You forget that I am a train fiend. At home in Exeter I used always to make up the timetables, to help my husband. Well, this has grown to be such a habit that I always make a study of the timetables now, wherever I go. I knew that, to get to Castle Dracula we should go by Galatz, or at any rate Bucharest, so I studied the times accordingly. Unhappily there are not many to remember, and the only train tomorrow leaves, as I say, at half-past six in the morning.'

'Wonderful woman!' murmured the Professor.

'Can't we get a special?' asked Art.

Van Helsing shook his head:

'I fear not. This land very different from yours or mine. Even if we get a special, it probably arrive later than regular train. Moreover, we have to

313

prepare. Think. Organize. You, friend Arthur, go get our tickets. Do you, friend Jonathan, get letters to the agent of ship in Galatz, with authority to make search the ship there. Quincey Morris, you see the Vice-Consul. Ask aid with his fellow in Galatz, and to make smooth our way – so no times be lost when over the Danube. Friend John will stay with Madame Mina and me, and we shall consult. So, if you delay, it matter not when the sun set, since I am here with Madame.'

'And I', said Mrs Harker brightly, and more like her old self than for many a long day, 'shall typewrite for you as before. Something is shifting from me, in some strange way, and I feel freer than of late!'

The three younger men looked happier the moment they attached significance to her words. But between Van Helsing and myself there flashed a grave and troubled glance. We said nothing at the time, however.

When the others had gone out to their tasks, Van Helsing asked Mrs Harker to look out Harker's journal of his stay at Castle Dracula. She went away to get it and when the door was shut upon her the Professor nodded to me:

'Speak your mind!'

'There is definitely some change. This gives rise to a hope that makes me sick, I have to say – for it may deceive us.'

'Quite so. Know you why I ask her to get the manuscript?'

'To get an opportunity of speaking with me alone?'

'In part right, friend John. Only part. I do want to tell you something, and oh! What terrible risk. But I believe it right, I do.'

'I am afraid I do not quite follow,' I informed him politely.

'In that moment where Madame Mina say those words that arrest our understanding, yes? Inspiration come to me!'

'What inspiration?'

'In the trance of three days ago the Count sent his spirit to read her mind. Or more like *he* took *her* to see *him* in his earth-box – in the ship, with water rushing, at rise and set of sun. He learn then that we are here. For she have more to tell in her open life, with eyes to see, than he shut in his box.

'Now he make his most effort to escape us!

'At present he want her not.

'He is sure with his so great knowledge that she will come when he call – but ah! There have I hope that our man-brains, that have not lose the grace of God, will achieve us higher than his child-brain, that lie for centuries in tomb – that grow not yet to our stature, and only work selfish and therefore small.

'But here come Madame Mina! Not a word to her as yet, friend John. It would overwhelm and make despair her, just when we want all her hope and courage – when most we want of all her great brain, like man's brain, but of sweet woman, and with special power which the Count give her, and which he may not altogether take away – though he think not so. Hush! Let *me* speak.'

The Professor was so excited that for a moment I feared he might break into hysterics, just as he had when Lucy died, but with a great effort he controlled himself and was poised with perfect nonchalance when Mrs Harker tripped into the room, happy-looking and – absorbed in useful work – seemingly forgetful of her misery. As she came in she handed a number of sheets of typewriting to Van Helsing. Gravely he began looking through them, but his face came alive as he read. Then, holding the pages between finger and thumb, he said:

'Friend John, to you with so much of experience already – and you, Madame Mina, still so young – here is a lesson:

'*Do not never fear to think.* A half-thought, I say, has buzz often in my brain, recent times, but I fear to let loose his wings. Here now, with more knowledge, I go back where that half-thought come, and I find he be *whole*. A big swan-thought that sail nobly on wide wings, when his time come to fly.' Nodding benignly at our incomprehension, the Professor continued:

'See? I read here what Jonathan have wrote:

'"That other of his race who, in a later age, again and again, brought his forces over The Great River into Turkey-Land; who, when he was beaten back, came again, and again; even all alone from the bloody field where his troops lay slaughtered, since he knew that he alone could ultimately triumph—"

'Now what this tell us? Ha! The Count's child-thought see nothing. *Therefore* he speak so free. Your man-thought see nothing. *My* man-thought see nothing – till just now, when pouf! Like a flash of heaven suddenly . . . '

Mrs Harker and I waited eagerly for the Professor to contain his brainstorm sufficiently to explain:

'The criminal too have not full man-brain. He is clever and cunning.

Resourceful. But he be not of man-stature as to brain. Now this criminal of ours – this Dracula – is predestinate to crime also. He too have child-brain, and like animal he learn not by principle, but all empiric.'

'What follows from that, Professor?' asked Mrs Harker attentively.

'"Give me a fulcrum," say Archimedes, "and I shall move the world!" To do *once*, there is the fulcrum whereby child-brain become man-brain. Until he have purpose to do more, he continue the same again, every time. Oh, my dear, I see your eyes open, and the lightning flash show you all leagues!'

For Mrs Harker had begun to clap her hands, and her eyes were sparkling with hope.

The Professor went on:

'Now *you* shall speak. Tell us dry men of science what you see with those so bright eyes.' He took her hand and ringed his fingers round her pulse – as she said:

'The Count is of criminal type. Nordau and Lombroso would so classify him, and *qua* criminal he is of imperfectly formed mind. Thus, in a difficulty he resorts to habit. His past is a clue, and the one page of it that we know – and that from his own lips – tells that once before, in what Mr Morris would call a "tight place", he went back to his own country from the land he had tried to invade, and thence, without losing purpose, prepared himself for a new effort. He came again, better equipped, and won. So, later, he also came to London: to invade a new land. Beaten, and with all hope of success in England lost, his very existence in danger, he fled back over the sea to his home. Just as, formerly, he had fled back over the Danube from Turkey-Land.'

'Good-good! Oh, you so clever lady!' applauded Van Helsing, swooping to kiss her hand. A moment later he said to me, calmly as in a routine sick-room consultation:

'Seventy-two only. And in all this excitement. I have hope!' Turning to Mrs Harker again, he said with keen expectation:

'But go on. Go on! there is more to tell if you will. Heh-heh?'

'I will try,' she replied modestly. 'But you must forgive me if I seem egotistical.'

'Fear not! You *must* be egotist, for it is of *you* that we think.'

'Well then,' she theorized with growing confidence, 'as Count Dracula is criminal, he is selfish. And as his intellect is small, and his actions are based on selfishness, he confines himself to a single purpose. But that purpose is remorseless. As he fled back over the Danube, leaving his forces to be cut to pieces, so now he is intent on being *safe*, careless of all else and all others. So, his own selfishness frees *my* soul somewhat of the terrible power which he acquired over me on that dreadful night. Oh, thank God for His great mercy! My soul feels freer today than ever since that awful hour. All that haunts me now is a fear lest, while I lay in trance for you, *he* may have used my knowledge for his ends.'

The Professor stood up, saying:

'He *has* so used your mind, and by so he leave us here in Varna, while his ship rush up through enveloping fog to Galatz. Thus for the moment he escape us. But his child-mind see only so far. And it may be that, as ever in God's Providence, the very thing the evil-doer most reckon for his selfish, turn out his chiefest harm. The hunter is take in his own snare, as the great Psalmist say. For now that he think him free from every trace of us, his selfish child-brain will whisper him to sleep. He think, too, that as he cut himself off from knowing your mind, there can be no knowledge of him to you.

'*There* is where he fail!

'That terrible baptism of blood he give you – it make you free to go to him in spirit, still, when the sun rise and set. At such times you go by *my* volition, and this power to good, of you and others, is win from your suffering at his own hands. This now is all more precious, since he know it not, and to guard himself have even cut away from his knowledge of our where. *We*, however, are not all selfish, and believe God still be with us in darkest hour. So shall we follow Dracula. Nor never flinch from him, even if we peril to become like him ourself. God forbid. Friend John, this great hour do much to advance us. Pray you be scribe and write him all down, so when others return they know all finest detail, and their grandchildren too.'

29 October.

This is written on the train from Varna to Galatz. Last night we all assembled a little before sunset. After more strenuous efforts by Van Helsing than has usually been necessary, Mrs Harker sank into her trance. Of late she has responded to his promptings with considerable freedom of speech, but this time the Professor had to question her closely.

At last, and with evident difficulty, she reported:

'I see nothing. We are still. No waves lapping, but only a steady swirl of water, softly running against the hawser. And men's voices calling, near and far. Now . . . the roll and creak of oars in the rowlocks. A gun is fired somewhere. Its echo seems far away. There is a tramping of feet overhead. Ropes and chains are dragged along. What is this? There is a gleam of light – cool air blowing in upon me . . . '

Mrs Harker had risen from where she lay on the sofa, and raised her hands, palms upwards, as if pushing at an attic trap-door.

Van Helsing and I looked at each other with understanding. Quincey raised his eyebrows slightly, and Harker's gaunt right hand closed and opened obsessively round the hilt of his kukri.

There was a long pause.

The time when Mrs Harker could speak was passing, but we felt it was useless to press her. Suddenly she sat up, opened her eyes, and said innocently:

'Would none of you like a cup of tea? You must all be so tired!'

To keep her happy we acquiesced, and she bustled off to get tea.

When she had gone Van Helsing said:

'You see, my friends. He is close to land and out of his chest. But yet to get on shore! In the night he may change his form and fly, like at Whitby. But if day come before he get on shore, then, unless he be carry he cannot move. We may so arrive still in time tomorrow. To discover him in day – still boxed and at our mercies.'

There was no more to be said for the moment, so we rested in patience until the dawn, hoping then to glean more from Mrs Harker's sunrise trance.

Later.

Early this morning we listened, with breathless anxiety, for the lady's hypnotic response. Deep trance was even longer in coming than before, and the time remaining until full sunrise was so short that we began to despair. Van Helsing seemed to throw his whole soul into the effort until, at last, in obedience to his will, Mrs Harker whispered:

'All is dark. Again lapping water, level with me, and some strange creaking – as of wood. Wood on wood.' She paused; the red sun shot up. We must wait till tonight.

Later.

Now we are on the train for Galatz, travelling in an agony of suspense. We were due to arrive between two and three in the morning; but already, at Bucharest, we are three hours late – so we cannot possibly get in till well after sun-up. Thus we shall have two more hypnotic messages from Mrs Harker. Let us pray they cast more light.

Later.

Sunset, fortunately, occurred between stations – otherwise we might not have secured the necessary calm. Mrs Harker yielded even less readily than this morning, and I fear her power of reading the Count's sensations may be dying away, just when we want it most. It seems to me that her own imagination is now beginning to work. In trance hitherto she has confined herself to facts, whereas now . . . if this alteration continues it may ultimately mislead us. Would that I thought the Count's power over her would die away equally, but I am afraid it may not – and what then?

And when she did speak, Mrs Harker's words were enigmatical:

'Something is going out. I feel it pass me like a cold wind. Afar I hear sounds – confused sounds – as of men talking in strange tongues. Then fierce-falling water, and the howling of wolves.' She broke off as a sudden shudder intensified into a palsy-like shaking for several seconds. When this ceased she would say no more, not even in answer to the Professor's imperative questioning. When she emerged from the trance she was cold, exhausted; physically languid. Yet her mind was all alert. She could not remember anything, but asked what she had said. When she was told, she pondered over it deeply. For a long time, and in silence.

30 October, 7 a.m.

We are near Galatz now, and I may not have time to write later. Sunrise this morning was an anxious time. Knowing of the increasing difficulty of procuring hypnosis, Van Helsing began his passes earlier than usual. They produced no effect, however, until the regular time, when Mrs Harker yielded only after an immense subconscious struggle, and only a minute before the sun rose. The Professor lost no time in his questioning, and her response came with equal speed:

'All dark. Water swirling by, level with my ears. Creaking, more creaking. Again. Wood on wood. Cattle low far off. There is another sound, a queer one like—' she stopped and turned terribly white, then whiter still.

'Go on! Speak. I command you!' said Van Helsing in an agonized voice – despair in his eyes, for the risen sun was reddening even

Mrs Harker's snow-white face. She opened her eyes, and we all started as she said, with exquisitely engaging concern:

'Oh, Professor, why ask me to do what you know I can't? I don't remember anything.' Then, seeing the amazement on our faces, she asked:

'What have I said? What have I done? I know nothing, you see. Only that I was lying here, half asleep, and I heard you say, "Go on! Speak. I command you!" It seemed so funny to hear you order me about, as if I were a naughty child.'

'Oh, Madame Mina,' lamented the Professor, 'it is only proof of how much I honour – indeed, *love* you. See? To command her I should be proud to obey.'

There are the whistles. We are nearing Galatz. All on fire with eager anxiety.

34

Where is Dracula?

30 October. Galatz.

Mr Morris took me to the hotel where our rooms had been ordered by telegraph, he being the man who could best be spared, since he speaks no foreign language. The forces were distributed much as at Varna, except that Lord Godalming went to the Vice-Consul, as his rank might carry some weight. Jonathan and the two doctors went to the shipping agent to learn particulars of the arrival of the *Czarina Catherine*.

Later.

Lord Godalming has returned. The Consul is away, and the Vice-Consul sick; so the papers have been processed by a clerk. He was very obliging, and offered to do anything in his power.

30 October.

At nine o'clock Professor Van Helsing, Dr Seward, and I called on Messrs Mackenzie & Steinkoff, agents of the London firm of Hapgood. They had received a wire from London, in answer to Lord Godalming's telegraphed request, asking them to render us all possible assistance. They were more than courteous, and took us at once on board the *Czarina Catherine*, which lay at anchor out in the river harbour. There we saw the captain, Donelson by name, who told us of his voyage. He claimed never, in all his life, to have had so favourable a run.

'Man, but it made us afeared!' he said.

'Why was that?' I asked him.

'We expeckit to pay for it wi' some rare ill luck by the end. It's no canny, ye ken, to run frae London to the Black Sea wi' a wind ahint ye, as though the Deil hisself were blawin' ye. An' a' the time we couldna speer a thing!'

'That means they couldn't see,' I explained quietly for the Professor's benefit.

'Gin we were nigh a ship, or port, or a headland, a fog fell and travelled wi' us, till when it lifted and we looked oot, the deil a thing could we see. We ran by Gibraltar wi'oot bein' able to signal; an' till we came to the Dardanelles and had to wait to get wur permit to pass, we never were within hail o' aught. At first I thocht to slack off sail and beat about till the fog would lift; but whiles, I thocht that if the Deil was minded to get us into the Black Sea quick, well – if we had a quick voyage it wadna be to our miscredit wi' the owers, an' the Auld Mon wad be decently grateful to us for no kinderin' him.'

That mixture of simplicity and cunning, of superstition and commercial reasoning, struck a chord in Van Helsing, who said:

'Mine friend, that Devil is more clever than many think him – yet he know when he meet his match!'

The skipper was not displeased with the compliment, and went on:

'When we got past the Bosphorus the men began to grumble. Some o' them Roomanians came and asked me to heave overboard a big box we took on board from a queer-lookin' old man just afore we started frae London. I seen them speer at the felly, and put out their twa fingers to him – agin the evil eye, ye ken. Man but the supersteetion of foreigners is pairfectly rideeculous! I sent them aboot their business pretty quick, but just after a dour fog closed down on us, and I felt a wee bitty masell as they did – anent *somethin'*, though I wouldna say it was partucular agin the box.

'Well, on we went.

'And as the fog didna let up for five days I joost let the wind carry us on. For if the Deil Hissell wanted to get somewheres – well, he would fetch it up a' reet. An' if he didna? Well, we'd keep a sharp look-out anyways. Sure enough, we had a fair way and deep water all the time. And two days ago – then the mornin' sun came through the fog – we found ourselves in the river just off Galatz. The Roomanians were wild by now, and wanted me, right or wrong, to fling the box straight in the river.'

'How did you react to that?' I asked, as the skipper's head shook in reflective wonder at the superstition of foreigners.

'I had to argy them aboot it wi' a handspike! An' when the last o' them rose off the deck, wi' his head in his hand, I had fair convinced them that, evil eye or no, the goods entrusted to my owners were better in my hands than at the bottom of the Danube. They had, mind you, taken the box on the deck, ready to heave, and as it was marked *Galatz via Varna* I thocht I'd let it lie till we discharged in the port an' got rid o't athegither. We didna do much clearin' that day, an' had to remain the nicht at anchor. But in the mornin' braw an' airly – an hour before sun-up, indeed – a man came aboord wi' an order from England, to receive a box marked for one Count Dracula, would ye believe?'

'Yes, yes!' cried the Professor. 'We believe. And what then?'

'He had his papers a' richt,' recalled the skipper. 'An' glad enough was I to be rid o' the dam' thing, for I was beginnin' masell to feel queer at it. If the Deil did have luggage aboord, ken, I'm thinkin' it was a' in yon damn box!'

'The name of the man who took it?' the Professor asked quickly.

'Nae prublem,' the skipper answered confidently. Stepping down to his cabin, he produced a receipt signed 'Immanuel Hildesheim', of '16 Burgenstrasse'.

Evidently that was all the captain knew, so with thanks we came away.

Hildesheim we found in his office: a Hebrew, rather of the Adelphi type – with a nose like a sheep, and a fez. After a little good-humoured haggling he told us what he knew. This turned out to be simple but important. He had received a letter from Mr de Ville of London, telling him to receive, if possible before sunrise so as to avoid Customs, a box which would arrive at Galatz in the *Czarina Catherine*. This he was to give in charge to a certain Petrof Skinsky, who dealt with Slovaks who traded down the river to the port. He had been paid for his work by an English bank-note, which had been duly cashed for gold at the Danube International Bank. When Skinsky had come to him, he had taken him to the ship and handed over the box, so as to save porterage. More than that he did not know.

We then sought Skinsky but were unable to find him. One of his neighbours, who seemed to bear him little affection, said he had gone away two days before, no-one knew whither. This was corroborated by his landlord, who had received by messenger the key of the house together with the rent due, paid in English money. This had been between ten and eleven o'clock last night.

Then, just when we were beginning to feel at a standstill once more, another neighbour came running and breathlessly gasped out that the body of Skinsky had been found inside the wall of the churchyard of St Peter, his throat torn open as if by some fearsome animal. All those we had been speaking with now ran off to see the horror with their own eyes, the women crying out loudly:

'This is the work of a Slovak!'

The Professor and I hurried away too, though in the opposite direction, to avoid becoming involved.

As we returned to our hotel we were unable to reach any sure conclusion. We were agreed that the box was on the move, quite likely by water, but . . . to where?

And how could we find out?

MINA HARKER'S JOURNAL

30 October. Evening.

They were so worn-out and dispirited that I asked them all to lie down for half an hour while I wrote everything up. I feel so grateful to the man who invented the 'Traveller's Typewriter', and to Mr Morris for getting this one for me. All this work with a pen would be such a bore.

Later.

All done. Poor Jonathan. What must he be suffering now? He lies on the sofa hardly seeming to breathe, and his whole body appears collapsed. His brows knit, his face is drawn and wrinkled with the pain of vexing thoughts. If only I could help him. But how?

While the men are resting, I shall carefully read all our papers through again, and who knows what I may not discover?

MINA HARKER'S MEMORANDUM

Ground of inquiry. Count Dracula's problem is to get back to his Castle unscathed.

(a) He must be *brought back* by someone, for had he the power to move entirely as he wished, he could go as a wolf or bat. He evidently fears discovery or interference, helplessly confined as he is, between dawn and sunset, in his earth-filled wooden box.

(b) *How* is he to be taken? Here a process of exclusion may help us. By road, by rail, or by water?

1. *By Road?* Here lie endless difficulties, especially in leaving a city. There are people; and people are curious, and investigate. An accidental

hint as to the contents of the box could destroy him. There might also be customs and octroi officers to pass.

2. *By Rail?* There is no-one in charge of the box. It would have to take its chance of being delayed; and delay could be fatal, with his enemies on the track. True, he might escape at night. But what if he were stranded in a strange place by day, with no refuge to fly to? This is not what the Count would risk.

3. *By Water?* Surely the safest way, in one respect, but with most danger in another. On water too he is powerless except at night. Even then he can only summon fog and storm, snow and his wolves. But were he wrecked, the living water would engulf him. Helpless, he would indeed be lost. He could have the vessel try for land; but if it were an unfriendly land, and he not free to move, his position would yet be desperate.

Now we know from the record that he *was* on water, but *what* water? He evidently intended all along to arrive at Galatz, and sent that invoice to Varna to deceive us. His immediate and sole purpose then was to *escape*. Proof of this is the instruction sent to Immanuel Hildesheim to remove the box *before sunrise*. There is also the message to Petrof Skinsky. This we can only guess at, but there must have been *some* order, since Skinsky came to Hildesheim.

We know that, so far, the Count's plans were successful. The *Czarina Catherine* made a phenomenally quick journey – so rapid that Captain Donelson's suspicions were aroused; but his superstition united with his canniness to play the Count's game for him, and he ran with his favouring wind through fogs and all till he brought up blindfold at Galatz. That the Count's arrangements there were well made has been proved. Hildesheim cleared the box, took it off, and gave it to Skinsky. Skinsky then – but here we lose the trail. We only know that the box is somewhere on the water, moving along. Customs and octroi have been avoided.

Now we come to what the Count must have done after his arrival – *on land*, at Galatz. The box was given to Skinsky, but *why* Skinsky? In my husband's diary, Skinsky is mentioned as dealing with the Slovaks who trade down the river to the port – and the man's remark, that the murder was the work of a Slovak, showed the general feeling against his class. So Skinsky was a lone individual, which suited the Count's desire for isolation.

My surmise then is that already in London the Count had decided to get back to his Castle by water, as the most safe and secret way. After all, he had been brought from the Castle by Szgany, and probably they delivered their cargo to Slovaks who took the boxes to Varna, for there they were shipped for London. Thus the Count already had knowledge of persons who could arrange this service. Once ashore, before sunrise or after sunset, he came out from his box, met Skinsky and instructed him to arrange carriage of the box up some river. When all that was in train, he blotted out his traces, as he thought, by murdering his agent.

From the map it seems the rivers most suitable for the Slovaks to have ascended are the Pruth and the Sereth. I read in the typescript that in my trance I heard cows low and water swirling level with my ears. Also the creaking of wood. The Count in his box, then, was on a river in an open boat – propelled by oars or perhaps poles, for the banks are near and the boat is working against the stream.

But *which* stream?

Of the two rivers, the Pruth is the more easily navigated, but the Sereth is, at Fundu, joined by the Bistritza, which runs up round the Borgo Pass. The loop it makes is manifestly as close to Castle Dracula as can be got by water.

MINA HARKER'S JOURNAL

When I had done reading out my memorandum, Jonathan took me in his arms and kissed me. The others kept shaking me by both hands, and Dr Van Helsing said:

'Our dear Madame Mina is once more our teacher. Her eyes have see where we blind. Now we are on the target again, and this time we may succeed. Our enemy is at his most helpless, and if we can come on him by day, on the water, our task will be over. He have a start, but is powerless to hasten, as he may not leave his box lest those who carry him sniff rats. For them to suspect would land him in his box in river, where he perish. This he know, and will not. And so, gentlemens, to war. What counsel?'

'I shall get a steam launch and follow him,' said Lord Godalming.

'And I, horses to follow on the bank, lest by chance he land,' said Mr Morris.

'Good, good!' said the Professor. 'But neither must go alone. There must be force to overcome force if force need. The Slovak is strong and rough, and he carry rude arms.'

The younger men smiled at this, for amongst them they carry an arsenal. Said Mr Morris:

'I have brought some Winchesters. They are pretty handy for crowd control, and plus there may be wolves.'

'Let me go with Quincey,' suggested Dr Seward. 'We are accustomed to hunt together, and we two, well armed, will be a match for no matter what. You too must not go alone, Art. You may have to fight the Slovaks, and a chance thrust – for I don't suppose these fellows carry guns – would undo all our plans. This time we must take no chances. Not till the Count's head and body are separated, and we are certain he cannot reincarnate.' Dr Seward looked at Jonathan as he spoke.

Jonathan looked at me.

I could see the poor dear torn about in his mind. Of course he wanted to be with me, yet the boat service would most likely be the one to destroy the . . . the . . . Vampire. (Why do I hesitate to write that word?)

During Jonathan's silence Professor Van Helsing spoke:

'Friend Jonathan, this is to you for twice reasons. First, you are young and brave and can fight, and all energies may be need at the last. Again, it be *your* right to destroy him – *that* – which bring such woe to your house. So be not afraid for Madame Mina. She will be *my* care, if you permit I may. For I am old, see? My legs not so quick to run as once. Nor am I use to ride so to pursue, or battle with lethal weapon. But I can fight in other ways. And die, if need, as well as younger man. Now what I would is this. While you, my Lord Godalming, and friend Jonathan go in your so swift little steamboat up the river, and while John and Quincey guard the bank where perchance the Count might land, old I will take Madame Mina right into the heart of the enemy's country. While the old fox is in his box, trapped on the running stream by day, not daring to raise his coffin lid lest his Slovak carriers should in fear him abandon to perish – we shall go, Madame Mina and I, in the track where Jonathan went. From Bistriz over the Borg – and find we our way to Dracula's Castle. Here Madame Mina's hypnotic power will surely help, and we shall find our way – all dark and unknown otherwise – after the first sunrise when we near that fateful place. There is much to do and other places to sanctify, so the nest of these vipers be obliter—'

'Do you mean to say, Professor,' Jonathan interrupted him hotly, 'that you would take Mina, in her sad case and tainted as she is with that devil's illness, right into the jaws of his death-trap? *No*, I say. Not for the world! Not for Heaven or Hell!' Struggling to keep his speech civil, Jonathan went on:

'Do you really know what kind of place that is? That den of hellish infamy – its very moonlight alive with grisly shapes, while every speck of dust the wind whirls up is a devouring monster in embryo? Have *you* felt the Vampire's lips upon *your* throat?' As he turned to me, Jonathan's eyes lit on my forehead. Throwing up his hands in despair, he cried:

'Oh, my God, what have we done to merit this terror?' and he collapsed on the sofa in misery.

The Professor's measured tones calmed us all;

'Oh, friend Jonathan, it is just because I would *save* Madame Mina from that awful place that I would go. But God forbid that I should take her *in* there – where waits such terrible work to do, that her eyes must not see. We men, all save Jonathan, have see already what must to do before his Castle be purify. Yet remember we voyage through perilous straits. If the Count escape us this time – with his strength and subtle and cunning – he may sleep him for a century! Then in time our dear one' – the Professor took my hand – 'would come to keep him company, and end as those others friend Jonathan saw: with their lips that gloat and their ghastly laugh as they clutch the moving bag Count Dracula he throw them.

'You shudder? And well! Forgive that I make you such pain, but it is needful. And so I too am giving, if need be, my life. Also, perhaps, my *soul* – who knows? But Madame Mina will be protect.'

'Do as you will,' sobbed Jonathan on the sofa. 'We are in all in God's hands now.'

Later.

How can women help loving men so earnest, so true, and so brave? Money, too. What good can it not do when properly applied? Evil too, I suppose. But today I felt so thankful that Lord Godalming is rich, and that both he and Mr Morris, who also has plenty of money, are willing to spend it so freely. But for them our little expedition could not begin so promptly, or so well equipped, as it will within the hour.

Now, after only three hours, Lord Godalming and Jonathan have a lovely launch, with steam up, ready to start at a moment's notice. Dr Seward and Mr Morris have six magnificent horses, all perfectly appointed. We have all the maps and outdoor gear that could be wished for. Professor Van Helsing and I are to leave by the 11.40 train tonight for Veresti, thence to drive to the Borgo Pass. We are taking a good deal of ready money, as we are to buy a carriage and horses in Veresti. And of course the Professor knows so many languages that I am sure we shall get on all right. We must drive ourselves, he has decided, for whom else could we possibly trust?

And with danger in mind, even I bear a large-bore revolver – imagine! For Jonathan would not be happy if I were not so armed against attack. Alas, that I may not carry a crucifix too, but the scar on my forehead forbids it. The Professor, dear man, makes light of this and tries to comfort me by saying that with a revolver the size of mine at least I need fear no wolves. The weather, however, is getting colder every hour, and there are some warning flurries of snow.

Later.

It took all my courage to say good-bye to my darling. To think we may never meet again. But I must be strong, for the Professor is looking at me keenly. So there must be no tears now. No, nor never again. Unless it be God's will that they fall in gladness.

JONATHAN HARKER'S JOURNAL

30 October. Night.

I am writing this in the light from the furnace door of the launch, as Lord Godalming fires up. He is an experienced hand, as he has a steam launch of his own on the Thames, and another on the Norfolk Broads. Regarding our plans, we are acting on Mina's surmise that if water is the means of Count Dracula's escape back to his Castle, the Sereth, and then the Bistritza at its junction, would be the way. We reckon that somewhere about the 47th parallel would be the place to cross the country between the river and the Carpathians.

In our launch we should make good speed up the river, even at night. There is plenty of water, and the banks are wide enough apart to make steaming easy enough, even in the dark. Now Lord Godalming has just told me to sleep for a while, but how can I? Not with such terrible danger hanging over my darling, and her venturing out into that awful place with only the Professor to protect her. My only comfort is that we are in the hands of God, and I feel that but for one's faith it would be easier to die than to live, and so be quit of all the trouble.

Mr Morris and Dr Seward were off on their long ride well before we started. They are to keep up the right bank, far enough off to get on higher ground, where they can see a good stretch of river yet avoid having to follow all its bends. For the first stages they have hired two men to ride and lead their spare horse – four in all – so as not to excite curiosity. When they dismiss the men, which will be shortly, they will look after all the horses themselves. It may be necessary for us to join forces, so we have mounts for all our party. One of the saddles has a movable horn, and can easily be adapted for Mina, if required.

What a wild adventure this is. Steaming through the darkness, cold from the river rising round us, all the mysterious whispers of the invisible night . . . I feel we are drifting into some eternal black unknown.

But there is practical reality: Godalming is closing the furnace door.

31 October.

Still hurrying along. Day has come, Godalming has had a short sleep, so I am again free to write. The morning is so bitterly cold that the furnace heat is most welcome, notwithstanding our heavy fur coats. As yet we have passed only a few open boats, and none big enough to conceal any box of the size we seek. In each case the boatmen were terrified when we turned our electric lamp on them, and fell on their knees to pray.

1 November. Evening.

No news all day, and no glimpse of what we seek. We have now passed into the Bistritza, and if we are wrong in our surmise – well, God help us. Meanwhile we overhaul every boat, large and small. Early this morning one crew took ours for a Government launch, and treated us with respect accordingly. We saw in this a means of expediting our subsequent inquiries, so at Fundu, where the Bistritza runs into the Sereth, we purchased a Romanian flag, which we now fly conspicuously. Every boat we have overhauled since then has paid us quite astonishing deference, and not once has any objection been raised against our queries. Alas, would that our results were in proportion.

Some of the Slovaks say a big boat passed them at more than usual speed, as she had a double crew on board. But this was before they reached Fundu, so no-one knows whether the fast boat turned into the Bistritza or continued on up the Sereth. At Fundu we heard nothing of any such boat, so she must have passed there in the night.

I am feeling very sleepy. No doubt the cold is beginning to tell upon me. Godalming seems less affected by it, and his stamina is remarkable. God bless him for all his goodness to poor dear Mina and me.

2 November. Morning.

It is broad daylight. That good fellow would not wake me – he says I was sleeping so peacefully. It seems brutally selfish of me to have slept so long, and let him watch all night; but he was quite right. I am a new man this morning; and feel my strength and energy returning. I wonder where Mina and Van Helsing are. They should have got to Veresti about noon on Wednesday. It would take them some time to get the carriage and horses; so if they then made good time they should now be nearing the Borgo Pass. God guide them. I am afraid to think what may happen. If only we could go faster . . .

But we cannot. Already the engines are throbbing their utmost. I wonder too how Dr Seward and Mr Morris are getting on. There seem to be endless streams running down from the mountains into this river, but as none is substantial at present, though doubtless they are terrible in winter, when the snow melts – the horsemen may not have met much obstruction. I hope we may see them before we get to Strasba, for if by then we have not overtaken the Count, we shall need to confer together on what to do next.

DR SEWARD'S DIARY

2 November.

Three days on the road. No news, and no time to write it if there had been. Every moment is precious. We have had only the rest needful for the horses; but we are both bearing it well – thanks, I dare say, to all our more youthful adventures together.

Now we must push on, for we shall not feel at ease till we get the launch in our sights again.

3 November.

We heard at Fundu that the launch had gone up the Bistritza. I wish it wasn't so cold. There are signs of snow coming; and a heavy fall would stop us. In that event, we must continue on sledge, Russian fashion.

4 November.

Today we heard the launch had been detained by an accident when trying to force its way up the rapids. The Slovak boats get up all right, by aid of a rope, and steering with knowledge. Some went up only a few hours before. Godalming is an amateur fitter himself, and evidently it was he who got the launch going again. Finally, with local help, they got up the rapids all right, and are off on the chase afresh. I fear, though, that the boat will be no better for the accident. The peasantry tell us that after she got up to smooth water again, she kept stopping and starting laboriously until she was no longer in sight.

So we must push on ever harder. Our help may be needed soon.

MINA HARKER'S JOURNAL

31 October.

Arrived at Veresti at noon. The Professor tells me that this morning at dawn he could hardly hypnotize me at all, and that all I could say was:

'Dark and quiet.'

He is off now buying a carriage and horses. He says he will later buy additional horses, so we can change them on the way. We have something like seventy miles before us. The scenery is lovely, and – if only we were under different conditions . . . If Jonathan and I were driving through this land alone, what a pleasure it would be. To stop and meet people, learn something of their life, and fill our memories with all the colour and picturesqueness of this wild, beautiful country and its fascinating people. But, alas . . .

Later.

Dr Van Helsing has returned with our carriage. We are to have some dinner, and set off in an hour. The landlady is preparing us a huge basket of provisions – enough, it seems to me, for a brigade of hungry soldiers. The Professor encourages her, and whispers to me that it may be a week before we see fresh food again. He has been shopping too, and has equipped us with fur coats and wraps, and all sorts of warm things. Little chance of our being cold!

Soon we shall be off, and I dread to think what may happen. Truly we are in the hands of God, and I pray, with all the strength of my sad and humble soul, that He will watch over my beloved husband. And that, whatever may happen, Jonathan shall know I loved and honoured him more than words can say, and that my fondest thoughts were always of him.

1 November.

All day long we have travelled. The horses must appreciate being kindly treated, for they go willingly and at good speed. During our stops the Professor is very laconic, telling the farmers only that we are hurrying to Bistritz, and paying them handsomely for their best fresh horses. We get hot soup, coffee, or tea; and off we go.

The country through which we speed is magnificent – full of all imaginable beauties – and the people are brave, strong, pleasant – and yet . . . *very* superstitious. In the first house where we stopped, the woman who served us, seeing the scar on my forehead, crossed herself furiously and put out two fingers towards me – *against* me – to keep off the evil eye. I believe too they deliberately put extra garlic into our food; and I can't abide garlic. Since then I have taken care not to take off my hat or veil, and so have avoided such local suspicions. We are travelling fast, and as we have no driver with us to carry tales, we ride ahead of scandal; but I dare say that fear of the evil eye will follow hard behind us.

The Professor seems tireless. All day he would not rest, though he made me sleep for a long spell. At sunset he hypnotizsed me, and he says my answer was as usual:

'Darkness, lapping water and creaking wood.'

So our enemy is still on the river.

I am afraid to *think* of Jonathan, yet curiously I have now no fear for his safety, or my own. I write this while we wait in a farmhouse for the horses to be got ready. The Professor is dozing. Poor dear, he looks very tired now – old and grey. But his mouth is set firmly as ever. Even in his sleep he is instinct with resolution. Soon I must make him rest while I drive. I shall tell him that we have arduous days before us, and he must not break down before his best strength shall be needed.

All is ready; we are off.

2 November. Morning.

I was successful, and we took turns driving all night. Now the day is upon us, bright though with a strange heaviness in the air – which oppresses us. It is very cold, too, and only our warm furs keep us comfortable. At dawn Van Helsing hypnotized me. He says I answered:

'Darkness. Creaking wood and roaring water.'

So the river is changing as the Count ascends. I do hope my darling is not in danger – no more than need be, at least. But we are in God's hands.

2 November. Night.

All day long driving. The country gets wider as we go, and the great spurs of the Carpathians, which at Veresti seemed so far away, and so low on the horizon, now seem to gather round us and tower in front. We both seem in good spirits, and Professor Van Helsing says that by morning we shall reach the Borgo Pass. The houses now are few, and the Professor fears we may find no further fresh horses. At our last stop he bought a further two, so that we have a rude four-in-hand. The dear horses are so patient, and no trouble. There are no other travellers on the road, and so even I can drive. We shall get to the Pass in daylight, as we do not want to arrive before. So till then we have a little time to rest.

Rest?

Oh, what will tomorrow bring? I, alas, am unclean in God's eyes, and so may incur His wrath. Yet do I trust in Him to watch over my husband, and those others so dear to us both — brave men in deadly peril.

Amen.

35

Memorandum by Van Helsing

4 November.

This to my old true friend John Seward MD, of Purfleet, London, in case I may not see him. It may explain. It is morning, and I write by a fire which all the night I have keep alive – Madame Mina aiding me. It is cold; so cold. The grey heavy sky is full of snow, which when it fall will settle for all winter as the ground he harden beneath. It make, this cold, Madame Mina so heavy of head all day that she not like herself.

She sleep so very much.

Of usual so alert, she now do nothing all the day. Even she lose her appetite, and in this so cold too. She make no entry into her little diary! She, who write so faithful at every pause. Something whisper me that all be ill.

However, tonight she is more *vif*. Her long sleep all day have refresh and restore her, for now she be bright again. At sunset I try to hypnotize her, but alas! The power grow less each day, and tonight it fail me total.

Well, God's will be done.

Now to the historical. For as Madame Mina not stenograph, I must write in my long old hand, that so no day of us go not record.

The Borgo Pass we reach just after sunrise yesterday. When I see the dawn I get ready for the hypnotism. We stop our carriage, I make couch with furs, and Madame Mina, lying down, yield herself as usual to the hypnotic sleep – but more slow and short than ever. As before, she answer:

'Darkness, and the swirling of water.'

Then she wake, all radiant, and we proceed us to the Pass. There she come all on fire with zeal. Some new guiding power be in her manifest, for she point one road and say:

'This way.'

'How know you it?' I ask.

She pause before to answer:

'Have not my Jonathan travel it and wrote?'

At first I doubt, but then see there be only one by-road such. It is use but little, and most different from the coach road from Bukovina to Bistritz, which be hard and wide, with much travellers too.

So came we down this road. When we meet other ways – not always were we sure they be roads at all, for they be neglect, and now with light snow cover. The horses know, and they only. So I give rein to them, and they go on so patient. By-and-by we find all things which Jonathan have wrote. Then we go on for long, long hours. Very long. At the first I tell Madame Mina to sleep. She try. She succeed. She sleep all the time. At the last I feel myself suspicious, and would wake her. But she sleep on and *will* not wake. I shake her not too hard lest I harm her, for I know she have suffer much, and sleep at times be her all.

I think too I drowse myself, for of sudden I feel guilt to discover me: bolt up, with my reins in hand. Yet the good horses jog-jog along, just as ever.

I look down.

Madame Mina still sleep.

It is now near dusking and over the snow the sunlight flow in yellow floods, making us to throw great long shadows into where the mountain rise so steep. For we are going up, and up; and all is – oh! So wild, so rocky, as like the ending of the world.

Then I arouse Madame Mina.

This time she wake with no trouble.

Then I try to put her to hypnotic. But she yield not, being as though I were null. Still I try and try again, till all at once I find us in darkness. So I look round, and of course the sun be down. Madame Mina she laugh. I turn to her. She is now bright awake, and look so well as never since that night at Carfax – when first we enter Count Dracula's house. I am amazing then, and not at ease. Yet she is so tender and thoughtful for me that I forget all fear.

I light some fire, for we bring dry wood with us. Madame Mina she prepare food while I undo the horses and set them tether in shelter, to feed. When I return to fire she have my supper ready. I go to help her. She smile and say she have eat already – so hungry she would not wait. I like it not and have grave doubts, but I fear to affright her, and so am silent of it. She serve me and I eat alone. Then we wrap us in furs and lie beside the fire. I tell her to sleep while I watch. But presently I forget. When all sudden I remember that I watch, I find Madame Mina her lying quiet, but awake. With so bright eyes she look at me. Twice more the same occur, and I get much sleep that way.

When I wake I try to hypnotize her; but alas! Though she shut her eyes obedient, she may not sleep. The sun rise up and up, and . . . her sleep come too late. Also so heavy that she will not wake. I have to lift and place her sleeping in the carriage when I have the horses harness. Madame Mina still sleep, and sleep. And in her sleep she look more healthy and more redder than before.

I like it not.

And I am afraid, poor old me — afraid of all things — even to think. Yet I must go on. The stake we play for is *life*. Life against death. More than that, even. So never must we flinch.

5 November. Morning.

Let me be accurate in everything, dear friend John. For though we have see some strange things together, you and I, you may now suspect that I, Van Helsing, am *mad* — that all the horrors and strain of nerves have turn my poor old brain.

All yesterday we travel, I say, ever closer to mountains, up into a more wilder and desert land. Here are great, frowning precipices, and much water falling. Nature she seem sometime to have hold here her carnival. Madame Mina still sleep and sleep. Myself I did have hunger and appease it, but I could not waken her — not even for hot food. So began I to fear the fatal spell of this place be upon her, baptized as she is with the Vampire.

'Well,' say I to myself, 'if she sleep all the day, then must I not sleep at night!'

As we travel the rough road, all ancient and imperfect, my head allow to nod. Again I wake with a stabber of guilt, and of time passed. Madame Mina I find still sleeping, and the sun low down.

But all was indeed change.

The frowning mountains seeming further away, and we near to top a steep-rising hill. On summit of him, such a castle as Jonathan describe. At once I exult and fear. Now, for good or ill, the end must be near. I wake Madame Mina. Again I try to hypnotize her. Alas, alas! All unavailing till too late. Then, ere the great dark he gobble us — for even after down-sun the heavens reflect pale on the snow — I take the horses to feed in shelter. Then I build fire. Near it I make Madame Mina, now more awakeful and charming than ever, sit comfortable amid her rugs. I get ready nice food but she will not eat, insisting she have no hunger. I know better than to pressing her, but I myself eat, for I must now be strong for us both.

Next with fear in my heart I draw a ring, so big for her comfort, round where Madame Mina sit. Over the ring I pass some Wafer, broke fine so guarding all. This while Madame Mina she is sitting − still as dead. And whiter she grow. Ever whiter, till the snow is not more pale. And no words. But when I draw near she is clinging to me, and the poor soul is shaking her, from head to feet, with tremors most painful to feel.

Presently I say to her, when she seem more calm:

'Will not you come, over to the fire?' To make test of what she can.

Madame Mina she rise obedient, but then stop as deadly stricken.

'Come on!' I say.

She shake her head and sit back down. Looking at me with eyes like new from sleep, she confess:

'I cannot,' and silent she remain.

I rejoice me then, for what *she* can not, none other vampire can neither. Though she live in danger of her body, yet her *soul* be safe.

Presently the horses scream, and tear their tetherings till I quiet them. When they feel my hands on them, they whinny low, as in joy, and lick my hands, and rest quiet for a time. Often through the night did I come to them so, till arrive the cold hour when all nature is at lowest.

In that coldest hour our fire begin to die.

I was about stepping forth to replenish him, for now it snow in flying sweeps and with a chill mist too. Even in the dark was a light of some kind, as ever over snow.

And now snow-flurries and wreaths of mist take shape, to me it seem, as of women with garments trailing. All in silence, grimly dead. Silence − only that the horses still whinny and shy, as in terror of the worst. I also now feel fear − most horrible fears; but then return a sense of safety in this ring where here I stand. Next I suspect my imaginings to be only of the night, the gloom, the unrest I go through, and all terrible anxieties. It seem like my memories of all friend Jonathan's most horrid experience befool − for the snowflakes in the mist begin to wheel and dance around me till I get as though a shadow glimpse of those women that would kiss him. And then the horses cower low, like dogs, and moan in terror as men in pain. Even the fright of madness is denying to them, so they cannot break away.

I dread now for my dear Madame Mina when these weird figures circle near. I look at her. She sit calm, and smile. When I would step to the fire, to replenish him, Madame Mina she catch me tight, and whisper, like in a dream, so low:

'No, no! Do not go without. *Here* you are safe.'

I turn to her. Looking in her eyes I say:

'But you? It is for *you* I fear.'

Hereat she laugh – a laugh deep unreal – and reply:

'Fear for *me*? But why? There is no-one safer in all the world from them than I – as I am . . . '

As I wonder at her words meaning, a puff of wind leap up the flame and I see her forehead scar – never redder. Then, alas, I *know*. Meanwhile the figures of snow in the the mist come wheeling ever closer, but remaining yet without the Holy Circle.

Gradually they materialize.

Becoming flesh, until – if God not take away my reason, for I *see* it, through my eyes – here before me are in bodily life the same three wicked women as Jonathan he see in the Castle chamber, when they would have . . . kiss his throat. Their swaying round forms, the bright hard eyes, white teeth so long, ruddy colour, and those so voluptuous lips.

Ever they smile at poor dear Madame Mina.

And as their laugh break hard through the snowy night, they twine their arms, they point to her, and entone in so evil sweetness – that Jonathan he liken to the water-glasses:

'Come, sister. Come to us. Come! Come!'

In fear I regard my poor Madame Mina, but now my heart with gladness leap like the flames – for oh! The terror in her so beautiful eyes, the horror, repulsion – all tell a story to my heart of hope not yet dead.

God be thanked.

Madame Mina is, I see, not yet of them.

So I seize some firewood by me, and holding high my Wafer I advance upon the she-devils that beckon.

And they?

Draw back before me they are oblige, though they make mock all the while, and laugh their ghastly laugh. I feed the fire and I fear them not, for I know they dare not approach me, so armed, nor Madame Mina within the Ring – which she can no more leave than they may enter.

The horses – poor, noble beasts. Long they have cease to moan. Upon their sides they lie still. The snow falls on them softly, and they grew whiter. No more of terror for them.

And so we are remaining till the red dawn creep up the snow-gloom. I so desolate, with weariness and woe, but when that gloryful sun he climb the horizon, life come to me again. The evil women figures melt with the mist. The snow in his wreaths of gloom he retreat back to the terrible Castle whence he come.

Encouraged by these signs of dawn, to Madame Mina I turn, to hypnotize her. Alas I find her in sudden deep sleep, like coma, from which I may not wake her. I have try to hypnotize *through* her sleep, but she make no response – no, none.

And now it is full day.

Fearing yet to stir, I have make my fire anew. The horses – all dead indeed. Today I have much to do here, so shall wait till sun be high. For there may be places I must go, where the bright light of him, though mist and snow obscure it, will be to me a strength.

Meanwhile, Madame Mina still she sleep. Calm, as innocent child. At least it so seem.

God be praised.

Myself I must warm me with breakfast, and then to my terrible work.

36

Home of the Vampire King

4 November. Evening.

The accident to the launch has been a terrible setback. But for that we should have overtaken the Count's boat long ago; and by now my darling Mina would be free. How I agonize to think of her, up in the wolds near that loathsome place.

We have horses now, however, and we follow on their track. I note this while Godalming gets ready. We have our weapons, too, so the Szgany had better look out if they mean to fight.

If only Morris and Seward were with us . . . but we can only hope, and pray. If I should write no more . . .

Goodbye, dearest Mina. God keep you.

DR SEWARD'S DIARY
5 November.

With the dawn we saw the body of Szgany before us dashing away from the river with their leiter-waggon. They surrounded it in a cluster, and hurried along as though demented. Snow is falling, and there is a strange excitement in the air. Far off I hear the howling of wolves – the snow brings them down from the mountains – and there are dangers on all sides. The horses are ready, and in a moment we shall be off.

We ride to the death of someone, but God alone knows whose – or how.

VAN HELSING'S MEMORANDUM
5 November. Afternoon.

I am at least sane, though the proving of it so dreadful. Thank God for His mercy. When I leave Madame Mina sleeping within the Holy Circle, I take my way to the Castle. The blacksmith hammer I bring from Veresti most useful now. Though Count Dracula's doors be all open I break them off from their hinges of rust, lest some ill-chance or malice lock them again behind me. The bitter experience of Jonathan serve me handsome here. By memory of his diary I find my way to the old chapel, for here must my work lie.

The air there oppressive as with sulphur fumes, which at times make me dizzy. Either a roaring in my ears, or far-off the howling of wolves. Or both. Yes, both. Then I bethink of my dear Madame Mina, and the dilemma have me sore on his horns. For her I had not dare bring to this place, but leave safe from the Vampire in that Holy Circle. Yet even there would be wolf. But I resolve me that my work lie here, and that to wolves we must submit, if so God will.

At any rate, that only death, and freedom ever beyond.

So I choose for her, though so hard. For only myself the choice easy: the maw of wolf so preferable to Vampire grave.

So I choose to go on with my work.

I know at least three graves are inhabit, so I search, and search, and one of them soon find. There she lie in her Vampire sleep, so full of volupturous beauty that I shudder as though come to do murder a pretty young girl. How to doubt that in old times many man with such task find at the last his heart failing, and then his nerve. So he delay, and delay, till seducing fascination of the wanton Un-Dead have hypnotise him. And he remain on till sunset come, and the Vampire sleep be over. Then the beautiful eyes of the fair seeming woman open and look love. The volupturous mouth present to kiss – and man is weak.

And soon?

One more victim thrall in Vampire fold. One more to swell his grisly Un-Dead ranks . . .

And lying as she, in a tomb fret with age, and heavy with centuries of dust, and even in such fetid odour as lairs of the Count all have, yes, even I be moved. I, Van Helsing, with all my motive for hate – yet feeling a yearn for delay freeze up my faculties, and bind my very soul. Mayhap my need of sleep, and strange oppression of this air, overcoming me. Certain anyway I lapse into open-eyed sleep as a man lulled by woman's beauty power, not mattering how evil, when then through the snow-stilled air wail a long, low wail, so full of woe and piteous that it it wake me clarion quick.

For this the voice of my dear Madame Mina that sting my ear.

Then I brace again to my gruesome task and find, by wrenching away of tomb-tops, one second sister, she dark. I dare not pause to look on her as on the first, lest again I fall enthral. Rather I search on until, in a high and special tomb, as made to one much belove, I find that thirdly sister – she too fair – which, like Jonathan, I see to gather herself out of atoms that swirl in mist.

Ah. So fair to look on, she, so radiant beautiful, so exquisite volupturous, that all instinct of man in me, which call my sex to loving and protecting hers, make now my head to whirl with new emotion. God I thank that the soul-wail of my dear Madame Mina ring still in my ears, for before the Vampire spell can bind me numb I have nerve myself anew.

By now I have search all like tombs in the chapel, and find only these three young women, phantoms seeming, so Un-Dead.

One great tomb however remain: more lordly than all other. Huge he be, and noble in his proportion. And on him carved:

DRACULA

Here then, I, at the home of the Vampire King. The emptiness of him speak eloquent, and before to restore these women to their rightful dead selves, through my awful work, I lay in Dracula's tomb some Wafer, so banish him from it – Un-Dead, for ever. Amen.

Then begin my ghastly task, which I dread. For if so terrible with the sweet Miss Lucy, how not worser far with these stranger creatures, experienced of centuries? With all their strength so stronger from the passing years?

Oh, my friend John, but that be butchery work. With not spur to think of others living, over them hanging such pall of fear, I could not have – to do what even now I tremble to write.

But thanks to God my nerve he stand, and is rewarding by sweet repose I see in that first face I kill, and the gladness stealing over her, just ere the final dissolution come, as she feel her immortal soul so won. This give me great heart to continue my butchery: to endure most horrid screeching as my stake drive home in their breasts; the plunging of writhing form; and their lips of bloody foam. But for my holy purpose I should have flee in terror, sure, and leave my work undone.

But done it now is – all over.

And the poor souls of them?

I can pity them now and weep, as I think of them placid – each in her full sleep of death, for a short moment ere fading. For know, friend John, hardly my knife he sever off the head of each, before her whole body melt thin and dry, and crumble into dust. As though their deaths they should have, in centuries bygone, at last assert loud to each:

'I am thou!'

Then before to leave the Castle I so fix the entrances that never more can the Count enter there Un-Dead.

And when I step inside my circle to Madame Mina where she lying, she wake most instantly and cry out in sympathetic pain that I endure so much, too much.

'Come on,' she say then. 'Away from this awful place. Let us go to meet my husband, who is, I can feel, coming near us.'

So thin and pale and weak, her body look, yet her eyes glow hot with fervouring. And so with trust and hope, yet full of fear, we go eastward to meet our friends – and . . . *him*.

A Miracle of Death

6 November.

It was late afternoon when the Professor and I started east, whence I knew Jonathan was coming. We did not go fast, though our way was downhill, for we had to carry heavy rugs and wraps in case of mishap in the cold and the snow. We had to take some provisions too, for we were in a wilderness of desolation, and, so far as we could see through the snowfall, there was no sign of habitation for leagues around.

When we had trudged about a mile, I felt so tired that I had to sit down to rest. Then we looked back to where the stark lines of Dracula's Castle cut the sky in all its grandeur, perched a thousand feet on the summit of a sheer precipice, with seemingly a great gap between it and the steep of the adjacent mountain on any side. There was something uniquely uncanny about the place – grim as hell, it was true, yet savagely majestic too.

Now, again, we heard the howling of distant wolves. Even though their dismal baying came from so far, muffled through the deadening snowfall, to me it was full of terror. As I sat resting, Professor Van Helsing went searching for some less exposed vantage, where we would be less vulnerable in case of attack. Before us the rough roadway still led downwards, just traceable through the drifted snow.

Presently the Professor signalled, and I struggled up to join him. He had found a wonderful spot, a sort of natural hollow in a rock, with an entrance like a doorway between two boulders. Taking me by the hand, he drew me in.

'See!' he said. 'Here you are in shelter. If wolves do come, I can meet them one by one.' He brought in our furs, made a snug nest for me, got out some provisions, and pressed me to take some food. But I could not eat. Even to try was repulsive to me, much as I would have liked to please him.

The Professor looked very sad, but did not reproach me. Taking his field-glasses from the case, he stood atop the rock and began to scan the horizon. Suddenly he called out:

'Look, Madame Mina! Look, look!'

I forced myself up beside him on the rock. He handed me his glasses and pointed. The snow was falling more heavily now, and swirled about fiercely, for a high wind had begun to blow. However, in lulls between the snow flurries, from our height we could see a great distance. Below and beyond the white waste of snow the river, like a discarded ribbon, wound its way in kinks and curls of black. Straight down in front of us, and not far off – so near, indeed, that I wondered we had not noticed them before – came a group of mounted men in whose midst was a cart, a long leiter-waggon, swaying from side to side, like a heavy dog's tail wagging, as it lurched to the uneven road. Outlined against the snow as they were, I could see from the men's clothes that they were peasants or gypsies of some kind.

Roped to the cart was a great square chest which my heart leaped to see, for I felt the end approaching. The evening was drawing close, and how well I knew that at sunset the Thing, till then imprisoned there, would take on new freedoms, and could in many forms elude pursuit. In fear I turned to the Professor, but to my consternation he was not there. An instant later I saw him below me. Round our rock he had drawn a circle, such as had sheltered us last night. When he had completed it he stood beside me again, saying:

'At least you shall be safe here – from *him*.' He took the glasses from me, and during the next pause in the snow he studied the vast space below us. 'See!' he exclaimed. 'They come quickly. Flog-flogging their horses, to gallop so hard they can.' He paused, then went on in a hollow voice:

'They race for the sunset. We may be too late. But God's will to be done!'

Down came another blinding belt of snow, and the whole landscape was obliterated. Minutes later there came a brief respite, and once more the Professor's glasses were fixed on the plain.

'Look, look!' he suddenly cried. 'See? Two horsemen follow fast, coming up from the south. Quincey and John, they must be. Take the glass, Madame Mina. Look, before the snow blot all away.'

I took the field-glasses and looked. The two men might indeed be Dr Seward and Mr Morris. I knew at all events that neither was Jonathan.

At the same time I *knew* that Jonathan was not far off. Looking around I now saw, on the north side of the coming party, a second pair of riders, galloping at break-neck speed. One of them was certainly Jonathan, and the other I took to be Lord Godalming.

They, too, were pursuing the party with the cart.

When I told the Professor he shouted in glee like a schoolboy and grabbed the glasses from me. After looking intently till a further snowfall made vision impossible, he laid his Winchester rifle ready for use against the boulder at the opening of our shelter.

'They all converging,' he said. 'When the time come we shall have gypsies on all sides.'

I got out my revolver ready to hand, for while we were speaking the howling of wolves came louder and nearer by the moment. When the snowstorm abated a little we looked again. It was strange to see snow fall in such heavy flakes so close – while beyond and above the sun shone ever more brightly as it sank towards the far mountain tops. Sweeping the glass all around us I could see here and there tiny dots growing bigger in twos and threes: wolves gathering for a kill.

Every instant seemed an age while we waited. The wind blew in fiercer bursts, and the snow as with fury drove against us in circling eddies. At times we could not see an arm's length before us. In other moments, as the hollow-moaning wind swept by, it seemed to clear the air-space around us – so we could once more see far off. We had of late been so accustomed to watch for sunset that we could *feel* with fair accuracy when it would be.

And we knew now that before long the sun must set.

It was hard to believe that, by our watches, it was less than an hour that we waited in that rocky shelter before the various bodies began to close upon us. The wind came now in ever sharper gusts, and more directly from the north. It seemingly had driven the snow clouds south, for the snow had ceased to fall except in odd sporadic flutters. This enabled us to distinguish clearly the individuals of each party: the pursuers and the pursued. Strangely, the latter seemed not to realize, or to care, that they *were* pursued. Rather they seemed to hasten with redoubled speed on account of the sun, dropping low to the mountain tops.

Closer and closer the riders approached.

Professor Van Helsing and I crouched down behind our rock and held our weapons ready – he being vibrant with determination that the leiter-waggon should not pass. On towards us the gypsies meanwhile sped, oblivious to our presence.

All at once two voices shouted out together:

'Halt!'

One was my Jonathan's, raised to a key of high passion. The other was Mr Morris, his strong tones bravely resolute. The gypsies may not have known the language, but there was no mistaking the command. Instinctively they reined in, and at that instant Lord Godalming and Jonathan dashed up at one side and Dr Seward and Mr Morris on the other. The leader of the gypsies, a splendid-looking fellow who sat his horse like a centaur, waved them back, and in a harsh voice ordered his companions to proceed. They lashed the horses, which obediently sprang forward, but now four raised Winchester rifles reaffirmed the command to stop. At the same moment Professor Van Helsing and I rose behind the rock and aimed our weapons down.

Seeing themselves surrounded, the gypsies tightened their reins and stood still. Their leader yelled at them – a single word, but one which caused every gypsy in the party to draw what weapon he carried, knife or pistol, and hold himself ready to attack.

Issue was joined in an instant.

The leader, with a snatch at his rein, threw his horse out in front. Pointing first to the sun – now half behind the peaks – and then to the Castle, he shouted something I did not understand. But in reply all four men of our party threw themselves from their horses and dashed towards the cart. I should have felt terrible trepidation at seeing Jonathan in such danger, but the ardour of battle must have risen within me too, and I felt no fear – only a wild, surging desire for action.

Seeing the threat from our parties, the gypsy leader yelled a further command. Instantly his men formed round the cart in a jostling circle of protective bodies, their various weapons pointing outwards. Jonathan I could see on one side of the ring of men, and Quincey Morris on the other, both determined to force their way to the cart before the sun should set.

Nothing, it seemed, could deter them.

Neither the levelled pistols and flashing knives of the gypsies in front, nor the howling wolves at their heels, appeared even to engage their attention. The towering singleness of Jonathan's purpose so overawed the gypsies in front of him that, as it were instinctively, they cowered aside to let him pass. In an instant he had jumped upon the cart and, with more than human strength, raised up the great box and flung it over the wheel to the snowy ground below.

Meanwhile Mr Morris had had to use force to break through the ring of Szgany on his side. The knives of the gypsies flashed viciously as they cut at him, and he parried with his long bowie-knife. At first I thought Mr Morris too had won through in safety, but as he sprang to aid Jonathan – who by now had jumped down from the cart – I could see that with his left hand he was clutching at his side, where blood was spurting dreadfully through his fingers. For the moment, however, his wound did not hinder him. As Jonathan, with desperate energy, attacked one end of the chest, prising at the lid with his kukri knife, Mr Morris attacked the other just as frantically with his bowie.

Before such forceful efforts at either end the lid began to yield. Soon the nails drew with a sudden screech, and Count Dracula's chest was thrown open.

By now the gypsies, seeing themselves covered by the Winchesters, and at the mercy of Lord Godalming and Dr Seward, had given in and made no further resistance. The sun was almost down behind the mountain tops, and the shadows of all the men fell long upon the snow. The Count I now could see lying upon the earth within his box. Some of the earth had been scattered over his face and clothes by his rude fall from the cart. He was deathly pale, like an image in wax, and those red eyes glared horribly with the vindictiveness I knew only too well.

As I looked down, the Count glimpsed the sinking sun and the hate in his eyes turned to triumph.

But in that very instant came the flashing arc of Jonathan's Gurkha knife. I shrieked as I saw it shear clear through the Count's white throat, then immediately again as Mr Morris's bowie-knife plunged like a stake through the Vampire's heart.

Then – sweet miracle of death – before our very eyes, and almost in the drawing of a breath, the Count's whole body crumbled into dust and blew away.

As long as I live I shall be glad that, even in that final dissolution, there passed over Count Dracula's face a moment of peace, such as I never could have imagined.

Castle Dracula now stood out black against the crimson sky, every stone of its broken battlements articulated hard against the dark light of the dying sun.

The gypsies, taking us to have caused the extraordinary disappearance of the dead Count, turned from us in shameless terror and galloped away to save their souls. Those who were unmounted jumped upon the leiter-waggon and shouted to the horsemen not to desert them. The wolves, which had withdrawn to look on from the trees, followed in the gypsies' wake.

In moments we were left alone.

Mr Morris, who had sunk to the ground, leaned on his elbow, hands pressed to his side where, through his fingers, the blood still gushed in torrents. I flew to him – for here no Holy Circle kept me back – and so did the two doctors. Jonathan knelt behind him, and Mr Morris laid his poor wounded head on my husband's shoulder. With a feeble sigh he pressed my hand to his lips. Seeing the anguish of my heart in my face, he smiled at me weakly and said:

'I am so happy to have been of service. Oh, God!' he cried suddenly, struggling to sit up as he pointed to me. 'Surely to die is worth this. Look, look!'

The sun was now invisible behind the mountains, but still an echo of red reflected down from the sky, to bathe my face in a dusky light. United in wonder the other men sank to their knees, and a deep and earnest 'Amen' broke from all their throats as their eyes followed Mr Morris's finger – as the dying man whispered:

'God be thanked it was all not in vain! See? The glacier snow is not more stainless than Mina's forehead! Her curse has passed away!'

Then, to our bitter grief – with a smile, then silence – our American friend Quincey Morris died, a supremely gallant gentleman.

Epilogue

Looking Back on Horror

It was seven years ago that we all went through the flames; and our happiness since has surely been well worth the pain we endured.

An added joy, to Mina and me, is that our boy's birthday is the exact anniversary of poor Quincey Morris's death. Mina cherishes, I know, the secret belief that some of our brave friend's spirit has passed into our son. His several names salute all our little band of men; but at home we call him Quincey.

This summer we journeyed back to Transylvania, and retraced our old footsteps, through those scenes of vivid horror. And in the bright sunlight of those warm days it seemed almost impossible to believe those dreadful things; things which we had seen with our own eyes, heard with our own ears, and felt with our own hearts.

All the countryside around seemed so normal now, so peaceful, and only Castle Dracula itself still reared gaunt and high, as a stark reminder of our adventure, like a hawk with a hood of haze.

One evening in the autumn, back in England, we got to talking over those times – looking back objectively, without despair, as Godalming and Seward, too, are married happily now.

When I took the papers from the safe, where they have lain these seven years, we were amazed to note how few handwritten documents survive, almost all the records having been typed later – except, of course, the later note-books of Mina, Seward and myself, and Van Helsing's memorandum.

We could hardly ask any stranger, therefore, even did we so wish, to accept our evidences as proof: that so terrible a tale was wholly true.

None of us, perhaps, could have summed it up better than the

Professor himself, as, bouncing our young Quincey upon his knee, he exclaimed:

'But we *want* no proofs! Outsiders we ask none to believe. Enough this boy will soon day learn what gallant woman is his mother. Already he know her sweetness, and loving care. Later he discover how brave men so love her, that they dare all for her sake.'